VICIOUS SPIRITS

ALSO BY KAT CHO

Wicked Fox

VICIOUS SPIRITS

KAT CHO

putnam

G. P. Putnam's Sons

G. P. Putnam's Sons
An imprint of Penguin Random House LLC, New York

Copyright © 2020 by Kat Cho
Penguin supports copyright. Copyright fuels creativity, encourages diverse voices, promotes free speech, and creates a vibrant culture. Thank you for buying an authorized edition of this book and for complying with copyright laws by not reproducing, scanning, or distributing any part of it in any form without permission. You are supporting writers and allowing Penguin to continue to publish books for every reader.

G. P. Putnam's Sons is a registered trademark of Penguin Random House LLC.

Visit us online at penguinrandomhouse.com

Library of Congress Cataloging-in-Publication Data
Names: Cho, Kat, author.
Title: Vicious spirits / Kat Cho.
Description: New York: G. P. Putnam's Sons, [2020] | Series: [Gumiho; #2]
Companion to: Wicked fox. | Summary: "Somin and Junu are helping
Miyoung and Jihoon heal from their recent trauma when
a new supernatural threat arises"—Provided by publisher.
Identifiers: LCCN 2020017237 (print) | LCCN 2020017238 (ebook)
ISBN 9781984812377 (hardcover) | ISBN 9781984812384 (ebook)
Subjects: CYAC: Supernatural—Fiction. | Murder—Fiction. | Soul—Fiction.
Animals, Mythical—Fiction. | Seoul (Korea)—Fiction. | Korea—Fiction.
Classification: LCC PZ7.1.C5312 Vic 2020 (print) |
LCC PZ7.1.C5312 (ebook) | DDC [Fic]—dc23
LC record available at https://lccn.loc.gov/2020017237
LC ebook record available at https://lccn.loc.gov/2020017238
Printed in the United States of America
ISBN 9781984812377
1 3 5 7 9 10 8 6 4 2

Design by Suki Boynton
Text set in Adobe Caslon Pro

This is a work of fiction. Names, characters, places, and incidents either are the product of the author's imagination or are used fictitiously, and any resemblance to actual persons, living or dead, businesses, companies, events, or locales is entirely coincidental.

For my sister, Jennifer Magiera,
you are my hero and my person!

VICIOUS SPIRITS

PROLOGUE

AS WITH ANY tragedy, it came about because he loved.

When he was on the cusp of manhood, a young man met a girl. She was beautiful, desired by everyone in town, and—unbeknownst to him—desired by a powerful sansin.

However, despite the many scholars and noblemen offering their love, she chose the young man who was only the forgotten last son of a lower noble family. She professed her love for him, and they planned to marry.

In preparation for their marriage, he commissioned a ceramic vase that he would present to her.

He didn't know that, as he prepared his gift, she was preparing one of her own. For the girl he loved was not a girl at all. She was a fox, a gumiho, and she wished to become human for him. But she was tricked by the sansin who coveted her. He persuaded her to kill to gain mortality. One hundred livers devoured in one hundred days. It would allow her to take the gi of her victims—energy that fuels all living things. She did not know that the world demanded balance. That if she took the souls of others, she was sacrificing her own.

The night before their wedding, she came to her young man.

He awoke to see her washed in the light of the moon.

He cringed in fear of her. For she wasn't human, but half

woman–half demon. Her nine tails wove around her as symbols of her true form, and her soul was shrouded in shadows.

He denied her love. The gi she'd devoured fueled her despair, and the gumiho lashed out, killing him in a blind rage.

But that wasn't to be his end, because he awoke again. This time not as a man but as a beast. A dokkaebi. He was cursed by a shaman that served the sansin to roam the earth as an unnatural goblin.

In despair, he planned to kill the shaman who turned him. But before he could, she told him that because of his rejection, the gumiho had hired the shaman to curse the man to this dokkaebi form. And the shaman gave him a chance for his own revenge. She helped him capture the gumiho for the rest of her immortal life. So the vase that was to be his wedding gift became the gumiho's prison.

And Junu lived the rest of his life as a dokkaebi.

1

MIYOUNG LOVED HER mother.

Miyoung mourned her mother.

Miyoung was haunted by her mother.

She didn't use to dream much, and when she did, they were often of her victims. But now, it seemed, she dreamed of her mother as well.

At night, Gu Yena came to Miyoung. Her skin so pale it seemed translucent. Perhaps that's what happened to gumiho when they died. They became spectral things that could haunt you.

"*Eomma,*" Miyoung said. *The innocent title a child gave their mother. The title she hadn't called Yena since she was a toddler. Except for once. Except when Yena lay dying in her arms. "I'm sorry."*

"*Sorry?" In death Yena's voice sounded hollow, distant. A shiver raced down Miyoung's back.*

"*I should have tried harder to save you."*

"*How could you when you can't even save yourself?" Yena asked, sorrow tingeing her words. They hung thick in the air. More accusation than question.*

"*What do you mean?" Miyoung asked, fear joining the chill that spread over her.*

"*You can't save yourself because you don't even know what trouble you're in. My sweet girl. My ignorant saekkiya."*

The words stung, but Miyoung couldn't dwell on that.

"What kind of trouble? Is it because I don't have my yeowu guseul?" Miyoung had always worried losing her fox bead would have dire consequences. She just didn't know it would involve her mother.

Yena's eyes shifted at the mention of Miyoung's bead. A light pulsed, then faded into nothing. "I didn't prepare you enough."

"No, you did everything you could for me."

"And now you must do for yourself."

"How?" The chill seeped into her, so deep it took root in her bones.

"I wish we had more time." Yena sighed, and it seemed as if she started to sift away, fading into the dark around her.

"Eomma!" Miyoung cried out as the cold spread from her spine to take over her limbs. She could barely move them, as if her very blood were freezing.

"How will you go on without me?" Yena asked. "How will you survive?"

"Maybe I won't," Miyoung said moments before her body petrified. Before she became stone, so cold she couldn't even release the tears that pooled.

"Maybe you won't," Yena repeated before the world faded to an icy void. Darker than dark, like a vacuum engulfing everything it touched.

And when Miyoung awoke, her eyes burned. Not from tears. Her cheeks were dry as bone.

When she'd first started having dreams about her mother after her death, she thought they were just that, dreams. A kind of coping mechanism. A way for Miyoung to mourn. But now she was worried they were more. Now she was worried something was wrong. Ever since she lost her fox bead, she'd felt like she was living in a weird kind of limbo. Not quite human, but not really a gumiho either. And it seemed that these visits from Yena were becoming more frequent. And her riddles becoming more threatening. They must be connected.

2

JUNU LOVED A good deal. Sometimes he hated doing business.

But a dollar was a dollar, no matter the hand that gave it to you.

This was what Junu repeated to himself over and over as the . . . customer explained what he needed.

"I think I understand," Junu said.

The creature in front of him huffed, his rancid breath blowing at Junu. His face was broad with a large nose and deep-set eyes. He wore baggy pants and an ill-fitting shirt. A threadbare coat covered him even though the early August heat was sweltering outside. His skin was ruddy, like a man who'd lived his life in the bottle. Or the hue of a creature that many humans refused to believe existed, unless they were under seven years old.

A dokkaebi. The kind of goblin that graced the pages of folktales and myths.

And the kind of thing that Junu was. Though, Junu was the first to point out that there were different *kinds* of dokkaebi and if anyone was to do their research, they'd know that.

Junu was a chonggak dokkaebi, the only ones made to be charming. The ones made so beautiful they could woo anyone they pleased.

So, even though the thick-muscled, slow-witted creature in

front of him shared the name *dokkaebi*, Junu would never call it kin.

"I think I might have something to help you with your . . . problem," Junu said delicately. He didn't want to give the dokkaebi an opening to start explaining the gruesome plan he wanted to enact.

"Good," the dokkaebi mumbled. "I didn't know if you would. I've never heard of one of our kind having to be a merchant."

"Ah, I see," Junu said calmly, though inside he burned from embarrassment and annoyance. Embarrassment because most dokkaebi, despite their horrendous hygiene and taste, looked down on him. And annoyance because he knew it shouldn't matter to him, but it did. "Tell me, how did you come to learn of my services?"

"I ain't been quiet about my plans, and one day this guy appeared, definitely no human. But I'd never seen someone like him before. He seemed almost godlike."

"A god told you about my business?" Junu asked.

"Nah, he wasn't no god, but he just had something about him like he was above us all."

Something sparked in Junu's mind at that.

"Anyway, he told me about you, but I wasn't sure, because buying stuff from a dokkaebi seemed like a scam." The goblin eyed Junu.

He would have been insulted, but it was true: Dokkaebi didn't usually need to do anything menial to earn cash, even though they were known for their healthy greed. They could summon riches with their bangmangi, a goblin staff that some of the more indelicate dokkaebi also liked to use as a club. The only thing dokkaebi liked more than money was mischief. So, to see one running a business—even a black-market one that traded in talismans—would definitely seem suspicious. Like a scam waiting to rob them of every dollar.

"Oh, he actually did want me to give you a message." The dokkaebi snapped his fingers. "He said to tell you 'Hyuk had sent me.' He said it would ensure good service."

"Ah, he did, did he?" Junu asked, turning to a large wooden chest to search through his wares. It also gave him a chance to hide his face and his obvious surprise. Hyuk. A jeoseung saja. And a figure from Junu's past he'd rather forget. What did that old reaper want from him? Junu wondered as he searched through dozens of small drawers that held different knickknacks and magical potions alike. He riffled through a few before he found what he was looking for.

The goblin let out a rumbling noise, and Junu worried it was signaling an attack. Then he realized it was a laugh, and he knew what was coming next.

"Can't you just summon it?"

"My bangmangi is in the shop."

"You don't have it? No dokkaebi would ever give up their staff," the dokkaebi said with a grunt.

"I guess I'm not like other dokkaebi," Junu muttered.

"So you have no magic?" The dokkaebi laughed.

Junu clenched his jaw so he couldn't bite out a reply. Better this way. Wouldn't do to lose his cool in front of a customer, even one as dense as this one. His palms burned, and he realized his nails were digging in so hard they almost broke skin. Slowly he loosened his grip and turned, placing a congenial smile on his face.

"Well, you're lucky that I won't need magic to fill your order." And Junu switched the envelope he'd first selected, plucking out the one next to it. "I think this will help you get far."

"What a strange dokkaebi you are. Having to work like a *human*." The goblin chuckled.

Junu gritted his teeth, then forced a smile. He pulled the golden talisman from its envelope. "I said, I think this will help."

The dokkaebi glowered, but he leaned forward to study the talisman. His coat swung a bit open, and Junu spotted a wooden handle. The dokkaebi's bangmangi.

Junu wondered if he could snatch it. Would it even work for him? He hadn't held one in so long.

His hands itched to reach out, but the dokkaebi's fist came up to grab the envelope. Thick and meaty. And something that could snap Junu in half. If he was good at anything, he was good at self-preservation.

Junu stepped back, pulling the envelope out of reach. "That's one million won." Twice the usual cost, but this goblin had annoyed him.

The dokkaebi sneered but took the staff out from beneath his coat. Unfortunately, he shook the dusty thing out, and from the smell that wafted forward, Junu was certain this dokkaebi didn't wash his clothes very often.

With a thud against the floor, the dokkaebi summoned a small stack of bills to his hand. It was the magic of the goblin staff. The ability to summon what the dokkaebi desired was a convenient trick, and one that meant all dokkaebi had a stash somewhere. In that Junu was just like his brethren, except he had to use his mind to earn the money instead of magic.

Speaking of money, Junu plucked the cash from the other dokkaebi's hand, holding out the envelope with a genteel grin. The small revenge he'd already enacted would have to be enough.

And he watched the hulking goblin exit his house, giving a silent prayer to whatever god that was listening that the talisman would carry this dokkaebi far, far away from Junu's doorstep.

As the door closed, Junu thought of the dokkaebi's words. Hyuk had sent him. Which meant Hyuk was in the mortal realm. Otherwise, he wouldn't have been able to talk to a dokkaebi. Junu almost took out his phone, but he didn't. Whatever the reaper was doing in the mortal realm, Junu wanted nothing to do with it.

THERE ONCE LIVED a boy from a poor family who went into the woods every day to chop firewood to sell in the village and help feed his family. One afternoon as he was out gathering wood, he came upon a walnut tree. He climbed it and gathered walnuts for his family and then sat among the branches eating his fill. However, he stayed too long, and soon it became dark. Knowing he could not find his way home through the forest in the dark, he remembered a small abandoned cottage a few kilometers back. He did not want to sleep on the floor for fear rodents would find him, so he climbed into the rafters and quickly fell asleep.

At midnight a cacophony of sound woke him. Below he saw a group of dokkaebi gathered. They were bragging about the mischief they'd spread that day. One had hung on the tail of an ox all day. Another had teased a naughty boy. Another had danced loudly under a floor, scaring the occupants of the house. Finally, another dokkaebi said it was time to stop chattering and feast.

The boy watched as the dokkaebi pulled out a staff and yelled, "Tudurak tak tak, come out, food, come out, drink!" as he banged his club on the ground.

No sooner had he finished banging his staff than food and

drink appeared out of nowhere. The staff was a bangmangi, a magical summoning club. The dokkaebi danced and ate their fill. And all the while the boy watched. Seeing the feast, the boy began to hunger. So he took out some walnuts and began cracking them with his teeth. The dokkaebi heard the cracking and started to shout, "The roof is breaking! It's going to collapse!" Then they all went running from the shack.

The boy climbed down, ate his fill of the feast, then retrieved the bangmangi from where the dokkaebi had dropped it.

The next morning, the boy made it home. His parents had been quite worried, afraid he was eaten by a tiger, but the boy told them his story and demonstrated the magic of the staff. They were elated; now they would never have to worry about how to feed their family.

But news traveled of the boy's adventure and his new treasure. The son of a rich merchant, who had never worked a day in his life, decided he wanted his own bangmangi, though his family had never been hungry or wanted for anything. He persuaded the poor boy to tell him the details of his adventure. Then he ran off into the forest. First, he found a walnut tree and ate his fill and stuffed his pockets with walnuts. Next, he ran to the shack, climbed into the rafters, and waited for midnight.

The dokkaebi arrived like clockwork and summoned their feast. The rich boy, seeing his prize, did not let the dokkaebi even begin to eat before he cracked a walnut in his teeth. But this time, the dokkaebi were not fooled. They looked straight up and saw the rich boy.

"You again!" they shouted, and pulled the rich boy from the rafters. They punished the boy by making his tongue grow *a hundred meters long. And when he tried to stumble home, he fell in the river. He would have drowned except the poor boy heard his screams and rescued him. From that day forward, the poor boy was no longer hungry and the rich boy never did anything selfish again.*

3

SOMIN HATED SUMMER. And in this first week of August, it was at its worst—sticky and humid and the air felt too thick. Plus, her shoulder-length hair, fried from too many at-home dye jobs, was not in the best shape, and the humidity of summer made it frizz in unflattering ways.

Sometimes she dreamed of leaving Seoul, just packing a duffel and leaving. And those fantasies tripled when the summer got truly unbearable like it was now. But Somin knew she could never really leave. She had too many responsibilities here.

One of those responsibilities lay in the small apartment above the dark, empty restaurant. Jihoon's halmeoni's little restaurant used to be a bustling place, a hub in the neighborhood. But it had been closed for months now. The landlord had used Halmeoni's illness as an excuse to change the terms of their lease. And as soon as it was clear he couldn't pay the rent, Jihoon had received an eviction notice. Even thinking about it made Somin's blood boil. The second-floor apartment door was unlocked. The space inside felt like it should be musty, like she was opening a time capsule. But she knew better. Jihoon and Miyoung had been living in the apartment for the past few months. A strange fast-forward in their relationship that would have worried Somin. Except now she knew that worrying about dating teens living together was nothing compared to knowing the real horrors that lurked in the shadows of the world. Things that could rip out your liver or your throat without a second thought.

Somin liked to think she was pretty tough. She didn't scare easily. She would never run from a fight, especially if it meant defending someone she loved. Still, knowing that the monsters in her childhood storybooks were real was a cold shock to the ever-practical Lee Somin. Now she had to readjust her whole way of looking at the world. And for a girl who always liked to be right, it was a hard thing to accept.

As Somin let the door close behind her, she wasn't sure what she expected, but Gu Miyoung in an apron, dusting the shelves, was not it.

"Did I step into an alternate universe?" Somin asked.

Miyoung glanced up. She was beautiful. With ebony hair that swung halfway down her back, long legs, thick lashes, full lips. But when she looked close enough, Somin saw the worry in the pursed set of Miyoung's mouth.

"I know how to clean an apartment," Miyoung said. "I'm not a total slob."

"Oh, I never thought that," Somin said. "I just figured dusting was beneath a gumiho."

"Well, I'm not really a gumiho anymore," Miyoung muttered.

The only thing weirder than realizing that her new friend had been a gumiho was learning how she'd become a not-gumiho. Betrayal, lost fox beads, a long-lost father, and an overprotective mother.

Somin had grown up hearing stories about gumiho—nine-tailed foxes with the ability to live forever as long as they devoured the energy of men. And in the span of one night, she'd had to accept that they existed and that there was one who wanted to kill her best friend, Jihoon. Miyoung's mother, Gu Yena, to be exact. A gumiho who had lived for hundreds of years and had been willing to do anything, even kill—even die—to protect Miyoung.

It had been a few months since she found out Miyoung's secret, and sometimes Somin still forgot that Miyoung wasn't just human.

Jihoon walked out of his bedroom, a tall boy with a lanky frame and hair that always looked mussed, probably because, more often than not, he'd just woken up from a nap. He spotted Somin and gave her a sad smile. It looked wrong on his handsome face. His face was better suited for wicked grins that made his dimples wink. But Somin supposed he had nothing to really smile about today.

"Jihoon-ah, are you putting your girlfriend to work while you sleep away the day?" Somin said, but there was no bite to the words.

His smile deepened a bit, so there was a hint of dimples. Like a ghostly trace of the affable boy Somin had grown up with.

"She volunteered for cleaning duty. Don't offer to do the boring work if you don't want me to accept." He shrugged. Jihoon was never one to make excuses, but his blunt honesty was part of his charm, usually.

"I'd rather dust than try to clean out the black hole you call a bedroom," Miyoung said.

"You make fun of it, but when the government pays me billions to study the natural phenomenon of a black hole right here in Seoul, you'll be sorry," Jihoon quipped.

Somin rolled her eyes, but secretly she was relieved her best friend was still able to make jokes on a day like today. "What job should I do?" She glanced at the empty boxes scattered throughout the room. Not even a dish towel packed away yet. Perhaps because these weren't just things. This was everything that Jihoon had left of his halmeoni—the woman who had raised him. And now she was gone. Somin understood why the boxes were still empty: because packing away these things was like packing away memories.

She started to reach for a box at the same time Miyoung did. When their hands brushed, she felt a spark, like static shock. It happened often when she came in contact with the former gumiho, as if Miyoung's latent fox abilities still hungered for energy.

"Sorry," Miyoung muttered.

"No worries," Somin assured her. "As long as you don't suck out all my gi, we can stay friends."

Miyoung pursed her lips at that. She still wasn't quite able to joke about her old gumiho life. Somin couldn't really blame her. After all, she figured it had to be traumatizing to survive by taking the lives of others.

"Knock, knock." Somin's mother opened the front door. "Sorry I'm late. Traffic was horrible. I *was* going to take the subway, but I just didn't want to deal with so many sweaty people. I hate public transportation during the summer. But then I guess everyone else had the same idea to drive, and it took way too long to get here."

Somin almost laughed. Usually, it was a toss-up who was taking care of whom between the two. Her mother was all spark and energy and light. But she was also so scattered she'd forget her own brain if it wasn't shut securely in her head. Even though Somin was just a nineteen-year-old high school senior, she was definitely the more responsible out of the two.

There was no one in this world Somin loved as much as her mother, except maybe Jihoon. They weren't quite a traditional family, but Somin considered them a unit.

"It's all right, Ms. Moon, we haven't even gotten started," Jihoon said.

"Some of us have," Miyoung muttered.

"Well, what should we tackle first?" Somin's mother clapped her hands together and looked expectantly at her daughter.

Now Somin did laugh. It always fell on her to take charge. "Jihoon, why don't you take care of your black-hole room. Miyoung, can you do the bathroom? Mom, can you do . . ." She hesitated, then said, "The back room?" because she couldn't quite bring herself to say "Halmeoni's room."

Her mom gave her a knowing smile. "Of course." She picked up a box and headed to the back.

Jihoon stared after Somin's mother as she opened the door to Halmeoni's room. He still didn't move as the door closed behind her.

"Jihoon-ah," Somin said.

"Clean my black hole of a room, got it," he said, his voice way too bright.

"Is he doing all right?" Somin asked Miyoung when Jihoon was gone.

"He's surviving," Miyoung said as she picked up a box and hauled it into the small bathroom.

Somin sighed. That wasn't what she had asked. But she knew that Miyoung had lived the first eighteen years of her life shutting the rest of the world out. For Miyoung, surviving was the main goal of life.

The living space of the apartment was small and cozy. The well-used couch slouching in the middle from decades of use. Yellow bujeoks fluttered against the door frame—talismans taped around the entryway to ward off bad energy.

Somin started on the kitchen, putting pots and pans into boxes. She wondered if they should save the mugs and dishes. Maybe Jihoon would want some later? Or was she overthinking this?

She wiped her arm against her sweaty forehead and turned to rummage through the fridge for a drink. It was empty. Honestly, Somin had no idea how those two had survived together in this apartment the last four months.

The front door opened and let in the noise of the outside.

That must be Oh Changwan, the final one of their motley crew. Late as usual. With some halfhearted plan to cheer herself up by giving Changwan hell, Somin stepped out of the kitchen. Changwan was tall and gangly. With a buzz cut that highlighted his too-big ears. He hated the cut, but his strict father insisted on it. Changwan was a sweet boy with a nervous energy that probably came from the high expectations his rich father had for his firstborn son. Somin always felt like Changwan would do much better with more carrot and less stick. But she also knew she couldn't poke her nose into another family's private business.

"I know, I know. I'm late. But I brought iced Americanos." Changwan was trying to balance a tray of iced drinks and Somin almost wept with gratitude. There was no air-conditioning in the apartment, and she was roasting. But she stopped short as she saw who stood behind Changwan.

Where Changwan was tall and gangly, this other boy was tall and lean in an almost athletic way. Though, Somin had never seen Junu exercise once since she'd known him. He had the kind of figure that wore clothes well. His hair was silky and perfectly styled. His eyes were striking as they met hers. And Somin glared in greeting.

"How did you get in here?" she demanded.

"Why? You thought I only existed in your dreams?" Junu winked.

She almost groaned. She really hated this dokkaebi.

4

JUNU WOULD NEVER claim the title of saint. Far from it, in fact. Even when he was human, he never pretended he held any more virtue than the average person. Still, he wasn't a complete monster, though many would argue he was, seeing as he was a goblin. And honestly, he found it much easier to meet expectations most of the time. Which was why he was a bit perplexed with finding himself standing inside the threshold of Ahn Jihoon's apartment. Or old apartment, he guessed, as he surveyed the packing boxes littering the floor.

He was really regretting all his decisions that day. Junu hated physical labor. This was not how he thought he'd be spending his Sunday when he woke up this morning.

Then there was Lee Somin, who stood, hands on hips, blocking his path. The pose was meant to threaten, but it only accentuated her short build. Junu acknowledged he was tall at 185 centimeters, but if he took a step forward, Somin's face would be squarely planted in his chest. A funny image, now that he thought of it.

"What the hell are you smiling at?" Somin demanded.

If he were a lesser man, it would have frightened him. Okay, fine, it did frighten him a bit. But over his centuries of life, Junu had learned the power of a good bluff. Added to that, he wasn't quite fully a man, per se.

"I bet I could pick you up and put you in my pocket," Junu said. He knew exactly what reaction he would get from that. And as if on cue, Somin's face reddened, her cheeks puffed out all cute, and her fists clenched. Junu shifted on his feet, ready to jump away if she came at him. He'd learned the hard way that Somin was as much bite as bark.

Still, it was worth it to see her eyes flare. They sparked like she held fire inside. It always intrigued him. This firecracker of a girl.

"What is he doing here?" Somin asked Changwan.

"I'm just here to help out. Looking to be assigned a job," Junu replied before Changwan could.

"Changwan-ah, you're here." Somin's mother rushed out of Halmeoni's room. "Let me have one of those coffees." Her mother took a sip, closing her eyes to savor the iced Americano.

"And, Junu," she said, turning to the dokkaebi with a dazzling smile. "I didn't know you were coming."

He gave her a congenial smile and a small flush rose in her cheeks. With a bow he said, "Good to see you again, Somin's eomeoni."

"Oh, that makes me sound so old," she said with a giggle.

"You *are* old, Mother," Somin said, taking a cup of coffee as well.

"Yes, but we don't have to always be talking about it," Somin's mother said, with a wink to Junu.

He laughed and wondered why the daughter had not inherited the mother's good humor.

"Well, where can we help?" Changwan asked, placing the tray of coffees on the living room table.

"Why don't you pack up the living room?" Somin's mother

said. With a grunt of disgust, Somin retreated back into the kitchen. Soon Junu heard the angry clatter of dishes.

"Wrap everything well," Somin's mother said before disappearing down the hall again.

Junu looked around at the knickknack-filled space. It would take a while to make sure everything was put away with care. He wondered if he was in over his head. Maybe it had been a mistake to volunteer for this. He could just leave, but Junu always kept his word. And if he said he was here to help, he was going to help. Even if the August heat was somehow worse in here than it was outside.

As Changwan took frames off the shelf, Junu started wrapping them in old newspapers. He wasn't sure whether he was doing a good job or not, but he figured the more padding the better.

"Maybe that's too much newspaper, Hyeong?" Changwan said.

"Really?" Junu asked, crossing his arms and studying the box that was probably 70 percent newspaper and only 30 percent actual things.

"Yeah, you might be great at strategizing video game battles, but I think we've failed at packing." Changwan frowned, and it made his too-big nose scrunch.

"Well, being good at packing is only a required life skill if your job is a mover," Junu said. "And I doubt any romantic pursuits will care if you can wrap frames in the right amount of newspaper. Make a note of that, Changwan-ah."

Just as he said it, Somin stomped out of the kitchen. "Don't take dating advice from him, unless you want to get slapped."

Junu held a hand over his heart. "Lee Somin, that hurts. I get slapped only like fifteen percent of the time. I swear."

Changwan laughed and earned a glare from Somin.

She looked down at their half-packed box. "You two are horrible at this."

"Are you out here to check up on us?" Junu asked.

"No, I needed more tape." She picked up the roll of packing tape as if that were proof enough. "But I'm glad I came out here. If you keep going at this rate, you'll use ten boxes for one bookshelf. Maybe you should wash the dishes instead."

"I don't really like doing dishes, they make my hands all pruney . . ." Changwan trailed off as Somin sent him a pointed look. "But then again, that's what they make dishwashing gloves for." He scurried into the kitchen like a frightened rabbit.

Somin had started unwrapping the frames and laying them on the table when Junu knelt beside her. "What are you doing?" she asked.

"Dishes is a one-man job. I figured you just wanted an excuse to be alone with me," Junu said, wiggling his brows.

"Fine, it's probably better than letting you fill Changwan's brain with your ridiculous advice. Why are you so obsessed with the idea of turning him into a clone of you, anyway?"

"Is that so bad?" He held up a hand before she could answer. "Never mind, I know already. To you, that would be a fate worse than death."

She carefully folded the paper around the delicate frames before stacking them in the box. "Well, I wasn't going to be quite so extreme, but yes. Let Changwan be his own person. He's nothing like you."

At that Junu almost laughed, but he knew Somin wouldn't

get the humor in what she said. And Junu wasn't about to give up any secrets from his past. If you asked Junu, the past was behind them for a reason.

Instead, he shrugged. "I just want to give him some more confidence. He's a smart boy; he can be anything he wants if he puts his mind to it."

"You don't know anything about Changwan." Somin's voice became harsh. The voice she got when she was being protective of her friends. Junu didn't know why it bothered him, except that the person she was protecting them from was so often Junu.

"Changwan and I are friends." It came out a bit more defensive than Junu had intended.

Somin let out a snort. "You're too selfish to have any friends."

That stung, and Junu was about to give a sharp retort when Somin's mother walked back in, extra boxes in her arms. "Found these in the back room, figured we could use them out here."

Somin jumped up to help her mother with the pile. Junu was debating whether to stick out his tongue at Somin's back when her eyes shot to him, an unspoken warning sharp in her brown irises. If he didn't know better, he'd have thought her a gwishin or other evil spirit descended on him as some kind of curse.

Somin's mother was on the shorter side; it was clear that's where Somin had gotten her height. Her black hair was pulled back in a bun, but a few wisps still fell around her forehead, giving her the illusion of youth. She was energetic, always ready with a smile that created lines around her eyes. Instead of adding age, it made her look like a warm welcome. She was more scattered than her tightly controlling daughter. But Somin also broke rules, like the dress code at her school, and got into fights. It would seem like a contradiction, except Junu could tell that it wasn't that Somin didn't live by rules; she just lived by *her* rules. She truly fascinated him.

"Junu, I can't say how nice it is for you to come and help," Ms. Moon said, and there was that kind smile.

"Of course. I'm always here for a *friend*." He emphasized the word and gave Somin a wink.

Her mouth formed a thin line, and he imagined she was trying to hold back harsh words that would earn her a smack from her mother.

Junu almost gave another wink just to annoy her, but Miyoung stepped out of the bathroom.

She was hauling what looked like a very full and very heavy box. The sight of her made Junu lose any of his glib words. He never knew the right thing to say in front of Miyoung these days. Every time he saw her, he felt a rolling in his stomach. In the past, when he felt uncomfortable around someone, he'd just leave. But for some reason the idea of leaving made him feel even worse. For the first time in his immortal life, he felt like he owed a debt to someone. And he hated it.

Despite her disheveled hair, tired eyes, and the light sheen of sweat on her brow, Miyoung was gorgeous. Though, Junu would expect nothing less from the former gumiho. A girl so beautiful men fell instantly in love with her only to find themselves missing a liver. He'd once thought they could be confidants, two immortals living with the burden of being seen one way and, when that glamour faded, labeled as monsters.

But that was the old Miyoung, and she hadn't even been that good at the whole predatory immortal lifestyle of the fabled nine-tailed fox.

Miyoung stopped short when she saw him. Her eyes narrowed as if deciding how to handle his presence. It was clear she wasn't happy to see him.

"Hello, Miyoung-ah," Junu said. "You need help with that?"

She tilted her head in a way that reminded him of a fox, then set down her packed box on a far pile and turned to Somin's mother. "I need another box."

"Here you go." Ms. Moon handed her one from her pile.

Without another word, Miyoung disappeared into the bathroom.

Junu watched her retreating back, wondering if she would ever truly talk to him again. It wasn't that he *missed* her conversation. Miyoung had always been a prickly companion at best. But he couldn't deny that her company had been an interesting change from his loner lifestyle. The three months they'd lived together had been quite eventful. And if he was being honest, he'd become quite invested in Miyoung's life.

But of course, he'd made mistakes that had cost them their unlikely alliance. Perhaps Junu could have even called it a friendship for a time.

Still, one mistake had cost a life. It had cost Miyoung her mother. A long time ago, Junu had sworn to himself he would no longer deal in games of life and death. So, whether she would accept it or not, Junu felt like he owed some kind of restitution to Miyoung for his actions. He would stick around until he'd paid back the debt. The problem was he wasn't sure when that would be. He might be an immortal dokkaebi, but even he couldn't know when this weight of guilt would ease from his chest. It was damned inconvenient if you asked him, but it was something he could not ignore.

"So, Junu, how are classes?" Ms. Moon brought him back to the present.

He thought about whatever lie they'd told Somin's mother.

"At Hongik University, right?"

"Ah yes," Junu said with a pleasant smile. "It's great. Love the area."

He forever looked like he was just leaving his teens. Some, Ms. Moon's daughter being one of them, might even claim he still had the maturity of a prepubescent child, but he was centuries old. Still, he accepted the fact that Ms. Moon lumped him in with her daughter's classmates, though the story was that he was a twenty-year-old student in his first year in university. He hadn't even remembered whether they'd told her an actual university when they made up the lie of who Junu was—Miyoung's cousin.

"So will Miyoung be moving back in with you?" Ms. Moon asked, and Junu didn't process the words at first. He'd just assumed Miyoung would find a place of her own, but he remembered that nineteen was still one year away from being a legal adult even though he could argue that it was an arbitrary designation. He still didn't feel like an "adult" half the time.

Somin paused in her packing, turning toward them. Her eyes were wide, as if warning Junu to tread carefully. So, of course, he wanted to do the exact opposite.

"Eomma, I don't think Miyoung has decided where she's going to stay yet," Somin said at the same time Junu blurted out, "Of course," without pausing too long to consider it.

Somin's mother let out a relieved sigh. "Oh, good. I was so worried about where Miyoung would go."

At the sound of her name, the girl in question poked her head out of the bathroom. "Did you call for me?"

"I was telling your cousin I'm so glad to hear you have a place to stay," Somin's mother said.

"What?" Miyoung's eyes shifted to Junu with suspicion.

"I told Somin's mother that you're moving back in with me, right, cuz?" Junu said, plastering a bright smile onto his face.

Miyoung's scowl was so immediate that he wondered if it was brought about by the mere sound of his voice. "I don't—"

"That's such a relief," Somin's mother said, giving a small laugh. "I really was worried when Somin said she had no idea where Miyoung was going to live. And with our place so cramped already with Jihoon now, I didn't know how we'd cram another teenager in there." It was almost cute, how Ms. Moon babbled to cover her obvious discomfort with the idea. She really wasn't one to filter her thoughts.

"Thank you for the thought. And I appreciate the offer . . . , cuz." Miyoung bit out the last word like it was a vile curse. "But I don't want to be a burden."

"Oh, it wouldn't be a burden at all. I'd be happy to have you." Junu added one of his charming smiles.

There was a minute of silence. Even Somin seemed frozen. But Ms. Moon, either completely unaware or willfully ignorant in the face of an easy solution to her guilt, spoke up. "I think it's best if you stay with Junu," she said. "Wouldn't you be happier to be with family?"

The look in Miyoung's eyes seemed to transmit a message clear as if she'd spoken the words. *You're going to regret this.*

So, because Junu couldn't help himself, he gave the hornet's nest one more poke. "That's right. Trust your oppa."

"Sure," Miyoung bit out.

5

AFTER MIYOUNG AND Junu had gotten into their non-fight, there was a palpable tension between them. Everyone felt it. Well, everyone except Somin's mother and Changwan, who was so oblivious to life that Somin sometimes wondered how he functioned.

But Changwan had to leave to meet a private tutor. Without his mindless chatter, Somin could feel the tension between Miyoung and Junu no matter where she went in the small apartment. And after two hours of it, she felt suffocated. She was debating the best way to escape when there was a knock on the door.

"Eomma," she called. "I think lunch is here."

Somin opened the door and blinked in confusion as she stared at the men with matching T-shirts. They carried reusable moving boxes she'd seen in nicer neighborhoods and padded furniture covers.

"This the Ahn household?" the first man asked.

"Yes, but I don't understand. We didn't hire movers."

"I did," Junu said, standing up from his packing. He let out a groan and bent to stretch his cramped legs. "Come on in. We've still got a lot to do in the living area." He turned to Somin. "Figured since we lost Changwan, this would be easier all around."

"You hired them?" Somin asked as the men brushed past her into the apartment. "Wait, no, don't touch that." She yanked a photo frame away from one of the movers. "We don't need movers."

"It's not a case of need. But why not take the help?" Junu asked.

"These aren't just *things*. They hold sentimental value." She shook the frame she still held at him.

"I hired movers, not circus jugglers. They'll take care of the stuff," Junu said, laughter in his voice.

Somin's anger drove her forward. "This is so typical." She jabbed a finger into Junu's chest. "You come in and create a scene and then throw your money around to get what you want. Why did you even come here in the first place if you didn't want to work?"

"Lee Somin!" Her mother's voice echoed through the apartment, effectively freezing Somin as she was about to drive her finger into Junu's chest again. Miyoung and Jihoon stood in the hallway behind her mother, watching the scene with curiosity. "I will not have my daughter speaking that way in front of guests."

"Guests?" Somin asked incredulously, but she let her hand drop.

"Well, we weren't expecting help, but it's appreciated. Why don't I show one of you what needs to be packed in the back room?" Somin's mother said to the movers. "Jihoon-ah, show the other gentleman what to do in the kitchen."

Somin waited for Jihoon to back her up, to say they didn't need help, but he just shrugged and walked into the kitchen to help the mover.

The other man followed Somin's mother. With a final look that clearly said *behave*, her mother disappeared down the hall.

"Miyoung-ah," Somin said, futilely searching for an ally.

But Miyoung just shrugged.

With a grunt of disgust, Somin turned back but spotted Junu watching her with his arms crossed. Instead of saying something she'd catch heat from her mother for, she grabbed a trash bag and stomped out the front door.

The air outside was thick and humid, almost unbearably so, but she had to get away for her own sanity.

She took her sweet time separating out the recycling from the trash and putting them all in the correct receptacles, stopping every so often to wipe sweat off her brow. There were no clouds in the summer sky to block the intense rays of the sun. It was as if the weather knew that today would be hard and just wanted to add more suffering on top of the pain.

She upended the bottom of the bag with the last of the recycling, but a can hit the edge of the receptacle and bounced across the asphalt, rolling down the incline. Hot, sweaty, and still annoyed from her fight with Junu, she wanted to just let it go, but she'd been raised better than that and jogged after it. The can came to rest centimeters from a pair of battered loafers.

"Oh, sorry," Somin said to the man. He had salt-and-pepper hair mostly covered by a baseball cap. His back was to her, but there was something about him that felt eerily familiar.

Why was she so intrigued by this man? He was just standing there. Perhaps it was because he stood so still, he could have been made of stone. Anyone else might turn, bend down to pick up the can for her, or at least acknowledge her, but he just stood there. Maybe he hadn't heard her. As she approached him, she could just make out the scent of licorice.

She picked up the can, but when she stood, the man was gone. Somin could have sworn he'd been there just a second ago. She scanned the road but saw no sign of him. She hadn't even heard his footsteps as he'd retreated. In fact, she might have convinced herself no one had been there at all except she could swear she still smelled the faint scent of licorice.

"Strange," she murmured to herself as she walked to the trash receptacles.

As she dropped the can into the recycling bin, a cold sensation washed over the back of Somin's neck. So chilly, it made the hairs at her nape stand. The wilted trees by the roadside stood still. There was no breeze, but she felt the chill again, a prickle against her skin.

Then Somin saw him, not the older man but a teenager. He stood out somehow. Like he didn't belong here. Not just in this neighborhood, but in this world.

Maybe it was because he was dressed head to toe in black with a brimmed black hat to match. He even had a matching black trench coat over his suit; he had to be roasting. But that wasn't the strangest thing about him. She was pretty sure he was staring straight at her. Though he was a few meters away, she could see his eyes. They were as black as his clothes and unblinking as they watched her.

He was tall, and even though half of his face was shaded by the hat, he was striking. Pale skin, full lips, dark eyes.

"Can I help you?" Somin asked.

The boy finally blinked. "You can see me?"

Somin frowned. "Yeah, you're standing right in front of me, staring like a byeontae."

"So strange," he said, but it seemed mostly to himself. He didn't even care that Somin had called him a pervert.

Somin let the lid of the recycling bin fall as she fumbled in her pocket for her phone, just in case she needed to call for help.

"You slam those lids any harder, you might break something," called the old woman who sat across the street.

She spun around, then bowed in apology. "Sorry."

Hwang Halmeoni was a fixture in this neighborhood, a woman hovering around the century mark who still ran her medicinal wine shop across the street from Jihoon's old apartment. She sat on the wooden deck outside of her shop, an umbrella perched to protect her from the sun and an electric fan blowing from the open doorway. Rain or shine, hot or cold, you could depend on Hwang Halmeoni to be on her perch watching the neighborhood.

Somin turned back to the boy, but he was gone. Just as suddenly as the old man. Strange. Was the heat affecting her somehow?

"Did you see that boy?" Somin asked Hwang Halmeoni, walking over to the medicinal wine store.

"Which one? That cute Junu that keeps hanging around here?" Hwang Halmeoni wiggled her brows. "He's sure been a treat for my eyes lately."

Somin didn't want to talk about Junu, so instead she asked, "Should you be sitting outside in this heat?"

Hwang Halmeoni waved away Somin's concern with the giant fan in her hand. "Inside. Outside. It's hot no matter where I sit. At least this way I can see the goings-on in the neighborhood."

Somin laughed and nodded.

"Moving day?" Hwang Halmeoni asked, her eyes sad as they focused on Jihoon's apartment.

"Yeah," Somin said. "We're packing everything up today."

"Mrs. Nam had been in this building for over forty years. It won't be the same without her, even if I did tell her she made her kimchi jjigae too spicy."

Somin laughed at that. Leave it to Hwang Halmeoni to be brutally honest. "I'm sad you and I won't be able to have our talks anymore."

"Well, you should still come visit me. One thing is for sure, I'll never leave."

"Why not?" Somin asked. She knew that Hwang Halmeoni had a daughter who'd moved south around Busan a while ago, but still Hwang Halmeoni had stayed.

"When I was younger, we were forced to leave our home. Not out of a desire to see the country, but out of a desire to survive."

Somin knew Hwang Halmeoni was old enough to remember a unified Korea, and how it was broken in two, but she realized she'd never heard the woman talk about it.

"We weren't able to come back for years, and when we did, everything seemed different to me. Perhaps when you're forced out of your home like that, you're willing to hold on to it with all you've got when you get it back. I'm sorry Jihoon wasn't allowed to hold on to his."

The way Hwang Halmeoni looked at Somin made her self-conscious, like the old woman was looking into Somin's soul. Like she could see the secret desire that Somin had never told anyone—that sometimes she wished she could just leave. To go and be anywhere but here. But she knew it was a pipe dream. Where would she even go? And where would she get the money for it? She should just take a lesson from Hwang Halmeoni's words and appreciate what she had: a good family, good friends, a place to call home.

Somin's mother stepped out of the apartment and lifted her

hand to her brow as if scanning the terrain, stopping when she zeroed in on Somin below.

"Your mother should find someone," Hwang Halmeoni said. "Such a pretty woman like that, a shame for her to be alone."

"She's not alone," Somin said. "She has me."

"Of course she does." Hwang Halmeoni patted Somin's hand.

"Somin-ah," her mother said, jogging across the street to join them. "Hello, Hwang Halmeoni." She dipped into a bow.

"Moon Soohyun, you look like you could be Sominie's sister instead of her mother."

Somin's mother blushed. It was true, Somin thought. Her mother always had such a youthful glow about her. Despite the things she'd been through—getting pregnant right after high school, losing her husband when Somin was still so young—she was ever the optimist. Somin wondered why she hadn't inherited any of that positivity.

"Somin-ah, I'm going to go buy some drinks for the movers. They're working so hard, and it's so hot, you could bake an egg in there. Can you keep everything in order here?"

"Sure," Somin said. She was used to her mother trusting her to take charge of things. It had been that way since she was a little girl. Her mother used to say she was so serious about everything she did, wanting it all to be absolutely perfect. *I'm so lucky to have a daughter like you,* her mother always said. *I had no idea what I was doing, but you made it so easy for me.*

Somin used to love that her mother said that. It made her feel so useful. Though the truth of her childhood was that Somin had raised her mother just as much as her mother had raised her.

On her way back to the apartment, Somin stopped short when she spotted Junu outside, fanning himself as he perched on the railing of the stairs. Somin considered just giving him a push. The two-story fall probably wouldn't kill him with his fast dokkaebi reflexes. But it would give Somin great satisfaction.

He lifted his head, perhaps alerted by the sound of her steps, or maybe it was those supernatural dokkaebi senses. He sent her a cocky grin.

Somin ignored him and tried to walk around, but he blocked her path.

"What's the rush?" Junu asked. "Didn't you leave to get away from the stuffy apartment?"

"I left to get away from *you*."

Junu laughed, the opposite reaction she'd wanted. "Lee Somin, your words hurt."

"Yeah, right."

"I mean it. I've never been quite so . . . intrigued by a person before. Can't you give me a chance?"

Somin glared at the suave words. Junu's beauty was both smooth and hard. The kind of face that looked better with a smirk. And Junu always took advantage of his best features, so his mocking smile was pretty much a permanent fixture.

It's why Somin had hated just the sight of his smug face from the day she'd met him. What did he have to be so confident about? It's not like he worked hard for that face. The luck of being born with good looks wasn't something to brag about. And to make matters worse, every time he spoke, heads turned. As if everything he said was the most important thing in the world. He probably thought so, as nine times out of ten, he spoke about himself. Pompous ass.

"Not if you were the last boy on earth."

"Good thing I'm not only a boy." Junu's grin widened.

Somin made a gagging noise deep in her throat. "Don't make me throw up."

"I bet I could change your mind if I put any effort into it."

She let out a short, sarcastic laugh. "I'd love to see you try." She'd blurted it out before she had time to think. Or remember the fact that the dokkaebi loved to take things literally just to piss her off.

Junu's grin turned into a full-fledged smile. "Would you, now?"

Something seemed to take over Somin, an overwhelming sense of competitiveness that she couldn't fight. She lifted her chin and said, "Of course. Give it your best shot."

He took a step forward and every muscle in Somin's body tensed, but she didn't step back. She knew Junu's type, and she knew he was bluffing. She refused to lose at this game.

"I'd say that I love everything about you. I love your hair." He picked up a strand of her shoulder-length hair and let it sift through his fingers. She held her head rigid, the sight of his fingers a blur in the corner of her eyes. She refused to take her gaze from his. This was a game of wills, and hers was made of steel.

"I love your hands," Junu said, picking one up. He studied it, letting a smile quirk the corner of his mouth. Somin searched for the mocking in the tilt of his lips, but instead he looked purely enamored as he let their fingers intertwine. He was good. But she wouldn't be swayed by pretty words and quick smiles.

"I love your lips." His eyes lifted again, landing on the new object of his faux affection. His hand tightened around hers, and his body moved closer. His eyes filled her vision. He tilted his head down. Her heart was sprinting at a breakneck speed. So fast it practically hummed in her chest. She wondered how it didn't cause her whole body to vibrate. Or was it and she was just numb to it? Still she didn't move. She waited as he brought his mouth within a centimeter of hers.

"I love everything you possess," he said, his words breathed over her lips. "I'd like to possess it, too."

Somin's heart was racing, and she told herself it was the heat.

"You use the word *love* so selfishly," Somin said.

And perhaps it was shock at her words, or perhaps it was him tiring of his own game, but Junu finally moved back. She'd won, though she didn't feel the triumph that she wanted as her heart continued to sprint.

"Selfish?" Junu asked, letting her hand drop from his.

"You use it to mean you want to own a person. That's a pretty selfish sentiment," Somin said, thanking the gods that her voice came out smooth and calm. "You love what a girl has, not what she is."

A silent beat passed before Junu threw his head back and let out a loud, guffawing laugh. "Oh, Lee Somin, you are definitely an opponent to be reckoned with." Junu spoke in such an antiquated way. And worse, he sounded good doing it.

"Is it any wonder I look forward to our little sparring matches?"

"They're not sparring matches. I genuinely hate you," Somin said.

"Hate to love," Junu said with a wiggle of his eyebrows.

Whatever Somin would have said in retort was interrupted by a gruff voice behind them. "This where Nam Soonboon lives?"

"Not anymore," Somin said, turning around.

"Where's my good-for-nothing son?" the man said, and Somin lifted a brow, surprised.

She only had a vague memory of Jihoon's father. But she could tell the years hadn't been kind to him. He was tall—it must be where Jihoon had gotten his height—but he hunched over like he hadn't the energy to hold his frame up. He had thinning gray hair, a pockmarked face, and lines radiating from his squinting eyes. A cigarette hung from his fingers, still lit, as if he'd just pulled it from between his lips.

This was the last person Jihoon needed to see today.

"Not sure who you're referring to, sir," Junu said, his voice pleasant, but there was a spark in his eye. A sharpness that Somin had never seen in the dokkaebi before.

"Who the hell do you think my son is? That good-for-nothing ingrate who doesn't even have the courtesy to pay any respects to his father in fifteen years."

That was it. Somin couldn't hold her tongue anymore. "Maybe he would have if he'd even known where you were."

"Do I know you?" Mr. Ahn drawled as he glared at her.

"I'm Jihoon's friend, and I've *been* in his life for the past fifteen years."

"Why, you little brat," Mr. Ahn said, clenching his yellowed teeth.

Somin started forward, but Junu's hand stopped her. It wasn't restraining, but it served to get her to pause, to take a beat. For the first time ever, Somin was grateful that he was here or else she didn't know what she'd say (or do) to Jihoon's father.

"Well, seeing as this is the first time we're meeting, I believe introductions are in order." Junu held out a hand. "I'm Junu, and you are . . . ?"

Mr. Ahn ignored him and turned to shout, "Ya, Ahn Jihoon! You come out and greet your father, you ungrateful boy."

The door opened, and Jihoon stepped out. His expression was blank and cold. Except Somin knew him well enough to notice the tic in his jaw. Miyoung stepped out as well, her eyes hard, like she was ready for a fight.

"What are you doing here?" Jihoon's voice was low and clipped.

"A few months ago, a private investigator came sniffing around. Said he was hired by some big-shot Seoul cop to find me. Said it had to do with my son. So I thought it was about time to come see how you were doing." Jihoon's father puffed on his cigarette, blowing out smoke in lazy clouds.

Big-shot Seoul cop. That could only mean one person. Hae Taewoo. Miyoung's fists clenched. She must have been thinking the same thing Somin was. That her father, a man who had gotten close to Jihoon in order to find Miyoung, was still messing with their lives from beyond the grave. He'd tried to kill Miyoung this past spring, and now his actions had brought Jihoon's father back to town.

It also wasn't lost on Somin that the private investigator had found Jihoon's father a few months ago, but he'd still waited to come. Probably because he needed something now.

"You guys, can I have a minute alone?" Jihoon asked.

Somin wanted to say no, and from Miyoung's silence, she seemed to feel the same way.

Jihoon must have sensed it as well, because he said to his father, "Can we go downstairs to talk in private?"

Instead of replying, the man gestured for Jihoon to lead the way.

When Somin moved to follow them down the stairs, Junu held her back. "He wants to handle this alone."

Somin wanted to object. She wanted to shout that this was unfair. That Jihoon didn't deserve this. But she'd learned that what was right and fair was rarely what happened in this world. Her friends' broken lives were all proof of that. So she turned back to Miyoung.

"We can't just stand here. That man is a bastard who abused Jihoon as a kid!"

Miyoung's eyes were glued to the top of the stairs. "I'd like to siphon away all his energy and leave his body to rot."

Even Somin was shocked by the vitriol she heard in Miyoung's voice. "Can you still do that?"

"There's only one way to find out." Then she sighed. "But when my father came back, I needed to be able to face him alone. Jihoon probably needs to do the same." Miyoung stepped into the apartment.

And, outnumbered, Somin followed behind her.

6

JUNU HAD TOLD Somin to allow Jihoon to face his father, but that didn't mean Jihoon should be left without backup. Junu could tell Mr. Ahn was the type of person who abandoned the ones who needed him most until he could come around and leech off them. There were only two reasons for a man like that to come around: He was running from something or he wanted something. Either way, he should be dealt with quickly and efficiently.

Junu leaned against the front of the building, out of sight from the front windows, but close enough that with his dokkaebi hearing he could make out what was being said inside.

"There's nothing for you here," Jihoon was saying.

Don't show weakness, Junu thought. *Make him think he doesn't affect you. Don't let him have a piece of your pride.*

"That's not for you to decide," Mr. Ahn said. There was the sound of lips puffing on the cigarette. A nasty habit, if you asked Junu.

"You can go through the place, but you won't find anything but dirt. Might be fitting, I guess," Jihoon said.

There was the sound of a smack. Skin against skin. The kind made from an open palm. A slap instead of a punch. A move meant to embarrass just as much as it was meant to hurt.

The sound of it painted Junu's vision red. He clenched his

fists, his skin burning hot with his anger. And he knew it wasn't just normal rage, but the beginning of dokkaebi fire. No, he hadn't used it in centuries, and he wouldn't break now. Not even as memories of his own broken childhood flooded back. Junu's father had liked to punish with equal parts pain and humiliation. But his father had been dead for centuries and Jihoon's father, though a bastard, was a human. It wouldn't do to intercede or to use supernatural means to do so.

"You can't hurt me anymore." Jihoon's voice was hard with defiance. Junu nodded in approval. *Good. Don't let him see your pain.*

"Ingrate. I clothed and fed you for your first four years, and this is the thanks I get?"

"You barely took care of me and only did it because you were too cowardly to admit you couldn't hack it as a husband and a father. When you went to jail, it was the best thing that ever happened to our family."

"I don't see your slut of a mother here!" Mr. Ahn shouted. "How is she any better than me?"

"Why did you come back?" Jihoon asked. "Was it for money?" There was the sound of coins hitting the floor. As if Jihoon had emptied his pockets.

"Here. It's all I have," Jihoon said.

"What about what your halmeoni left you? She must have had loads. Was always harping on me to save for your college. Where's that money?"

"It's all gone now, used to pay rent so I didn't have to live on the streets. And even if there was any left, I wouldn't give it to you."

"Oh yeah? What makes you think you can stop me from just taking it?" Mr. Ahn asked with a grating laugh.

"Want to find out?" Jihoon asked.

Junu worried now. Mr. Ahn was a bully, which meant challenging him could cause him to lash out. Like a rabid animal afraid of losing ground. Junu thought it was time to intercede.

"Don't think this is the last you'll see of me," Mr. Ahn said, his voice a low hiss.

Ah, so he was the other kind of bully. The coward kind.

Junu heard the approach of footsteps and sank back into the shadows of the alley. He waited as Mr. Ahn started to storm past, then reached out and pulled the man into the darkness with him.

"What the fu—"

"I'm going to give this warning once," Junu said, throwing Mr. Ahn against the wall. The man crumpled and fell on all fours. "You stay away from Jihoon and never come back."

Junu took a few bills from his wallet, large enough to make Mr. Ahn's eyes widen. "This is all you'll see from us, so be grateful for it and leave. Trust me when I say I know the right people to make you disappear quietly. Do you understand?"

Mr. Ahn's eyes didn't leave the money in Junu's hand as he nodded frantically.

Junu threw the bills at him, letting them flutter on the ground.

Jihoon's father went scrambling on his hands and knees, scraping his knuckles against the asphalt in his rush to grab the money. Then he clambered to his feet. "I deserve more than this for all the trouble I went through over that boy."

"I doubt you troubled yourself at all for your son. And I don't believe you have any plans to do so in the future. So take that money and go."

Mr. Ahn's eyes darted around, like he was wondering if he had a chance. He lunged toward the wallet, but Junu grabbed the old man's wrist before he could reach. Mr. Ahn let out a yelp, yanking free, a red burn circling his skin. "What the hell?"

"Get out of here. Now. Before I change my mind," Junu said through clenched teeth.

Mr. Ahn didn't need to be told twice as he turned and raced out of the alley.

Junu was left to stare at his palms. They still burned hot from his anger. Dokkaebi fire was tied to strong emotions. And though his own father hadn't been a pathetic alcoholic bully like Jihoon's, he'd still been a man who cared more about himself than raising his own son. Seeing Mr. Ahn's selfishness had triggered too many memories Junu had spent a long time burying.

"You always did know how to make an impression."

Junu winced at the familiar voice. He almost pretended he didn't hear it, but knew it would be futile.

He'd been trying to avoid this. Ever since that dim-witted dokkaebi had arrived on his doorstep yesterday claiming "Hyuk" sent him. In fact, it had been an anxious energy that had caused him to leave his apartment today, seeking out company.

Turning, Junu took in the sight of the reaper. He was beautiful. Taller than even Junu with a lean build. Full lips with a perfect Cupid's bow. Thick lashes. Alabaster skin that made him look like he was carved from marble. His beauty felt almost otherworldly. Though, Junu supposed that made sense, as Hyuk didn't belong in this world. It's what had originally drawn Junu to him, a being with the face of youth but an old soul. Someone that reminded Junu of his own predicament. Forever frozen at the end of his teen years but with the burden of eternity on his soul. Although Hyuk never seemed truly weighed down by his immortality, it was a balance that Junu used to seek, before he gave up on any kind of inner peace.

Hyuk was dressed head to toe in black with a black wool fedora to match. If he were a mere mortal, Junu would worry the guy would get heat stroke, but he knew that jeoseung saja felt things differently, even when they visited the mortal world.

"What are you doing here?" Junu asked, pasting a neutral expression on his face. Reapers weren't known for being able to read human expressions; they were almost comically bad at it. But Hyuk had developed the ability to read Junu from their time together.

"I would have thought you'd be expecting me. You did get my referral, didn't you?"

"Well, you've gone through a bit to get my attention," Junu said. "What do you want?"

Hyuk gave a stilted smile, but Junu knew the awkwardness in the reaper came from being unused to expressing human emotion. "I want nothing from you, old friend. In fact, I am here because I want to *help* you."

"How kind of you." Junu made his voice so smooth you'd slip off it. His patience was wearing thin. And he knew Hyuk would take it for the subtle warning he meant.

"It seems there's something affecting our worlds."

"Something other than the normal, horrible ailments?" Junu asked with a lifted brow.

"There is something in the Between. Something that's connected to the land of the living, creating a tear."

"The Between?" Junu asked. He'd spent a lot of time with Hyuk, but even so, he had never fully understood the world of the reaper.

"The Between is where souls stay before they're able to pass on to the afterlife."

That did not sound good. "So, like a ghost realm? What could be connecting it to the world of the living?"

"That's what I'm here to find out. It's already affecting things. Ghosts are appearing in this world. And my abilities are not working the way they should. Earlier today, I was following one of these ghosts that slipped through and a mortal was able to see me when I should have been cloaked."

"Ghosts have been able to come to the mortal realm before," Junu pointed out.

"Yes, *temporarily*, and in places where the boundaries between the world of the living and the world Between are thin. But if a ghost spends significant time in the mortal world, they could have negative effects on the living."

"So they have a little fun in the mortal realm, haunt a few people they hold grudges against. Why is that so bad?"

"If they stay too long, they could have undue influence on the psyche of the living. They could cause those in the mortal realm to go slowly mad, with fatal consequences," Hyuk said. "It would upset the balance of life and death."

Junu didn't like the ominous sound of Hyuk's words, but still, he had no idea what this had to do with him. "Why are you coming to me with this?"

"I don't know much, but I can tell that the source of the tear is currently coming from near here. It's like a thread of energy connecting the two worlds."

A thread of energy near here. One that had ties to someone who might have recently entered the ghost realm. Junu's heart dropped as his mind went to a certain former gumiho who'd recently lost her mother and her fox bead in a horrific incident. But he kept it to himself and just shrugged. "Sorry, I haven't seen any thread of energy lately."

"You forget, I know you better than most. I can tell you know something."

Hyuk had never played along with Junu's games. Something he'd never really liked about the reaper.

"I suppose I could offer my services. After all, I've been living in Seoul for a few years now and it's my business to find out information."

"You should of course tell me anything you hear," Hyuk said. "But in the meantime, you should be careful. There are things in the Between other than ghosts and restless spirits. Supernatural souls that are trapped."

Junu's heart skipped a beat. He sucked in a sharp breath. "She's trapped by multiple forms of magic. There's no way for her to get free."

"If there's a way into a trap, there's always a way out. No matter how completely you believe you've sealed it."

"She won't get free," Junu insisted. "I was promised."

"I hope so, for your sake. I'd hate to have someone like that free, knowing they'd come after me the way she'll most definitely come after you."

"I'll handle my own problems," Junu said. "I don't need your advice."

"You didn't use to think that."

"Well, times change, as you well know."

Hyuk nodded, accepting Junu's rejection in stride. Something that was equal parts admirable and frustrating about the reaper. "I hope you take this as I meant it. For old times' sake."

"Sure," Junu said before turning away. "Do you really think—" he started to say, turning back again, but the reaper was gone. He was talking to no one. Junu ran his hands roughly over his face, like he was trying to rub away the conversation.

He hadn't seen Hyuk in over a century. But the jeoseung saja had tied his feelings into a complicated knot. He knew that the reaper did not present himself to those in the mortal world lightly. That's why the jeoseung saja's warnings worried Junu so much.

Slowly, he started back to the apartment and stopped halfway up the steps as Miyoung descended the stairs carrying a bag of trash. Despite the thousands of concerns winding through his thoughts, he noticed that she looked worn out. Junu didn't like the pale pallor of her cheeks.

"I can take that," he said, reaching for the trash bag, but she pulled back.

"Kkeojyeo," she said through gritted teeth. But the threat was tempered by the fatigue in her voice.

This close, he saw the bags under her eyes that he hadn't noticed before. She was stuck in some limbo state that he'd never heard of in his centuries of existence. A gumiho who'd lost her fox bead and had gone over a hundred days without feeding on human energy, yet still walked the earth. He wouldn't have believed it if Miyoung wasn't standing in front of him. Pale and disheveled, sweat beading her brow, but definitely whole and alive. One thing was for sure: Junu knew that Miyoung wasn't fully human. She was still tied to the supernatural world.

Sometimes he wanted to ask her why she did it. Why did she sacrifice her bead to save her dying mother? And now Yena was dead anyway, and the bead was gone with her. Was it worth it?

Then Junu remembered what Hyuk had told him and studied

Miyoung more closely. Was there anything about her, any aura that might be a sign that she was somehow connected to the Between? Would Junu even recognize the sign if he saw it?

"How are you feeling?" Junu ventured.

"Like there's an annoying bug that keeps buzzing around me. And no matter how much I swat at him, he doesn't go away."

"Ha-ha," Junu said dryly. "You're spending too much time around Somin. Your insults are getting very barbed."

"You're insufferable."

"Miyoung-ah," he started. "Let me help you." He wasn't sure if he was just talking about the trash bags now.

"No," Miyoung said, her voice hard. "I don't understand why you're still here. You pretended like you cared if I got my bead back, but the whole time you were only looking at your bottom line. Well, you got paid, and all you had to do was betray me and keep me from finding Jihoon and my mother until it was too late and my father already had them both."

"That's not fair," Junu said. "I was only doing what Yena asked me to do. I had no idea that your father wanted to hurt either of you." He started to reach out, but she gave a low warning growl in the back of her throat, a habit she hadn't lost from her more predatory days, and swatted his hand away.

Then she paused. "What have you been up to?"

"What?" Junu asked, unsure how to react to the suspicion on her face.

"You have the energy of death on you," she said quietly. "Like gi that's rotted."

"You can still taste gi?" Junu asked.

"Just answer my question," Miyoung said.

"I don't know," Junu said, shrugging. He didn't want to reveal his conversation with Hyuk just yet, not until he'd done more research on his own. "I don't always interact with the most savory clients. Maybe you're tasting one of them."

Miyoung stared at Junu another second before she turned away. "Whatever," she said. But as she started down the steps, she stumbled. Her ankle rolled. She cried out in surprise, and the bag went flying from her hands as she tumbled down the rest of the stairs. Junu raced forward as she came to a jarring stop at the base of the stairs.

Bruises mottled her arms, and the skin of her palms was torn where she'd tried to stop her downward momentum.

It was unsettling to see. A girl who used to be an immortal now lying in a pile of bruises and cuts.

All this pain just so she didn't have to feel the guilt of devouring a few souls.

Was it worth it? Junu wondered again.

7

AS MIYOUNG WALKED *through the forest, she knew it was hap-*
pening again. Another lucid dream. She stood beside the maehwa tree
where she'd placed a plaque in memory of her mother. The tree was
missing its leaves, and the air felt cold with winter even though Mi-
young knew that in the real world the heat of summer cooked the city.

She started looking for her mother before she heard the movement
in the trees. The rustle of leaves echoed through her ears like thunder.

"Eomma?" Her voice shook. "Eomma, if you're here, then say
something."

There was a snap of a twig, a flash of shapes, and Miyoung spun
to face whoever emerged from the forest. There was nothing there. And
when a hand dropped onto her shoulder, she jumped with a scream.

"Why do you keep coming back?" Yena asked, concern lacing the
question.

"I don't mean to," Miyoung said, breathy from the scare. "Where
are we? In a dream?"

"Not entirely." Yena hummed and didn't continue.

"Then where?" Miyoung asked, frustration pushing away the fear
that had filled her.

"You cannot keep coming here," Yena said instead. "It's not safe.
They know."

"Who knows?" Miyoung surveyed the area for this mysterious they.

"Leave." Yena stepped away, her form becoming transparent, bleeding into the maehwa tree behind her. "Don't come back."

"Eomma, wait." Miyoung stepped forward, but it felt like she was walking through molasses and she couldn't reach her mother in time. "Don't leave. Tell me what you mean. Who knows?"

Yena didn't reply. Her skin became pale, then gray, as her form joined the tree. And then she wasn't there at all.

"Eomma!" Miyoung called, trying to will her mother back.

Her voice echoed into the forest. A place that was a dream but wasn't at the same time. She felt cold down to her bones, like she was somewhere she wasn't supposed to be. Like it was rejecting her, and if she didn't leave, she had no idea what would become of her.

8

SOMIN HATED WAITING, but it's all they could do once they'd rushed Miyoung to the hospital. The doctors had let Jihoon sit with her, mostly because he stubbornly refused to budge. But Somin and Junu had been relegated to the large waiting area where dozens of chairs sat in rows facing a large television tuned to a news channel.

She pretended to watch the screen but absorbed nothing that the news anchors were discussing.

The anxious monotony of waiting was broken as Changwan hurried in, ran to the desk. Probably babbled some nonsensical question.

He was directed to the waiting area and rushed over. "Somin-ah, Hyeong, what happened?"

"They're still waiting for some blood work to come back," Somin said. She could practically feel the waves of nervous energy emanating off Changwan. He didn't deal with crisis well.

"Changwan-ah, why don't you sit and wait with us?" Junu said. His voice was soft and calm. One might even call it comforting, if one weren't Somin.

"I'd rather do something," Changwan said. "Do you want coffee?"

"No," Somin said at the same time Junu said, "Sure."

Junu gave her a hard look that seemed to imply she was being difficult. She wanted to stubbornly hold her ground, but as Changwan looked nervously between them, she realized it wasn't about the coffee to her friend. It was about being able to do something instead of sitting and waiting. The very thing she had been lamenting two minutes earlier.

"Sure," Somin said. "I could use something to drink."

"On it." Changwan took off in search of the caffeine he obviously did not need.

"Look, I know you're worried—" Junu started to say.

"Then you should leave me alone, because you're not going to help with my nerves," Somin said, turning to find another section to sit in.

"I get it that you don't like me, but I'm worried about Miyoung, too. I have a right to be here."

"Oh yeah?" Somin asked, spinning on him. "You have a right to be around a person whose life you upended with your secrets and lies not four months ago?"

"That's not fair. I thought I was helping her. There were more players in that game than I'd anticipated," Junu said, running his hands through his hair. It stood on end, and for the first time, Somin realized he didn't look perfectly done up. His shirt was untucked, his hair now mussed, and there was a line of worry that sat between his brows.

Still, Somin refused to soften toward him. "I find it hard to believe a guy who claims to be able to find out anything had no idea that Miyoung's father was back and what he intended. You could have warned her. You could have protected them both."

"Just because I can find things out doesn't mean I go looking for information that is none of my business. I just do what I get paid to do."

Somin shook her head. "Whatever. Do what you want, just don't bother me."

"What exactly have I done to you to make you hate me so much?" Junu asked, throwing his hands in the air.

Somin let out a derisive laugh. "Didn't I just tell you?"

"No, you were like this to me way before anything really happened with Miyoung. You've had it out for me since the moment you laid eyes on me." Junu took a step closer, his eyes focused, like he was piecing parts of her together.

"I just don't like people like you."

"People like me?" Junu let his lips quirk in an amused smile, and Somin wanted nothing more than to wipe it from his face. "You mean the devilishly handsome kind?"

"Well, the devilish kind at least," Somin said.

"You have to admit that we'd have fun," Junu said with a cajoling grin.

Somin made a gagging noise. "Trust me. I don't go for your type."

"What type is that?"

"The type that's all smoke and no substance. You want people to think you're so hot and mysterious, but I bet behind all of your shine and smiles, there's nothing to back up your big talk."

Somin was used to her words hitting home. They were how she kept bullies in line at school. After all, she knew Junu was like the kids who stole lunch money from first-years, someone who was so insecure that he buried it in bravado. But one poke and they deflated like an old balloon.

Instead of the effect she was hoping for, Junu's smile spread as he leaned a little closer. "You should just admit that you're intrigued by what could be behind the smoke. Or are you afraid of getting burned?"

"I'm afraid of getting emphysema," Somin said, crossing her arms. Refusing to let him see how he affected her even as her pulse raced.

Changwan came around the corner, carefully balancing three overfilled cups of coffee, and Somin latched on to the excuse to turn her back on Junu's unflinching grin. Changwan must have gotten the coffee from one of the vending machines, because none of them had lids, which was a huge mistake, as she could see some of the coffee had already splashed and stained his shirt.

"Changwan-ah," Somin said. "You shouldn't walk so fast while carrying these."

"I didn't want them to get cold," he said, wincing as more hot coffee splashed onto his bare hand, already pink from previous spills.

Before Somin could reach out, Junu had deftly plucked two cups from Changwan's hands and held one out to her. She debated not taking it. Or better yet, upending it on him. But she knew it would be a childish move, so she took it, being careful to make sure her hand never came in contact with his.

She blew on it, but even so, when she sipped it, the coffee was a bit too hot and she let out a hiss as it went down.

"Careful, you don't want to get burned," Junu said, watching her over the rim of his own cup. The way he said it, with that smug tone, Somin knew that he meant more than the coffee.

A booming voice echoed across the hospital waiting room: "Changwan!" It wasn't a shout, but it was deep and authoritative.

"How dare you leave your study session." Changwan's father came over to jab his finger in his son's chest to emphasize his displeasure. He was tall, like his son. But where Changwan was all gangly limbs and awkward angles, his father had a filled-out frame that Somin knew came from regular workouts with a trainer. Changwan had once been forced to train with them for a week. He'd been so sore that he could barely walk and claimed he had bruises in places he'd never knew existed before. Soon, his father had given up on getting his son to build up muscle, just like he'd given up on so many things when it came to Changwan.

"But, Abeoji, my friend was—"

Changwan was cut off as his father slapped him on the back of the head, the thwack of his palm against Changwan's skull loud and jarring. Somin wanted to intervene somehow. But instead, it was Junu who acted.

Somin watched, openmouthed, as the dokkaebi planted himself like a living shield between Changwan and his seething father.

"Sir, I don't believe we've met. I'm Junu," he said, but his voice was cold and he didn't give a respectful bow of greeting. Instead he just slightly inclined his head. Something that definitely wouldn't be lost on Changwan's father.

Mr. Oh's jaw clenched. "I don't have time to make small talk with your friends, Changwan. Get in the car."

"Yes, Abeoji."

"Surely, he can visit a sick friend," Junu said.

"Is she dying?" Mr. Oh asked.

"Not that I'm aware of," Junu said, and Somin realized the dokkaebi's fist was clenched tightly at his side, like he held it there instead of letting it slam into Mr. Oh's face.

"Then he can see her when she gets out of the hospital. Changwan!" Mr. Oh boomed as he turned toward the exit. He didn't even look back to ensure his son followed him, so complete was his confidence in his authority.

"I'll see you later, Hyeong. Somin-ah," Changwan mumbled, his eyes lowered with embarrassment. Somin started to reach out, thinking to comfort Changwan. But he darted after his father with his shoulders hunched.

"What was that?" Somin asked, turning to Junu.

"Nothing."

"You looked like you wanted to punch Changwan's father in the face."

"I just hate men like that," Junu said. "They push everyone down, crushing them into nothing so they can feel superior. That man's a coward and a bully."

Somin's brows lifted into her bangs. She was shocked that there was actually something they agreed on. "Wow, you surprise me."

"Why? Does it not bother you how Changwan's father talks to him? How he belittles him?" Junu asked, and from the vitriol in his voice, Somin wondered if there was more going on here than just indignation about Mr. Oh's rudeness.

"Of course I hate how he talks to Changwan, but what am I supposed to do about that? He's his father."

"Just because someone's a father doesn't mean he knows what's best for his children," Junu muttered.

"What's that supposed to mean?" Somin asked, genuinely curious about the dokkaebi for the first time. It seemed that perhaps his waters didn't run as shallow as she'd assumed. The cup of coffee still in Junu's hand started to bubble and steam.

"Um, Junu?" Somin said. "Your coffee is . . . boiling."

Junu glanced down, then pulled it behind his back. "I'm going to take a walk." He turned on his heel, throwing the steaming cup in the trash before turning down a random hallway.

Somin almost went after him. There was an odd feeling in her gut. Junu was definitely hurting even if he wasn't admitting it. But that wasn't the part that worried Somin. What worried her was that she had a strange need to comfort him.

Snap out of it, she told herself. She started to go to the waiting area, but a chill raced down her spine. And she turned toward the hallway Junu had just gone down. A figure stood there. Salt-and-pepper hair sticking out from under a baseball cap that shaded his eyes. That same strange man from the street.

"Excuse me," she said. The man started down the hall and she went after him. "Hey! I just wanted to ask you something." There was something so familiar about the figure, and she had to find out what it was.

She walked until she was in a completely different wing. It was quiet. And it looked like most of the rooms down here weren't being used. Without the beeps of machines and the chatter of nurses, Somin felt like she could hear strange noises. Like whispers in the air.

"Hello?" she called, wondering where the man could have gone. She strained to hear his footsteps, but all she heard was the whoosh of the air-conditioning.

Somin was about to give up and go back when she noticed an old man. He stood with his face practically pressed against a door. He wore the outfit of a patient, and Somin wondered if maybe he'd gotten locked out of his room. Could the rooms even lock in a hospital?

"Sir, are you okay?" Somin asked, looking around for a nurse or someone to help.

He turned, and she jerked back, letting out an involuntary yelp.

His eyes were white as snow, and she could see right through him to the doorway beyond.

Somin slapped her hands over her mouth, worried the sound might agitate the man. But he just turned down the hall. He didn't walk; his feet didn't even touch the ground. He just floated gently down the corridor.

Then, at the end of the hall, he faded into the beige wall.

Somin blinked so hard that lights bloomed in her vision. She had to be seeing things. This couldn't be real. She just had delayed heat stroke or something.

Hands came down on her shoulders, and she let out another yelp. She spun around, swinging out. But instead of a ghostly figure, she saw Junu.

"Whoa, I come in peace. I'm not here to fight." Junu lifted his hands, palms out.

Somin closed her eyes and crossed her fists over her speeding heart. "Don't sneak up on people like that."

"I was calling your name. I thought you heard me."

She took a deep, steadying breath. "No, I was . . . I was distracted."

"By this completely empty hallway?" Junu asked, glancing behind her.

"By none of your business." Somin started down the hall, then thought twice. If this was where that . . . man had gone, she wasn't sure if she wanted to be here anymore. At least not alone. She turned back and considered Junu. Trying to decide what was better: his company, or ghosts.

"I can practically hear the thoughts churning in your head."

"No, you can't," Somin said, but a part of her wondered whether he could somehow read her mind.

"Well, I can tell you're spooked. Let's get out of here."

She nodded and let Junu lead the way back toward the main hospital wing.

"Were you trying to follow me?" Junu asked.

Somin let out a laugh. "Of course not. You're the last person I'd want to voluntarily spend time with. I just got lost."

Junu stopped, and Somin had to stop, too, or else run into him. He turned and tilted his head to the side as if contemplating her.

"Isn't it tiring to hate me so much, Lee Somin?" Junu asked.

It was annoying how smooth he sounded. How his confident words were almost purred. "Obviously, it's my defense mechanism against my intense attraction to you."

Surprise creased Junu's brow. "Really?"

"No." Somin shook her head. "I hate you. You really should learn to trust your instincts."

His smile returned but with a razor-sharp edge. "Do you actually hate me or are you scared?"

Somin scoffed. "You think I'm scared of you?"

He leaned in suggestively. "Maybe you're scared of what you feel."

There was that flush of competitiveness again, rising in her like steam in a pressure cooker. She could feel the dare hovering over her, and she didn't want to lose.

Letting out a harsh laugh, Somin reached out and grabbed his collar. For the first time ever, Junu looked shocked. She reveled in the wide-eyed surprise before she crushed her lips against his.

It only took ten seconds for her to regret her decision. Not because of the kiss. Well, yes, because of the kiss. Because it was doing things to her that she'd never felt before. It was as if every nerve in her body was suddenly ten times more sensitive. She could feel her heartbeat racing. And her limbs felt restless. Made her want to hold on. So she let go of his collar and wrapped her arms around his neck.

She felt his hands come around her, hesitant at first. Then his palms flattened against her back, pulling her into him. And as their bodies collided, he changed the angle, deepened it.

Somin hadn't thought it was possible for the kiss to get . . . more. But it did. He let out a moan of satisfaction, and it echoed through her. Made her want even more of him.

Then, as if a switch flicked in her brain, she realized what she was doing and pushed away. They'd been holding on to each other so tightly a second ago, but as soon as she pulled away, he released her. Like he knew she needed space or she wouldn't be able to breathe anymore. Or at least, that's what it felt like as she gulped in air.

She didn't want to look at him but couldn't tear her gaze away from his face. His eyes were blurry, like he was still lost in what had just happened. Like he didn't know what to do or say next.

That made two of them, as Somin couldn't figure out how to get words out of her mouth.

And then thinking of her mouth made her think of her lips. And then about his lips. And then about what they'd just done, and she wanted to melt into a puddle and just slide into the floor drain behind them.

"I guess you proved me wrong," he said.

And Somin couldn't even recall what they'd been arguing about. She only knew she had to get away from him. She couldn't stand to be close to him right now. Or, if she was being honest, she wanted to be closer to him again, and she couldn't stand that fact.

"I'm going to check on Miyoung," she said, and hurried down the hallway, desperate to escape with what was left of her pride intact.

9

THE SMELL OF antiseptic and the vinegary tinge of cleanser filled Miyoung's nostrils as she woke. So, before she even opened her eyes, she guessed she must be in the hospital. She hated the hospital. The only times she'd ever been here were when Jihoon was hurt and when his halmeoni had been dying. To Miyoung, the hospital was not a place people came to heal.

When she opened her eyes, she saw Jihoon pacing the room, his hands clenched into tight fists.

"You didn't have to stay," she croaked out.

"Miyoung-ah." Jihoon was by her side in two quick strides. "You scared me," he said, sitting on the edge of the bed. His body heat felt good against her side.

She looped her arms around his waist. Now she could smell him, the last vestiges of laundry detergent that clung to his shirt, and beneath that, his skin smelled almost sweet, like cream. Jihoon stroked Miyoung's hair, his fingers working through her strands. It felt good, like a gentle massage of her scalp.

She wanted to stay like this forever. Just feeling him close to her. The silence sitting comfortably between them. She tasted his gi, sweet and effervescent like cider, but underneath it was a bitter anxiousness.

"You're tired and worried," Miyoung said. "I can taste it on you."

"Hey, didn't we make a deal that you don't use your residual fox powers on me, and I won't force you to listen to me talk about L-o-L anymore?" Jihoon said.

Miyoung scooted back. "Here, lie down with me."

Jihoon smiled. "Well, if you wanted to get me into bed, you just needed to ask."

She tried to hold back her smile, but it didn't work. Jihoon knew how to make her laugh despite herself.

"Did the doctors say anything?" she asked as they lay face-to-face on the small hospital bed.

"They think you're just overtired and dehydrated."

"When can I leave?" she asked.

"Are you uncomfortable?" Jihoon frowned.

Miyoung remembered what he'd told her about the three months he was in and out of the hospital. How much he'd hated it. How the feeling of being sick had weighed on her heart as much as his body.

"No, I'm fine. I'm just sorry if I scared you," Miyoung said, running her hands down his cheek. She felt a bit of stubble, scratchy against her palm.

"I love you," Jihoon whispered.

And Miyoung's heart squeezed, but she couldn't say it back. For some reason she could never say those words. Instead she leaned forward and kissed him. He let out a sound of surprise and appreciation. She felt a warmth move over her skin. And suddenly she wasn't as tired anymore. Miyoung started to scoot closer, but he pulled back.

"Why don't you try to get some sleep?" Jihoon said, clearing his throat, obviously affected by the kiss.

"I can't," Miyoung said.

"I can tell you about the latest RPG I bought. That always puts you to sleep quickly," Jihoon said with a grin.

Miyoung rolled her eyes and punched him lightly. "No, it's not that. I just . . . I don't *want* to sleep. I don't want to dream."

"Why not?" Jihoon asked, and she could taste his concern growing, like the acidity of citrus in his energy.

"It's not safe in my dreams." The idea of going to that dark place with Yena made her heart hammer. Not because she feared Yena, but because she worried the yearning to be with her mother would cause her to linger in her dreams until she forsook the waking world.

"But if you don't sleep, you can't get better. I'm no doctor, but that's pretty commonsense."

Miyoung's laugh was interrupted by a yawn. She felt her eyes weighing down, exhaustion coming over her. And with Jihoon there, she was the most relaxed she'd felt in a week.

"I'm afraid to see her again," Miyoung admitted.

"Who?" She felt Jihoon brush her hair back gently.

"My mother," Miyoung murmured as she started to drift off. She tried to keep her eyes open, but they refused to obey. And despite herself, she fell asleep.

10

JUNU STOOD OUTSIDE of Miyoung's room. Somin had finally convinced Jihoon to grab food in the cafeteria. It was hours past lunchtime, and none of them had eaten. Junu figured if he was going to check on Miyoung, it should be now, but he wasn't sure if it would help her to see him. Still, he had to check on her. After his conversation with Hyuk, this accident couldn't be a coincidence. If Miyoung was somehow connected to the Between, then it would explain why she hadn't gotten better after her mother died. And if Miyoung was the reason for the tear between the ghost realm and the mortal realm, then it meant Hyuk was going to come for her sooner or later. He needed to know if his suspicions were true.

He found Miyoung sitting up in bed.

"What do you want?" she asked.

Her dismissive tone made his stomach drop, but Junu was skilled at hiding when he was hurt. "I'm just checking on the patient. Do you need your pillows fluffed? I'm pretty good at that. I was around when they were invented, after all."

"I'd love to stuff a pillow over your face until you stop breathing," Miyoung muttered under her breath. But Junu heard it loud and clear.

"Oh, come on." Junu tried his brightest smile. But it felt tight and made his cheeks hurt. "You can't hate me that badly. I do provide a bit of comic relief to your serious, angsty life."

"Why are you still here?" Miyoung asked.

That made his smile dim a bit. "I told you, I wanted to check on the patient."

Miyoung sneered. "No, why are you still in Seoul, bothering me? I don't understand why you don't just leave. You've done your damage, made your money. You have to know there's no way I'd use your services for anything, so why are you still here?"

Junu supposed he deserved that. Didn't mean the words hurt any less. To buy himself time, he turned to pour a cup of water and find a good response. He held out the cup, and when Miyoung refused to take it, he gulped down the water himself.

"I'm not one to admit when I'm wrong," Junu began. "But I feel bad about the part I played in everything."

"You act like you accidentally slipped and let Yena kidnap Jihoon."

"I thought she was doing it to protect you. How was I to know that your father was manipulating things so he could kill you?"

"Isn't it your job to know things?" Miyoung lifted a brow.

She had him there. And if Junu was being honest, he hadn't trusted Miyoung's father from the moment he'd heard the man was sniffing around. But it hadn't been his business to have suspicions. It was his business to do what Yena paid him for. "Look, I've survived a very long time by choosing the winning team. And Yena seemed like the sure winner. I could never have anticipated your father. I could never have predicted how much your love for Jihoon would affect things."

Miyoung crossed her arms, her expression cold as winter. He could see why the kids at her school gave her the nickname Ice

Queen. "So, what? You want to apologize to me? It'd be a waste of breath. I won't accept it. I won't forgive you."

"I know," Junu said. "Maybe that's why I haven't apologized."

Miyoung scoffed. "What a weak excuse. If you really cared, you'd say you're sorry every day."

She was right, and yet Junu still couldn't say the words. Some might call it pride. But what do you call it when that feeling has been compounded by centuries of needing to be above everyone, to the point that their judgment couldn't touch him? Couldn't hurt him?

"I'm not used to being wrong," Junu said.

Miyoung snorted at that.

"Fine, I'm not used to *admitting* when I'm wrong," Junu said. "But I do feel I owe you a debt. Which is horribly inconvenient for me. And until I feel like it's paid, here I'll be."

"Don't try to be something you're not," Miyoung said. "I tried to do that for a long time, and it didn't work out. I lost almost everything because I tried to hide who I really am."

Junu scowled. "And the person you think I really am is a selfish, callous goblin?"

Miyoung shrugged. "More or less."

"Well, maybe I don't want to be like that anymore." The words were out before Junu could measure them.

"I don't believe you," Miyoung said. So blunt that it should have been shocking, but Junu was used to Miyoung's brusque nature.

"It's true. Sometimes . . ." Junu let the word trail into silence, not sure how to finish. No, that was a lie. He knew exactly what he wanted to say. And nothing he'd tried to gain Miyoung's forgiveness in the past four months had worked. So why not a little honesty? He'd never tried it before. "Sometimes I think I want the chance to show that I'm more than a fairy-tale monster. Humans make up these stories that paint us as things to blame all their sins on. We should get a chance to defend ourselves. Don't you feel the same way?"

"I don't think about that anymore. That life is behind me now."

That was a failure. Miyoung still looked at him with suspicious eyes, trying to figure out if he had some alternative motive.

"Well, I do hope you feel better. I know you don't believe anything I say. But it's true."

He left before she could throw another barbed gibe.

Closing the door, Junu wondered if he really was wasting his time on all of this. He had better things to do. He'd been neglecting the business. And though he was comfortably well-off, he shouldn't let his business slide for too long.

Then something caught his eye. It shouldn't have. There were half a dozen people moving through the hallway, nurses and patients, doctors and family members. But this swatch of black grabbed his attention, like something had tickled at his skin. And his eyes met Hyuk's before the jeoseung saja disappeared down a side hallway.

Junu didn't run. The reaper obviously wanted Junu to come after him. And as Junu turned the corner, he caught sight of a door slowly closing down the hall.

Slipping into the dark room, Junu realized it was a storage closet. And Hyuk stood at the end, examining a box of gauze as if it were the most fascinating thing in the world.

"What are you doing here?" Junu asked.

"Is that any way to greet an old friend?"

Junu ground his teeth at the title. "I'm not in the mood for cryptic riddles, Hyuk. What are you doing here?"

"I was just wondering how you're doing. How is your . . . friend?"

This made Junu's instincts tingle. Hyuk wasn't one to waste his time on trivial things.

"Why are you here?" Junu asked.

"You know why."

"Don't."

"Don't what?"

"Don't do whatever you came here to do to her," Junu said.

Hyuk shook his head. "You know you can't stop me from doing anything."

"That's why I'm asking you not to," Junu said. "Please. For old times' sake."

The reaper sighed before pursing his lips. The look he got when he was thinking things through. This was a good sign because, nine times out of ten, the reaper was so set in his goals that he didn't even stop to consider. It was a trait all the jeoseung saja shared; once they're given a task, they're dogged in their pursuit of it. Nothing can change their minds. That's why so many called them supernatural bureaucrats.

"There is an energy connected to that gumiho," Hyuk said. "It's tying her to something in the Between."

"Do you know what it is?" Junu asked, even as he had his own suspicions.

"You ever ask yourself how a gumiho could survive after not feeding for a hundred days?" the reaper said instead of truly answering.

"Of course," Junu said. "But we figured it's because her bead is gone." Even as he spoke, he was hit with a realization. "It's not truly gone. It's in the Between."

"And it's still connected to her," the reaper said.

"How do we find it?" Junu wondered aloud. "And what could be holding it in the Between?"

"That's not my concern. I just want that connection cut. I don't care how."

There it was, Junu's in. "So give me a chance."

"A chance?" Hyuk laughed. "What can you do? A dokkaebi without his bangmangi?"

That sliced at Junu, and he realized that he and the reaper were no longer quite so close. Hyuk had to know bringing up his dokkaebi staff would hurt Junu. "I'm resourceful. You know that."

Hyuk nodded. "You have seven days to sever her bond to the bead and the Between."

Before he could feel grateful, Junu realized it had been too easy. This is what the reaper had wanted all along. Junu had never stopped to wonder why Hyuk had come to him first instead of going after Miyoung directly.

"Why are you giving me this chance?" Junu asked.

"Because you can get me what I want without an unscheduled death. We don't like to interfere in the world of the living. A reaper's job is not to be judge and executioner but to guide the souls once they're dead. I was ready to kill the girl, since it served the greater purpose of righting the balance between worlds, but I was surprised to see you with her."

Junu nodded. He knew there would be no use getting annoyed. It would make no difference with Hyuk. "So, what? You've been watching us?"

"You're attached to that gumiho for some reason. At first I thought it was romantic."

Junu's eyes widened. "Oh no, definitely not."

Hyuk let out a chuckle, a surprisingly warm sound. "I figured that out. But you're sticking around for her. I wonder what it is about her."

"I owe a debt," Junu said. "And apparently I have seven days to repay it."

"I'm giving you this chance because I know your word is good," Hyuk said. "But you know mine is as well. And if you can't get rid of the connection between that energy and that girl, we'll do it. I can promise you that."

"And who is 'we'?" Junu asked, though he had a feeling he knew. When he'd known Hyuk before, they tried to pretend they were separate from the worlds that claimed them. Junu's world of supernatural creatures that roamed the earth. And Hyuk's world of the jeoseung saja—beings that reaped souls of the dead and brought them down Hwangcheon Road to the afterlife.

Soon those worlds did come back to claim them. They were fools to think otherwise.

And Junu wasn't in the mood to meet Hyuk's reaper friends. Or to watch them come and take Miyoung to the afterlife.

"Fix it," Hyuk said, instead of answering Junu's question. "Or we will. You have seven days."

He left Junu alone among the bandages and clean bedpans in the cramped storage space.

THERE ONCE WAS a boy named Sinui who grew into a fine man, then a great general.

Though he was accomplished and respected in life, he wanted one thing above all: to cheat death.

One day, a jeoseung saja came to Sinui's house, and Sinui knew that the reaper had come for his spirit. The jeoseung saja tried to enter Sinui's house, but he couldn't cross the orange trees that surrounded it. In his studies, Sinui had learned that oranges warded off evil. So he'd planted them around his home.

For three days, the jeoseung saja could not enter. But on the fourth day, he found a peach tree, a plant of evil. The jeoseung saja crossed the walls using the peach tree.

However, when the jeoseung saja entered the home, Sinui stood with a silver pin piercing on his head. Sinui had learned that silver warded off evil gods.

The jeoseung saja did not leave, but he hid himself under the floors. When Sinui went to wash his face, he removed the pin, and the jeoseung saja appeared and reaped him with an iron hammer.

So Sinui was taken to the underworld, but he was not done fighting. For he was a clever man and had prepared for this eventuality. He fought the gaekgwi, the spirits between the underworld and the mortal world that barred reentry to the land of the living. And with his great fighting skills, he defeated them and reentered the mortal world.

However, when Sinui reentered his body, he found that his family had already buried him. He had not prepared a way to escape his own grave. So he suffocated, returning to the underworld once more.

Because no matter how Sinui fought, the reapers had marked him for death. And no spirit can escape the grasp of the jeoseung saja once they set their eyes on you.

11

MIYOUNG FELT LIKE a burden. She'd lived her whole life trying to be unassuming, to be invisible. And now she was the center of attention as Ms. Moon hurried around her apartment, cleaning up for an unexpected guest, rambling about going to the store to buy oxtail for soup. Jihoon's small white dog, Dubu, jumped around, stopping every once in a while to snarl in Miyoung's general direction. Dogs hated foxes, and Dubu had always seen Miyoung for what she really was.

Somin and Jihoon were arguing over the best way to set the table for family dinner. The excuse for why Miyoung had to come here after the hospital. Ms. Moon said they used to have family dinner every Sunday when Jihoon and Somin were younger and claimed she wanted to start the tradition again.

She almost got up and left half a dozen times, but every time, she could feel how weak her legs were. How her head spun. How she couldn't seem to quite catch her breath. The doctor had said she was sleep deprived. That seemed like an understatement. She was afraid to go to sleep; she didn't know what her mother's constant visits meant. But she knew in her heart that Yena wasn't fully gone, at least not for her. And a part of her worried that the dreams weren't supernatural at all, but a sign that she was going slowly mad.

"Somin-ah, where did you put my shoes, the ones with the

tassels?" Ms. Moon called, digging through the shoe cabinet in the foyer. Shoes kept spilling out as she shoved the piles back and forth.

"You threw them away," Somin called from the kitchen. "You said they made your ankles look fat."

"No. Those were the loafers," Ms. Moon called back, taking out a pair of white tennis shoes, studying them, then shaking her head and letting them fall at her feet.

Somin came out of the kitchen and started picking up the mess. "The ones with the tassels *were* the loafers. You threw them away."

"I did?" Ms. Moon said with a frown, staring at a pair of sandals. "Ugh, I really loved those shoes."

Somin started shoving discarded shoes back into the cabinet. She took out the pair of sneakers her mother had worn to the hospital and handed them to Ms. Moon. "Last week you called them a waste of money and said you regretted letting the saleswoman talk you into buying them."

Ms. Moon bent down to put on her sneakers. "Yes, but that was *last week*. This week I remember that they're my favorite."

"Well, if you still miss them next week, we can go shopping for another pair."

"Aw, thanks, Daughter, I'd love that," Ms. Moon said. Then she turned to Miyoung. "You just rest. I'm going to go to the store to buy ingredients for miyeokguk."

"Seolleongtang," Somin corrected her.

"Yes, seolleongtang," Ms. Moon said, kissing Somin's cheek. "Call if you need anything."

As the door swung shut behind her mother, Somin bent to organize the fallen shoes.

"She's not like any mother I've ever seen," Miyoung said before she could stop herself.

"Yeah, I know." Somin laughed. "Half the time I worry she'll forget to put on shoes altogether when she leaves the house."

"But she loves you," Miyoung said, and felt her chest constrict. "It's so obvious how much she loves you."

Somin smiled and sat next to Miyoung on the couch. She picked up the forgotten tea that Miyoung hadn't started drinking and held it out. "Drink your tea or my loving mom is going to lecture me about not catering to our guest."

"You're lucky, you know, to have a mother like that," Miyoung said, sipping her tea. "One that can love you with no strings attached."

"Your mother loved you—she just showed it differently."

"Yeah, maybe," Miyoung said.

"And listen, just because my mom is fun and cool doesn't mean it's easy to be her daughter. Half the time I feel like I'm the parent."

Miyoung laughed. She could see that. Ms. Moon seemed so carefree. And she let Somin do pretty much whatever she wanted. Miyoung wondered what that was like. To have a mother who trusted you so explicitly.

"I really shouldn't stay the night. Your mother said there was barely enough room now with Jihoon. I can just go to a hotel."

"Are you not staying with Junu?"

The way Somin said Junu's name struck Miyoung as odd. Like she wanted to spit it out as quickly as possible. Like she was afraid to say it.

"I don't know. Maybe I will. It is someplace familiar. And

I guess that would be nice right now. I just don't know if I can trust him."

"Yeah, I guess he's not the most trustworthy guy."

"You guess? I thought you were the president of the anti-Junu club."

"I am. I guess I'm just wondering if there's anything else to him that I'm not seeing." Somin turned to face Miyoung. "What do you think of him? Like, really think?"

"I think he's annoying. Presumptuous. Exhausting. Pushy."

"So the worst being to ever walk the earth," Somin said with a nod. And for some reason, Miyoung thought she hadn't given Somin the answer she'd wanted.

"Well, he's not all-the-way bad. But I'd never tell him that to his face."

"Are you happy he's still here?" Somin asked.

"I wouldn't say *happy*," Miyoung said, but she remembered what Junu had said to her in the hospital. *Sometimes I think I want the chance to show that I'm more than a fairy-tale monster.* Maybe all this time he'd been hiding his insecurity behind his bravado. It made sense. But that didn't undo all the bad he'd done. "I think Junu is a complicated person. I think even he doesn't know who the real Junu is most of the time."

"Do you think, underneath it all, he's a good person?"

"What is 'good'?" Miyoung asked. "What is 'bad'? Is a bad person someone who lies and cheats and kills? If so, then I'm a bad person."

"You don't do that anymore," Somin said with a frown.

"But I lived like that for nineteen years. I can't forget that."

"Are you telling me to give Junu a chance?"

"A chance at what?" Miyoung asked. If she didn't know better, she'd say there was a bit of longing in Somin's voice.

"I mean just in general." Somin's eyes wouldn't quite meet Miyoung's. "Like not being so hard on him or whatever. You know what? Never mind. I'm going to finish setting the table." And with that, she zoomed out of the room.

Miyoung was left to wonder what was going on between Somin and Junu. Then she told herself not to worry about it. She wasn't one to get involved in other people's business. Except, now that she had these people who wanted to take care of her, shouldn't she be doing that right back? It felt unnatural to care, to worry. But wasn't that what being a friend was about?

"Miyoung-ah."

She jerked upright, then let her shoulders relax again as Jihoon returned to the living room and sat on the couch.

Miyoung let her head fall onto his shoulder; the day had been too long.

"What do we do now?"

"Nothing. Just wait for Somin's mother to get back from the market."

"I'm sorry for being such a nuisance," she mumbled, blinking furiously, and she realized she felt like crying. Which was silly. Why should she cry now when she felt safe with Jihoon beside her?

"You're not a nuisance. You're sick. We're all worried about you . . . which bothers you, doesn't it?" The realization in Jihoon's voice made Miyoung's burden deepen. He knew her so well. Too well at times.

"It's strange," Miyoung mused. "I always thought I was the strong one. But I realize now it was a lie I told myself. I'm slowly uncovering all of my lies, and it's not very pleasant."

Jihoon shifted so she had to lift her head from his shoulder and face him. "What do you mean? What kind of lies?"

"Like when I'd say that I needed no one but my mother. When I said I didn't care about the men I killed so I could survive. When I told myself I was strong. That I could handle anything that life threw at me, but now . . ." Should she tell Jihoon about her dreams? About her mother coming to her?

"You *are* strong," Jihoon said, caressing her arms. "You're one of the strongest people I know."

Miyoung shook her head. "I'm not talking about physically. Though, I guess that's gone now, too. I mean I'm realizing how much of this world my mother shielded me from. I don't know what to do now that she's gone."

Jihoon nodded. "I get it. She was your world. It's not easy to get over that."

"So you understand that I can't just move on."

"Are you saying you don't like that we're trying to take care of you?" Jihoon frowned.

Miyoung didn't know the right answer to that, so she picked up her tea, which had become lukewarm now. "I'm saying that I'm not used to this stuff. People waiting at the hospital half the day for me and insisting I come over for family dinners. It makes me feel like a burden."

"You're not. This is what family does. And you're part of our weird, abnormal family. You know that, right?"

Miyoung couldn't answer. If she said yes, did that mean she was throwing Yena away? If she said no, did that mean she would never get this offer again? She'd always thought that being a human would make things easier, but somehow it had made everything so much more complicated.

She shook her head. "Would you hate me if I said I don't know what I know yet?"

Jihoon took her hands in his. "Of course I wouldn't hate you. I don't know a lot of things. Just ask Somin."

Miyoung laughed at that and knew it's what he'd intended. To lighten the mood. It's what Jihoon did best. She rested her forehead against his. "I know one thing. And it's that, no matter what, I can trust in you."

"Always," Jihoon whispered, then leaned in, hesitating a moment before their lips touched. As if he was asking permission.

Miyoung smiled and closed the last of the distance. The kiss was sweet. Meant to comfort. A gentle brush of lips to soothe away her anxieties. But she didn't want something sweet right now. She didn't want easy or comfortable. She wanted to forget the things that gnawed away at the back of her mind. She wanted to stop thinking. So she shifted until she was straddling him. He let out a sound of surprise, his hands fluttering to her hips. She nipped at his lip and heard his sharp intake of breath. She smiled at the power she had over him in this moment and tilted her head to find another angle of the kiss.

His hands tightened as she took more and more. She wanted to lose herself in him completely. She wanted to become a part of him so she wouldn't have to be herself anymore.

She shifted, started to pull up his shirt, but Jihoon pushed at her shoulders until they separated.

"We can't. Not here. Not right now."

"I'm feeling much better," she said, but he held fast, sliding her off his lap and back onto the couch. She let out a groan of protest.

"Somin or her mother could walk in at any minute."

"So?" Miyoung pouted, annoyed that she was being reminded of her recklessness.

A line of worry formed between Jihoon's brows. "What's going on? Please tell me."

"Nothing." She crossed her arms and sank back into the couch cushions. "I guess you aren't in the mood."

Jihoon sighed. "Well, I'm always in the mood for that. I just . . . are you sure you're okay?"

He knew her so well. Too well at times. And in this moment, Miyoung hated him for that.

"I'm fine. I'm just tired."

"Okay, maybe you should rest before dinner." He stood, and without his body heat beside her, she was suddenly cold. "Miyoung-ah."

She didn't reply, just stared resolutely at the blank television screen in front of her.

"I love you," he whispered. There was a beat of silence where she knew he was waiting for her to reply. It was a strange routine, Jihoon saying those words that made her heart swell and soar, but Miyoung unable to return them. He left, and she heard the clatter of dishes in the kitchen as he joined Somin.

Miyoung didn't mean to close her eyes, but she felt completely drained. And soon she fell into sleep and dreams, where her mother waited for her.

12

DUSK WAS FALLING when Somin walked down the road. She shouldn't have come here, Somin thought for maybe the hundredth time. But still she made her way down the narrow alleyway that led to Junu's apartment. Somin practiced what she wanted to say in her head again. It was silly, this need to figure out her words first. She never had a problem telling people exactly what she was thinking. But Junu flustered her. It was annoying.

Somin had stewed over that kiss all evening. Well . . . *stewed* might be the wrong word. Worried over. Stressed over. But Mi-young had said that Junu had more layers than they knew. That maybe, underneath it all, he was something . . . more. What it was, Somin wasn't sure. But knowing about the supernatural world had shown Somin that there was so much more that she couldn't understand on this earth. So perhaps there was more about Junu that she didn't know. Still, she did know that she should nip this—whatever *this* was—in the bud before it grew out of control.

So, after dinner, she'd told her mother that she wanted to go to the study room where most seniors rented a cubicle. During the short summer break, it would be packed with third-year high school students preparing for the suneung exam in November. Somin had claimed that she'd fallen behind on her study schedule after everything that had happened today, carefully omitting the fact that she'd set aside the whole day long ago to help Jihoon move. Her mother didn't need to know that. And if Miyoung had sent Somin a curious look when she'd left, she could take solace in the fact that Miyoung was not one to gossip about other people's business.

Somin's shoulder banged into a pipe bolted to the stained concrete wall beside her. She hissed in pain, rubbing her arm and cursing herself for being distracted. She hated this narrow alley. It seemed like a deterrent, telling people that nothing worthwhile was down this way. Which, Somin supposed, was the point. Junu lived in a world that hid in plain sight. Beings that lived in legends, ones that no one truly believed in anymore. Except those superstitious enough to be wary.

A whisper of wind blew down the alley. Strange, as it always felt like the air down here was so stagnant. Any good breeze was shut away by the tall, narrow buildings. But her hair fluttered against her ears, and with it she could hear something. A whisper. It slowly formed syllables until she was almost certain it was her name. A soft hiss of sound that called to her.

She picked up the faint scent of licorice.

There was a tickle along her neck. A feeling like she was being watched.

Don't turn around, she told herself. *Just keep walking. You're almost at the door.*

But like a girl in a horror film, she ignored her inner voice and turned her head slowly to the side. Out of the corner of her eye she could make out a form. It was less than two steps behind her. Its face so pale it was almost translucent. Dark hair peppered with silver. Cheeks sunken in. And a cap low over its eyes.

"Who—?" she started to say, but before the words were free, the figure was gone. And so was the wind. The summer air suddenly weighed on her despite the setting sun. Like it pressed all of the humidity of Seoul onto her chest. Somin felt light-headed, her vision wavering as her ears began to ring. She thumped her fist against her chest as her lungs struggled to fill. She coughed, and it seemed to help as she sucked in a breath.

"Get yourself together, Lee Somin," she told herself, taking two huge gulps of air. It helped.

Somin pushed away the strange feeling that still shivered down her spine and rang Junu's doorbell. She counted out her breaths and had only gotten to thirteen when the door opened and Junu stood in front of her. He wore a simple outfit of jeans and a T-shirt. He'd changed after the hospital, and his hair was a bit damp, like he'd taken a shower. A bead of water clung to a strand of hair. She watched it drip onto his shoulder. Had she ever noticed how broad his shoulders were before? Not too big, but they showed he had strength under his wiry frame.

"Somin-ah?" Junu said, and she realized they'd been standing in silence as she stared at him.

"Oh, sorry." She cleared her throat, ready to launch into her monologue. "I just—"

"Do you want to come in?" Junu asked, and ruined her carefully practiced flow.

"What?"

"Why don't you come in. I just started a kettle for tea." He walked back inside. The door swung shut behind him, and Somin just caught it before it slammed in her face.

Had he done that on purpose? No, she wouldn't dwell on this. She needed to be clearheaded, get her speech out, and leave once he agreed that the kiss had been a mistake. A lapse in judgment. It had been like an unspoken dare. One of Junu's many games. And Somin was here to tell him the game had ended on a draw.

She made her way into the apartment, toeing off her shoes in the foyer. It was gleaming and spotless. The floors were cool under her feet. It felt nice and refreshing after the heat of outside.

As she walked down the hall, searching for the kitchen, a side room caught her eye. Inside was a giant, gleaming grand piano and shelves and shelves of books. She gaped at how many there were as she realized that every wall was covered in shelves.

Somin selected a book at random. It was a cookbook. The second was a collection of old European fairy tales. She flipped the pages to find elaborately illustrated pictures of fairies, mermaids, and witches.

The next book was about a boy wizard. It was written in English, so when she flipped it open, she couldn't read it. But she recognized the cover art; any kid born in the last thirty years would know this story.

"That's a first edition."

She spun around, hugging the book tightly to her chest.

Junu stood in the doorway with two cups of steaming tea.

He set them on a table next to an armchair Somin hadn't noticed. It looked well-used, like a person could spend hours in it without moving an inch.

"This room is so . . . cozy," she said. "Different from what I'd imagine from you."

"I like comfort, too," Junu said with a shrug.

"I've always dreamed of having a library at home," Somin said, glancing around at the towering shelves. "It just needs a fireplace and it would be perfect."

"No fireplace," Junu said firmly. "I hate fire."

Such a strange fact. Especially for a dokkaebi. Somin remembered the stories of how a tall blue flame called dokkaebi fire heralded the arrival of some. Was that just a myth?

"I didn't know you liked to read," Somin said, placing the book back on the shelf.

"Who says I do?" Junu asked. "Many of these are collector's editions, worth a lot of money."

Somin tried to read him and failed. Then reached behind her and took out a battered secondhand edition of *Howl's Moving Castle*. "And how much is this worth?" she asked, glancing at the heavily dog-eared pages. "Five hundred won?"

Junu grinned, comfortable in being caught in his lie. "I do enjoy a good book now and then. After all, I lived in a time before television. But you're not here to inquire about my favorite ways to pass the time, are you?" Junu took a step toward her. If he took another one, he would be entering uncomfortably close territory. She could just smell his scent, a mix of shampoo and aftershave.

Somin knew she better get talking or else she'd forget her whole reason for coming here. "I came over because—" She cut off because she couldn't remember the rest of her carefully cultivated speech.

"Yes, please tell me what you came over for," Junu said with a grin as he took another step toward her. She took a step back and held up a hand. It stopped him. Thank God. She didn't know what she'd do if he touched her. She felt like a bundle of live wires, sparking at just the presence of him.

"I came over to discuss what happened." Somin almost winced. When she wanted to sound more self-assured, she ended up sounding like a kid playing office. But it was too late now.

Junu let out an amused chuckle. "Discuss it? Is that all?"

"Yes, as it seems like we have a misunderstanding about what . . . transpired, I'm glad I came over." There it was again, a child pretending to be an adult.

"I'm glad you came over, too." Junu's grin became a full smile, but it was too wicked to be called friendly.

"Stop it," Somin said sternly, and Junu finally moved back.

She realized that whenever she told him she didn't like something, he actually listened to her. As if, when it came down to it, he really did care about her comfort. It was hard to reconcile that with the contemptible flirt and con she'd labeled him as.

"That kiss was . . ." She trailed off again as she latched on to the memory. She didn't want it to be so fresh in her mind. Or to have a part of her want to try the taste of him again. Like a dessert she knew she shouldn't eat. One that she should be allergic to. That would probably give her hives.

"Yes?" Junu asked, expectantly watching her with a patient look on his face. It was just a mask, she knew. He was waiting for a good moment to break her resolve.

"It can't happen again," she finally said.

"And why is that?" Junu asked pleasantly. Too pleasantly.

"Because we don't . . . we can't. It's just not going to happen . . . it can't happen again." She stumbled over words like she was just learning to talk. She couldn't seem to string a convincing sentence together.

"I see," Junu said. "Well, I can't force you to do anything you don't want to do. So, if that's it." He started back toward the foyer.

Somin couldn't believe this had been so easy. And she worried that there was still some kind of misunderstanding. She needed to make him understand why the kiss meant less than nothing. It was important he know that. Because she was starting to doubt it herself.

"Hold on." She grabbed his hand, but she must have yanked a little too hard (she tended to use her strength too much when she was anxious). And the momentum hauled him into her. They would have fallen to the ground if he hadn't grabbed her arms, somehow keeping their balance for them.

A part of her wanted to shrug out of his embrace. But a stronger part of her wanted to step into it. Somin was a girl who followed her own rules. And her rules strictly forbid her from starting anything with a guy like Junu. But she was also one who took something if she wanted it. And she wanted Junu right now.

So she lifted onto her toes. That alone wouldn't have reached him; she was so short and he was so tall. But in the same moment, he leaned into her and their lips connected.

They clung to each other, and Somin stumbled back, pulling him with her. Something hard dug into her hip. A clash of sound echoed into the room. She didn't care as she reached up to loop her hands behind Junu's neck, to hold him securely to her.

She loved the feel of his mouth on hers. It drove all logical thought out of her mind. It made her feel weightless. And she hadn't realized how tense she was before until she felt all the pressure leave her temples and her shoulders. She let out a satisfied hum and felt his grin against her lips.

He shifted the kiss to be deeper. They met each other like two hurricanes crashing in the middle of the ocean. Feelings battered into her, but they were too strong and too varied for her to sort through. And she didn't want to think. She just wanted to experience and touch and feel. It was good to just feel.

Then Junu broke free, desperately dragging in air. Somin clung to him, her legs too shaky to stand on her own.

She finally realized what the source of the jarring noise had been. The grand piano was wedged into her back.

Her eyes slid to Junu, whose breaths were matching her rapid puffs. She wanted him to kiss her again. She wanted him to keep going. His gaze glinted as he read her unspoken request, and his hands went to her hips. He lifted her so effortlessly, she felt like smoke and vapor instead of solid flesh. As if she would drift away. Maybe she would—her body vibrated with anticipation—maybe she would shatter into a million particles. Then she was plopped unceremoniously onto the top of the polished wood, her sock-covered toes pressing into the piano keys, causing another cacophony of noise. She could feel the vibration of it through the top of the piano beneath her.

Junu moved in, his legs pressing against the keys. So the sound of their movement became a clash of notes. His hand wrapped around the nape of her neck. She held on to him as if he were an anchor. And his mouth claimed hers.

She felt like she was burning up, like she would evaporate into steam. Her clothes felt too tight, and she tugged at her shirt, trying to yank it off. Junu pushed her hands down.

"Don't be so rushed," he said with a smile that somehow didn't annoy the living daylights out of her. In fact, she kind of thought it was cute. "We have plenty of time."

"I feel like maybe I'm going to start overthinking this soon if you don't keep kissing me," Somin gasped out. She tried to kiss him again, but a pounding echoed down the hall. At first,

Somin thought it was a figment of her imagination. Or maybe the loud echo of her own heart. But it came again, and this time a bellowing voice joined.

"Junu, gaesaekki-ya! Get out here!"

Somin lifted a brow. "Friend of yours?"

Junu seemed to realize who it could be and let out a groan as he rested his forehead against hers. His hands gripped her waist, like he was reluctant to let go.

"So more of an acquaintance?" Somin asked.

"Stay in here," Junu said before he stomped down the hall.

Somin considered ignoring him and following after, but figured it was best to stay out of whatever shady business Junu was involved in. She took stock of herself. Her hair had fallen out of its tie. And her shirt was rumpled and pulled halfway up. She jerked it down. This was probably for the best. She would definitely hate herself in the morning if things had gone any further.

A loud crash echoed down the hall, followed by a heavy thump. Somin ignored Junu's command to stay and ran into the foyer, her mouth dropping open in shock.

If she hadn't learned that one of her close friends was really a mythical nine-tailed fox, she wouldn't believe what she saw with her own eyes. Except, she still didn't think she believed it.

The man standing in the foyer looked like a hulking beast with a bulbous nose and dark, glaring eyes. His hair was coarse and tangled. His clothing was torn and frayed. He was at least two hundred centimeters tall. And in front of him sprawled Junu, the vase that used to sit in the entryway shattered beneath him. There were lines of cuts along his arms and one across his chin. But Somin stared in bewilderment as she realized there was no blood.

The creature above Junu pulled something out of his disgusting coat. It looked like a narrow club. And suddenly it came to her. A dokkaebi. Or at least what she and millions of Korean kids had been taught dokkaebi looked like.

At first, she hadn't believed Junu was a dokkaebi because he'd looked too smooth. Too perfect. Too beautiful. But this creature was exactly how she'd imagined them.

And this perfect model of a dokkaebi was about to smash his club into Junu's face.

"Ya!" Somin yelled, instinct taking over. The creature paused mid-swing, glancing up in bewilderment. It was all Somin needed. She snatched the club before he could use it.

"Give that back," the dokkaebi rumbled, lurching forward.

Somin danced away and hoped the giant beast wouldn't trample Junu as he tried to lumber after her.

"It's rude to come into someone's house and assault them," Somin said.

"Somin, drop that and get out of here," Junu said, gaining his feet. His voice was so serious that Somin almost did what he said. She'd never heard Junu sound scared. But he seemed terrified, and as his eyes latched on to hers, she realized with a flash that he was scared *for* her.

The dokkaebi let out a guttural yell as he charged toward Somin. But Junu launched himself into the larger goblin. Together they stumbled to the side. The beast flung out an arm, smacking Junu in the gut and throwing him back. He had to have known he wouldn't have any effect on this hulking thing.

He'd done it to distract the dokkaebi from Somin. And she watched in wide-eyed horror as the goblin slammed Junu against the wall.

"Stop it!" Somin shouted, jumping onto the dokkaebi's back. She tried to use the club to batter at his thick skull. He easily dislodged her, and Somin crashed into the marble floor.

Her vision spun and a loud ringing filled her ears. For a second the world was a blur, and she could only make out colorful shapes around her.

A figure loomed over her. Not the dokkaebi. And not Junu. But someone who looked eerily familiar, except she couldn't quite focus on their face.

"Somin-ah," they whispered in a raspy voice, and it itched at her memory. She started to reach for them, but her fingers passed through nothing but cold air.

The dokkaebi let out an angry roar, and she blinked hard, finally clearing her vision. The dokkaebi still held Junu pinned to the wall, a meaty fist slamming into his stomach. Junu doubled over but didn't fall as the dokkaebi dragged him up and shoved him against the wall again.

He was going to die if she didn't do something.

She picked up the club. It had splintered from the fall. With a deep breath, she sprinted forward and thrust the jagged end of the club into the dokkaebi's shoulder. He let out a roar and reared back, throwing her across the room. Somin heard a loud crack as her head connected with the gleaming wall. The sound was so loud, she wondered if her skull had split open. She watched in a daze as the dokkaebi turned and leapt at her. She lifted her hands, which somehow still held the splintered staff. And as the dokkaebi fell on her, she felt the staff pierce his hide.

The dokkaebi's face was centimeters from hers, and even with her blurring vision, she could see his eyes widen in surprise. Then he let out a roar just as he burst into dust.

A whistling sound rang in her ears. Was it coming from the dokkaebi? No, he'd turned into dust and air. She'd killed it. *Him*, she corrected herself.

Though the dokkaebi had been a beast, he had still been a living thing. And Somin had killed him. This wasn't like when she swatted a fly or a mosquito.

She'd killed someone. She was a killer.

The whistling grew, so high that she pressed her palms against her ears. And then, suddenly, it stopped. And the world seemed completely quiet.

"Somin-ah." The word was whispered into her ear, and she jerked her head up. She saw nothing but darkness. Where was she? Had she died, too? Was she being judged and punished so quickly?

Then she saw something, a blur of light in the dark. It became opaque, forming a shape that looked strange and familiar at the same time. She squinted to make it out, then blinked hard to clear her vision. Because she must have been hallucinating. Standing before her was Jihoon's halmeoni.

"Somin-ah," Halmeoni said with a kind smile. "You cannot blame yourself."

"What are you doing here?" she asked. "Am I seeing things? Or am I . . . am I dead?"

"You're not dead. And I don't know how much time I have. I am not meant to be here, but I could feel that you needed me."

"Did you . . . did you see what I did?" Her words came out in a hiccupping sob as tears pooled in her eyes. She wiped them away with the back of her hand. Even if Halmeoni was a hallucination or a dream, Somin wanted to see her this one last time.

"I did, and you had no choice. Do not blame yourself. If you hadn't stopped him, he would have killed you both."

"This isn't who I am," Somin said, holding out her hands. The hands of someone who'd taken a life. "I don't want to be like this."

Halmeoni took them between hers. And her palms were warm and comforting, just how Somin remembered them. She lifted their joined hands to her cheek and felt Halmeoni's papery-thin skin against hers. "I'm sorry, my child. But this world we've stumbled into is not an easy place to exist. You must realign your morals if you're going to protect the ones you care about. Including my grandson."

"Have you seen Jihoon? Are you watching over him, too?"

Halmeoni gave a sad smile. "I've seen him, but right now, you are the one who is in need."

"He hasn't been the same since you . . . left," Somin said. "I'm worried about him."

"Yes, I know. That is why I know he is in good hands. You are a protector. You will make sure my Jihoonie stays safe."

"I will," Somin said.

"Good, but first, you must wake up."

"What?"

"Wake up." Halmeoni's voice faded into an echo. Then the pain came. A throbbing in the back of Somin's skull. She let out a low groan as she opened her eyes. And as her vision cleared, she made out Junu's foyer.

She was sprawled across the tile floor. And when she lifted her hand to the back of her head, she felt a lump that throbbed as she pressed it.

Somin stood slowly and saw Junu's unconscious form. Was he still breathing?

She leaned over him, and before she could check his pulse,

Junu's eyes flew open. He reached out, lightning quick, pulling her head down until her face was centimeters from his.

"You saved my life," he mumbled. "My hero." Then he planted a hard kiss on her. Before she could react, he fell back to the floor with a thud, unconscious.

Somin stood, warily nudging at his ribs with her toe.

"Ya," she said with another nudge. He didn't move.

She nudged him again, so hard it could be called a soft kick. His head wobbled a bit, but he didn't wake. She saw his swollen eye and winced, admitting to herself that he probably wasn't faking it.

Not seeing any other choice, she hoisted Junu up, flopping his weight over her, piggyback style. His limbs were so long that his hands batted at her legs as she walked. She heard his feet dragging on the floor behind her. But it was the best she could do. He'd probably be pissed at her when he woke up. Claim that she scratched his floor or something. But it was really his fault for growing so tall.

When Junu was unceremoniously delivered onto his bed, Somin gave a grunt of discomfort and bent over to stretch her back. What should she do now? Probably just leave. But she couldn't bring herself to do it. Not because she cared about Junu, she told herself. But he had put himself in harm's way to protect her. She owed it to him to stick around. At least until she could assure herself he was going to be okay.

But first she needed something to help with her throbbing headache. She found medicine in the bathroom and took twice the dosage suggestion. She winced as she poked tenderly at the lump on the back of her head and went in search of ice.

When she returned to the bedroom, Junu lay flat on his

back, his hands crossed over his belly. It should have made him look stiff, like a body being prepared for eternal rest. But instead, he looked calm and peaceful. Young, like he truly was a high school or college student. Not for the first time, Somin wondered how Junu had come to exist. The stories said that dokkaebi were made from things. Like vases or pots. But Somin had a hard time believing the lively, sarcastic, often infuriating being that was Junu had come from anything as cold and lifeless as a vase.

"Stop staring, byeontae," Junu said without opening his eyes.

Somin jumped, her fist clutched against her heart. "I was just checking on the patient. And I've confirmed he's just as annoying as when I left him. So I'll be going now."

"Stay," Junu said, opening his eyes now. He watched her earnestly.

"Why?"

He smiled. "Would you believe me if I said I'm afraid of monsters?"

She didn't answer, but she dragged the armchair from the corner of the room closer. There was no way she'd sit on his bed. Knowing Junu, he'd take that as an invitation for something.

"What are you thinking?" he asked, watching her intently.

"I was actually just thinking about how dangerous you are. A boy who's never been told no."

That pulled a laugh out of Junu, but oddly, it had a bite of bitterness to it.

"Am I wrong?" she asked.

"Does it bother you?" Junu said instead of answering. "The

idea that I get whatever I want. Or—" He paused with a suggestive grin. "Is it the fact that you know you want to give me everything I want?"

"I don't want or need to give you anything," Somin retorted, standing, finally ready to storm out of this place.

"Thank you," he said, and it stopped her. "For saving my life."

She turned back toward him. "You said that already."

Junu smiled. It wasn't like the mocking grins he usually gave her. It was small and thoughtful. "Sorry about that. I think my whole life was flashing before my eyes. I was delirious."

"Now, that I can believe," Somin said, and sat on the edge of the bed before she realized what she was doing. She started to stand again, but Junu's hand came to rest over hers.

"I'm sorry that you had to do that," he said, his eyes sober and steady.

Somin looked at their joined hands. She realized she wanted to lace their fingers together. But instead she pulled away. "I did what I had to do." She thought of Halmeoni's words. She still wasn't certain Jihoon's halmeoni had truly come to her. It could have been a dream, but if it was, then these were her words anyway. "In this world, things are harsher. We have to move our moral lines in order to survive."

"But I don't want that for you," Junu murmured as if he were talking more to himself than to her.

"You can't decide what's best for me. Only I can."

Junu chuckled. "Well, I sure know that. You're not one to let others make decisions for you. Though, you do make so many of your decisions because of others."

"What is that supposed to mean?"

Junu shook his head, and she knew he had no intention of answering.

Now Somin did stand. She shouldn't stay, she told herself again. But something held her in place. An unfinished thought. Something that had been nagging at her all day.

"I know why it's happening," Somin finally said. "It's because I hate you."

"Well, you're not the first human to do things because of hatred for my kind. Still, I'm curious to know where you're going with this." He folded his hands patiently, waiting for her to continue.

"I know I should stay away from you. I know you're bad for me. It's like when I was little and my mom told me not to touch the flame of a candle. But the more I watched it, the more I had to know what it was like to touch it," Somin said. "My mother always said she was worried one day my curiosity would get me into trouble."

"Did you touch the candle?"

She didn't want to answer. She was afraid of how he'd take it, but she'd come this far. "Yes."

Junu's lips spread into a slow smile. "So what's stopping you from . . . touching the candle now?"

Somin frowned at how he made that sound so sensual. "You're missing the point."

"No, I get it. You say that it's because you hate me? The reason you kissed me . . . twice." Junu held up two fingers and wiggled them playfully. "You sure have a funny way of showing your hatred."

"It's because I feel *something* whenever you're around," Somin snapped. Only he could make this ten times harder for her. She was trying to explain something to him, and he continuously insisted on misunderstanding. "I wish I could feel nothing about you. But for some reason you make me *react*."

Junu stopped at that. He seemed to be pondering something, and then he said, with surprising sobriety, "I'm not sorry that I get reactions out of you. I'd much rather you notice me. I like it when you notice me. But a rational person doesn't kiss a person they hate."

"I know," Somin said, frustrated.

"So you ever consider that maybe you don't actually hate me?"

"I have to," Somin whispered, her throat tight.

"Why?"

"Because otherwise I'd have to be worried that I kissed you. Twice."

"True," Junu said, lying back again and letting his eyes closed.

She started to go when he spoke again. "Will you stay tonight?"

She hesitated; there was nothing keeping her here. But she found herself saying, "Yes."

13

THE FOREST WAS quiet. So still that Miyoung knew immediately it was a dream.

She walked down the path, her eyes moving back and forth, watching for any shifting shapes.

She thought she saw movement to her left and edged away.

"Does it frighten you so much? The idea of me being here?"

Miyoung spun around to face Yena. A sharp pang ripped through her chest. Whether it was born from fear or anticipation, she wasn't sure.

"You don't frighten me, Mother." Miyoung knew the reedy sound of her voice gave away her lie.

"Why do you fear me?" Yena asked. "I am only here to help you."

"But all you've done is talk in riddles and threaten me."

"Threaten?" Yena's eyes widened as her voice rose. "I only want the best for you."

Miyoung cringed away, lifting her hands as a shield.

Yena's face fell as she moved back, her hands coming up in apology. "I'm sorry. I'm not . . . stable."

"What are you?" Miyoung asked.

"I'm not sure," Yena said, and her form seemed to fade a bit with the uncertainty.

"You're really here," Miyoung said, confident of that. "But how?"

"I don't know. Something holds me here."

"What?" Miyoung asked, heat settling in her stomach.

"Perhaps . . ." Yena's eyes shifted down.

Miyoung followed her gaze and saw a golden thread between them.

Yena smiled. "Do you feel it, Daughter? That we are still connected?"

A hope bloomed in Miyoung like a flower on a maehwa tree, fighting its way into the world in the cold of winter.

"Help me, Daughter. Help me find you again," Yena said.

Miyoung reached for the thread. She worried it would pass right through her hands, but it was warm as she wrapped her fingers around it. Yena's smile widened, became bright with anticipation. And Miyoung pulled.

The string tightened, became so bright it blinded her. Then it blinked out. Disappearing into the night and leaving her in total darkness.

She tried to move but couldn't see even two centimeters in front of her nose.

The ground shook as something heavy fell beside her.

It felt like the world was falling away. Crumbling pieces crashing around her.

"What's happening?" Miyoung yelled around the thunderous noise. A chill started to seep into her, so deep it took root in her bones. And she knew something was wrong.

14

JUNU WOKE THE next morning with a headache and a mouth so dry it felt like his tongue was made of sand. Rolling over, he noticed a full glass of water on his nightstand. Somin. She was a saint. He gulped the whole thing down.

Feeling slightly revived, he wandered out to find her. He planned to show his gratitude, and he had a few ideas of how he could do so. But as he made his way toward the kitchen, he heard a suspicious thud from the opposite direction. He followed the noise and then watched Somin try, and fail, to open the many drawers of his ancient chest. The one where he kept his very delicate and very hard-to-procure wares.

"Lee Somin, shame on you for snooping," Junu said with a click of his tongue.

"I thought maybe there'd be medicine or something in here to help you," Somin said.

Junu almost laughed. "You're not a great liar. You should work on that."

"This is where you keep it, isn't it?" Somin asked, not even bothering to look contrite. "All that magic stuff."

"Magic stuff?" Now Junu couldn't help but laugh. She made him sound like a second-rate magician.

"Should it all just be sitting out here like this?" Somin stared intently at the chest like it was a thing that had greatly offended her.

"I know what I'm doing."

"Do you? Why was that dokkaebi so mad last night? You sold him something bad, didn't you?" Somin shook her head, judgment in every movement. "And it's one thing when you put your own life at risk with your business, but what about the other people you've hurt?"

"Are you saying you regret last night?" Junu asked quietly.

"What part of last night?"

He closed his eyes and tried to ignore the uncomfortable fire that rolled through his chest. "I guess I'm asking if you regret coming here last night."

Somin chewed on her lip. Giving the question far too much thought. The answer wasn't an easy one for her, and Junu had wanted it to be.

"I'm sorry that you seem to have been forced to do things you regret," he said, unable to stop his voice from becoming ice cold.

"Can't you just give me a minute?" she asked. "I killed someone last night."

"You protected us from a *monster* that wanted to kill us."

"A monster?" Somin asked, her eyes dark as they watched him. "You mean a dokkaebi. Like you."

Junu shook his head, but the words to deny it didn't come out. "He would have killed me. And then he'd have killed you, too, just for fun."

"I know that," Somin whispered. "Doesn't make it any easier."

"So why are you still here, then?" Junu asked, frustration biting at him. "Why did you stay all night if you feel that way?"

"I don't know," she admitted, turning back toward the chest.

"You think so little of me. I didn't mind when I thought it was part of a game we were playing. But if I truly disgust you so much, then perhaps we should just call an end to all of this. Whatever it was." *You don't want that*, a voice inside him said. But he'd always moved on when things got too complicated. And things with Somin were like trying to make his way through a minefield. He told himself it was time to walk away.

"Maybe you're right," Somin said, though she didn't quite meet his eyes when she said it.

Say something, dammit. Stop her, that voice inside him said. But he didn't. He watched as she jerked the door open. Was that a pause? Or was she just getting her bearings as the bright sunlight flooded the foyer? Before he could come up with an answer, she was gone.

He clenched his fists. Partly to direct his frustration somewhere and partly to stop himself from going after her. What had he wanted her to say? That she believed in him? That he was worth crossing a moral line for? It was better this way. She didn't belong in his world. Ending it now would save them both time and heartache.

He started back to the kitchen. He'd make some breakfast, then take a shower and wash all of the doubt away.

He was only halfway through frying an egg before he threw it in the trash and went after Somin.

15

SOMIN COULDN'T STOP thinking of Junu. Of random things he'd said. Of the way he looked when he'd finally fallen asleep. His face serene, almost innocent.

But Junu had been right. There was no reason for them to see each other anymore. Even if Miyoung was living with him, it's not like Somin went to all of her friends' homes. After all, she'd been friends with Oh Changwan for three years and never set foot in his house.

It was better this way, she told herself for maybe the dozenth time since she left Junu's apartment. And she believed it even less than the first time she'd thought it.

Somin rubbed the heel of her palm over her chest. It felt tight, like it was bound by something. But her loose T-shirt was hardly even touching her skin. Still her heart strained in her chest and her breaths felt labored.

She felt light-headed, too. Probably from the heat. Except, she wasn't hot. Wasn't even sweating like she usually was after walking from the bus stop to her apartment building in the middle of summer. In fact, she realized as she hugged her arms around herself, she felt chilled. Goose bumps ran along her arms as she shivered.

It was then she realized the empty street was eerily silent, even for a Monday morning. With only the sound of the dull thud of her sneakers as they hit the pavement.

The hairs on the back of her neck stood up.

"Halmeoni?" Somin's voice shook. "Halmeoni, is that you? Are you here?"

But she picked up the scent of licorice, and she knew that it wasn't Halmeoni before she turned and saw the figure, standing with his back to her. She blinked.

"Hello?" she called out, taking a stumbling step forward. Why were her legs suddenly so weak? Like they were afraid of approaching this man. "Why are you following me? Who are you?"

He finally moved, a slow shake of his head, like he was warning her of something. Then he started down the road, and before he took two steps, he'd evaporated into thin air.

Somin pressed her hand against her racing heart. What was happening? Was she hallucinating? Why was she seeing these figures?

The silence was unceremoniously broken by the sound of running feet. A man old enough to be her father burst out from a side alley, his eyes wild and wheeling. Somin lifted her fists in case it was an attack.

"He's back! He's after me!" the man stuttered. He dropped to his knees at Somin's feet. "Don't let him take me. Please don't let him."

Somin searched the street for the man's pursuer. But they were the only ones there.

She knelt down and waited for him to look at her. He was drenched with sweat. His hands shook as he clasped them together, as if in prayer. "He shouldn't be here," he muttered. "He should be gone."

"Who?" Somin asked. This man's face was pale as snow. His eyes were so wide she could see the white around his iris.

"My brother. He's back. He knows what I did. He wants to punish me for it!" The man's head jerked to the side, his eyes darting up the road.

"I don't see him," Somin said, trying to add reassurance to her voice.

"He's dead. He died a year ago. And he knows what I did. He's come back to take me to the afterlife with him." He took hold of her wrists. Despite his tremors, he had strength, and she couldn't twist free.

Ice seeped into her veins. Somin didn't know this man. She had no idea what he was capable of. "What did you do?"

Instead of answering, the man's eyes stared over Somin's shoulder. He scrambled back, letting go of Somin in the process. "Get away from me!" the man screeched. "Don't touch me!" He jumped up and darted down the road.

Relief flooded Somin, and then a sense of guilt. What if this man really was in trouble? If anything, he was suffering from delusions, maybe born from overheating. He thought his dead brother had come back to life. But Somin remembered Halmeoni's strange visit to her last night. And the man that kept appearing with the salt-and-pepper hair. The scent of licorice was still faint in her nostrils now. No, there was a perfectly good explanation for these things. And it wasn't ghosts.

That tingling sensation returned. The feeling that told her she was being watched. And this time it wasn't a light prickle but a chill that made her shiver. Like it had force behind it. The force of rage.

It couldn't be, she thought, reluctant to turn around. Still, she willed herself to do it. Somin had always been a rationalist, and she wouldn't let the ravings of a stranger change that. So she slowly turned and stopped short when she saw him: a man standing just up the road. Not the now-familiar man with the cap. This one's face was clearly visible. His expression was filled with cold satisfaction. An expression that sat on a face bloated and rotting. A face that Somin could see right through to the buildings beyond. She took a stumbling step back, letting out an involuntary gasp. The figure turned his white eyes to her before he disappeared completely.

"What is this?" she whispered to herself.

"Somin." She let out a scream before she could stop herself. She felt her legs buckle and would have fallen if Junu hadn't grabbed her arms to hold her up.

"Come on," he said. "Let's get you inside."

"Did you see him? Am I losing my mind?"

"No, you're not. I saw him. We need to talk."

"I—I can't right now." She shook her head; there were too many things racing through her mind. "I can't fight with you right now."

"I know," Junu said, his voice calm, his eyes soft. "That's not what we need to talk about. It's time I told you something. Told *all* of you."

Somin finally looked at Junu now, and his somber expression got through to her. Something was going on. And she latched on to it. She didn't know how to deal with whatever she just saw, but if there was a problem that needed fixing, she could do that. She was good at that.

"Let's go," she said, taking another deep breath to steady herself.

∘ ∘ ∘

The minute she opened the door to her apartment, Dubu came running down the hall, closely followed by Jihoon. Somin scooped up the small, yipping dog, cuddling her close. She needed this right now. The unfiltered, simple love of a canine.

"What's he doing here?" Jihoon asked, eyeing Junu.

"Jihoon, not now. I've had a really . . . weird morning," Somin said.

"That's what worries me." Jihoon crossed his arms. "Please tell me you actually spent the night in the study room and not somewhere else." He bit out the last words as he gave Junu an accusing glare.

"I thought you hated lies," Somin said.

"I don't hate them when they let me believe you weren't alone with that dokkaebi all night."

"Nothing happened." Lies. "You don't need to worry about me." More lies. "I can handle things." Even more lies.

"Well, as much as I love being the center of attention," Junu said, "I'm not here to be interrogated by Ahn Jihoon."

"What are you here for?" Miyoung walked down the hall. Suddenly, Dubu started barking so wildly her whole body shook.

"Dubu, stop it," Somin said.

"It's all right," Miyoung said with a shrug. "I'm used to it by now."

Somin moved past them to put Dubu in her mother's room; she hoped the task would let her escape Jihoon's scrutiny, but he just followed her down the hall.

"What happened last night? Why is Junu here?"

"He said he needs to talk to us," Somin said, closing the door behind her to muffle the dog's frantic barks. She hurried back to the living room before Jihoon could ask her more whispered questions.

"Where's my mother?" Somin asked, looking around.

"She just went to the store to get some meat for miyeokguk. And we lied and told her you were still sleeping."

"Thanks." Somin's gratitude was peppered with guilt.

"What are you here for?" Miyoung repeated. She'd been watching Junu since he'd stepped inside.

"I'm just here to help," Junu said, lifting his hands in innocence.

"And how much will that cost us?" Miyoung asked.

Maybe because she was watching him, Somin saw Junu's jerk of surprise. He let a smile spread on his face, and now Somin saw it for the mask it was. Not one of manipulation, like she'd always thought, but one to hide his hurt. How had she not seen this before?

"I'll do it pro bono," Junu said. "Out of the goodness of my heart."

"You don't have a heart," Miyoung said before turning to plop onto the lumpy couch.

"I know what's ailing you," Junu said, his voice smooth as butter. But now Somin was paying attention. She saw how his fists were clutched by his sides, knuckles white from being held so tight.

"And how could you know that?" Miyoung asked.

"It's my job to know things."

"It's your job to manipulate people with what you know," Miyoung retorted.

"Let's just hear what he has to say," Somin found herself saying. Three pairs of eyes shot to her with varying degrees of surprise.

"I mean it can't hurt, right?" Somin shrugged. But she couldn't quite meet any of the eyes that followed her as she moved to sit on the other end of the couch.

"Sure," Jihoon said, ever the easygoing one. "Let's hear his theory."

"It's not a theory," Junu said, gritting his teeth. "I have it on good authority that there is an energy lingering. Something powerful, kind of like a yeowu guseul. You know, the thing you mysteriously lost this spring."

"I didn't misplace it like a set of keys," Miyoung said.

"Well, you did lose it. And you had no idea what happened to it. But it's still connected to you. We've always wondered why you're still alive after not feeding for a hundred days. I think it's because the bead isn't in the mortal realm anymore."

"What do you mean?" Somin asked. She didn't like the sound of all of this as she remembered the ghostly figures she'd been seeing the last few days.

"I mean the bead is in the ghost realm, which might not matter, except it's still connected to Miyoung, and the energy of that connection is creating a rip."

"A rip?" Jihoon asked, frowning.

"I've heard rumors that the world of the living and the ghost realm might be crossing."

That surprised Somin. He knew about this? He knew that

there were ghosts? And he hadn't said anything. But why would he? It's not like Somin had told anyone about the weird figures she'd been seeing. Still, there was a strange feeling of betrayal that sat in her gut, like she wanted Junu's trust enough to tell her things. When had that desire started?

"The connection between a gumiho and her bead is strong," Junu explained. "If one of you is in the mortal realm and the other is in the ghost world, then the energy of your connection to your bead could affect the barrier. After months of this energy piercing the barrier, it's making a tear, one large enough to let ghosts cross into this world."

"That's why you're finally telling us," Somin said. "Because of what we just saw."

"What are you talking about?" Jihoon asked. "What have you seen?"

The concern in her best friend's voice made Somin feel guilty. It wasn't too long ago that she'd been pissed at Jihoon for keeping secrets from her, and now she realized she'd been keeping secrets from him. Whether intentional or not.

"I didn't think it was anything. And with all the stuff going on with Miyoung yesterday, it didn't seem important. I honestly thought I was imagining things at first, but then, that man just now. And Junu said he saw it, too."

"Somin-ah, you're rambling," Jihoon said gently. And it was the worry in his eyes that calmed Somin enough to take a deep breath and start again.

"I've been seeing weird figures. At first I thought it was just a strange guy who was following me." And then, like a snap, it all came together. Salt-and-pepper hair. The battered black cap. Her father had worn that thing every time he'd gone into the hospital to hide his thinning hair. The chemo had made half of it fall out and the other half turn gray. But whenever he came home, he always had licorice for her, like they were celebrating something. Because he'd never wanted Somin to worry.

"Um, you say that like a stalker isn't a big deal. Why didn't you tell anyone?" Jihoon demanded.

"He's not a stalker. He's my . . ." She couldn't finish the sentence, not with Jihoon and Miyoung watching her with unease. "He's a ghost." Somin felt so strange saying that. But if she was going to say it to anyone, it would be this group. "And then that old man at the hospital, he walked into a wall. And just now, that ghost haunting his brother. I just . . . It's a lot to take in."

"So you're saying you've been seeing ghosts?" Miyoung asked, glancing around like she could catch sight of one right now.

"I tried to come up with other explanations for it, but I just can't." And the tight expression on Miyoung's face made her want to apologize, like she'd done something wrong by seeing ghosts.

"No, this can't be possible." Miyoung shook her head. "And even if it was, how can Somin see them? She doesn't have the sight like Nara did."

Somin had never met the young shaman who had once befriended and then betrayed Miyoung. She just knew Nara had been able to see spirits.

"Because of the tear, the ghosts are stronger than they should be. Able to appear more clearly, able to interact with our world," Junu said. "Not everyone will see them immediately, mortals often see what they want to see, which is why when ghosts normally come to our world, they have little to no effect. But soon, as the tear grows and as the ghosts linger, more and more will notice them. Somin can probably see them because she's already aware of our world. Her mind is more willing to accept what she sees."

"Oh goody," Somin muttered. It was almost ironic. Somin had been feeling useless and left out of the strange paranormal club that her friends were a part of. But now that she could see these ghosts, she wanted to give that ability back. Classic case of be careful what you wish for. "How do we fix this?" she asked.

"We get the bead back," Junu said. "If it's in the mortal realm, then the energy should no longer affect the barrier between worlds and the tear should fix itself."

"How do we get it?" Somin asked.

Junu shook his head. "I don't know."

"If there's a rip, can we go to the ghost realm?" Jihoon asked.

"No," Miyoung said. "The Between is no place for the living."

"Then how are we supposed to get the bead back?" Somin asked.

Miyoung was quiet too long. Then she finally looked up. "You guys are forgetting that if there are two anchors to this connection, removing the bead from the equation isn't the only solution."

"What are you saying?" Jihoon asked.

"If I'm not here anymore, then there won't be an anchor in the mortal realm to create this connection." Miyoung said it like it was so simple, her voice eerily calm.

"No. You can't give up this quickly. We can fight," Somin insisted.

"It's the simplest solution. Maybe it's what was always meant to happen. I've cheated death too many times already," Miyoung whispered.

"Let's just slow down," Jihoon said. "We have time to figure this out."

Junu shook his head. "No, the longer the tear stays open, the worse it'll be. It's allowing ghosts to stay in our world for much longer than they should. The longer they're here, the more people will start to see them, and they'll start affecting people."

"How?" Somin asked, remembering the wild ravings of the man on the street.

"Once people start to see the ghosts, they won't be able to handle it. At best, they'll go a little mad; at worst . . ." Junu paused. "It could affect the order of death itself."

"How long do we have?" Somin asked.

"Five days, maybe six?" he said. And there was more in his expression. Like there was something he wasn't telling them.

"Well, there has to be a way to find Miyoung's bead," Somin said. "Some kind of talisman. A shaman ritual. You guys are freaking mythical beings. You can live forever, but you can't figure out how to find one fox bead?" She racked her brain, trying to remember Halmeoni's old stories. Ones about magpies bringing good news. Or rabbits tricking tigers into holes. But it wasn't a story that caught her memory but something from last night. Among the chaos and the violence. The dokkaebi. And his club. But Somin remembered that it wasn't a club, not in the stories. It was a bangmangi—a dokkaebi staff—and it could summon things. "The bangmangi."

"What?" Jihoon asked, but she could see recognition in Junu's eyes.

"The dokkaebi staff," Somin clarified. "It can summon things like food and gold, right? Can it summon anything you want? Is that story real?"

"I've heard tales of it," Miyoung said, her eyes considering Junu. "Could it work?"

"We could try," Somin said. "We have one. The dokkaebi last night—"

Junu shook his head. "No, it broke. It won't work anymore."

"Dammit." Somin huffed. She'd thought she'd hit on something there.

"I hate to bring it up, but . . . aren't *you* a dokkaebi?" Jihoon said to Junu.

"And?" Junu lifted his brow imperviously.

"Yeah," Somin said. Why hadn't she thought of this herself? It was a solution staring them all in the face. "Don't you have a bangmangi, too? Could you use it to find Miyoung's bead?"

Junu shook his head. "No."

"No, you can't use it? Or no, you don't *want* to use it?" Jihoon asked.

"I don't have it anymore," Junu said.

"Anymore? So you did have one. Where is it now?" Jihoon asked.

"Not here."

"Okay, well, tell us where it is and we'll go get it," Somin said.

"No."

"Why not?" Somin wanted to shake Junu. He was usually so chatty, and now he was barely answering them.

"It's somewhere I can't go," Junu said, turning his back to them. His shoulders were hunched defensively. Classic avoidance pose.

"Can't? Or won't?" Miyoung asked.

"I'm sorry, it's not possible," Junu said. "We'll have to find another way."

"There is no other way," Jihoon said. "We should have known. You said you were here to help, but you're still the same selfish jerk we've always known. Why don't you just go?"

And Junu did. Without so much as a reply, he opened the door and left.

"Jihoon-ah," Somin chastised. "Why did you have to say that?"

"What? He never listens to me. How was I to know he'd do it now?"

Somin shook her head and chased after Junu.

She caught up with him as he waited for the elevator. "You can't just leave like that."

"I don't see the point in staying. None of you trust me. I have nothing to offer you. Why should I be here?" Junu wouldn't even look at her.

There was a moment where the words seemed to encompass more than just this moment. But Somin couldn't think of that right now. She knew that if Junu left, then their chances of saving Miyoung would be leaving with him.

"Please, your bangmangi might be the only hope we have to save Miyoung," Somin said.

"There's no guarantee of that," Junu said, finally looking at her. "And even if there was, it's not in a place we can ever enter. It's not safe."

"Why not?"

Junu shook his head. "I can't talk about that."

"Please, Junu. I wouldn't ask this for myself, but it's Miyoung. She needs us. She's had everything taken from her. She has no one."

"And that's my fault, right? That's what you're trying to say?" Junu turned away from her, but he didn't leave. He paced a few steps away, then paced back, rubbing his hands over his face.

"I'm not saying that—" Somin began, but Junu held up his

hand. He closed his eyes, and it seemed Junu was having an internal war with himself.

"Dammit," Junu muttered, and Somin knew she'd won. "Well, let's go back inside if we're going to figure this out. It's not going to be fun. I can promise you that."

"Thank you," Somin said, but he'd already started back down the hall and she had to jog to catch up with his long strides.

He stopped in front of her apartment. "Just open the door before I change my mind."

16

MIYOUNG STOOD UP, needing to move. Needing to do something with the anxious energy that was building up inside of her.

"We'll figure something out," Jihoon said.

"*I'll* figure something out," Miyoung corrected him.

Jihoon stood and took her hand in his to stop her pacing. "When are you going to realize you're not alone in all of this?"

"When the people I care about aren't being forced to risk themselves because of mistakes I made," Miyoung said, pulling her hand free.

Before Jihoon could reply, Junu walked back in with Somin.

"If we do this, then you need to be aware of a few things," Junu said. "First, there's no guarantee that the bangmangi can summon Miyoung's bead. The magic isn't all-powerful; it has limits. A dokkaebi usually uses it to summon riches or food from a stash he has close by, usually small, inconsequential things. I've never heard of one reaching beyond the world of the living. And I've never heard of one summoning something as powerful as a yeowu guseul. So it's very possible it won't work."

Somin started to speak, but he shook his head to stop her.

"Plus, I haven't used my own bangmangi since I first became a dokkaebi. I don't know if I have the skill to help Miyoung find her bead."

"It's our only hope," Miyoung said.

"I know, but it's a shaky hope at best," Junu said.

"But you'll still go get it? You'll at least try?" Somin asked.

"I'll leave first thing tomorrow morning," Junu said.

"Why?" Jihoon asked. "If you say we only have days, why not go today?"

"I have to make some preparations first," Junu said vaguely. "And if I'm going to do this, it means you all have to trust me. No second-guessing how I do things."

"Fine," Somin said.

"I'm going with you," Miyoung said.

"Are you sure you're up for that?" Somin asked.

"Of course," Miyoung said, but her declaration was weak and breathy.

"I'll move faster without you," Junu said.

"This is my life you're talking about," Miyoung said. "I should do *something*."

Instead of replying, Junu pushed against her shoulder. Miyoung fell back, plopping onto the couch. "You're too weak. It's a long hike to get to the bangmangi," Junu said. "You'll have to trust me on this, whether you like it or not."

"Fine, I have a headache. I'm going to go lie down." Miyoung knew she sounded like a petulant child, but she didn't want to stand around discussing how weak and useless she was right now.

So she stormed into the bedroom, closing the door behind her.

She was frustrated at how weak she still felt and tired of depending on other people to solve her problems. Just like her mother. Always like her mother.

"Miyoung," Junu said, slipping into the room.

"Usually when someone closes a door, it means they want you to stay on the other side," Miyoung said.

"Yeah, but I was never really good at taking a hint," Junu said with a smile.

"Yeah, I know," she muttered.

Junu stood by the door, not moving to come farther into the room but not leaving. He seemed to be debating something, so Miyoung finally rolled her eyes and said, "What?"

"You should know something," he finally said.

Miyoung wondered what game Junu was playing here. It had been hard enough to accept that he'd help by going to find his bangmangi, but Junu loved to keep information to himself so he could use it as leverage later. She wondered what price she'd have to pay for what he was about to tell her.

"There's a reason I know about the tear," Junu said.

"Yes, one of your mysterious confidential sources," Miyoung said. "I know all about your privacy policy."

"Yeah, except this time it doesn't apply," Junu said. "Because I made a promise to help you, so I think you deserve to know this, especially since it affects your life. Or the length of it at least."

"What are you trying to say?" Miyoung asked, trepidation sparking in her chest.

"A jeoseung saja told me about the tear. Because it's affecting the order of death."

"A reaper?" Miyoung whispered, and her knees went so weak she had to sit on the bed. "Are they coming for me?"

"A reaper?" Jihoon said from the doorway.

"Does no one respect privacy anymore?" Miyoung complained.

"I would, except I know you two and your habit of keeping dangerous secrets," Jihoon said.

"Where's Somin?" Junu asked.

"Her mother just came home. She's helping with the groceries."

"Well, why don't we invite both of them in here? Since we're having a party now," Miyoung said sarcastically.

"Tell me about the reaper," Jihoon said, turning to Junu.

"There's nothing much to tell. They're here because of the tear between the worlds. But we'll fix it before they have a reason to go after Miyoung."

"That's why you said we didn't have much time," Jihoon said.

"We don't, but we *will* fix this," Junu said. "I don't make promises I can't keep."

"Then I'm coming with you to find the bangmangi," Jihoon said.

"What? No," Miyoung said, standing again.

"Please, let me do this," Jihoon said, taking her hand in his. "After everything you did for me last spring."

"Our relationship isn't a scorecard," Miyoung said with a scowl. "You don't owe me anything."

"No, but I want to do this," Jihoon said. "There are still people in this world who love you."

"You can't use that against me," Miyoung said.

"What? Me use something against you?" Jihoon said with an easy grin. "That doesn't sound like me. I'm too charming and easygoing to resort to those games."

"This isn't a joke," Miyoung said.

"Of course it's not; it's your life. I take that very seriously."

"And I'm serious when I tell you that you're *not* going. And I won't forgive you if you do," Miyoung said, adding a hard finality to her voice.

"But—"

"Give it up," Junu said, laying a hand on Jihoon's shoulder. "I don't think you're going to win this one."

Jihoon shrugged off Junu's hand, but he didn't try to argue again.

"I'll leave in the morning," Junu said. "Just rest, Miyoung, and don't worry."

She looked up at him, and if she didn't know better, she'd have said she saw sincere concern on his handsome face.

"I'll stop worrying when we find my bead."

17

USUALLY IF JUNU wanted to take a trip, he'd just book some luxury tickets on the mode of transportation he wished. Maybe a five-star hotel. A reservation at a nice restaurant if he had the time.

But today he wanted to move quickly, which meant he was traveling light.

He was already annoyed that he had to wake up at such an ungodly hour on a Tuesday. But he supposed this was what he'd signed up for.

He'd already taken his car out of storage—a bright yellow Porsche 911—it begged for speeding tickets, but he loved it. And if he had to travel hours across the country, then at least he'd do it in style.

At the knock on his front door, he opened it to find Somin. Déjà vu struck him from the other night, and suddenly he was remembering what had gone down the last time she'd shown up unexpectedly. He was grateful he didn't blush or else his pale complexion would have given him away.

"What are you doing here?" he asked. "Want to come along?"

"No, I wanted to talk to you in private." Somin stepped into the foyer.

Junu let a smile spread over his lips, and he couldn't help glancing at the doorway to the library. "Is that so?"

"Get your brain out of the gutter," Somin said. "I need to ask you a favor."

"What *kind* of favor?" Junu asked, wiggling his brows.

"Can you be serious for one freaking second?" The frustration in her voice wouldn't have bothered him, but he heard fear beneath it and sobered.

"Okay, what do you need?"

"I know Jihoon's going on this trip no matter what," Somin said.

"Miyoung said no."

"Yeah, well, whatever conversation they had didn't work. He told me he's determined."

"Then why are you here? Why don't you try to talk to him directly?"

"Of course I tried," Somin said. "But he's so bullheaded—" She cut off with a sigh.

Junu wondered if she realized she was just as hardheaded as her best friend, two peas in a very annoyingly stubborn pod.

"Since he insists on going with you," Somin said, "I need you to promise you'll take care of him. I need you to promise it in a way that will make me believe you."

Junu almost laughed at how she phrased it. Like no matter what, she truly thought he could never make her believe in him. It made him more determined to prove her wrong. This time it was easy to be sincere, because he had every intention of protecting Ahn Jihoon. There was no way he'd lose face by letting a mortal die while with him. And maybe Junu did kind of like Jihoon sometimes. Of course, he couldn't let *him* know that. They had such a great frenemy thing going on.

"I'll take care of him," Junu said. "If I make a promise, I keep it. It's how I stay in business."

Somin nodded. "Thank you. And please don't tell Jihoon that I asked you to look after him. It'll just annoy him."

"So what?" Junu asked. "You're his friend, aren't you?"

"He won't like it if he knows I talked to you about him behind his back."

"Am I really so bad that Jihoon doesn't want you talking about him to me?" Junu asked.

"It's not just you," Somin said. Which meant it was still partially him, and that made Junu's hackles rise. "Recently, Jihoon has felt like he's had no control over things."

"Well, can you blame the guy?" Junu asked. Even he thought that Ahn Jihoon had gone through an avalanche of unfortunate events in the few months Junu had known him. Almost dying. Miyoung secretly putting her own fox bead into him to save his life. Having that same fox bead almost kill him. Losing his halmeoni. And now losing his childhood home. If Junu were one who cared about such things, he'd feel bad for the guy.

"So, if he thought you were asking me this favor behind his back, then he'd feel like you were taking some kind of control away from him? That's bull," Junu said. "He'd care if you were hurting because of him."

"I'm not hurting. I'm just a little worried, but I can get over it on my own."

"You do this all the time for him, don't you?" Junu mused. "You bury your own feelings and prioritize him over yourself. That's not healthy. You need to just be honest with people sometimes. It makes things much easier."

"You mean how you're *so* honest?" Somin asked, raising a brow.

"What was it?" Junu asked, not letting her derail him. "What happened to make you put Jihoon before yourself all the time?"

"What makes you think something happened?"

"I can read people well."

"It's none of your business," Somin said.

Junu also knew when he wasn't going to get far with a person. And Somin was like a vault locked tight. "Fine, you don't have to tell me," he said. "But you know exactly why you give up so much of yourself for him, and maybe it's time for you to consider whether that's good for either of you."

"You don't know what you're talking about." Somin lowered her head, but not before Junu saw the glint of tears in her eyes.

"I don't like seeing you unhappy," Junu admitted. "Which you might find hard to believe. But at least believe that I'm an observant person. I see that you hide your own unhappiness so you can focus on Jihoon, and it's rotting your soul," Junu said, reaching forward to catch one of her tears with his finger. Somin pushed his hand away and rubbed at her face with her sleeve. It should have looked like a petulant motion, but it just made Junu want to hold her. Why did she bring out this protective feeling in him? He knew she didn't need his protection. But if he *could* protect her, he knew it would make him feel good, like he was somehow proving himself? But to whom?

"You're so dramatic," Somin said. "'Rotting your soul'! We're not in an Edgar Allan Poe poem."

"Ah, what a nice reference," Junu said. "You're paying attention in class."

"I know what you're doing," Somin said. "You're trying to distract me from my worries by being annoying."

"Is it working?" Junu asked with a wry grin.

She cracked a smile, and he knew it was.

18

"YOU WANT COFFEE?" Junu asked, and it was such a sudden shift in the conversation that Somin blinked in confusion.

"Come on, I'll make you a latte." Junu led the way to his kitchen, and Somin had no choice but to follow him. Her eyes slid to the door to the library before she rushed after him.

"I didn't come here to socialize," Somin said.

"Of course you didn't," Junu said, starting up the espresso machine. He held out the first mug, and when she reached for it, he held on a moment. "What do you wish to accomplish in this life?" he asked.

"What do you mean?" Somin frowned.

Junu shrugged and finally let go of the mug. "It's something someone asked me once. I think it means what's your most secret, selfish desire."

"I want to leave," Somin said. It surprised her to hear those words coming out of her own lips. She never thought she'd say them aloud. Like speaking about it would feed it. And she'd spent so long waiting for the desire to die from malnutrition.

"Where would you go?" Junu asked as he picked up the other mug and took a sip.

"I don't know," she admitted. "Just somewhere that wasn't here. Somewhere I could *experience*."

Junu smiled. "I think I know what you mean. That's not so selfish. It seems like a good wish."

She shook her head and put her mug on the counter. She was suddenly feeling too wired for coffee. "That's all it is. A wish. It'll never become reality. I could never leave my mother and Jihoon all alone."

"I don't think you give them enough credit. You can all survive without each other for a little while."

"You wouldn't understand," Somin said, shaking her head.

That seemed to darken Junu's mood. He lowered his eyes. "Perhaps not."

Had she hurt him? It was so strange, this feeling that he had . . . well, feelings. But it was ridiculous to think her words had any power over him. Still, a guilt rooted deep within her, and Somin hated to feel like she'd somehow hurt someone unless she'd deliberately meant to.

"You're brave for helping Miyoung," Somin said, hoping it turned Junu's mood.

"Where's that coming from?" Junu asked.

Somin shrugged. "Even though you annoy me, it doesn't mean I can't acknowledge when you do something good."

Junu laughed. "Oh, don't worry, I don't need your compliments. I know I never do anything good. I'm much better at being bad." He winked, and it made her insides squeeze.

"You say that like it's a good thing."

"Well, I've never heard anyone complain," he said with a sly grin.

"You know, there are only three kinds of people who are so self-absorbed: assholes, people who are genuinely oblivious, and people trying to hide some kind of pain."

Junu's eyes went dark and flat for a moment before he pasted on that megawatt smile again, a hint of mocking to add flavor. "And let me guess. You've convinced yourself that I'm the third and that you're going to save me from my demons."

"Well, you're half right," Somin said, not letting him get to her. "I do think you're the third. But I'm still trying to decide if you deserve to be saved. Maybe it's all your fault."

The flash of indignation was the reward she'd been looking for, but it was followed so closely by a hint of something raw that ate into her fleeting victory.

"What if I asked you?" His voice was smooth as velvet, but there was a strange, serious undertone.

"What?" Somin asked, unsure if she'd heard right.

"What if I asked you to save me?" he said, his eyes so intense they seemed to bore into hers. "Would you consider it then?"

"You can't be serious," she breathed, uncertain of where to tread here.

Then the tension broke as Junu gave a wide, reckless grin. "You know me too well."

Before Somin could reply, the doorbell chimed. Junu started for the foyer, but Somin stopped him. "He can't know I was here."

"Stay back here and wait until we leave," Junu said.

"You won't tell him what we talked about?" Somin asked, worry creasing her brow.

"I gave you my word," Junu said. "No matter how foolish I think the request is."

The doorbell chimed again and again with impatience.

"I'm trusting you," Somin said, trying to search out any seeds of doubt on his face. But it was placid, unreadable.

"And I'm sure that it's killing you to do so. Now, if you don't want Jihoon to know about your little visit, then wait here and stay quiet."

Somin nodded as Junu walked to the front door.

"Ah, Ahn Jihoon, why am I not surprised to see you?" Junu said as he opened the door, and for a moment Somin thought the dokkaebi was going to give her up.

"I'm coming with you," Jihoon said.

"I figured as much," Junu replied. "Well, come on, we're wasting time just standing here."

"You're not going to argue with me?" Jihoon asked.

Somin almost cursed. Junu was being too obvious.

"Well, I could argue, and then we'd waste about twenty minutes going back and forth about the pros and cons of you coming along. Like this is Miyoung's life and she told you explicitly not to get involved. Or how it would be easier for me to move quickly if I were alone. Or how you have no idea how dangerous this place can be."

"Those all sound like cons," Jihoon said.

"Well, I guess you *are* smarter than I gave you credit for. Come on, then. We've already wasted three minutes with this non-argument."

Somin heard the shuffling of feet, and then the door closed with a chime of notes. And she was left alone, worrying whether she'd made a mistake letting Jihoon go with Junu.

19

MIYOUNG WAS BACK *by the maehwa tree. The large X scarring the bark like a morbid mark on a treasure map. Mist hung so heavy she could barely see a meter in front of her. But she knew Yena was there. She could feel it.*

"Mother, what is all this? Is this just a dream or are you really here?"

Yena moved out of the mist. Her face was blank; there was no way to read any emotion from it, but Miyoung still convinced herself she saw anger there.

"Do you really want the answer to that?" Yena said, this time a spark of something in her eyes.

"I don't know." If Junu was telling the truth, then was her mother haunting her? Miyoung knew enough about gwishin to know that they were a shadow of their living selves. And the longer they lingered in the mortal realm, the more they lost parts of their humanity. But maybe . . . since Yena hadn't been truly human to begin with . . . maybe she was different?

"Something else worries you, Daughter. Tell me." Yena reached out to run her fingers over Miyoung's cheek; they were cold as ice.

"My bead," she said. "Do you know where it is?"

"It is your life and you've rejected it," Yena said, her eyes fierce and accusing.

"It's not the life I wanted," Miyoung said.

"So you reject the life I fought for? The life I died for?" Yena's voice rose, her teeth clenched in barely contained rage.

"No, I'm sorry. I'm sorry," Miyoung said quickly.

Yena settled, a small smile playing across her features. Such a sudden change that Miyoung's heart still raced. "My daughter. Tell me what worries you."

Miyoung frowned, confusion pricking at her anxiety. "I— I don't know."

"Tell me," Yena said, her eyes narrowing in anger.

"Junu," Miyoung said quickly. "I don't know if I can trust him, but it feels like he's the only one who can help me right now."

"Those boys don't know what awaits them."

The words sent a shiver down Miyoung's spine. "What do you mean?"

"He'll come against one that he can't deny."

"You're making no sense, Mother."

"They're approaching an enemy that has been waiting for her chance."

"If you know what's going to happen, then tell me!" Miyoung's chest tightened, and she couldn't draw a full breath.

"I don't know the future."

"Please just tell me what the danger is." Miyoung frantically reached out to her mother, but her hand went right through air. Where her mother's arm had previously been was wisps and vapors. She began to fade into nothingness, like pollen on the wind.

"No, Mother! I need an answer," Miyoung insisted.

But Yena floated away, sifting into the air as she had the night she died in Miyoung's arms.

"Mother!" Miyoung jerked awake, lashing out at a weight

pushing her down before she realized they were hands. And they were attached to a worried Somin.

"Bad dream?" Somin asked, sitting on the edge of the bed.

"I'm fine," Miyoung said. "Where's Jihoon?"

Somin was silent too long. And Yena's words still haunted her. *Those boys don't know what awaits them . . . They're approaching an enemy that has been waiting for her chance.*

"'*They're approaching*,'" Miyoung whispered to herself.

"What?" Somin asked.

"Jihoon went with Junu, didn't he?"

"Yes, and before you say anything, I tried to talk him out of it."

"You should have tried harder." Miyoung fought back a mix of anger and fear.

"You know how stubborn Jihoon can be."

"And I know he almost died because of me once already. I'm not risking him like that again."

"He's not going to die. Junu will take care of him."

Miyoung eyed Somin, looking for a mocking tone, but didn't find it. "You seem to have changed your tune when it comes to Junu. Why's that?"

"Because I have to trust him. It's the only option I can see right now."

"Well, right now, I need to be alone," Miyoung said. "And then I think I should go back to Junu's to wait for them."

"I'll go with you."

Miyoung wanted to say no, but she knew none of this was really Somin's fault. "Fine, just give me a little time to get ready."

"Okay," Somin said, worry clear in her voice, even as she abided by Miyoung's request.

Alone now, Miyoung listened to the quiet room. There was nothing. Just the sound of her ragged breathing.

How could Yena have known? What were these dreams? Junu had said Miyoung was connected to the ghost realm. Could that mean that Yena was truly visiting her?

"Mother?" Miyoung said aloud. "Are you here?"

She waited, not sure whether she wanted a reply or not.

But none came.

20

JUNU HAD SAT through tense silence before. He was good at compartmentalizing, so it didn't usually bother him. But Jihoon's presence weighed on him and wouldn't let him ignore it. So instead, he leaned into it.

"I like driving, feeling the power of the car in your hands," Junu mused as he pressed on the gas to pass an SUV. "Cars are a magnificent invention. Sometimes I wonder if people take them for granted."

"What are you talking about?" Jihoon asked.

"Figured it would be nice to get to know each other. You know, since we have so many friends in common."

Jihoon scoffed. "Friends? Who is your friend?"

Junu placed his hand over his heart in mock injury, though there was a real throb under his palm. "That's cruel. You know how I care for our Changwanie. And I think of Miyoung as a little sister of sorts. And Somin." He paused, unsure how to label that relationship.

"You and Somin are what?" Jihoon asked.

"Exploring things," Junu said with a shrug.

"Why are you so interested in Somin? You don't have a chance with her."

Usually, in a situation like this, Junu would feel smug.

Knowing he'd done something a person told him would never happen. But instead he tensed at Jihoon's words.

"You really think so?" Junu asked, maybe too seriously, because Jihoon gave him a confused look.

"I mean, you're just not her type," Jihoon said, the sharpness of his voice toned down.

"What's her type?" Junu asked, trying to keep the question casual-sounding. Staring at the road instead of at Jihoon.

"Why do you care? You're only hitting on her to annoy her. It's just one of your strange dokkaebi games."

"You think that's all I do? Mess with people for entertainment?"

"Well." Jihoon pretended to think it over, then emphatically nodded. "Yes. Yes, I do think that's what you do. Can you honestly say that you don't?"

Junu scowled because Jihoon wasn't completely wrong. Miyoung always claimed Jihoon was more observant than he let on, and Junu was starting to suspect that might be true.

"I do, but I don't *always* do that. Sometimes I'm being genuine."

"Well, that's really hard to tell." Jihoon shrugged. "Maybe if you spent as much time having an honest conversation as you did talking about how amazing you think you are—"

"Rude," Junu said.

"The truth," Jihoon said with a knowing smile. "Listen, I don't mind a person who keeps their feelings to themselves. I mean, we all do it. But you always act like you don't care about anything but yourself, so what else are we supposed to do but believe it?"

Junu scowled. He'd heard that Jihoon could be brutally honest.

A boy who hated to lie. Junu had thought it was an exaggeration when Miyoung first told him.

"Fine, let's have a moment of honesty because we're not just going on a leisurely hike."

"When is a hike ever leisurely?" Jihoon muttered, and Junu smiled despite himself. If they'd met any other way, Junu had always thought he and Jihoon could have gotten along. A shame, really, that they had to be frenemies.

"The mountain we're going to isn't just a mountain."

"What is it? Like, your evil lair?"

"What? No, you watch too many movies." Junu realized he should just spit it out. "There's a sansin that isn't really a fan of mine."

"A sansin? Like a god?" Jihoon turned now to stare at Junu.

"Do you know any other kind of sansin?"

"Why does this one hate you?"

"*Hate* is kind of a strong word. This one just doesn't like me that much. And, to be honest, I don't really like him either."

"Care to elaborate?" Jihoon asked. "Is there anything else I should know?"

"No," Junu said. And he meant it. There wasn't anything Jihoon *had* to know, and Junu was risking enough going back to this place. The place where everything had begun. The place where she was.

"If he's a god, then won't he *know* you're on his mountain?"

"Even a sansin has limits to his abilities. And that's why I needed to prepare yesterday. Here." He popped open the center console and took out a bujeok. The yellow paper waved like a flag as he handed it to Jihoon. "It should help hide our presence."

"Oh great, more bujeoks," Jihoon said, but he took it and tucked it carefully into his pocket.

"Just be cautious while we're on the mountain and stick close. We're going straight to the bangmangi and straight back down. No detours. No dawdling."

"I'm fine with that," Jihoon said.

THE FIRST TIME *Junu saw Sinhye was in the market.*

Junu's mother and sister had dragged him out to hold their purchases as they shopped. His mother said it was because she wanted all the women to see her youngest son and how filial he was.

He would believe her, except she already had a son who'd achieved great things. She didn't need her useless second son to help increase her pride. She just wanted someone to hold her things. But at least that meant she wanted him around. So he went along.

Before the war, their city had had a variety of classes. Now there was no in-between. If you weren't noble, then you were slave class. Junu's family was part of the noble class, barely. And his parents always worried about their place in society and the maintenance of their precarious hold on the claim of nobility. The market was the only place the two levels of society mingled.

The girl wasn't entirely visible through the crowd of men surrounding her.

Junu could barely make out her fair complexion, her raven-dark hair, long and flowing. Not the way a noble would wear it, but she still held herself with such grace and class. And the men surrounding her were from some of the most noble houses in town. Her clothes were made of fine silk. Brightly colored, but still not enough to take attention from her beautiful smile.

Then her eyes lifted and latched on to Junu's. A quick second later, someone shifted, and she was swallowed again by the crowd of her admirers.

Junu felt drawn to her, but his mother placed a hand on his arm.

"Come, Junu, there are more vendors down this street."

He tried to crane his neck to catch another glimpse, but she was gone.

She found him later.

As he waited for his mother and sisters to finish perusing a table of shoes, the girl approached him.

"You are one who observes more often than he partakes." She did not say it like a question, but like a statement.

"And you are one who can't seem to move much without attracting a dozen distractions."

She gave a small chuckle and gazed at the sky, taking in the sight of a kite flying above.

"I envy that kite. How beautiful and free it must feel all alone in the sky."

"But a string holds it down. How free could it really be?" Junu asked.

She nodded in agreement and said, "What do you wish to accomplish in this life?"

He was surprised at the question but too polite not to answer. "I would like it if I were free of social constraints. If I could be who I wish without the expectations of family and others. Though I have a plain face and my family expects me to become a scholar, I have more interest in art."

"Are you any good?"

"I'm great. I could sketch something for you if you'd like."

"Could you sketch me?" she asked.

He was speechless, so he just nodded.

And so they started spending time together. He'd steal out of the house to meet her in the nearby forest. She said that it was easier away from the crowds of town. And it would give them the space and privacy to finish the painting.

His family never noticed what he was doing unless they were looking for him to do some chore. So it was easy for him to spend hours and hours away.

And in the course of this painting, they fell in love.

He loved her under a new moon sky, lit only by stars. And that night, he asked her to marry him. When she accepted, he brought her home to meet his family and they laughed at him. They said there was no way a lady so beautiful would want to be with him. He was so homely and nervous and mediocre. His head was always in the clouds instead of trying to get an appointment that would make his family proud.

Plus, Junu's love of making art was no life for the son of a nobleman. Even though he was the second son, he was still a son of a noble house.

Junu vowed to leave his family behind once he was married. He no longer needed their disdain if he had Sinhye. He rented a small room and waited for the day he'd marry his bride.

But that wasn't to happen. His death came while he was still unwed.

21

SOMIN OPENED THE cabinet in Junu's kitchen for the third time without taking anything out. She kept opening it only to forget what she was doing and close it again. Then she'd remember a few minutes later, open the cabinet again, and immediately forget.

She wasn't usually this scattered. It was more her mother's forte to be so forgetful. But Somin had a lot on her mind. Not only was she worried about Jihoon—and Junu, to a lesser degree (or so she told herself)—but there was also something that had been eating away at her already raw nerves.

When Junu had accused her of sacrificing her own comfort for Jihoon's, he hadn't been completely wrong (which she hated). Somin had spent most of the day trying to convince herself he'd been full of it, but the damned dokkaebi was right.

She hated to think of that time when both she and Jihoon had lost their fathers. One might have thought the shared trauma was what made them so close. But it was actually the only thing they could never connect on. Through an act of fate or perhaps on a tragic whim of the gods, the day of her father's memorial was the same day Jihoon's father was arrested. So when she'd needed her best friend most, he wasn't there for her.

They both no longer had a father, but through such different paths. Even though Somin had been young, she'd known Jihoon's parents were cruel. And though Jihoon never said it out loud, she knew he'd lived a horrible childhood under his father's roof. Living with his halmeoni was the first time Jihoon had felt genuine love. Somin had never wondered if she was loved. And because of that, she felt a need to protect Jihoon.

Later, Jihoon always said he barely remembered his father. And Somin said the same thing, but it was a lie. A lie started when she was too young to understand the consequences. She thought that if she talked about how much she missed her father, how much she loved him, then it would make Jihoon sad. It was the first time she'd laid aside her own pain for Jihoon. And she'd never stopped since.

So she mourned her father in private, remembered him in private. Her father had been kind and loving and good. He was taken by cancer. It had been quick, at least according to her mother. Somin wondered if her mother thought that was a comfort. To know he died so fast. For Somin, it felt like an injustice that he was taken from her so quickly.

The last thing he ever said to Somin was a promise. He said he'd take her to Lotte World when he got out of the hospital. Now Somin knew he was far too weak to ever leave the hospital. She wondered if he knew. She wondered whether he was lying to her or to himself. He'd died the next day.

Somin closed the fridge again, not finding anything that caught her attention inside. She turned and almost let out a scream. In the doorway to the kitchen stood a dark figure, tall and thin with gray hair and pale skin.

"Appa?" she whispered before she remembered Junu's warning. That her father was a ghost and it wouldn't be smart to interact with him. It was too late now. "Why are you here? Are you trying to warn me about something?"

"Somin?"

She whipped around to see Miyoung standing behind her. "I thought you were going to take a nap."

"I couldn't sleep," Miyoung said, rubbing at her eyes like a fussy child. "Who were you talking to?"

Somin looked back toward the hallway. It was empty. "I was just talking to myself."

"Well, you sounded mad at yourself," Miyoung said, taking out a cup.

Somin considered telling Miyoung about her father and thought better of it. She had enough to worry about right now. "I guess I'm wondering if you were right. If I could have done more to persuade Jihoon to stay."

"I'm sorry I said that to you," Miyoung said. "I was lashing out at you because I felt guilty."

"Guilty?"

"Yeah, Jihoon was right. Junu shouldn't have to go alone. But I should have been the one to go with him."

"You couldn't have," Somin said as she busied herself making boricha. A comforting and familiar drink. Turning to the sink, she filled the electric kettle. "You already look exhausted and you've barely even done anything today. That's why they're going to that mountain. To help you get better."

"And shouldn't *I* be the one searching for an answer?" Miyoung asked, her voice rising in agitation. "The last time I sat on my butt and let someone else try to save me, she died."

That stumped Somin. She didn't know how to comfort

Miyoung and yell at her at the same time. And that's what she wanted to do. To tell Miyoung she was an idiot for continuing to blame herself for Yena's death, but she also wanted to comfort her friend who was still mourning her mother. And Somin knew that when you were grieving, words meant nothing if your mind didn't want to believe them. "It's not just about you—it's about closing the tear between worlds. You're too weak to make the journey. Trust them to do it. They'll be fine."

"Will they?" Miyoung asked. "Jihoon shouldn't be trying to take care of me; he's still grieving his halmeoni. You know he went back to the old restaurant the night after we moved out? Just stood out front, never went in."

Somin was surprised at that. "How do you know?"

"Hwang Halmeoni," Miyoung said. "She was worried, so she called me. I told her to keep letting me know whenever he's there."

"Wow, Gu Miyoung, taking a page out of my book."

"You mean I'm meddling," Miyoung said.

"Is that what you think I do?"

Miyoung's face fell. "Oh no, I don't . . ."

Somin laughed. "No, it's fine, I know I'm a meddler, but I can't help it."

"Do you really think they'll be okay?"

"Don't worry," Somin said, even though it was all she was doing. "Junu is smarter and stronger than he looks."

Miyoung lifted her brow. "Those are not words I'd have thought would come out of your mouth."

"Maybe he's not the worst person I've ever met," Somin said with a shrug, turning to take out mugs and to hide her flushed cheeks.

"I'm not really good at this whole friendship thing," Miyoung said. "But I think I'm supposed to ask you if there's something you need to talk about."

"No, of course not," Somin said. "I mean, if there was something to talk about, then that would make me weak, right? I'd have been swayed by a pretty face. If there was something to talk about, it would be so embarrassing, right?" She was rambling but couldn't seem to stop herself.

"I'm not sure if you're asking me an actual question," Miyoung said, looking like she'd just stepped into a room on fire and had no idea how to put it out. Somin would have laughed if she wasn't currently spiraling.

"I don't really know if I'm asking one either," Somin admitted as she filled two mugs with the steaming tea.

"Am I supposed to ask a question right now?" It sounded like Miyoung hated being part of this conversation, which made it that much more meaningful to Somin. Because however much her face said she wanted to run away, Miyoung stayed.

"I just can't stop feeling . . . things," Somin admitted. "Isn't it weird for me to feel anything for him? He's, like, hundreds of years old."

"Do you really want me to answer?" Miyoung asked, still looking slightly perplexed.

Somin handed Miyoung a mug of boricha. "Yeah, sure."

"Well, when it comes to immortals, just because someone's lived for a long time doesn't mean they're mature," Miyoung said, taking a sip and hissing through her teeth when the tea was still too hot.

"Are you talking about everyone? Or just Junu?" Somin asked.

"Someone who's immortal doesn't keep aging in the normal sense. They just keep existing."

"What does that even mean?" Somin asked in frustration.

"My mother once explained it to me. I guess she wanted me to be prepared for what it would feel like once I stopped aging. I wouldn't have felt old the way a human feels old when they age. I'd have felt . . . eternal." Miyoung blew on her tea and tried another sip.

"Do you think that's how Junu feels?"

"Junu has lived for a dozen lifetimes with a twenty-year-old face," Miyoung said, and when Somin gave her a blank stare, she continued. "You can't expect someone who's physically unchanging to change emotionally the same way you would."

"So you're telling me that even though he's lived for hundreds of years, he's still got the emotional capacity of an immature boy?" Somin asked, and Miyoung smiled. "That checks out."

"I'm saying that Junu has more emotional similarities with Jihoon than with your harabeoji."

"You're not so bad at this friendship thing," Somin said, finally taking a sip of her tea. It was still a bit too hot, but it felt good going down, a warm comfort.

"Maybe not, but this whole caring-about-people thing is still really new to me, and I think it's affecting Jihoon." Miyoung blew out a frustrated breath.

"Should I be asking questions now?" Somin asked. She'd stopped worrying about Jihoon and Miyoung's relationship after last spring. When two people are willing to risk their lives for each other, it seemed ridiculous to question their commitment to each other.

"I just have a hard time telling him how I feel. And I think that it's upsetting him. I'm worried that's why he felt like he needed to go with Junu. On some ridiculous, over-the-top attempt to prove his love."

"Do you doubt his love?" Somin asked.

"Of course not."

"Then, if you really think Jihoon is hurt because you can't tell him how you feel, maybe you should just practice telling him what he means to you."

"Practice?" Miyoung asked.

"Yeah." Somin laughed, finally in a position she was comfortable with, confidante and advisor. "Let's do it now. Tell me what Jihoon means to you."

Miyoung started to shake her head. "I don't think—"

"Come on, you can trust me. Do you love him?"

"Of course I do," Miyoung said. "I just . . . it's hard for me to say that word. Yena hated it. It feels so loaded."

"Okay, then tell me how you feel about Jihoon without using that word."

"How?" Miyoung glared into her tea.

"Just try. What does Jihoon mean to you?"

Miyoung pursed her lips as she thought. "He's my . . . umbrella."

"Umbrella?" Somin asked. Maybe she'd made the assignment too abstract.

"Yeah, it's like an inside joke to us. There was this umbrella that meant something to us once."

"Okay, and why is Jihoon this umbrella?"

"Because he's . . ." Miyoung trailed off.

"What? He's round? He's made of waterproof material?"

Miyoung laughed at that, and her shoulders finally relaxed. "No, he's my shelter. Even in the strongest of downpours, he keeps me dry and warm. I know that with him I'm safe."

Somin smiled. "Well, that's a really sweet way to put it. See? You're not that bad with expressing your feelings." Then she sighed. "Makes me want to find my umbrella one day."

"Oh, you don't need an umbrella," Miyoung said with a laugh.

Somin narrowed her eyes. "Okay, I'll bite; what do I need?"

Miyoung smiled. "You need someone who'll stand in the rain with you and face the storm."

22

"ARE WE THERE yet?" Jihoon asked for perhaps the fifteenth time. It was just as annoying now as it was the last fourteen times.

"When we get there," Junu said through gritted teeth, "I will tell you."

"How much farther is it?" Jihoon asked, his voice becoming nasally with whining.

Junu finally stopped to stare at his pitiful companion. Jihoon looked like a wilted flower. His shirt clung to him and sweat saturated his hair under the blazing sun.

Junu realized that maybe insisting they hike immediately up the mountainside instead of waiting until the sun wasn't directly above them had been a callous decision. He wasn't used to the limitations of a human body.

He searched the area and spotted a shady area under an overhang. "Come on," he said. "We can take a rest here."

Jihoon let out a noise halfway between a moan and a wheeze as he followed. "I guess I really shouldn't have slacked off so much in gym class."

"Yeah, or you shouldn't have given up that fox bead." Junu took out a bottle of water and handed it to Jihoon, who drank it gratefully.

"Oh yeah, you mean the thing that was slowly draining my

life force and giving me seizures? So much fun. Highly recommend, you should definitely try it."

Junu laughed. "I'll pass. But I do always wonder, if you'd have known you had it, if you could have harnessed the energy."

Jihoon eyed Junu. "You're making that up."

Junu shrugged. "Maybe. Guess we'll never know now. Though if I were you, I'd want to know exactly what side effects come from being a glorified safety deposit box for a gumiho bead."

Jihoon rolled his eyes, but there was a hint of curiosity in them, and perhaps a bit of fear.

Junu wanted to poke at Jihoon again, to see if he could get the boy to believe more tall tales, but he heard the shuffling of approaching footsteps and he turned to face the new person.

It was an ajumma. Her steps slow and labored.

"I see you've found a nice spot. Any shade to share?"

"Of course," Junu said, shoving Jihoon aside to offer her a prime spot in the center of the shade.

"You're sweet," she said, patting him on the arm. Her hand froze a second, her fingers tightened a tad on his wrist. Then she smiled as she leaned back and let out a long, grateful breath.

"I'm reminded I'm not as young as I used to be. Every time I come up here, it gets harder and harder."

"Do you like hiking?" Jihoon asked, starting to hold out his water bottle before realizing it was empty.

Junu pulled another bottle from his pack and offered it.

She shook her head with a pursed smile. "I'm not one for hiking for pleasure. But when there's a purpose, I can do it."

Something about how she spoke struck a nerve in Junu. His voice was measured as he asked, "And what purpose is that?"

"Oh, I think you already know. A creature such as yourself. You're good at observing others."

"Are you a ghost or a demon?" Junu asked.

"Do I strike you as either one?" she asked, her smile becoming sharper as she watched him.

"No," Junu said slowly. "Shaman, then."

That made Jihoon's eyes widen, and he took a small step away. Junu wondered if he even realized he did it. Not that Junu blamed him. The last time Jihoon had come up against a shaman, he nearly died.

"It's odd to see a dokkaebi and a human traveling together. And as you're on my mountain, it seems like something I should take seriously."

"Is your god the sansin of this mountain?" Junu asked, glancing up at the craggy peaks.

"He is." She nodded. "And if you're here to cause mischief or make problems, then I'm afraid I'm going to have to ask you to leave."

"We're not here to disturb your god," Junu assured her. "In fact, we weren't planning on letting him know we were here at all." He didn't add that the last time he'd been on this mountain, the sansin had banned Junu.

The shaman turned to Jihoon again, who gave a weak smile. Then she nodded. "Make sure your business is done before nightfall."

"We will," Junu promised.

With that, the shaman turned to make her way up the path again. She stopped and turned back, looking intently at Jihoon.

"There's a strange energy in you," she said. "Like you've held more than one soul."

Jihoon seemed at a loss for words. He looked imploringly at Junu for help.

"He's a very generous boy," Junu said. "Some might say his heart is two times the normal size."

The shaman's eyes narrowed; then she let out a dry laugh. "You know, I never did like you chonggak dokkaebi. Too smooth for my liking." She turned to go and shouted a reminder over her shoulder. "Done before nightfall."

THERE ARE AS many sansin as there are mountains in Korea. They usually don't leave their mountain. So, if one does not do anything to disrespect a sansin on his mountain, they are safe from his wrath.

Unfortunately, Junu got on the bad side of a sansin.

He only met the god once and it was not a pleasant experience.

Desperate from losing everything that connected him to his human life, Junu thought to take out his rage on the shaman that had turned him into a dokkaebi. She'd promised that revenge would soothe his battered soul. But it had only served to break his spirit.

He found the shaman praying beside an altar of rocks, stacked high in honor of her god.

"Stand and face me, witch!" he shouted.

She kept her back to him and did not speak, just continued to pray to the sansin.

"I said stand. Or I will strike you down where you sit." Junu pressed forward, a knife grasped tightly in his sweat-slicked hand.

Now she did speak, her back still facing him. "You have one chance to leave."

Junu let out a bitter laugh. "You think you're the one who has a right to make demands? I am the one who holds your life in my hands."

Now she rose and turned to face him, and as she did, a roar shook the trees.

A tiger, so giant he reached the woman's shoulders in height, leapt from the forest. He pinned Junu to the ground, teeth gnashing centimeters from his face.

Junu tried to lash out with his knife when a sudden pain lanced through his whole body as if fire raced through his veins.

"What is this? What magic do you wield?" Junu cried.

"You will not threaten one of my loyal shamans." An old man emerged from the forest.

His hair was white as the moon. A beard trailed down across his silk robes. He wore the garb of a noble.

Junu knew immediately that this was no mortal. Call it his new dokkaebi senses, but he knew without asking that this was a god.

"Please, make it stop," Junu cried. His body felt like it might tear apart.

Slowly the fire abated, but the tiger still sat on his chest, compressing his lungs.

"You will leave my mountain. You will never come back. Or you will pay for the slight with your life," the sansin said.

"Of course," Junu grunted out, his voice reedy as the tiger still pressed on his chest.

"If I see you again, your life is forfeit."

The tiger stepped back, and Junu scrambled up, gasping in breaths. He reached for his fallen knife, but a spark slashed across his palm and Junu screamed. There was a gash in the middle of his hand, but no blood spilled. He gaped at the sight, proof that he was truly a monster. Like his father had shouted at him with his final breaths.

"Leave it and go," the sansin roared, and the sound boomed through Junu's head so loudly his ears rang.

Junu bowed and stuttered out an apology before he turned and fled.

23

MIYOUNG GLARED AT her phone. Jihoon wasn't picking up. Junu wasn't picking up. Were they ignoring her calls? Jihoon had snuck out so early that morning to do the exact opposite of what she'd asked. Was he ignoring her because he was afraid of what she'd say? He'd be right, because she was planning to tear into him as soon as she saw him again. But was she a hypocrite for being upset? After all, she'd gone months lying to Jihoon, thinking she knew what was best for him last winter. But that had been different. Miyoung hadn't wanted to upset Jihoon because he'd held her fox bead inside of him. It had weakened him; she'd had no idea if he could handle the strain of knowing his life was in danger because of her.

Still lost in her thoughts, she went into the kitchen for a glass of water and stopped short when she saw Somin at the fridge.

"Somin-ah, what are you doing in here with all the lights off?" she asked, shuffling to the cabinets for a glass. "Can you pass me the water?"

Then she blinked, thinking perhaps she was just tired from stress. That's why she thought she could see the fridge through Somin.

Then the figure turned. The glass fell from Miyoung's hand, crashing against the tile at her feet.

"Mother?" she whispered.

Free me, Daughter.

"What are you doing here?"

Don't you want me to visit you? Don't you call me to you?

"No, I'm not doing anything. I promise," Miyoung said.

Yena held out her palm, and in it she held a thread, which shone bright and gold and sliced through the air to connect to Miyoung.

We are connected. It's how I can come to you. Back and forth. Back and forth.

"Mother?" Miyoung sobbed, stepping forward. But Yena faded into nothing before Miyoung could reach her.

"Miyoung?" Somin rushed to her. "What happened?"

"What?" Miyoung turned, dazed, barely registering Somin frantically dragging her to the high-top chairs around the island.

"You stepped in glass. You're bleeding everywhere." Somin grabbed a towel and knelt in front of Miyoung. "What happened?"

"I saw her," Miyoung murmured.

"Stay here, I'm going to find the first aid kit."

No, this isn't happening, Miyoung thought. Because if this was happening, it meant Junu was right about ghosts coming to this world. That her mother really was haunting her. And her mother must have the bead, which was how she'd been able to visit Miyoung this whole time, using her connection to her bead. Was Yena making the tear wider by coming to Miyoung so often in her dreams? How big was it now that Yena was appearing before Miyoung?

Somin rushed back with tweezers, ointment, and bandages. Miyoung barely felt it as Somin pulled the glass shards from her feet while chastising her. She might as well have been speaking in a foreign language; Miyoung was barely listening to her lecture.

"Miyoung!" Somin shouted. "Are you listening to me? What the hell happened here?"

"I . . . I can't . . . I don't . . ." And finally the pressure that had been building in Miyoung's chest broke free and she burst into sobs.

Without a word, Somin wrapped Miyoung in her arms. And Miyoung held on, her whole body shaking.

Junu was right; ghosts shouldn't linger in this world too long. Miyoung hated admitting it. But she'd been seeing Yena in her dreams for months and she had been ignoring it. No. She was lying to herself. She'd been holding on to it, just like she was somehow holding on to Yena. Her mother had said to set her free, but Miyoung didn't know how to do that.

When Miyoung's sobs had quieted to slow hiccupping tears, Somin pulled away. "Tell me what's happening. Let me help. Please."

Miyoung started to tell Somin. That her mother was haunting her. That her mother was a ghost and must be the reason that her yeowu guseul was in the ghost realm. But she couldn't bring herself to say it. Because there was nothing to say. No, because Miyoung knew that if Somin knew about Yena, she'd ask Miyoung to give her up. And Miyoung didn't know if she could do it.

24

JIHOON TRIED TO ask Junu questions about the shaman and what she could mean. But Junu ignored him until he finally fell into a sullen silence. Now all Junu could hear was Jihoon's labored breaths, but he no longer complained about the hike.

In the woods he could make out shapes moving through the trees. It was so miserably hot today that Junu doubted it was someone out for a leisurely hike. It was more likely a wayward spirit. Though, if they kept to themselves, there was no reason for the ghosts to bother them.

As Junu stepped past a giant pine, he had a sense of déjà vu. He didn't recognize anything, not the shape of the rocks beside him or anything else along the path. Yet something inside him knew they were close.

"Why are we stopping?" It was the first time Jihoon had spoken in hours, and his voice was breathy.

Junu held a finger to his lips, squinting as he scanned the rock face. Then he saw them, the stacks of rocks. Altars to the sansin. He spun around, searching the trees for the mountain god. If he knew Junu was here, then they were in a lot of trouble. Junu was definitely not a fighter. And he doubted Jihoon, currently bent over and wheezing, would be any help. Then he saw it, the cave opening. He realized the reason things didn't look familiar was because it had been centuries, and the flora had grown larger than he remembered. But he saw a dark shadow in the rocks beneath the looming branches of a tree. It had been a mere sapling the last time Junu had seen it, but now it stretched high into the sky. And now it practically hid the opening to the cave.

"You stay out here," Junu said.

"No way," Jihoon said, following him. "I came all this way. I'm not waiting out here as random ghost bait."

So he had seen the spirits.

"Fine," Junu said. "Come along. But if you get your soul sucked out, it's not my fault."

He made his way into the cave and heard the hesitant shuffle of Jihoon behind him.

"You weren't serious, right?" Jihoon whispered, nerves clear in his shaky voice.

"About what?" Junu asked. "You'll have to be specific because I'm so rarely serious about anything."

"Could my soul really get sucked out?"

Junu chuckled softly. It seemed that despite his bravado, Jihoon's sense of self-preservation was still healthy. It was a trait Junu could appreciate.

"I mean," Jihoon continued nervously, "I wouldn't normally believe that, but since I literally had a gumiho bead *inside* of my chest for like three months, I am a bit wary of anything essential leaving or inhabiting me."

Junu turned to Jihoon and patted him on the cheek. "Don't worry, I won't let anything happen to your frail human body."

Jihoon batted his hand away, and Junu laughed again. Perhaps letting Jihoon come wasn't all bad. At least the boy provided some entertainment.

Junu walked deeper into the cave, carefully making his way

around rocks jutting from the walls. The deeper they went, the less light there was until Junu was forced to pull out the flashlight he'd packed. He could still see fairly well, but he knew Jihoon's eyes wouldn't be able to adjust to the dark. He heard Jihoon grunt as he ran into a low boulder Junu had just skirted, but Junu had no desire to tease Jihoon anymore. The farther they traveled into the cave, the colder it became, like something leached out all the warmth from the air.

"There's no sound," Jihoon whispered. And Junu almost jumped at the echo of his voice.

But Jihoon was right; even now the only sound was the tap of their footsteps.

Sinhye, are you in here? Junu said to himself. *Can you hear me?*

Junu almost expected to hear a reply in his head. But there was nothing, just a deep, endless silence broken only by their steps.

The cave sloped lower as they walked and both boys had to crouch to pass through. The top of Junu's head scraped against something hanging from the ceiling, and he didn't dare reach up to check what it was. If he was lucky, it was just a stalactite. If he wasn't . . . What creatures might dwell in such a dark place?

Suddenly, it felt like the silence was no longer so thick. Instead there was a low hum in the air.

"Keep behind me," Junu said. And as if on cue, they stepped into a round cavern. It was tall enough for them to stand straight, barely.

"Where are we?" Jihoon whispered, the reverent voice of someone who knew he was somewhere sacred. Or somewhere cursed. He stepped out from behind Junu, despite the warning, to see what was inside the cave. He held up his phone flashlight, letting it sweep across the space. It lit up an object in the center of the cavern. "A jar? *That's* what all this fuss is about?"

Junu didn't reply. He had no time to explain to Jihoon what his weak human eyes couldn't see. Junu stared at the jar. It looked too new, too shiny. The pattern of branches more blue than black because of the ink used on the pale ceramic. Just as it had been the day he'd had it commissioned. And around the smooth ceramic, there was a shadow. Like the flow of energy that surrounded many supernatural creatures. The energy of a being so strong that she could barely be contained.

Except by love. Words spoken to him hundreds of years ago. Words that told him only he could truly trap the woman he once professed to love above anything else.

But the jar was not what he was here for. He turned toward the perimeter of the cave.

"Can you hear that?" Jihoon asked.

"What?" Junu asked as he ran his hand over the stone wall.

"It sounds like . . . a whisper. You can't hear that?"

Junu stared at Jihoon, who looked both confused and mesmerized. Was Jihoon really hearing something? Junu willed himself to listen, but all he heard was the echo of his own breathing.

"It's probably just the wind," Junu said, even though he couldn't feel a breeze on his skin. "Just stay put. I need to concentrate." He turned to the walls, running his hands over them. The rock was cold to the touch, like it was ice instead of stone. It felt like Sinhye had leached all the energy from the space around her prison. Feeding on anything she could reach.

He tried to remember the movements of a day that he'd spent hundreds of years trying to forget. How he followed the shaman into this cave. How he scraped his head that time, too. Except he lifted his hand frantically, expecting to find blood, before he realized he no longer bled. And it had fueled his fire. Sinhye had cursed him to this fate, so he would enact his revenge.

And with this rage running through him, he didn't even flinch when he saw her lying unconscious in the middle of the cave, surrounded by talismans pasted to the walls. His jar sat beside her. It was to be a wedding gift and instead sat as her future prison.

What was once made with love would be sealed with hate.

And the shaman guided him through the process. One that ended with him piercing a large bujeok pasted at the north end of the cave. He'd expected to find the stone resistant, but his bang-mangi sliced through the wall like butter.

He found that spot now. But instead of the knob of his staff, he found a hole the size of his fist. Empty.

"It's gone," he murmured.

"You really don't hear that?" Jihoon asked as if he hadn't heard Junu, and when the dokkaebi turned, Jihoon stood right next to the jar. His hands on the lid. "She says it's in here." There was a scrape as he started to lift the lid.

With a garbled shout, Junu sprinted across the cave and slammed the lid back with a crack. He almost expected the thing to break in half from the pressure, but it held strong.

"You stupid human. Do you know what you almost did?"

"What?" Jihoon's voice shook. And for the first time, he stared at Junu with fear.

"If she got out and—" Junu couldn't even finish the thought, his eyes darting around the cave, trying to measure the feel of the space. Was it somehow colder? Was there a strange breeze? Or was that Jihoon's ragged breath?

"How did you even move it?" Junu whispered, staring at the jar.

"Was it supposed to be . . . locked?" Jihoon asked.

"It wouldn't be a proper prison if it wasn't."

"A prison?" Jihoon squeaked.

"Yes, and you don't want what's trapped in here to get out."

"Why not?"

"She's not likely to be a benevolent spirit."

"What is she likely to be?" Jihoon asked, and it was clear he wasn't letting this go.

"A gumiho."

"*Why* is a gumiho trapped in this jar?" Jihoon's voice wavered.

"That's not important. What's important is that she was dangerous and I helped trap her," Junu murmured, remembering that fateful night when his life had changed. How the moonlight flooded the room. Bathed Sinhye in its glow. How she looked like a demon come to take his soul.

Jihoon's eyes widened and he took a step back, his hands out as if trying to ward away evil. "And I touched it. I think I'm going to be sick. I feel nauseous. Ugh, my head hurts." He pinched the bridge of his nose as he leaned his head back.

"Let's just get out of here before you have a stroke."

Jihoon looked around. "But we came here for your staff. What do we do now?"

"I guess we start from square one," Junu said. "But there's nothing for us to do here anymore. And I'd like to be away from this damned place as soon as possible. But first"—Junu slapped a hand on Jihoon's back hard enough to make him stumble a step—"we eat."

JUNU WOKE WITH a start. His brain foggy, like tendrils of smoke wound through it, trying to form shapes that dissipated before he could make them out. Memories nipping at the edges of his mind and dancing away when he reached for them.

Then everything cleared. As he remembered, he'd swung out in defense. But it was too late. He'd already died. And the moment of his death was replaying in his head no matter how he tried to push it away.

The woman he'd loved. The woman he'd trusted. She had revealed herself to be a demon and then killed him.

He opened his eyes to see a different woman standing in front of him. Not his murderer. Not his Sinhye.

She was a shaman. And she explained to him that after he died, his beloved hired her to trap his soul in a new form. Because he shunned Sinhye as a demon, she made him one as well: a dokkaebi.

Though, she could not bring herself to make him hideous, so she gave him a beautiful face and form. This way he would truly know her pain. Because though his face would attract humans, soon they would see his demonic side and they would shun him as he had shunned her.

Unable to accept this, Junu had run home, desperate to see his family. They did not recognize him. He wore a new face; he walked in a new body. And he stood outside the gates, staring at the signs of mourning on his household, unable to tell them he was still alive. Unsure if he was alive.

Dejected, penniless, alone, Junu returned to the cave where the shaman awaited him. She told him that he could get his revenge on the gumiho who trapped him in this form. And in return, he merely had to give up his dokkaebi staff.

Junu hated the thing and what it symbolized to him. He wanted nothing to do with the magic associated with his dokkaebi form. So he readily agreed. Magic had done this to him, and he would use every last bit he'd been cursed with to trap Sinhye forever.

25

SOMIN HATED HAVING nothing to do. Especially when people she cared about were out there risking their lives. She wanted to be in the action, to do *something* other than pacing the gleaming floors of Junu's apartment. So she went to his library hoping to find a good book to distract herself with. As she ran her fingers over the piano keys, the sound brought memories of the last time she was here, and she blushed.

Somin purposefully turned her back on the piano and moved to the opposite end of the room. There was no rhyme or reason to the organization of the books on the shelves. But she could tell that most were well-used.

Smiling, she shook her head at Junu's previous claim that these books were just for show. Her mother had always said that a well-read book was a well-loved book. And as she pulled some out at random, she found that most of them were dog-eared and worn. Some even had writing in the margins. Small notes Junu had made. Some of them his musings about the characters. Some little notes to someone—who, Somin wasn't exactly sure.

Piggy has a point, there do need to be rules. Otherwise how can you break them? But what an unfortunate name Piggy is.

An agency that only exists to apologize? What a futile endeavor. This book was almost pristine except for this note, a sign to Somin that Junu hadn't liked this novel.

Just tell her you like her. Rejection is fleeting and then there's wine was scratched into *Pride and Prejudice* and made Somin laugh. Like Junu would know what rejection felt like.

She placed a copy of *Persuasion* back on the shelf and tried to pull out the next book, but it wouldn't budge. She yanked again, gritting her teeth with the effort. With a click it jutted out of the shelf but didn't come completely free; instead the bookshelf swung out on a hinge like a door.

Somin almost laughed. Of course he would have a hidden room in this place. Probably where he kept his vault so he could sit in piles of his money. But when she pulled the hidden door open, she was shocked at what she saw.

Instead of the sleek steel safe she'd expected to find, she found a room filled with paintings and sculptures. Delicate ceramics sat on tables that lined the walls. Canvases were stacked on top of one another. The middle of the room had paint splatters marring the floor. Something that shocked Somin, as she knew what a stickler Junu was for cleanliness in his space. But here there was chaos. There was color. There was beauty. She was amazed at the gorgeous paintings. Why would Junu keep them in here and not display them proudly? They were obviously his own work.

How could a person who loved to brag about all of his accolades hide such obvious talent?

Somin stepped to a ceramic jar. It was smooth and delicate, decorated with birds and flowers painted in blue. Another had a leering tiger. And yet another had a fox. Perhaps inspired by Junu's new housemate.

She turned to the finished paintings leaning against the wall in a small stack. They looked like they were painted in styles from across the centuries. Some were sweeping watercolors. Some were bold acrylics and oils. She found one that looked as abstract as a Picasso, though it was the only one of its kind. Perhaps a phase where Junu had wanted to experiment?

Another pile had a tarp thrown over it. And when she moved it, dust flew into the air like it hadn't been disturbed in years.

These were done in the muted golds, reds, and earth tones of ancient Korean paintings Somin had seen in museums. Each of them was a portrait of a single person. Three different girls of varying ages. A man who could be anywhere from his late teens to his late twenties (it was always hard for Somin to tell with these older paintings). A woman old enough to be Somin's mother. There was something in her eyes that Junu had captured. A spark as if her soul were truly living inside this painting. As if she felt love for the person who painted her. And then she found a final painting, if you could call it that. It was mostly a splotch of colors—blacks and reds and browns—streaked over it like someone had thrown whole jars of paint over the canvas. But there, in the middle, peeked out an eye, brown and bold, staring so sharply that Somin felt it would come alive. She felt sweat bead at the base of her neck, a strange feeling like she was being watched. There had clearly been a portrait of someone on this canvas once, and Junu chose to cover it up, but not throw it out . . .

Suddenly, Somin felt like she was invading something private. There was something about these paintings that felt very personal. Like something she didn't have a right to see without permission. So she stepped back out and, with one final look inside, closed the door.

26

THE NEXT DAY, the trip back to Seoul was a sullen ride.

Junu had ushered them off the mountain as quickly as he could with Jihoon's slow, stumbling pace. He didn't want to stay there any longer than he had to. Every extra minute spent there meant more time for the god of the mountain to find out he'd come back and punish him for it.

But the long hike and the disappointment of the day soon caught up with both Jihoon and Junu. After dinner, Junu was faced with a dilemma. Try to drive through the night or find a place to sleep. Jihoon didn't have a license, and Junu would never have let him drive the Porsche anyway. So, as the sun set, he decided they better get a room at a small inn at the edge of the town close to the mountain. Junu had lain awake most of the night listening to Jihoon toss and turn.

Now they drove with the sun rising behind them, carrying the weight of failure with them. If his bangmangi wasn't in that cave, Junu had no clue where to start searching for it. Who had the power to take the staff? Another dokkaebi?

They were stuck in standstill traffic, strange for this highway, and it made Junu anxious. He tapped his fingers against the steering wheel as he craned his neck to see if he could spot the source of the traffic jam.

Jihoon's phone buzzed, and he silenced it. But when it buzzed again, Junu got a quick glance of Somin's name before Jihoon hit the ignore button.

"If you don't answer, it will just make her angrier."

"I think I know how to handle my best friend, thanks," Jihoon said irritably.

"Fine," Junu said with a shrug. But Somin's voice echoed in his memory, *I need you to promise you'll take care of him. I need you to promise it in a way that will make me believe you.*

"She worries about you a lot," Junu said conversationally.

"Who?" Jihoon asked, still busy on his phone.

"Somin. She worries so much about you that she ignores her own needs to make you happy."

Jihoon looked up at that, his expression twisted in disbelief. "That's ridiculous. Somin can take care of herself."

"Of course she can," Junu agreed. "That's why the perfect person to hurt her is herself. And she is constantly ignoring what she wants to make sure you get what you want."

"You have no idea what you're talking about." Jihoon glared back down at his phone. "Somin and I want the same things. Why would she have to give up anything for me?"

"Really? She wanted you to come with me on this trip?" Junu asked.

Jihoon's expression became pinched.

"She was really worried yesterday, but she knew that this is what you wanted. So she let you come with me even though it upset her."

"How could you know what Somin was like yesterday? When did you see her?"

Dammit. Centuries of a pristine record of keeping his promises, and he slipped up this one time because he'd let himself become too involved. This is why you don't mix business with personal. Or have nothing that's personal at all, much cleaner that way.

Junu sighed. "Just remember that your choices affect other people before you go riding off into danger. And I'd appreciate it if you didn't tell Somin about this conversation. If it gets out that I had loose lips, then my business could suffer."

"Sure, whatever."

Jihoon let out a yawn, and Junu realized for the first time how exhausted Jihoon looked. Maybe Junu had been wrong to assume Jihoon wasn't worrying. It seemed he hadn't gotten any sleep either.

"You doing okay?" Junu asked.

"I'm fine, I just didn't sleep well last night. I had the weirdest dreams, but I can't remember them now," Jihoon muttered as if talking to himself.

They finally reached the end of the traffic jam. It was a car accident that had closed two lanes. Police were talking to both drivers and neither looked very happy. One was animatedly gesturing toward the road, and the officers were staring at him like he was spouting nonsense. But Junu saw what had caused the accident. A ghostly woman stood in the middle of the lanes, her hair hanging in her face, dripping wet. A mul gwishin. And it seemed only one of the drivers could see her. Had probably swerved to avoid her.

"It's getting worse," Jihoon said. "The tear between the worlds."

"We need to get home," Junu said, stepping on the gas now that they were clear of the bottleneck.

27

SOMIN DISCOVERED THAT, though Junu's kitchen had all the state-of-the-art cooking tools one would desire, it had no food. When she asked Miyoung, she was informed that Junu liked owning shiny things but he hated cooking, so he ordered in more often than not.

Annoyed, Somin reluctantly went out to buy food before they starved to death. Okay, fine, maybe that was an exaggeration, but she felt better being annoyed with Junu than being worried about him. So she held on to the feeling as she traversed the neighborhood to the closest market.

She was baking under the sun and out of breath as she lugged her groceries. Maybe she'd let her anger push her too far, as she'd bought enough food to make a full banquet. Sweat dripped into her eyes, and since both of her hands were filled, she tried to wipe it away with her shoulder. She heard shouts but ignored them as she shifted the bags digging into her palms. She didn't realize that people were shouting at her to get out of the way until someone slammed into her and she went sprawling, groceries spilling into the road.

More people were shouting, yelling things she couldn't process at first.

"What are you doing?"

"Wait, don't!"

"Somebody stop him!"

She pulled herself up in time to see a man race into the street, right into oncoming traffic.

He turned for just a second, so Somin could see his face. His wide eyes were shifting wildly. And she had a moment of recognition as he howled, "He's after me!"

Then a cab screeched as it slammed on the brakes and swerved to avoid him. But the cab clipped the man with the edge of its hood and he went flying. For a moment, as he soared through the air, she saw a moment of clarity on his face. And the madness was replaced with terror. Somin turned away, not wanting to see what happened next.

She heard the screams. People shouting about calling an ambulance, about getting help.

It's that man, Somin thought. *The one who said he was being haunted.*

"The ghost drove him mad," said a low, clear voice.

A shiver raced down Somin's spine before she looked up. The boy in black stood beside her. The one she saw outside of Jihoon's apartment. This close, she could see that he was gorgeous. Smooth pale skin, a long thin nose, and full lips. He was again dressed head to toe in black, including a black trench coat that was inappropriate for the sweltering weather.

"I've seen you before," she said.

"This will happen again if he does not hurry."

"Who has to hurry? What happened here?"

"Spirits should not spend too much time in the world of the living. Their influence can be . . . harmful."

"Like driving a man to throw himself into traffic?"

"He must hurry," the boy said, instead of answering her question. "The tear between the worlds is widening. This will happen again."

"What are you?" Somin asked, because she knew that this beautiful boy could not be human.

"My list changes every day, every hour, every minute. The souls I must reap are no longer set."

"You're a jeoseung saja," Somin said, taking a step back. She'd never met a reaper before. Never knew she could while still living. She was just getting used to the idea of there being gumiho and dokkaebi. She wasn't ready to meet a servant of King Yeomra. "What do you want from me?"

"Tell him to hurry. Tell him that his time is running out." And the boy disappeared into a haze of vapors like heat waves fading into the sun.

She didn't know how, but Somin knew that the reaper spoke of Junu. She took off down the street, leaving her groceries behind as she ran.

o o o

Somin ran so fast she was gasping for breath when she rounded the corner toward Junu's apartment. Relief and anxiety raced through her, braiding together as she spotted Junu and Jihoon approaching the front door.

"Junu!" she called. He turned in time for her to barrel into him.

"I see you missed me desperately." Junu's voice rumbled in Somin's ear.

She pulled away and cleared her throat as she tried to find

something sharp and clever to say. But she was still wheezing for breath and her hair was plastered to her face with sweat. It wasn't the most dignified look. So she turned to Jihoon instead.

"Are you okay?"

He was watching her curiously, like he was trying to figure out how to react to what he'd just seen. Somin blushed under his stare. She knew Jihoon would probably give her an earful later. But right now, he just nodded.

"We're fine. It was a very quick trip." His eyes slid to Junu meaningfully.

"You sure?" Somin asked. Her best friend had dark bags under his eyes. He looked like he hadn't slept since he left.

"I'm fine," Jihoon insisted. "Let's go inside. I'm melting out here." He turned to open the front door, and as soon as it beeped, Miyoung came rushing toward them.

"Thank the gods you're back," Miyoung said, wrapping Jihoon into a hug.

"So . . ." Jihoon hesitated. "You're not mad?"

"Of course I'm mad. You did the exact opposite of what I asked you to do. What happened to 'people don't like martyrs'?"

Jihoon hunched his shoulders like he used to when Halmeoni scolded him. "I wasn't going off to die. We were just trying to get Junu's staff."

"Did you get it?" Miyoung asked, turning to Junu.

He shifted, his eyes not quite meeting anyone else's, and Somin knew the answer before he replied. "It wasn't there."

"Wasn't there?" Miyoung asked. "Then where is it?"

"That's a great question," Jihoon said.

"What are we going to do?" Somin asked.

"I don't know," Junu admitted.

"Well, we have to do something," Somin insisted. "I just saw . . . it was horrible. And this jeoseung saja said—"

"Wait, what jeoseung saja?" Junu's voice was sharp.

"I don't know. Just this boy, he appeared like from nowhere. He said you had to hurry."

Junu and Miyoung shared a pointed look.

"What is it?" she asked.

"So the reapers really are here," Miyoung said.

"I told you," Junu said.

"You *knew*?" Somin asked. "You both knew that there were reapers here?"

She turned to Jihoon, who didn't look surprised either.

"Did you *all* know?" she asked, her chest constricting with that familiar feeling of being left out. It happened so often these days.

"That's not important," Miyoung said. "What else happened? You said you saw something?"

Somin wanted to demand more answers. She felt like the kid that had been locked out of the secret clubhouse. But she knew that her feelings weren't the important thing right now. "I just saw a man run into traffic. I saw him yesterday and he was scared, but he didn't look like he was ready to jump in front of a speeding taxi. It's getting bad. Just like Junu said it would. We have to do something."

"Yes, we do," Junu murmured. "And we will. I just . . . I need to think."

"Think? We need to make a plan. Where else could your bangmangi be?" Somin asked, and if her voice was a little higher and louder than normal, then she felt she had an excuse after what she'd just witnessed.

"I need a minute." Junu turned and retreated into his room, closing the door on any protests Somin might have made.

She spun on Jihoon. "What exactly happened?"

"We got to the cave and there was just a random jar." Jihoon shrugged, then started to walk back toward the kitchen. Miyoung and Somin gave each other a confused look. Jihoon wasn't one to give up the chance to share a good story. They followed him to find Jihoon staring at the fridge, frozen like the appliance was perplexing to him.

"What did you say?" he asked.

"I didn't say anything," Somin replied.

"Oh," Jihoon said with a frown.

"Did you want water?" Somin asked, stepping forward and opening the fridge.

Jihoon blinked, his eyes clearing as he focused on her. "Oh yeah, that would be great."

"Tell us what else happened," Somin said, placing a cup in front of him.

"Well, he said that the cave was dangerous because"—Jihoon's eyes slid to Miyoung—"because he'd helped trap a gumiho in that jar. He'd used his bangmangi to do it. That's why he was convinced it would still be there. But it wasn't."

"Why would he do that?" Miyoung whispered. "Why would he capture a gumiho?"

"I guess you have to ask the guy," Jihoon said, lowering his head into his hands. "Is there any aspirin? I have a splitting headache."

"Sure," Miyoung said. "I think Junu has some in his medicine cabinet." She went into the bathroom to fetch it.

"What else did he say?" Somin asked. "Where else could his staff be? What else did you guys do?"

"I don't know. We didn't talk much. Why don't you go to Junu behind my back and ask him what else I did?"

"What?" Somin asked, her spine straightening in defense. "Why would you think I'd do that?"

Jihoon let out a hard laugh. "Come on, Junu told me that you don't think I'm capable of taking care of myself. You really think I'm that useless?"

Junu, that snake, Somin thought. She should have known better than to trust him. But she also hadn't expected the intense anger in Jihoon's eyes.

"No, of course I don't think that about you," Somin said. "I was just worried."

Jihoon let his head drop into his hands again, rubbing them roughly over his face. "I'm sorry. I shouldn't have said it like that. I just . . . I have a really bad headache."

"Here," Miyoung said, returning with the aspirin. "Take these and then go lie down."

"Yeah, okay," Jihoon murmured, throwing the pills back. "Maybe I'll do that."

"And I'm going to go have a little chat with Junu," Somin said. She wanted to give the dokkaebi a piece of her mind.

28

JUNU PULLED ON a fresh shirt, throwing the old one in the hamper. He actually considered burning it as it held a day's worth of sweat. But it was designer, so in the hamper it went.

He almost groaned when he heard the brisk knock on his door. Before he could answer, Somin stormed in.

"Listen, I don't—"

"No, you listen. I can't believe you told Jihoon about our conversation. What happened to that whole my-business-depends-on-my-discretion nonsense?"

"This is the last time I confide anything in Ahn Jihoon," Junu muttered. It felt like more of a betrayal than he'd have thought. He'd always thought Jihoon was steadfast when he made a promise. After all, he always guarded Miyoung's secrets so carefully. But perhaps that consideration wasn't extended to Junu. And that stung.

"Don't get mad at Jihoon," Somin said. "You're the one who broke your word to me."

"I brought him back in one piece," Junu said. "I kept that promise. I don't know what else you want from me. I'm not in the mood for the third degree about the last twenty-four hours."

"Is that why you escaped into here, because you're hiding out?"

"I'm not hiding," Junu said. "Not exactly. I just, I don't know what to tell Miyoung."

"I'm a big girl," Miyoung said from the open doorway, and Junu sighed. It seemed there was no escape, even in his own home. "Tell me what happened with your staff. The whole story. You know I wouldn't ask if I didn't need to know."

Junu nodded. He'd started this, so he would take responsibility. "I used it to trap something."

"A gumiho," Miyoung said.

Junu shouldn't have been surprised. Of course Jihoon had told them. Apparently, none of Junu's secrets were worth protecting. "I didn't know what she was when I first met her."

"I get it. You fell in love with her and then when you found out what she was, you betrayed her," Miyoung said.

"No, it's not as simple as all that." Junu closed his eyes to hide his frustration. Why did Somin have to be here right now? This was not a part of his past he'd ever planned to share with her. Or anyone, for that matter. "I thought I loved her. You don't know how much that meant to—" He couldn't continue without exposing more about his past than he was willing to. He took a breath to collect himself before continuing. "When she finally revealed herself to me, I was scared. She woke me in the middle of the damn night. Of course a guy needs a moment to react to the demon fox standing over his bed at midnight."

"Demon fox?" Miyoung said quietly.

"It's how it seemed to me at the time." Junu shrugged. "And Sinhye always did have a temper. She killed me for what she perceived as rejection. Next thing I knew, I woke up like this."

"You were something before you were a dokkaebi?" Somin asked.

"Yeah, once upon a time, I was human. Sinhye got a shaman to trap my soul in a dokkaebi form. A punishment for rejecting her." Junu gave a sardonic smile. Because in his human life, he'd always been the one being rejected.

"Some punishment. Immortality and beauty?" Somin said with a scoff.

"She wanted me to know her specific pain. A monster wearing a beautiful face. Cursed to incite lust but never real love." His eyes slid to Miyoung, who gave a small nod of understanding.

"Did all dokkaebi used to be human?" Somin asked.

"No, some of us are just special little prisoners," Junu said. "After the shaman turned me, she felt bad for her part in my curse and she offered me vengeance."

"And you took it?" Somin sounded incredulous. "I thought you said you loved her."

Junu stiffened at the accusation. "What upsets you? That I sought revenge for being cursed to wander the world a monster, or that I once loved another?"

"I don't care about your exes," Somin said. "I just can't imagine turning on someone you claimed to love."

"Well, I suppose you don't know me that well, do you?"

"I guess not." And Somin's expression seemed to shutter, like she was locking away her emotions.

"And when you trapped your former love, you used your staff," Miyoung continued the story quietly. Junu and Somin both turned to her. In the heat of the fight, they'd forgotten she was there.

"Yeah," Junu said. "And now it's gone. I left it in that cave. I thought it was what held her there. But I must have been wrong, because someone took it."

"So . . . it's over." Miyoung's head hung, her shoulders hunched.

"No," Junu insisted. "I'll figure this out."

From the expression on Miyoung's face, it was clear she still had no faith in him. What did he have to do to prove himself? And why did he still need to?

"We don't have time to come up with any more big plans. The reapers are already here. We have to close the tear, or they'll take care of matters. And I'm assuming they're not really motivated to keep me alive." She paused and closed her eyes, pinching the bridge of her nose. "I'll figure something out. I need to learn how to clean up my own messes or to at least face the consequences of them." She left before Somin or Junu could respond.

Junu clenched his fists. He wasn't sure if he was more frustrated or annoyed, but it didn't matter. He didn't want to deal with the disappointment that still hung heavy in the air. He waited for Somin to leave, but she didn't.

"Is there anything else I can do for you?" Junu asked, his tone sharp. Filled with all of his pent-up frustration. "Is there another traumatizing story from my past you'd like to hear?"

"I just don't get you," Somin said quietly. "I thought maybe you were different from what I initially thought. I was willing to admit I was wrong. But it's like you're constantly asking me to hate you."

"Then maybe you should," Junu said, suddenly wanting to punch something. "Maybe you're trying to look for something in me that just doesn't exist."

"I don't want to believe that."

"Why? Because otherwise you'd be ashamed of kissing me? Well, I absolve you of any responsibility there. I was already getting bored of you anyway."

He started to turn, and Somin grabbed his arm to stop him.

"Do you really mean that?" she asked, her eyes searching. "If you say yes, then that's it. But once the door is shut, I'm not opening it again."

Junu started to say yes. But he couldn't. The frustration that burned through him was sliced by the chill of fear. He was afraid of losing her. And suddenly all his anger seeped away and he was left feeling drained. "I don't know what to say to you. I don't know what to do here."

"Will you just tell me the truth?"

"I don't know if the truth will help," Junu said, but he knew he'd give it to her.

"Why did you do what you did? Why would you turn against someone you loved like that?"

He yanked his arm free like a petulant child. "You don't know what it's like to have everyone in your life tell you you're nothing. And then, when you think you've found someone who says they'll love you no matter what, they betray you, too. Worse, they turn you into a monster. You'd gladly take back the pathetic life you used to hate because anything is better than the hell you're living through now, living through it against your will. *Living* against your will."

"Do you really wish she had let you die?"

"She *did* let me die," Junu said. "She was the reason I died."

"Fine, do you really wish she'd let you *stay* dead?" Somin asked.

"I wish that I'd been given a choice." Maybe if his family had let him have a choice, then he wouldn't have been so enamored by Sinhye. He wouldn't have been so taken in by her.

"But you loved her."

Junu measured his reply. This felt like some kind of trap, but he couldn't tell what kind. And he'd promised Somin he'd tell her the truth. Stupid promises. Junu hated that he felt so honor bound to keep them. "It wasn't a healthy love."

"What does that mean?"

"Not all love is good for you," Junu said with a harsh chuckle.

Somin looked confused, like he was speaking in a language she couldn't understand. Of course she didn't. She'd grown up with a loving mother, good friends, loyal companionship. She never had to question if she was loved. Not like Junu had.

"Sometimes love can be so big that it consumes us," Junu explained. "And we see nothing else. That's dangerous. That's when it starts to move from love to obsession."

Somin shook her head. "You're just being cynical again. Letting your immortal boredom affect how you see things. Love is a *good* thing."

"No," Junu said. "In this I've done a lot of studies. Even love can be a crutch we lean on. Something we use to hide from our real problems. Trust me. I know."

"What were you hiding from?"

"Everything I was. And everything I couldn't be."

"I don't understand."

Junu shook his head. "You don't need to. It's not important anymore. What's in the past should not affect our present."

"That's ridiculous. How can you just ignore your past?"

"With a lot of whiskey." With that, Junu left in search of just that.

JUNU KNEW TWO things from an early age. That his father had certain expectations of him. And that he would never live up to them.

It didn't matter that he was the youngest of five and the second son. It didn't matter that he would not inherit the responsibilities of being the head of the family. He was too weak. Too mediocre. Too obsessed with flighty things like his art. He was not good enough in his father's eyes. And in the family, his father's opinion was law.

So Junu retreated behind his mother and his nunas. The women in the family fawned over him. Perhaps because he'd been sickly as a child and left in the care of his three nunas— older sisters who catered to his every need.

When he got older and he was bigger and stronger than his nunas, he would often accompany them to the market. Carry their shopping. Be an arm for them to hold on to. It wouldn't do for a daughter of a well-off household to be wandering the market alone.

But soon it was apparent that his father disapproved of how much time he spent with the girls. And sometimes that disapproval would culminate in a quick slap.

There were only a handful of times that Junu earned a real beating, and he always sought never to commit those infractions again. But for Junu, his own personal punishments weren't the worst. It was when his nunas were punished that it hurt the most. Sometimes it would be because they kept Junu out too long and he ignored his studies. So Junu's father would have their mother use a switch on the back of their legs. Or it would be when he heard them laughing too loudly with Junu in the courtyard. And they'd be denied dinner that night. Junu was left unscathed, but alone in his room, he'd hear the sounds of his nunas' cries as they endured their punishment. And every time they knew it was his fault. The one and only time his hyeong had spoken up on Junu's behalf, he couldn't sit easily for a day. Hyeong never stood up for Junu again. And Junu could see that it was a tactic of his father's. To drive a wedge between Junu and anyone who might defend him. Anyone that his father saw as coddling Junu. Until Junu felt completely isolated and alone.

This was the way Junu lived for the first nineteen years of his life. This was what drove him into the arms of the first girl who smiled at him. The first girl who said kind words to him. He was too enamored by her beautiful face and sweet words to realize that he was joining himself with a monster until it was too late.

29

DUBU SHOT OUT of the back room to greet Somin and Jihoon when they returned to the apartment. She barked happily when she saw Somin, before her mood suddenly turned. The small dog started growling, barking so much that her body jumped. But it wasn't directed at Somin; it was aimed at Jihoon.

Surprised, Somin scooped the dog into her arms. "Dubu, what's gotten into you? Jihoon hasn't been gone that long."

"Maybe I still smell like the road," Jihoon said. "I'll go wash up."

"Okay," Somin said. "I'll make lunch. You hungry?"

"Sure," Jihoon replied, and Somin watched as he paused a second in front of the first door before turning and trying the handle across the way. He looked disoriented and dazed. Like the travel had gotten to him.

Somin made a mental note to get those vitamin shots at the grocery store. The last thing they needed was for him to get sick, too, because he was so worried about Miyoung.

"Don't give him such a hard time," Somin said to the small dog, whose body still vibrated in her arms. "He's been through a lot. He'll give you more attention later."

She moved into the kitchen to give Dubu breakfast and found a note from her mother.

If you get home when it's still breakfast time, there's toast in the fridge. Hope you were studying and not partying, my daughter.

Somin almost laughed. She would definitely not count last night as a party. Even if she thought it skirted the line of being a mom-approved activity. Good thing her mom rarely asked questions as long as Somin's grades were good and she didn't have any open wounds.

As she set the dog bowl on the floor, the doorbell rang. She wondered who it could be and considered ignoring it. But the bell rang again and again, so persistently that Somin gave in and answered. And when she swung open the door, she immediately regretted it.

"Jihoon's not here," she said, glaring at Jihoon's father.

"I know he is. I saw you walk up here together. So go get that boy before I cause a scene."

"This is private property. I could call the police."

"Somin," Jihoon said from the hallway. "I can handle this."

"Good to see you know what's best for you," his father replied.

"Oh yes, I know," Jihoon said. There was a gleam in his eyes. Something sharp that confused Somin. She'd never seen such a harsh look on her best friend before.

Then Jihoon stepped forward and slammed his fist into his father's face.

Mr. Ahn stumbled back and might have fallen if Jihoon hadn't grabbed him by the collar.

"You here for a handout?" Jihoon asked through gritted teeth. "You think I'm an easy target because you remember when I was small and weak? Well, obviously I'm not anymore."

Somin grabbed Jihoon's arm. "Jihoon, let go. This isn't what you want."

"You think you know what I want?" Jihoon said, his face contorted in rage. Somin almost stepped back, but she knew if she did, Jihoon might do something he regretted. She pried his hands free, trying to drag him away. He felt like solid steel, unmoving. But at least he let his arms drop.

"You'll regret that," Jihoon's father said, smoothing his collar.

"I don't think so." Jihoon slammed the door closed.

"Jihoon-ah—" Somin began, ready to chastise him.

He spun on her. "How dare you."

Somin was taken aback by the venom in Jihoon's voice. "How dare I? You were attacking your father! In a public hallway where any of my neighbors could have walked by."

"So you're upset I could have gotten caught?"

"Jihoon-ah, this isn't like you. What's gotten into you?"

Jihoon shook his head, lifting a hand to his temple like he was fighting off a headache. "I don't know. I just got so angry. I couldn't stop myself."

"I get it; he makes me angry, too—"

"No, you don't get it. You don't know what it's like to have a father like that. To have him haunting your life. You don't even remember your father."

Somin considered letting it go. Even as the pain of Jihoon's words stung her, she tried to work on agreeing with him because she knew he was hurt. But instead she whispered, "You're wrong. I do remember him."

"What are you talking about?" Jihoon asked. "You always said . . ."

"I know what I said. But I lied."

"Why would you lie about something like that?"

Somin considered changing the subject. Why was she even

bringing this up now? They had bigger problems to worry about. But Junu had been right, damn him. She needed to stop pushing her pain aside just to cater to Jihoon's. "I lied because I didn't want to hurt you. My father was a good man. He loved me, and I really loved him. But I felt like if I said that, if I was sad about him in front of you, then it would hurt your feelings. Because your father was so . . ." She couldn't think of an easy way to describe Jihoon's horrible father.

"So you lied to me? For over a decade? Why would you think that's better?" He was looking at her like she was a stranger, like he thought she'd done something shameful.

"I did it to protect you," Somin said, suddenly defensive. "I did it because it's what you needed."

"Maybe you should stop thinking you know what's best," Jihoon said. "And start thinking about why you feel like you need to control everyone around you instead of letting us just live our lives." Jihoon slammed into his room.

"Fine!" Somin shouted after him, the word echoing uselessly in the empty room.

30

MIYOUNG WALKED THROUGH mist so thick she could barely see in front of her.

"Mother," she called. "Mother, if you're here, say something."

"I'm lost." Yena's voice sifted out of the fog.

"I am, too. Just follow my voice."

"I cannot find you."

"Mother, please. I have so many questions," Miyoung said. "Do you know where my bead is? We need it back and if you can help—"

"It's all that keeps us together," Yena said.

Miyoung's limbs shook. Her stomach felt like it held rocks. "Does that mean it's here? Is my bead with you?"

"It is lost."

"I know," Miyoung said. "Please, help me find it."

"He is lost."

"Who?" There was a shadow of movement to her right and Miyoung turned to follow it. "Mother, stop moving. Let me come to you."

"You'll lose him. You've already lost so much. My poor daughter."

"Who are you talking about?" Miyoung's vision wavered. "Please, Mother, you're scaring me."

"Good, you should be scared."

That made goose bumps rise on her skin, but still she moved forward, determined to find her way out of this. Determined not to let her mother's cryptic words stop her. "Tell me who you're talking about, Mother. I can't do anything if I don't know what the threat is!"

Yena's laughter rang through the mist. "Oh, my foolish daughter. You think you have the strength to fix this? A problem of your own making, because you were too sentimental to protect yourself over others?"

"That's not true!" Miyoung shouted, her tears making warm tracks down her cheeks. "I refuse to be alone any longer. I refuse to push people away."

"And when you pull others close, you put them in danger. He is lost because he loves you."

Miyoung's pulse leapt with knowledge now. "Jihoon-ah? Where is he?"

"Even he no longer knows. He runs and runs. Dirt and sticks." The dark shape moved closer, so fast that Miyoung barely blinked before Yena's pale face melted out of the mist, her eyes wide but unseeing. Her teeth bared. Miyoung tried to jerk back, but Yena clasped onto her shoulder, her nails digging into flesh. "He runs, but he cannot escape. Because the threat is coming from inside."

Then Yena shoved Miyoung away and she fell through the mist.

And she woke with a start at the moment she was sure she would have hit the ground. She lifted a hand to her sore shoulder, and it came away with a streak of blood. She leapt up and ran to the mirror above her dresser. Twisting so she could see the back of her shirt, she made out the smudge of blood above her shoulder blade.

If this was real, then . . .

"Jihoon," Miyoung whispered before running for the door.

31

SOMIN WOKE TO the ring of her phone. When she picked it up, she saw Junu's name and pressed ignore.

Just as she was about to fall back asleep, it rang again. And with a jab at the screen, she sat up. Fine, she'd just be awake.

She'd almost forgotten what day today was. She wished she'd forgotten. But as if her mind wanted to remind Somin to be miserable for the next twenty-four hours, she'd woken up at 3:00 A.M. and noticed the date. It had taken her over an hour to fall back to sleep.

Somin told herself lack of sleep was the main reason she was so irritable, but she knew it was a lie. She hated being alone on this day. So she waited for others to join her in the land of the awake. Finally, with a frown she glared at the clock on her phone. It told her it was already 9:00 A.M., which meant either everyone had overslept or she was alone. But that couldn't be right.

She walked to Jihoon's room and hesitated before knocking. Jihoon was not a morning person. But shouldn't today be different? He'd never miss today. In fourteen years, he hadn't.

So Somin rapped on the door. When there was no reply, she knocked again. Slowly, she chanced opening the door a crack. If he was a grump, then so be it. She'd dealt with angry morning Jihoon before. But when she poked her head in, the room was empty.

Where could he have gone so early in the morning? She dialed his number, but it went straight to voice mail. As if he'd turned it off. Or was screening her call. Could he really have forgotten?

Her phone buzzed, but it wasn't Jihoon. It was her mother.

I'm sorry I had to leave so early. The office called and asked me to come in. But I left soup on the stove, or there's bread if you want toast. I'll see you tonight for our family dinner. I love you.

The message was a small comfort. She knew her mother wouldn't be having an easy time of it today either. And though Somin knew it was selfish, she wished her mother had played hooky and spent the day at home. At least then Somin wouldn't be alone. But her mother probably thought Jihoon would be here.

Somin and Jihoon had a tradition for this day. For her father's birthday. Since it always fell during summer break, she and Jihoon would go out and eat ice cream, go to an arcade, maybe go to a movie. It varied, but Jihoon always planned a full day to keep her preoccupied. It was the one day a year that Somin let herself be the one taken care of. But now he was nowhere to be found. How could he forget today?

Or maybe he hadn't forgotten. Maybe he was still angry from their fight yesterday.

It stung that Jihoon could be so mad he'd abandon her on today of all days. But a part of her was worried she deserved it. Jihoon's parting words still echoed in her head. Was it so bad that she wanted to help her friends? Was she really so controlling she couldn't let the people she loved live their own lives?

She'd already been feeling useless the past week, unable to do anything to help her friends. But maybe Jihoon was right. Maybe they didn't need her help. She balled her fists, her useless fists, and slammed them into her pockets.

And before she knew it, she was crying. Just letting loose with all of her frustration, and fear, and anger. She gave the door a couple of punches for good measure.

She was crying so hard she barely heard the doorbell. But when it rang again, she answered with an angry jerk.

Junu's eyes widened as they took in her blotchy, tear-stained face.

"I take it this is a bad time."

"I take it you're an asshole and I don't want to talk to you right now." She tried to slam the door shut, but he reached out and stopped it.

"Listen, can you just tell me if you've seen Miyoung today?"

Somin frowned up at him. "You're looking for Miyoung?"

"Yeah, I woke up, and she was just gone. She's not answering her phone and neither are you, apparently."

She was confused for a second before she remembered what had woken her up on this already awful day.

"I don't know. I'm sorry, now's not a good time. Today's not a good day." Somin suddenly felt too drained and just sat on the step between the foyer and the living space.

"What is today?" She felt Junu's hand come down on her shoulder and the warmth of his body as he sat next to her.

"Today," Somin said into her knees, "is a day I don't want to be alone."

She heard Junu's sigh before he said, "Tell me what to do for you."

"Will you take me somewhere?" Somin asked without looking up.

"Anywhere."

32

MIYOUNG RAN THROUGH the forest quickly and quietly.

Jihoon hadn't answered her dozens of calls. And though it had been so early the sun had barely peeked over the horizon, Miyoung knew in her heart that it wasn't because Jihoon was sleeping. Something was wrong. Yena had said Jihoon was running. *Dirt and sticks*, she'd said. The forest.

There was a hum in the woods. A low rumbling that settled into Miyoung's ears. It felt like every tree, every beast, whispered around her. Wondering why she was here. Warning her away. Because in this forest she'd done unnatural things. She'd stolen life. She'd destroyed lives.

Miyoung tried to shake the thought out of her head. But it wouldn't break free. As morbid as it was, she realized it was fitting as she broke free of the trees into a clearing. Her mother's grave.

She almost turned and made her way back into the forest, but the hum seemed louder here and she moved out of the shelter of the trees. As she approached the maehwa tree, her steps slowed as she searched the area for any threats. Old habits were hard to kill, and to Miyoung, the forest was a place where she'd learned that threats could lurk in every shadow. The dappled sunlight that fell on the forest floor should have seemed beautiful, even magical. Instead, it felt like shapes that could twist into monsters to pull at her.

Still, she stepped toward the tree, close enough that she could place her palm against the trunk. It felt warm to the touch. Was that because of the summer heat that permeated down here despite the shade? Or was it because of something else?

"Mother," she whispered to the tree. "Can you hear me?"

Miyoung closed her eyes, waited for that whisper of a voice. Waited to see if she could call Yena forth when she wanted. But there was nothing but the whisper of wind through the trees.

"Please, if you're here, help me find him." Her voice trembled.

There was a rustle of sound and her eyes shifted, half expecting a spectral Yena to step out of the foliage. Instead a small rabbit scurried through the underbrush, and Miyoung laughed in embarrassment. The sound faded, but in its place she heard a soft huffing.

Her ears perked. Miyoung might not have super gumiho hearing anymore, but she recognized that sound. The sound of crying.

She stepped slowly around the maehwa tree and let out a breath of relief.

"Jihoon," she said. "I found you."

He was slumped against the tree, his knees hugged close to his chest. He looked up at her with bloodshot eyes.

"Miyoung-ah?" Her name came out like a hoarse question.

"What are you doing out here?" She bent down beside him.

"I can't—I can't—" Jihoon pressed his hands against his temples. "My head. It hurts."

"Tell me what's wrong."

"I can't sleep. I keep waking up like I'm having nightmares, but I can't remember them." Bags sat under his eyes as physical proof of his sleepless nights.

"Do you need to go to the hospital?"

"No, no more doctors. I just . . . I need you. I have such a need for you." He grabbed her shoulders, fingers digging into her cuts, making them sting, but she didn't pull away.

"I'm here," she said. "I'm always here for you."

Jihoon squeezed his eyes shut. Miyoung wrapped him in her arms, and she could feel his whole body trembling, like a live wire. And she realized he was the source of the humming. Like every cell of his body was vibrating so fast that it let off a buzz.

"It hurts," he mumbled. "Fighting hurts."

"What are you fighting?" Miyoung asked. She could taste his gi even though she wasn't trying to. It was too bright, too sharp. How long had he been out here?

"I can't fall asleep again. If I do . . . bad things wait for me there."

His words were an eerie echo of Miyoung's. In her dreams, Yena waited with her frightening proclamations and accusations.

"What waits for you in your dreams?"

"I don't know. She doesn't like it when I fight. She wants control," Jihoon moaned.

Now Miyoung pulled back and saw that Jihoon had started quietly sobbing. "Don't let her. Don't let her take me!"

"Who?" Miyoung asked as fear sliced through her. *Yena?* But she didn't dare ask the question aloud. What was her mother doing?

"No! I don't want to!" Jihoon shouted, fisting his hands in his hair and jerking his head back and forth.

"Jihoon-ah, stop it." Miyoung tried to stop him; she was afraid he'd rip out his own hair at this rate.

He slumped into her, his face pressing into her throat.

"Hold on to me," he said, his lips moving against her skin. "I'm so tired. I don't think I can take it anymore."

"What do you need from me?" Miyoung asked, desperately holding him close. "Tell me."

"Don't let me go."

"I won't," Miyoung said. "Of course I won't."

"Miyoung-ah," Jihoon murmured.

"What?"

"Miyoung-ah!" This time he choked on her name before he started to seize, shaking so hard that she couldn't hold on to him and he fell to the forest floor.

She reached out for him again with the half-formed idea of holding him still to stop him from shaking. But at her touch, he stopped. Like she'd pressed a switch, his eyes rolled into the back of his head and he flopped back.

"Oh gods. Oh gods. What do I do?" Miyoung stammered. "Hospital. We need to go to the hospital." She started to rise when Jihoon grabbed her wrist.

He sat up, his eyes clear again, no longer hazed with fear and confusion.

"Miyoung?" he said again. And this time his voice was stronger.

"I'm here. I'm right here. I'm going to take you to the hospital."

"I don't need the hospital," Jihoon said, standing and brushing off his pajama pants so casually, you'd never have thought he'd just had a seizure in the middle of the forest.

"Something is wrong with you," Miyoung said, reaching for him. But when she touched him, a spark raced across her palm. She jerked her hand back. It had felt like pure energy sizzling under her skin.

Jihoon chuckled, but it sounded jarring while Miyoung's heart was still racing with fear for him.

"I was just disoriented. I think I was sleepwalking last night and I had no idea how I got out here."

Call it instinct, but Miyoung wasn't sure if she fully believed this sudden story. But what reason did Jihoon have to lie? "You've never mentioned sleepwalking before."

"Well, that's because this is the first time it's happened. It's why I was so freaked out." Jihoon gave a quick smile.

"Then shouldn't you get checked out? I know you hate the hospital, but I think we should see your old neurologist, just in case," Miyoung said, trying to wrap her arm around him for support.

"Fine, if it will get you off my case, I'll go," Jihoon said, rolling his eyes, like she was overreacting.

"Why are you acting like this?" Miyoung asked. This wasn't like him. He wasn't mean or callous.

He closed his eyes, and when he opened them again, they were filled with tears. "I'm just . . . I think I'm just stressed. I'm scared every day that I might lose you."

Miyoung let out a deep breath, which eased a bit of the tension that still sat in her chest. "You won't lose me," she assured him.

"Of course I won't," Jihoon said, his eyes suddenly dry again. "We love each other. Love can conquer anything." He gave a sly smile that looked like he was making a clever joke, but what he was joking about, Miyoung couldn't tell.

She remembered her conversation with Somin. How those words were hard to push out, but how Jihoon needed to hear them. And it seemed he needed them now more than ever. So she took a deep breath, held it, and then dove in. "Jihoon-ah."

"Yeah?"

"I do love you. You know that, right?"

He gave her a crooked grin. "Of course I do. Now let's get going, the faster we see the doctor, the faster we can eat breakfast, and I'm starving!"

"Okay," Miyoung said with a frown. That wasn't the reaction she'd been expecting to her first true declaration of love. But she supposed after everything they'd been through, words could pale in comparison. She tried to push away the worry that still poked at her. She wasn't so insecure that she'd assume her boyfriend was sick just because he didn't react the way she'd wanted to her confession.

So she let Jihoon guide her out of the forest. But as they left, she heard Yena's voice echo behind her, *Be careful, Daughter.*

33

"I DON'T KNOW about this," Junu said warily.

"You said you'd take me anywhere," Somin reminded him, pulling him through the lobby. His shoes squeaked against the gleaming floor as they dragged. Then, finally, with a sigh, he let her drag him to the entrance of the indoor amusement park.

"I can already hear the creatures screeching."

"You mean the happy laughter of *children*?" Somin asked, rolling her eyes. "I never knew you were afraid of kids."

"I'm not *afraid*," Junu insisted. "I just keep a safe distance. They have sticky hands and sharp teeth. They're like trolls."

"Are trolls real?" Somin asked, eyes wide with curiosity.

Junu laughed. Throwing an arm over her shoulder, he said, "Let's get this over with."

With a whoop of joy, she raced forward to give her ticket to the boy standing at the entrance, Junu trailing slowly after. As they rode the escalator up, she felt butterflies in her stomach as she remembered staring at pictures of this place as a child. It's where her father had promised to take her. A promise he'd never been able to keep.

It felt like one of those clichéd slow-motion reveals as she started to see the park above the escalator platform. The rides rising up, the lights, the colors. She saw the famous air balloon ride that hung in the sky, showing people the aerial view of the park. She could make out the tracks that wound through the air and led to the outside portion of the park, like a trail to more adventures. As she entered the park, she closed her eyes and breathed in the smell, mostly the scent of fried food and sugary snacks.

I finally made it. Happy birthday, Appa.

And for a second, she thought she saw a man in the crowd, holding his hand out as if he'd been waiting for her.

"Why would you want to come here voluntarily? How can you stand the crowds?" Junu whined. Somin jumped at the sound of his voice. She'd been focusing so hard on the man, she hadn't heard Junu come up behind her. When she looked again, the man was gone, if he'd even been there at all.

But she did see other figures moving throughout the crowd. At least a handful of them that others didn't seem to notice, or perhaps they didn't realize these forms were floating instead of walking. Ghosts. Somin squeezed her eyes shut; she didn't want to deal with the supernatural. Not today. But when she opened them again, the ghosts were still there and the parkgoers remained mostly oblivious.

"They really can't see them," she breathed.

"Most of them, anyway," Junu said, gesturing to a little boy who stared openmouthed at an elderly ghost beside him. The boy seemed equal parts in awe and terrified, like maybe he thought this was part of the park's offerings.

"They can't hurt you," Junu said, taking her hand. He squeezed it comfortingly, and it helped calm her. "Not if you just ignore them."

"Maybe this is a bad idea. Maybe this is selfish, coming here when the world is turning upside down."

Junu sighed, "No, I promised I'd take you here. I keep my promises. Even when those promises lead to a day of torture."

Somin laughed at his morose tone. Like he was being forced into hard labor instead of a day at an amusement park.

She craned her neck back to glance up at the glass dome above. It let in the sky and the sun while protecting the parkgoers from the elements. She'd just take today, no, just half of a day, and have fun. Then she'd return to the real world and the problems that plagued her friends.

"Fine, but no more complaining. I'm not calling you out for buying *two* youth passes."

"What's the matter with that?" Junu asked.

Somin gave Junu a knowing look. "You're not quite a youth anymore, Junu. Haven't been that for a few hundred years."

"Well, the woman in the ticket booth didn't care." Junu shrugged. "And she seemed to like me. It's almost like she *wanted* to give me the discount."

"*Everyone* thinks they like you at first. Because people are innately shallow." She playfully grabbed his chin.

"Everyone except you, my love." Junu scrunched his nose playfully.

Somin stopped at that. She knew the words were said in casual jest. That they didn't mean anything. But they made her heart stutter regardless.

"Come on, I want to go on the pirate ship," Somin said, grabbing his hand, trying to ignore her erratic pulse.

"I don't do fast rides." Junu glared at the swinging pirate ship. Riders screamed in delight as it rocked back and forth, each time threatening to go all the way upside down.

"Why?" Somin teased. "Are you scared?"

"I'm just not willing to give up my breakfast right now."

Somin laughed at the fear he couldn't quite hide. She found she liked this new scared version of Junu. Made him seem more real. More human.

"Mortals love a thrill. They love to be reminded of their frailty. Nothing like knowing you'll die to make you really want to live."

"I can't tell if you think mortality is a good or a bad thing."

"I think it's . . . limiting." Junu shrugged. "I knew a boy once who was a disappointment. He couldn't do anything right. He brought a lot of shame to the family. He was worth only what honor he could bring to the family name in his short lifetime. Everything, including his happiness, came second to the family honor. And when he rebelled and tried to find a sliver of joy, he was kicked out of the family. And he died alone. And no one remembers him now."

"I don't care how others measure my life. I care how I feel about how I've lived." She gestured to a ghost standing by a trash receptacle. Actually, it was standing half inside the trash receptacle. "It seems like now more than ever, I'm being reminded that death is an inescapable fact of life, so why let the fear of dying stop me from living?"

That made Junu's brows rise. "I can't decide if I'm impressed by how cavalier you are or scared."

"Well, while you're deciding, let's get in a line. I've heard if we want to ride the roller coaster, it's a long wait," Somin mused.

"No." Junu firmly shook his head. "I refuse to get on that death trap."

"Fine, let's do the carousel first." Somin turned toward the large carousel, with glimmering bulbs and gleaming horses.

When she was younger, she thought that the carousel was a ride for princesses because of how the horses were decorated. She'd always wanted to ride one. And now she felt silly at the thrill she got from hearing the tinkling music. Wasn't she too old to be this excited?

"Ah yes, a much more civilized ride."

Somin laughed. "I can't believe you're scared of fast rides."

"It's not being scared when it's a healthy aversion to potential bodily harm. I refuse to spend eternity with the crooked profile caused by a broken nose."

"They're perfectly safe," Somin said, rolling her eyes as they lined up to wait for the next ride to start. "You're just being a big baby."

"Well, maybe I like the carousel because it allows you to do some secondary activities." Junu wiggled his brows.

"Yeah, that's not going to happen."

"Why don't you take a minute to consider it, at least?" Junu said.

"I don't need a minute. You know, for a guy who claims to be so smooth, I don't see it. You'd think after so many centuries on this earth, you could at least be a little persuasive."

Junu laughed. "Somin-ah, you really know how to hit a guy in the ego."

"Thanks." She smiled brightly.

"Is that all you like me for?" Junu asked as they were let onto the carousel. "As a punching bag?"

"Maybe," Somin teased, weaving in and out of horses frozen in various poses. She was in a weirdly playful mood. Perhaps it was the smell of fried amusement park food. Or maybe it was the laughter that lifted into the air, winding around her. She could even imagine it was the company. She was big enough to admit that she was starting to enjoy having Junu around.

She hooked her arm around a pole and let her forward momentum carry her around. She'd have gone swinging in a complete circle if Junu hadn't caught her. He leaned forward so their eyes were aligned, their noses touching.

"It says a lot that I don't mind being beat up on. I wonder what it is about you," he murmured.

Her hands flexed involuntarily.

"Why do I let you abuse me like this? Why do I stick around?" Junu mused.

"Maybe you're a secret masochist?" Somin breathed, her voice shaky.

She felt like the world was spinning and then realized the carousel had started, the amusement park swirling around them. Lights turning, the faces of other parkgoers becoming a blur. She heard the delighted squeal of a child from the other side of the carousel and thought, *I know exactly how you feel, kid. This is thrilling.*

Junu leaned forward, and she squeezed her eyes shut in anticipation. But instead of kissing her, he whispered in her ear, "Maybe being close to you helps soothe away the pain." He lowered his lips toward her neck. She craned her head back, an invitation, and she felt his lips curve as he pressed them against her skin. He'd won, and he knew it.

Somin had a fleeting thought that this wasn't appropriate. They were in public. Little kids were around. But she couldn't bring herself to care.

She looped her arms around his neck, fitting her lips to his.

She felt his mouth curl into a grin against hers as his arm

tightened around her, holding her in place. But still she felt like she was spinning out of control. Like her body was a top that was dancing along an uneven surface. She'd have toppled over if he hadn't been holding her so close. Then he leaned back, his eyes searching hers. She started to lift onto her toes, wanting more. He let out a chuckle.

"Ride's over. I don't think we're going to be let on again after the show we put on." His eyes slid to the side, and hers followed. She saw a group of disapproving parents ushering their kids away.

With a groan of embarrassment, she untangled herself from him and darted off the carousel. She couldn't even look at the ride operator as she slunk away.

"Don't worry," Junu said, slinging his arm around her shoulders. "It's a rite of passage to horrify a few parents when you're a teenager."

Somin shook her head and asked, "What's next?"

34

AS LONG AS Junu had lived (and that was a very long time), he'd never regretted anything more.

As soon as the ride stopped, he lurched off the faux pirate ship and pushed through the crowd of exiting riders. Making a beeline for the closest trash can, he leaned over it and dry-heaved.

He heard the squeals of kids as they passed by. He'd never been more embarrassed in his life.

"Aw, poor baby," Somin taunted as she walked up. There was laughter in her voice, and Junu vowed he'd get his revenge. One way or another.

"I never should have let you persuade me to get on that death trap."

"I swear, I didn't know you were so prone to motion sickness."

Junu tried to straighten, but his stomach rolled and he leaned heavily on the trash can. He stared at Somin through narrowed eyes, silently daring her to laugh. "You're enjoying this way too much."

"No." Somin shook her head soberly. "I think I'm enjoying this just enough." Her giggle turned into a snort as she tried to hold it in.

"We will never talk of this again. Ever. Even to ourselves," Junu said.

"I mean, I can't promise that. I'm already planning a lot of late-night gab sessions with myself where we go over everything in detail."

"You are a cruel person, Lee Somin. I rue the day I ever met you."

"Go ahead, rue away. I'm still buying one of those ride photos of you screaming your head off. Wait here," she said before skipping away. As if Junu could do anything but lean pitifully against the disgusting trash can. He watched her go and saw a figure standing in the crowd watching Somin as well.

Junu almost called out to the man. He wore a battered cap over salt-and-pepper hair and looked old enough to be Somin's father. But before Junu could say anything, the figure disappeared. Junu blinked, then glanced around at a dozen more spirits, floating in and out of the crowd. Some of the children seemed to notice them as well. Pointing or staring with wide eyes. But their parents either didn't notice or didn't believe their kids' exclamations of wonder.

One of the ghosts floated through a teenage girl, who squealed and clung to her boyfriend.

"What?" the boyfriend asked with a laugh.

"You didn't feel that?" she said, still hanging on to him. "It felt so cold, I've got goose bumps."

"Don't worry. I'll keep you warm," the boyfriend said, hugging her close and guiding her through the crowd.

The ghosts were becoming bolder. Floating among the living, visible, at least to those open to believe. The tear was getting worse.

"Excuse me."

Junu almost ignored the small voice, but there was a tug on his shirt. A girl blinked up at him with curious eyes. Her hand was still fisted around the bottom of his shirt. She couldn't have been older than six or seven.

"Can I help you?" Junu asked, eyeing her hand and wondering what mystery sticky substances she might be rubbing into his shirt.

"I've never met one of you before," the girl said, tilting her head as she stared at him.

"One of whom?" Junu asked, trying to make his voice friendly and not confused.

"A dokkaebi. You're much more handsome than I thought you'd be." Her small lips pursed as if she was contemplating this fact.

Junu glanced around furitively as he knelt down and lowered his voice to a low whisper. "I don't know what someone told you, but—"

"My halmeoni wanted me to give you this," she interrupted him, and held out a business card.

Junu was so surprised, he took it automatically. She was a precocious one. And didn't seem at all scared to be talking to a fabled dokkaebi.

The card was plain white with only a phone number printed across it. He flipped it over in his hand, but the rest was completely blank.

"What is this for?" he asked.

"To call, duh." The girl rolled her eyes like he was the child, not her.

It would have made Junu laugh, but suspicion had taken ahold of his chest. "Why would I call this number?"

"She says that you'll be too curious not to." She gave a smile that showed she was missing her two front teeth.

"I don't usually go looking for things I know nothing about."

The girl giggled. "My halmeoni said you might say something like that. She said if you did, I should tell you something else." She scrunched up her face as she raised her eyes to the sky in an exaggerated thinking face. Then she smiled. "Oh yeah, she said when you find hidden the one that seeks to harm, you'll call."

Then, without another word, she turned and skipped into the crowd. Junu stared at the card in his hand.

"Thirty thousand won!"

Junu spun around, pocketing the card as Somin stomped over to him.

"What?" he asked, trying to push the strange conversation out of his mind.

"It costs thirty thousand won for just one photo. They're thieves!"

Junu chuckled. "I could have told you that."

"Well, I'm not wasting my money on that. Even if it was the greatest photo of all time."

"You should have expected those kinds of prices at an amusement park," Junu said, leading her away from the pirate ship ride. "You know, I could take you so many better places. You said you want to travel. Maybe we could just get out of here, travel the world. Go global like BTS on the hallyu wave."

That surprised a laugh out of Somin. "You know, for a guy who's hundreds of years old, you're pretty obsessed with pop culture."

Junu shrugged. "Being eternal doesn't mean I have to be boring."

"What's it like?" Somin asked, her expression suddenly somber. "Being immortal."

"Why? You considering a new lifestyle?"

"Is immortality an option for someone like me?" Somin asked, her eyes drifting to a spectral form in the corner. As if these ghosts were making her ponder her own mortality.

"No." Her words worried Junu, and he couldn't quite put his finger on why. "You shouldn't be immortal. Your mortality is what makes you shine, Somin-ah. Don't ever let anyone tell you otherwise."

Somin became contemplative. "Do you regret it? Your immortality?"

"There's no use regretting something you have no control over," Junu said, a heavy weight settling in his gut. He lifted his shoulders, as if trying to shrug off the troublesome sensation.

"I'm sorry," Somin said quietly. "How could she do this to you when she once claimed to love you?"

Junu hated the sorrow in her voice. "I used to ask myself that every day. And then I realized, I'm immortal. I don't need to spend the rest of eternity worrying about things that don't matter anymore."

"Of course it matters." Somin reached for him, but he didn't want to be comforted right now. He didn't think he could handle it. "She betrayed you. You loved her. That means something."

"I thought I loved her," Junu said, searching her eyes. But what he found wasn't the pity he thought he'd see. He saw a fire in her, the kind she got when she tried to protect one of her friends. And now it was burning for him. But would it last? He couldn't be sure. It was like standing at the threshold of a warm room after being out in a blizzard for too long, but being too scared to step inside. "Now I'm starting to think that maybe what I felt then wasn't real," he whispered.

"What are you saying?" Somin asked, her eyes boring into his, like they were trying to find all his secrets. It wasn't the first time someone wanted to figure him out, but it was the first time he was rooting for them to. It was dangerous. She was dangerous.

They stood in this moment, both unwilling to move. Two bodies frozen in place as the sounds and lights of the amusement park still swirled around them. Junu had lived hundreds of years. He'd been with dozens of people. And none of them had made his heart stutter the way Somin could with one look. He wanted to haul her to him, never let her go. But at the same time, he knew that would be wrong. The thing that made Somin shine was how separate she was from his world. Untouched by the darkness he held inside him. If she knew half the things he'd done, she wouldn't be looking at him with this soft look. So he'd have to accept that, no matter how much he wanted to keep her close to him, he couldn't. And one day, she'd see him clearly enough to know that he didn't deserve her. Perhaps that was for the best. For both of them.

A spirit floated by, and Somin jerked back, a gasp escaping her. "Maybe we should get going. I feel like there are more of them now."

"We could go," Junu said, but realized he was reluctant to end their time together. "Or we could go somewhere the ghosts aren't." His eyes moved to the air balloon ride overhead.

Somin smiled. "Okay."

Junu took her hand in his, gave it a light squeeze, and waited. It took a couple of seconds, but then he felt Somin squeeze back. And he promised himself that he'd just take today. Make it a perfect memory. And then he'd let her go.

35

THE LINE FOR the air balloons was one of the longest, but they made small talk as they waited. Never touching on anything too serious. And neither addressing the spirits that floated through the park. Perhaps they both knew that they needed a reprieve. Somin could feel a tension in Junu that slowly sifted away as the line moved. She'd become so attuned to his moods, and now she found herself worrying about him. Wanting to comfort him. Wanting to be around him. She didn't know what to do with that realization, so she just pocketed it to take out later.

As they settled in their assigned balloon, Somin said, "Thank you for today."

"I'm glad it was helpful," Junu said with a gentle smile. She loved the shape of this smile on him. It made his face look so different. Where Junu usually seemed so wickedly sly, now he looked young, almost sweet.

"Can I ask you something?" Somin asked.

"If I said no, would that even stop you?" Junu said.

Somin laughed because he was right. "Why do you always insist on acting like you don't care about anything but yourself when you have the ability to be so kind?"

"Being kind doesn't get you things in life," Junu said.

"That's not true. Being kind gets you friendship, family, love."

"Not in my family it didn't."

This piqued Somin's interest. She'd been wanting to know more about who Junu was as a person. What made him tick. What had shaped him into the strangely complicated person who sat beside her. And this was the first time he'd ever voluntarily mentioned his family. "You never talk about them. Why is that?"

"Because they're not worth talking about."

Junu tried to turn away, but Somin stopped him even as a part of her warned her to let this go. It was obvious Junu didn't want to talk about this. But she had to know. She had a growing need to know more of him. And she was finally admitting it was because her feelings for him had grown beyond her control. It made her desperate for any scraps about the person who was embedding himself into her heart. "But they're who raised you."

"Well, that was hundreds of years ago. I've done a lot of living since then."

"I hate it when you do that." Somin huffed.

"What?"

"Use your immortality as a weapon against me. Because you know I can't argue against it, since I have no idea what it's like to be immortal."

"Oh, have I finally made the great Lee Somin feel like she can't be right about everything?"

Frustration washed through her. "I feel like I'm constantly on unequal footing with you. Even when I'm *so sure* I'm right, I feel like that doesn't make a difference with you."

Junu chuckled. "Because I'm immortal?"

"That. How nothing ever fazes you. Even the way you say my name 'Lee Somin' like you're just toying with me. I don't even know your family name. I feel like I'm lacking a tool when I can't use your full name when I'm yelling at you."

"Things faze me, but I'm just good at recovering. After centuries doing black-market deals with unreliable clientele, you learn how to hold your cards close." Junu shrugged. "And despite what you might think, I don't use a single name because I think it makes me sound cooler."

Somin waited for him to continue, and when he didn't, she asked, "Okay, then why do you do it? To keep up an air of mystery with your disreputable clientele?"

Junu shook his head. "No, it's because that name is a reminder of my family. I don't like remembering them. My mother was indifferent, and my father was very strict. They didn't have much patience for me, probably because I wasn't the good studious son they wanted."

The raw emotion that sprinted across his face was such an unfamiliar sight that it took Somin by surprise. "I'm sorry," she said.

"There's nothing to be sorry about. They've been gone a long time now. I've moved past it."

"That story you told me, about the boy who was a disappointment to his family name. Was that you?" Somin asked.

Junu's silence was answer enough.

Let it go, Somin told herself. *Don't push at it*. But she couldn't help herself. "If it's still upsetting, then maybe keeping it buried inside isn't working."

Junu shrugged. "Leaving something behind means you don't have to talk or think about it again."

Somin shook her head. "You should be able to talk about things. If you can't, then doesn't that mean the memories are still hurting you?"

"What do you want from me?" Junu's voice rose. Somin flinched; she'd never seen Junu lose his temper, he was always so poised, so controlled. "Do you want me to bare my soul to you? To fix all the broken pieces of my heart so I can realize I just want to be a normal boy who can fall in love with a normal girl?" He shook his head. "If that's what you want, then you're wasting your time."

"What? No, I don't want . . . I mean, I don't know what I want." Somin remembered what Miyoung had said once. *What's the point of worrying who we'll be in a year? Right now,* he *is what's right for me.* Could she say that Junu was right for her now? Or were they fooling themselves to think they could make anything of this . . . whatever this was. "What do *you* want?"

Junu's brows drew together, as if the question stumped him.

"What? No smart reply?" She couldn't help herself; the sarcasm was like a defense mechanism that spilled out of her. Because the truth was, she was scared. Scared that after a day of realizing how much she wanted to be around Junu, she'd inadvertently pushed him away.

"I know I like being with you." The words could have calmed her nerves if not for the silent "but" hanging at the end of the sentence.

"And?" she asked despite her trepidation.

"And I also know that you ask a lot of me just by being who you are. I've always lived exactly how I pleased. I promised myself a long time ago that I would never change myself to be what another wanted. But being around you makes me need to be different. I can't tell if it's what *I* want or what I think *you* want."

"I told you I don't know what I want," Somin whispered. She felt like she was losing hold of something here, like sand sifting through her fingers.

"But that's a lie," Junu said, running his hands up her arms. His smile was almost sad, like he was already saying goodbye.

It made Somin feel edgy. "I can't stop myself from wanting to help you. It's what happens when I care about someone."

That stopped Junu, his face pinched.

"Is it really that bad?" she asked. "To have someone care about you?"

"Yes," Junu breathed, and Somin closed her eyes, embarrassed at the easy rejection.

She tried to pull away, but his hands tightened.

"It's bad because I don't deserve it," Junu continued. "I don't deserve *you*. Why do you always insist on giving everything of yourself to people?"

"As opposed to you?" Somin asked. "Who gives nothing and tries to convince himself he can live alone because he's scared to let go of any part of himself?"

"I'm not scared. I just know who and what I am," Junu said. "I should never have started this. I'll only ruin you like I ruin everything I touch."

"What?" Fire rose up in her now, anger fed by this drawn-out game of hot and cold Junu was playing. She jerked away. "Ruin me?" she said. "Like I am just this innocent little flower that you're going to crush in your dangerous dokkaebi hand?"

Junu stared at her, his mouth agape. "No," he stammered. "I just meant—"

"I don't need to hear what you *think* you meant. You spent so long teasing me, pursuing me. And now that I'm here, now that I care, you're trying to pull away because you think you know what's best for me? I can make my own choices. I'm not a weak, delicate thing that needs your protection."

Junu shook his head. "I've never thought that."

"Well, you could have fooled me. You know, for someone who insists we leave the past behind us, you're still stuck there."

"You're one to talk," Junu said.

"What's that supposed to mean?" Somin asked.

"What's today?"

Somin couldn't answer. No, Somin didn't want to answer.

"Come on, I'm not completely oblivious. You were upset this morning. And you said Jihoon forgot today. Which means it's important. You say I'm stuck in the past, but today seems to have some kind of past significance for you."

"It's my abeoji's birthday," Somin murmured.

"Ah," Junu said, drawing out the syllable. "And because he was good to you, you miss him."

His words rubbed at an old wound. "You say that like it's wrong for me to mourn him."

"No, of course you should. I'm sorry that today causes you pain." But Junu's voice was wooden, his body stiff. Despite herself, it made Somin feel embarrassed that she'd shared something so personal with him when he seemed almost bored by it.

"I didn't tell you to get your sympathy," Somin snapped. "And I didn't *force* you to come here. I'm only here with you because—" She broke off and snapped her lips closed, but it was too late.

"And you'd never be caught dead out with me, right? Except, you didn't want to be alone and I just happened to be there."

"That's not true," Somin said.

"Then if I hadn't come when I did, would you have sought me out? Would you have called me and trusted me to be there for you?"

"I don't know." Somin couldn't quite look him in the eye,

because he was right. She'd never have gone to him first. She'd never have trusted him to be the one to comfort her, but she was wrong. He was what she needed today. Why couldn't she say that? Why couldn't she make herself say the words?

"It's wrong to latch on to the closest person just because you're afraid of being alone. People don't realize that loneliness isn't just about being alone," Junu said quietly. Words spoken so casually that it took a moment for her to recognize the sorrow in them.

"Junu, I never meant—" Somin broke off as the ride came to a stop and the door opened.

"Hope you enjoyed your ride," the attendant chirped.

Junu got up without a word and exited. Somin followed him, giving a small cursory bow of thanks to the attendant.

"Junu," Somin started to say, but she stopped short as a scream pierced the air.

A woman dropped to her knees, her hands folding like she was praying. "My mother! It's my mother. She's come back from the dead." She was staring at the ghost of an old woman who stood before her. The old ghost's eyes were blank and uncaring, like it couldn't recognize its own flesh and blood.

Many looked confused and concerned for the woman and her hysterics. But some seemed to finally notice the ghosts among them. Like her cries were a switch.

A woman ushered her children toward the exit, eyeing a spectral form that floated beside an ice cream stand, her youngest child crying as he clung to his mother.

"Do you see them?" a little boy asked his parents, who were pulling him toward the information center. "Gwishin, Eomma! Do you see them?"

An older man was gathering his granddaughter close as she

hid her eyes in his collar. "Don't worry, Harabeoji is here. No one can hurt you."

Suddenly a voice came on the speaker. "We apologize, but Lotte World is closing for the day. Please make your way to the exits, and if you have any questions, then you can call our customer service line. We apologize for the inconvenience."

"Junu," Somin said, fear heavy in her voice. "What do we do?"

"I need to find Miyoung," Junu said.

"But what should I—?" Somin was interrupted by the ring of her phone. She picked it up. "Mom? Already? Oh, okay, yeah, I can come back now." She hung up, staring at the screen instead of looking at Junu. "My mom got off work early. She said she has something important to tell me."

"We should get going," Junu said, walking toward the exit.

"Okay," Somin said, and cursed her voice for wobbling as she hurried after him.

36

HE SHOULDN'T HAVE overreacted the way he did, Junu thought as he walked up the path to his apartment. Should he just turn around and find Somin? Tell her he was sorry and a jerk and sorry for being a jerk. She'd told him today was her father's birthday, and instead of comforting her, he'd blown up at her. He was more than a jerk. But he was too caught up in his guilt to think of a good expletive to call himself right now.

No, he had to find Miyoung first. The tear was obviously growing, and he didn't know how the reapers would react to that. He had to make sure she was safe. His fight with Somin would have to wait.

Junu almost didn't notice the person sitting in the living room as he walked through the apartment. But it rose and spoke his name.

Junu jumped back. "What are you doing sitting in the dark?" he asked, flipping on a switch.

"I was waiting for you." Jihoon stepped around the table until he was uncomfortably close to Junu.

"Okay," Junu said, drawing out the word and taking a step back. "Well, I had a really bad day, so maybe this can wait until morning?"

"Oh, I'm done waiting."

"Well, sorry I wasn't around today. Maybe you should give

Lee Somin a call?" he said, hoping perhaps this might be the first step in making things up to her. Reminding her absentee best friend that she needed him.

"Why would I call her?" Jihoon asked, sincere puzzlement wrinkling his brow.

"What?" Junu hesitated at the disinterest on Jihoon's face. "Because she's hurting."

"Ah, and of course you want to save her from that. I see you still have that foolhardy notion that you can be someone's savior. Are you going to save her from her lonely life as well?"

"What are you talking about?" Something about Jihoon's tone, more than his confusing words, rang an alarm. "What's going on here? Where's Miyoung?"

"She went to the market. I think she wants to take care of me, since I haven't been sleeping well and all." But despite Jihoon's claim, he looked fine. His skin was bright, and his eyes were wide and watchful. Had they always been this dark? Like endless black pits?

"Jihoon-ah, if this is some kind of game, can you just tell me? I'm not in the mood for any surprises."

"Ah yes, I remember you hate surprises. Though I tried to prepare one for you. You see, I knew you'd never accept me for what I really was. You were far too simple. Far too cowardly." Jihoon ran his finger behind his ear. A motion that was too familiar. A motion that sparked an unnerving recognition. He could see that same motion in his memories, pushing long strands of dark hair behind a pale ear. A small, clever smile quirking rosebud lips, a smile like Jihoon had right now.

"Sinhye," he breathed with grim certainty. "This isn't possible."

"Oh, Junu-ya, you of all people should believe in the

impossible by now. Didn't I teach you that?" There was a spark of light in Jihoon's eyes before he leapt forward, pushing Junu so hard his head slammed into the wall. He heard a sharp crack resonate through his skull as lights exploded behind his eyes.

"I've waited so long for this. I'm going to enjoy destroying your world." The shape of Jihoon's face became warped as Junu's vision wavered. He tried to reply, but his words were swallowed by a nauseating darkness that overtook him.

37

WHEN JUNU OPENED his eyes, Hyuk stood over him.

His head ached and his limbs felt shaky and Jihoon was nowhere to be seen. "Ugh, please tell me I'm dead."

"Is that truly something you wish for?" the jeoseung saja asked, his head tilting curiously to the side.

"You've been away from the mortal world too long. You used to be better at reading sarcasm," Junu said, pushing himself up.

"You told me sarcasm was a form of humor. Were you trying to be funny just now?" Hyuk asked.

Junu shook his head, and the movement made him dizzy all over again. "Never mind. I guess you're here because of Sinhye."

Hyuk's brows lifted. "No, but I am surprised it took you this long to identify her threat."

"Sorry that I don't live in an immortal realm where the spirits tell me all I wish to know."

Hyuk laughed. "That one was meant as a joke, right?"

Junu closed his eyes in frustration.

"Sinhye is dangerous," Hyuk said.

"I know that."

"Spirits are not meant to possess human bodies this long. It goes against the command of King Yeomra. If a spirit is lucky enough to find a host vessel, their energy is expelled within twenty-four hours."

Junu opened his eyes at that. "But we went to the cave two days ago. How can she hold on to Jihoon this long?"

"Something about that human makes him the perfect vessel."

"What? He's just a normal kid," Junu said.

"Something created a space, an energy, that is perfect for Sinhye's soul."

Junu's stomach dropped as he pieced it together. "Dammit, Miyoung's yeowu guseul. Of all the humans to take to that cave, I had to bring the one person in this world that's had a fox bead inside of him. I should have known better."

"Could you? Could even someone as clever as you have anticipated this?"

Junu knew that, despite his cold demeanor, this was Hyuk's way of comforting him. Of telling Junu that he could never have known.

"You could have warned me," Junu said.

"You know that jeoseung saja do not interfere with the affairs of the living," Hyuk said.

"But you're here now," Junu said.

"I shouldn't be," Hyuk admitted. "I just wanted to check on my old friend."

"What do I do now?"

"When something like this happens—a spirit finds the perfect vessel—the longer they spend within it, the more their energies fuse. The longer she stays in him, the more it will take to pull her free."

"What will it take?" Junu asked.

Before Hyuk could reply, the door opened with a beep and let Miyoung in. She paused at the sight of Hyuk and Junu.

"I didn't realize you had a guest," Miyoung said, holding two bags from the local fried chicken restaurant. "Where's Jihoon?"

"So you are the source of all this trouble," Hyuk murmured. "I can see it now. The energy around you, it reeks of death. You hold on to it like a lifeline, but you know you should let it go."

"Who are you?" Miyoung looked ready to attack at a moment's notice if Hyuk so much as breathed wrong.

Not wanting to see the result of a fight between a reaper and a former gumiho in the middle of his pristine house, Junu stepped between them. "He's leaving," Junu said. Then he turned back to Hyuk. "You promised. I have three days left."

The reaper was still a moment before lowering his chin in a nod. "Then I'll be back in three days."

"Yes, and try to actually give me the full three days. No more check-ins."

"Her life is in your hands. Be sure to keep your promise. Because I will keep mine."

"What are you talking about?" Miyoung demanded. But Hyuk ignored her.

"Tell her about your ghosts. And ask her about hers." And he turned to go, disappearing into vapors that sifted through the air.

Miyoung jerked back in surprise. "What is going on here? Who was that? Why did he say my life is in your hands?"

Junu frowned, wondering how many of those questions he could skirt around. He decided to answer the easiest one first. "He's a jeoseung saja."

Miyoung's eyes widened. "If he's a jeoseung saja, then has he come for me?"

"No, there's still time. We just have to get your bead back."

Miyoung shook her head, her expression one of guarded distrust. "A reaper's list doesn't change. When they come for you, you can't do anything to fight it."

"You heard him. We still have time."

"How do you know this reaper? Why would he come to you? Why would he give you this time?"

"I knew him in a past life," Junu said quietly, unwilling to elaborate. His private life was never something he liked to discuss.

"That's how you got him to wait? Because you're friends with this reaper?"

"I don't know if I'd call us friends. And he wouldn't have given us more time if he didn't benefit from it. The reapers want this resolved without getting their own hands dirty. The reapers don't like to get involved in matters of the mortal world."

"But if we can't solve this in three days, he'll come for me, right?"

And Junu couldn't lie, so he just nodded.

"I don't get it." Miyoung frowned. "You always said you don't get involved in things unless it benefits you. Why are you helping me like this?"

"I owe you a debt for the part I played in your mother's death," Junu said.

Miyoung laughed bitterly. "Is that what this is really all about? You paying off a debt?"

"Isn't that what it looks like?"

She nodded, pursing her lips. "It could be that. It would be so much simpler if it was that. But I can't help but think there's more going on here."

"When will you finally trust me?"

"I don't know," Miyoung said. "Maybe never."

"Never?" Junu let out a harsh laugh because what he really

wanted to do was throw something. "Just because I made one mistake?"

"*One* mistake?" Miyoung shouted. "You say that like it's about the quantity of the betrayal and not the glaring, awful quality of it. What you did cost me my mother."

"And I'm trying to make up for that. I'm trying to do the right thing here."

"You're trying to do the right thing for the wrong reason," Miyoung said. "You're not doing this for *me*. You're doing it because you hate feeling guilty. You're selfish, Junu. You always have been and you always will be."

She was right, Junu realized. He used all the bad things that had happened to him as an excuse for being selfish. He'd always thought that because no one would care about him, he had to do it himself. But seeing how hard it was for Miyoung to trust him hurt. Somin's words came back to taunt him: *You, who gives nothing and tries to convince himself he can live alone because he's scared to let go of any part of himself?*

As she turned to leave, he spoke, one final last-ditch effort to get her to understand: "I *am* sorry for what I did."

"I know you are," Miyoung said without turning back to look at him. "But I don't want to forgive you."

"Fine," Junu said, throwing his hands up in frustration. "Don't forgive me. But we've got bigger problems right now."

Miyoung's eyes narrowed in suspicion. "Like what?"

"Jihoon."

HEOUNGAEGI WAS A mother with many children. So, when she died and was sent to the underworld, she wept with worry for her children. The king of the underworld saw her tears and felt compassion for her. He gave her permission to travel to the human world by night to care for her children. There was only one rule: She had to return to the underworld before morning came. And so Heoungaegi was able to spend each night with her children. For a time they were happy. But an elderly neighbor soon became suspicious that the children were always well-kept and cared for despite losing their mother. When the neighbor questioned one of the younger children, they said that their mother came back from the underworld every night.

The neighbor, thinking that this was no proper way to live, told the children that she would come up with a way to keep their mother from returning to the underworld. She tied one end of a string to her foot and the other end to the foot of the eldest. She told the children to signal her when their mother came by pulling on the string. When they did, she hid the mother's spirit to keep it in the world of the living. When morning came and Heoungaegi did not return to the underworld, the king was enraged. He came to the world of the living himself, found her spirit, and took her back. And for this breach of trust, he said that no spirit would ever be allowed to enter the world of the living again.

38

AS SOON AS Somin stepped into the apartment, she was pulled into the whirlwind that was her mother.

"Somin-ah," her mother said, rushing out of the back room. She had on her robe, thrown over a camisole that she often wore under her work clothes. "Have you seen him?"

Him? Who? Jihoon? Somin wondered. Or did her mother know who she'd spent the day with? She truly hoped not. Her mother always had weird questions for Somin every time she started dating someone new. And she really wasn't in the mood for it now.

Maybe because her mom had been too young when she got pregnant. And instead of raising Somin like a daughter, she'd raised her like a friend.

It had been great when Somin was a kid. And when she'd discovered makeup and fashion. But as soon as puberty had hit, her mother's questions had started to make her uncomfortable.

"He's back, and I just don't know what to wear if he comes by again. I just don't know what to do when we see him," Somin's mother said, her words tumbling over one another.

Her mother had started toward the bedroom when Somin grabbed her arm and turned her. Her eyes were overly bright. Like she'd drunk too much espresso.

"Who's back? Who are you talking about?"

"Your father," her mother said. And Somin's hands dropped in shock. Her mother spun around to rush into her room.

Your father—the words echoed in her head like a cruel joke. Except her mother would never do that, not about this. *Your father.* She'd said it with such conviction. With such hope. With such manic joy.

"Eomma," Somin said, walking back to the master bedroom. Her mother stood in front of her closet, dresses clutched in her hands.

"Which one looks best on me? I mean, which one makes me look less *old*? It's been so long. I don't want him to think I look old."

"Eomma!" Somin shouted, pulling the dresses from her mother's hands. "What are you talking about? Appa is . . . he's not here anymore."

"I know he's not *supposed* to be here. But we were given a miracle. I don't know how. I didn't believe it at first, but then he said my name. And I'd never forget your father's voice. It was him. It was really him!" her mother said, her eyes becoming wider, almost panicked. Like she needed Somin to believe her. Like she'd break if Somin didn't.

"Oh, Eomma," Somin said as she realized what was happening. "I have to tell you something." Her voice cracked; she wasn't sure how to say it.

But she was saved from it by the chime of the doorbell.

"That might be him!" her mother said, rushing to answer.

"Eomma!" Somin called, starting after her, when her phone dinged. It was a text from Miyoung: *Jihoon is not Jihoon.*

Somin frowned. What was that supposed to mean?

"Jihoon-ah," she heard her mother say. "You didn't have to ring the bell."

Jihoon was here? Where had he been all day? Maybe he could help Somin explain things to her mother.

"Interesting." Jihoon's voice echoed down the hall. "You've been touched by a spirit."

"A spirit?" Somin's mother asked with a light laugh, but there was tension in the sound. Somin knew her mother well enough to recognize it.

What was Jihoon doing? Somin wondered. This wasn't the way to tell her mother about the supernatural world. She glanced down at Miyoung's text again. What was wrong with Jihoon? What did it mean that he wasn't being himself?

"Oh, I see. You were hoping he was real, weren't you? Hoping a dead loved one had returned to you through some kind of magic of what? True love?"

"Jihoon-ah?" Her mother's voice shook.

"Jihoon!" Somin barked, stepping into the foyer, intent on giving him a piece of her mind. But instead, she watched as he swung out, slamming her mother into the large shoe cabinet. Her head smacked against the wood with a heavy thud before she dropped.

"Eomma!" Somin yelled, bending to catch her mother.

"She'll be fine," Jihoon said, stepping around them. "I just didn't want her listening in on our conversation."

Somin stood, positioning herself between her mother and Jihoon.

"Get the hell away from us," she said, her fists clenching. Never in her life had she wanted to strike Jihoon. Not even during their worst fights. But she also never thought she'd be forced to choose between her mother's safety and Jihoon.

Jihoon laughed, a low rumble that sounded unnaturally cruel.

She'd never seen such violence from her friend who usually had a friendly smile for everyone.

"This isn't like you," she said. "You've been acting off since . . ." Her breath caught. *Jihoon is not Jihoon.*

Jihoon's lips spread into a nasty grin. It looked less like a smile and more like he was baring his teeth. It was cold. It was cruel. It was not her best friend. "I guess I should stop with the charade, huh?"

"Who are you?" Somin asked, her voice hard as iron. She looked around for a weapon. There was an umbrella she'd forgotten to store and the neatly organized shoes in the foyer. If she had to, she'd use anything she could to keep him away from her mother.

"If I told you, it wouldn't make a difference," not-Jihoon said with a shrug as he turned to pace the living room. His motions looked so smooth. His gait different from the way he usually walked.

"Where did you come from?"

"That also doesn't matter."

"Get out of my friend," Somin said.

Not-Jihoon gave a sharp grin. It made him look like a stranger. "I can't do that until I finish what I've started."

"What have you started?" Somin asked.

"Something I've been waiting centuries for." Not-Jihoon smiled again in that teeth-baring way. It looked like a tiger eyeing her prey.

"What do we have to do with your plans?"

"It's unfortunate, really. I have nothing against you, but it seems like hurting you could hurt him."

"Who? Jihoon?"

Not-Jihoon gave her a look of pity. A look one gave a small child or a bug that they were about to crush.

"Junu," Somin said now with conviction. "You're trying to hurt Junu."

"When I'm done with him, he'll wish he was dead. Again."

Somin shifted her stance, picking up the umbrella and wielding it like a club. "Not if I have anything to say about it."

Not-Jihoon let out a harsh laugh. "I've been watching you. You like to stick your nose where it doesn't belong. You have no business in this world, little girl. Does it make you feel important to pretend like you have anything to do with our affairs?"

That stung, and if it had been actual-Jihoon saying it, Somin would have thought of backing down. But there was no way she was letting this . . . whatever it was get into her head. "I might just be human. But when you put my friends' lives in danger, it becomes my business."

The doorbell rang, and they both froze.

"Somin-ah!" Junu yelled from outside.

She reached for the handle, but not-Jihoon grabbed her wrist and spun her around. "Don't."

Somin pulled back, but not-Jihoon held tight, surprising her. She was usually stronger than Jihoon. She swung out with the umbrella, but he caught it easily and yanked it out of her hands.

"You don't seem to realize how dangerous I can be." With a jerk of his arm, not-Jihoon pulled Somin toward him and encircled her neck with his hand. "Perhaps I should show you just how wrong you are to underestimate me."

Somin was slammed against the door so the knob dug into her back. She clawed at his hands, realizing for the first time how big they were as they cut off her air. Somin could count on her fingers the amount of times she'd felt true fear. And in this moment, seeing the face of her best friend contorted into rage as his hands tried to choke the life out of her, she was terrified.

The ringing doorbell continued, becoming insistent.

"Somin-ah!" Junu shouted.

She tried to choke out a word but could barely breathe, let alone speak. No matter how she struggled, whatever was in Jihoon wasn't letting go. So she let her hands fall, running them over the door behind her.

"Maybe if he finds your body, he'll know that I'm not playing around here," not-Jihoon mused.

White dots began dancing in Somin's vision. She worried she was on the edge of passing out. Then her fingers found the knob and she used the last of her strength to twist it.

The door unlocked with a series of chirps.

It swung open with such force that Somin went flying forward, her body tangling with not-Jihoon's. His grip finally loosened, and she gasped desperately. As her wheezing turned to coughs, she shifted and bumped into something—her mother. Reaching out, she thought to pull her mother to her, to find some comfort in the unconscious arms, but Junu rushed to her side. He pulled her up so she was lying half in his lap.

She let out a hiss of pain at the jarring movement.

"Somin-ah, are you okay?"

"I'm fine," she croaked.

Miyoung leapt on top of not-Jihoon to hold him down. His arms came up in defense or, perhaps, in surrender.

"This body doesn't belong to you." A spark flared in Miyoung's eyes as she shook not-Jihoon.

"I guess a gumiho without her yeowu guseul can still have

some fire, huh?" the thing with Jihoon's face said with a chuckle, and turned to spit blood from his mouth. A bruise was forming on his jaw from the fall.

"I'm going to give you ten seconds to get out of that body, or else you're going to see how much fire I have left in me," Miyoung snarled.

Somin would have been pleased to see Miyoung look almost like her normal self if her vision wasn't wavering from a splitting headache.

"Oh, I'd love to see it," not-Jihoon said, his face straining forward so it was mere centimeters from Miyoung's. Then he slammed his forehead into hers.

Miyoung went flying back.

Not-Jihoon leapt up and stalked toward her.

"Sinhye," Junu shouted, and not-Jihoon froze, turning to Junu with a vicious grin. "Let her go. Your fight is with me."

"Are you going to stop me?" not-Jihoon asked, lifting an arm as if to strike Miyoung. But at that moment, an avenging ball of fur came racing down the hall. With a growl that Somin had never heard come from Dubu before, the little dog launched herself at not-Jihoon's leg, biting him on the thigh. He let out a howl and pulled at the dog, but her teeth were dug in. With a hard yank, he finally wrenched her free, flinging her aside.

Somin screamed.

Before anyone could stop him, not-Jihoon jumped up and sprinted away, out the front door.

39

STILL TOO DIZZY to stand, Somin crawled to Dubu. The dog stood, snarling at the closing door. Jihoon's blood stained her mouth, and Somin tried to wipe it away, but it was too matted.

She scooped Dubu into her arms. The dog's growls made her body vibrate, but Somin didn't care. She hugged Dubu close and knelt beside her mother, whose chest rose and fell evenly, a bruise blooming at her temple.

"Somin-ah," Junu said, kneeling beside her.

"We have to call 1-1-9, get my mom to the hospital," Somin said, trying to stand, but found it impossible while still holding a squirming Dubu tight to her side.

"Somin-ah, we have to talk."

"I have to take care of my mother. And Dubu. She might be hurt. Oh God, what if she has internal bleeding?" Somin didn't even know who she was talking about anymore as she finally managed to sit up, still cradling Dubu in her arms.

"Somin-ah." Junu turned her to face him. "You're in shock. Just take a deep breath. Miyoung is calling an ambulance."

Somin's muscles trembled as she let them relax a fraction, letting the wiggling dog free. She finally focused on Junu. And suddenly her anxiety coalesced into a new emotion: anger. "What the hell just happened?"

Junu winced, but Somin didn't care.

"She's back," he said.

"Who is?"

Junu's brow furrowed as he hesitated.

"*Who* is?" Somin asked again.

"My evil ex."

"Your *what*?"

"These idiots opened some kind of magical jar and let out that damn fox spirit," Miyoung said, pocketing her phone. She stepped over to them, and Somin could make out the start of a bruise on Miyoung's cheek.

"The jar itself isn't magical," Junu began, then stopped when Miyoung's and Somin's eyes whipped to him accusingly.

"So you took Jihoon to some kind of supernatural prison and let him *open it*?" Somin asked, pushing her fingers against her temples, trying to stave off her headache.

"When we went to find my bangmangi, Jihoon touched the vase before I could tell him what it was."

"Oh yeah? Or did you purposefully not tell him because you love withholding things and you thought that Jihoon was too beneath you to deserve to know?"

Junu lowered his eyes, and Somin knew she'd hit on the truth.

"Usually a human body is not a good vessel for a spirit. I didn't even think it was a possibility that Sinhye would get free, let alone get hold of the perfect vessel."

"What does that mean?" Somin asked.

"Jihoon's held the energy of a gumiho before. It's like he was conditioned to hold Sinhye's soul."

"I can't believe you didn't tell us any of this before."

"I just figured out what happened. I didn't realize the tear between the worlds had weakened the lock on Sinhye's prison."

"I should never have let Jihoon go with you," Somin said.

"You can't control everyone around you," Junu said. "No matter how much you might want to."

That caused Somin's anger to flare. "You're one to talk when you're always manipulating everyone around you all the time. I can't believe I let myself forget that." The doorbell rang, interrupting her tirade.

"Somin," Junu said, reaching for her hand. But she turned away from him to open the door for the paramedics.

40

SOMIN DIDN'T KNOW what was stronger right now, her headache or her fear.

Her friend was somehow possessed by an evil spirit. A spirit that wanted to hurt Junu. Would do anything to hurt him, it seemed. What if she hurt Jihoon?

The thought scared Somin so much she didn't even realize she was pacing until she rammed into an empty hospital bed and stubbed her toe. She cursed, then looked furtively at her mother asleep on the other bed.

She had lain there after the doctors left, staring at the ceiling. "Your appa isn't back, is he," her mother had said. It hadn't been a question.

"No, he's not back," Somin replied. And her mother had turned on her side and gone to sleep. As if being awake in a world without the man she still loved had sapped all of her energy.

And leaving Somin alone with nothing but her thoughts and her worry to keep her company. Well, and the ghosts. They floated through the halls, seemingly unnoticed by most. Though some of the nurses seemed more nervous than normal. Things were getting bad. Even if people couldn't see the ghosts, they could definitely sense them. There was a tenseness in the air here. Less chatter than normal and more people keeping their heads down as they made their way through the halls.

Somin wanted to bring her mother home, but the hospital wanted to keep her overnight for observation, and when Somin had tried to argue, they didn't budge.

When her mother had first woken up, she claimed she remembered nothing. She didn't even know Jihoon had been at their house. Somin wondered whether that was true or whether it was her mother's strange way of protecting Jihoon.

Miyoung and Junu went to search for Sinhye, and despite her intense desire to go with them, she'd been too worried about her mother. So she stayed in the hospital.

Somin was rubbing her throbbing toe when her phone beeped. When she saw Jihoon's number flash across the screen, she slipped out of the hospital room quietly and swiped to answer.

"Where are you?" she asked, praying that Jihoon had somehow regained control.

"Somin-ah," rang Changwan's bright voice. "We're in Jihoon's old neighborhood, at that food cart in front of the kalguksu restaurant."

"Why are you using Jihoon's phone?" Somin asked carefully. Changwan's tone was casual and calm, not the voice of someone who was being held against his will. Still, Somin's heart beat so fast that she thought it would break free from her chest and flop onto the ground.

"Oh, I can't find mine. I hope I left it at home and didn't lose it. Again. My dad would kill me; it would be the second phone I've lost this month."

"Why are you calling me?" Somin asked, careful to keep her tone even.

"Oh, Jihoon-ah said I should call and ask you to come out and meet us. Are you busy?"

What game is this fox spirit playing? Somin wondered. "No, I'm not busy."

"Great," Changwan said. "We'll just hang out until you get here."

There was a murmur of a voice that Somin recognized as Jihoon's and she strained to listen, but the words were too muted. She didn't have to wonder long, because Changwan said, "Jihoon says you should hurry."

Somin checked her phone again to see if Junu or Miyoung had texted her back as she hurried up the street from the bus stop. Her message sat in the chat: *I found Jihoon. He's in his old neighborhood.*

But neither had replied. She started to call Miyoung again, when someone stepped out of the corner convenience store and blocked her path.

"Excuse me," Somin said as she tried to skirt past, but the person moved to block her.

She finally looked up, about to tell them off, and stopped short. Mr. Ahn sneered at her, a half-drunk bottle of soju in his fist. "Where's that good-for-nothin' son of mine?" His breath reeked and his words slurred.

I don't have time for this. "I don't know."

"I know he's staying with you. Mooching off you while he keeps all that money for himself."

"Mr. Ahn, please, I don't know where he is, and I have somewhere to be." She tried to step to the left and he came with her, but she'd anticipated it this time and swerved back to the right, sprinting past him before he could recover.

"Ya!" he shouted after her. "I want my money."

Somin raised a hand in a wave (when, really, she wanted to

raise just one particular finger) and raced down the street. She hoped she wasn't too late.

o   o   o

Somin wasn't sure if she should be grateful or terrified to find Changwan and not-Jihoon chatting amicably at the plastic stools beside the food cart. The ajumma manning it was lazily stirring the broth that held the eomuk, usually Somin's favorite. She could smell the scent of fish cakes wafting through the air. It joined the spicy aroma of the tteok-bokki, little rice cake tubules, simmering in a sauce so red it would burn your lips and stain your clothes.

The light from the sign of the neighboring kalguksu store lit the street with a neon glow. EOMMA SOHN. Mother's touch. It reminded Somin of her mother lying in a hospital bed, sparking her anger.

Not-Jihoon spotted her first. No, Junu said her name was Sinhye, back when she'd had her own body and wasn't stealing one from Somin's best friend.

Sinhye let a smile spread on Jihoon's face. Sharp and predatory. Then she smoothed it out, like an expert actress.

"Somin-ah, took you long enough," Sinhye sang out.

Changwan turned, a wooden skewer with a half-eaten eomuk clutched in his hand. "Somin-ah," he said, waving, but he'd forgotten he held the skewer and the eomuk went flying off, falling to the ground with a splat. Changwan's face fell like a puppy who'd lost his treat.

"Changwan-ah," Somin said, and purposefully didn't address Sinhye. "What are you doing here? Shouldn't you be at your hakwon studying for the suneung exam?"

"The class doesn't start for another hour," Changwan said

with a bright grin, like he expected Somin to be happy about this fact.

Instead it made her search her brain for another reason to get Changwan to go. She didn't trust Sinhye to leave him unscathed. He was obviously a tool in whatever sick, twisted game the fox spirit was playing.

And though Somin never liked to take advantage of Changwan's kind soul, she did it now for his own good. "I am just not in the mood for tteok-bokki or eomuk."

"They have kimbap," Changwan offered.

"I just really want Shin ramyeon from the convenience store," Somin said, pouting. "I'm really craving it, actually."

"I can go get it," Changwan offered, jumping up. And Somin felt her chest constrict a bit with guilt. He was so sweet, and if she got her way, they'd be long gone when he came back. But any hurt feelings would be worth it to protect him.

"Thank you, Changwan-ah. And don't forget the cheese slice," she said, gifting him with a giant smile.

He nodded emphatically to let her know he'd heard. "Do you want anything, Jihoon-ah?"

"No, I'm stuffed," Sinhye said, her eyes never leaving Somin.

They both waited until Changwan had jogged down the street before either spoke.

"You could have let him stay. He was so cute. I wasn't done playing," Sinhye said, her eyes tilting with malice.

"What do you want?"

"Ah, I see we won't be exchanging pleasantries." Sinhye stood up, eating the last bite of eomuk, letting her teeth run along the skewer. "That's fine. I like to get down to business, too."

"And what's that?"

"Not here. Let's take a walk."

"I'm not going anywhere with you," Somin said.

"If you don't, then I'll be very upset and I might have to take it out on your sweet friend Changwan."

Somin didn't want to believe Sinhye would actually hurt Changwan, but from what Junu had said, it sounded like this fox spirit could be capable of anything, so she nodded. "Where are we going?"

"I don't know this area that well. So you decide. Somewhere private. And remember that if you try to lose me, I'll just double back and let Changwan help me with my little task." Sinhye grinned, and there was no kindness in it.

"Fine," Somin said, her mind spinning. She wasn't someone who would willingly walk into a trap. And that's definitely what this was. But she also hadn't had time to plan any countermoves. For the first time, she cursed herself for looking down at Jihoon's computer games; at least they required strategic thinking. But now, when she needed something clever, her mind was a blank. Then she remembered something Miyoung had told her. It seemed far-fetched, but it was better than nothing. "I know where we can go."

They walked up the steep road, and Somin watched Sinhye closely. She was trying to find some kind of weakness to take advantage of. But if it was possible, Jihoon's body seemed even more invigorated. Like it was powered by the fox spirit inside.

Somin stared at the abandoned building. Jihoon's old home. Halmeoni's old restaurant. She felt a petty satisfaction in the fact that Jihoon's old landlord hadn't found someone to rent the space yet. Served him right for pushing Jihoon out of the lease and raising the rent.

Somin scanned the street but tried to look like she wasn't. It was empty. Had it always been this quiet? Or did it just seem that way because she was so desperate for help?

"This will do," the fox spirit said.

"Well, I guess I'll leave you to your nefarious plans, then." Somin turned to go, but Sinhye was too quick and grabbed Somin's arm.

"You can't go before you give me the tour." A sharp smile, maniacal as a jack-o'-lantern's, split Sinhye's face.

Somin's mouth was suddenly dry. What would happen to her if she went into the building with this gumiho? Would she ever come out again?

"Well, look who we have here."

Somin's knees weakened with relief at the sound of the voice.

"Hwang Halmeoni." Somin hoped her voice sounded steady. She couldn't give away her nerves. Not now. The old woman stepped out onto the platform outside the medicinal wine store. "Are you well?"

The woman gave a gruff chuckle. She sat and started to unscrew a small glass jar. It must be what she'd been inside fetching. Usually Hwang Halmeoni sat all day long on her platform, observing the neighborhood. It's what Somin had been counting on. The woman started to rub the ointment on her legs.

"What is this?" Sinhye hissed, her hand tightening on Somin's arm.

Somin lowered her voice so only Sinhye could hear. "If you don't want to look suspicious, then follow my lead. It would be weird for Jihoon *not* to say hello to Hwang Halmeoni."

Sinhye studied Somin's face. Somin tried to keep her expression neutral. It felt like her lips were quivering, but it seemed

Sinhye accepted the story, because she let go and turned to Hwang Halmeoni with an overly bright smile and a bow.

"I've missed you two sorely," Hwang Halmeoni said, her eyes shifting to take in Sinhye as well. They narrowed ever so slightly before returning to Somin. "What brings you back my way?"

"We're just visiting the old place. We've missed it," Somin said, hoping her voice sounded casual.

"Something odd is happening," Hwang Halmeoni said ominously, and Somin could feel Sinhye stiffen beside her.

"Have you seen them? The spirits?" Hwang Halmeoni said, and Somin let out a breath of relief.

"Yes, I have, but don't worry, you're safe," she said.

"Oh, don't worry, I know how to handle a wayward ghost or two. Though I've never seen so many at a time before," she said. "You two take care, and don't be a stranger after this. I hardly get any visitors anymore with the restaurant closed."

"Of course," Somin said with a smile. Then she hesitated. It took all her willpower not to glance at Sinhye. Somin had to tread carefully here. "I hear you've kept in touch with Miyoung lately. I'll bring her by, too."

Hwang Halmeoni nodded with a mild smile, and anxiety sliced through Somin. Had her message not gotten across? Miyoung said that Hwang Halmeoni was supposed to call her whenever Jihoon came by to visit the restaurant. Would she do so now? Or had she forgotten about her promise?

"Come on," Sinhye said.

Somin was barely able to give a bow of goodbye before she was yanked toward the restaurant.

"I thought people from your time were more respectful to elders," Somin muttered as she almost tripped over her own feet.

"I didn't mingle with the people that much," Sinhye said. "Being a monster and all."

The words might have garnered some sympathy from Somin, but seeing as she was currently being held hostage, she didn't have much pity to spare for the gumiho.

Most of the doors of the building were locked, but Somin knew a trick with the back door. If you jiggled it in just the right way, then it would come loose. She didn't know how many times she and Jihoon had nagged Halmeoni to get it fixed.

It looked weird to see the back of the restaurant without any dirty dishware waiting to be washed. Now it was just a cold industrial room with scuffed counters and a wide, dripping sink. There were so many memories Somin could practically hear the echo of voices. As if the space were haunted. Somin's eyes drifted to the fox spirit. "What now?"

"Now I do my villain monologue," Sinhye said.

The declaration shocked Somin into silence.

Sinhye moved about the room. It was so odd. Somin was used to Jihoon in this space. It should have looked familiar. But there was a way the fox spirit moved that was so foreign to her. Like watching a puppet master move Jihoon in unnatural ways.

"I was trapped for a millennium. Can you imagine what that feels like?" Sinhye gave Somin a dismissive look. "No, of course you can't. Betrayed by the one you thought you loved. Kept in that damned jar by his own magic. Floating in a nothingness. But I could hear the whisper of other spirits. I could hear them talking. And one day, I could hear that they were excited. Something had changed. And it was like a veil was lifted. I could feel the energy of the world. I could practically taste it. I knew it would be my only chance to open my prison. But I knew I'd have to bide my time. I didn't want to be a bodiless spirit floating through the world. I needed a vessel." She wandered the room, running her hands over the shelving. Opening empty cabinets. Somin winced every time they slammed shut again. "I thought about taking hold of Junu. But a dokkaebi's body is a strange thing. A vessel already, built especially for his soul. It would not stretch to accommodate another. But your friend." She gestured down toward Jihoon's body. "Fits like a glove. I could taste the energy of another gumiho on him. It was all so deliciously perfect."

Perfect was not the word Somin would have chosen for it, but she refused to reply.

Sinhye walked to the sink and played with the faucet, turning the water on and off. "You all don't know how good you have it these days," she murmured.

Somin was finally annoyed enough to reply. "I'm not really interested in hearing how hard it was before indoor plumbing."

"I'm getting carried away," Sinhye said with a light laugh. "I have to admit I was very intrigued to meet you. Junu's new great love."

Somin's breath hitched, but she kept her face impassive. "Junu and I aren't that serious."

Sinhye laughed. "You think just because I've been trapped away for centuries, I can't see what's right in front of me? I've been watching you all the past two days as your friend unwittingly carried me around. I've seen how he looks at you. How he talks about you."

Somin's lips pressed into a thin line. This wasn't exactly a topic she wanted to talk about with an evil spirit possessing her best friend.

"Why are we here?" Somin finally asked. "What do you want?"

"I want the people who trapped me to pay!" Sinhye shouted. "Starting with your boyfriend."

"You killed him," Somin said, unable to hold back her anger. "You trapped his soul instead of letting him move on. You had the shaman turn him into a dokkaebi. He lost everything because of that. Wasn't that enough?"

"This is the problem with humans. You see everything that's different from you as monstrous, as lesser. Do you know where the first dokkaebi came from?"

"What?" Somin frowned.

"The first dokkaebi was a mix of man and spirit. A king once loved a lady, but she was already married. But, as powerful men are wont to do, he couldn't let go of something he wanted. Something he coveted. And so, even after he died, he desired this lady. He came to her as a spirit, and she became with child. The first dokkaebi. A coming together of two worlds. A dokkaebi is not a monster because he is evil; he is seen as evil because people do not understand him." Sinhye shrugged. "What is so wrong about making Junu a dokkaebi? What is so wrong about it except that he is no longer human?"

Somin shook her head. She wouldn't let Sinhye's pretty words distract her. She wouldn't let herself be confused. "You took a choice away from him. You made him something he never chose to be."

"And greedy, lustful men made me what I didn't choose to be," Sinhye snapped, and the look in her eyes was enough to have Somin shrink back. "Junu was far from the only victim."

"What's that supposed to mean?" Somin asked despite herself.

"When I lived, if women were beautiful, we were both coveted and punished."

"I don't need a history lesson," Somin said. Especially not one that would soften her to the evil thing inside her best friend. She tried to keep her heart hard. Tried to keep it cold.

"Everything that happened to me happened because I was seen as property. A sansin wanted me, but I loved Junu. I turned the mountain god down. I wanted a simple life, a mortal one with the boy I loved. And for that horrible crime." She paused, let the words sink in. "For that crime, he cursed me. He convinced me that I could gain my mortality only if I ate one hundred livers for one hundred days. Instead it cursed me and all who came after to be immortal monsters."

"Those who came after you?" Somin asked, *like Miyoung?* "So that's it? There's really no way for a gumiho to become mortal?"

"Oh, there is," Sinhye said with a grim smile. "Just because I was in that prison didn't mean that I couldn't hear the spirits in the Between. And they watched the world of the living. They told me things. Like how some gumiho found they could become human if they refused to feed for one hundred days, three moons. And then at the end they severed their ties with their bead. A painful process, from what I've heard; some of them didn't survive it. Severing yourself from your yeowu guseul is like trying to rip out a part of your own soul. But the ones who lived could be free from the curse of the gumiho. Could be human."

Somin couldn't help but think of Miyoung. She hadn't fed for one hundred days, and they'd all been wondering how she survived. Was it possible for her to become fully human if she just severed her bond with her bead?

"You're thinking of your friend, aren't you?" Sinhye said. "Such an interesting creature. Not quite human, not quite gumiho. She's sitting in a fragile limbo. Still attached to her lost bead. She'll be a fun toy after I'm done playing with you."

"I know that you've suffered," Somin said, carefully choosing her words. "You didn't deserve it. Maybe we can help you find peace."

Sinhye was quiet for a moment. She circled the room, as if taking its measure. She let her fingers run along surfaces, creating lines and patterns in the dust. "You really think you can somehow get through to me?" She raised pitying eyes, and the seed of hope in Somin disappeared. "Any humanity in me died a long time ago. After those who coveted and betrayed me locked me away in that prison for centuries."

Somin almost stepped back at the venom in Sinhye's voice.

"And now," Sinhye said, her voice quiet again, "I will repay those who cursed me. Starting with Junu. It's so hard to decide just how I'm going to make him suffer the most."

Now Somin did back away. She didn't like how calm Sinhye sounded. How resolved.

"Should I wait until he's here to watch? Or perhaps I'll just let him find your body. It's really so hard to choose." Sinhye let out a macabre laugh.

"He's not coming," Somin said. "He doesn't even know where I am."

"But didn't your little message get to him?" Sinhye asked.

Now Somin froze, her heart skipping a beat. "What?"

"I assume that's what you were doing with that halmeoni out front," Sinhye said calmly. Like she hadn't caught Somin trying to pull one on her. "I mean, that's why I let you choose the location. I figured a girl like you wouldn't be able to resist trying to get a message to her friends. And now they'll come for you, but it'll be too late. Oops!"

"Michin-nyeon!" Somin couldn't hold back her anger anymore and swung a fist. But she miscalculated. She was so used to Jihoon being slower, she could clock him without any effort. But Sinhye was too fast. And she dodged the punch and swung out with her own fist. Stars exploded behind Somin's eyes as she went sprawling onto the floor.

"I think I've made up my mind," Sinhye said. "I think I don't want to wait to snap your pretty little neck."

Somin scrambled back, crab-walking to get away from Sinhye. But, of course, it was futile. She was nowhere near as fast as the gumiho. So she pushed to her feet. If she was going to die, then she'd go down fighting. She'd just lifted her fists and stepped forward when the kitchen door slammed open and Mr. Ahn stumbled in. Somin considered using the momentary distraction to make a run for it, but Sinhye wrapped her in a choke hold.

"Well, what did I just walk into?" Mr. Ahn asked, his bleary eyes taking in the scene.

"Get out of here or I'll snap her neck," Sinhye growled, holding Somin like a human shield.

"Wow, Son, I didn't know you had it in you. But I don't care about that brat," Mr. Ahn said with a low, gravelly chuckle. "I just want the money you've been hiding from me."

"Money?" Sinhye asked with a laugh. "What nonsense are you talking about?"

This enraged Mr. Ahn, who was already sloppy from drink. "I know your halmeoni had money secreted away. Even when we asked her for help, she wouldn't give it to us. Said it was in a college fund for you. Well, now that she's dead, you've got to have it. And I raised you, so I'm entitled to at least half."

"Mr. Ahn, get out of here," Somin choked out.

"I see now. I see what type of man you are," Sinhye said, and Somin didn't like the glee she heard in the words. "I see that there is so much greed in your heart that your soul is black. I wonder what it will taste like."

Sinhye flung Somin aside. The momentum threw her into a metal column holding up one of the industrial shelves. Her head slammed against it with a thud that echoed through her ears. The sound reverberated. Her vision blurred. The world spun and twisted into three rotating layers as she fell. The last thing she saw was Sinhye lunging at Mr. Ahn.

KING JINJI FELL in love with Lady Dohwa and asked her to be with him, but she refused, as she was already married. Even if she didn't love her husband, she was loyal. So King Jinji was forced to live without the woman he loved until his untimely death. But as a spirit, he returned and found that Lady Dohwa's husband had died as well. She accepted him into her bed, and King Jinji stayed with her for seven days before leaving again.

Lady Dohwa became pregnant and gave birth to a son that she named Bihyeong. He was born of a mortal and a spirit, so he was unlike any other who'd come before him. He was extraordinary, and the new king, Jinpyeong, recognized this and raised him at the palace. But despite his royal heritage, Bihyeong much preferred to spend his nights on the hills by the river west of the city, in the company of ghosts instead of humans. These ghosts served as friends and confidants of Bihyeong. When the king ordered Bihyeong to build a bridge, he did so with the help of the ghosts and finished it in one night. Once they'd finished, they named it Gwigyo—Ghost Bridge.

But despite his unwavering friendship, Bihyeong's ghost friends did not stay by his side. They left him eventually and he was alone in the world of mortals, not quite human and not quite spirit. A new breed of creature that came to be known as dokkaebi.

41

MIYOUNG RAN AROUND the back of the old building that Jihoon used to call home. Her heart hadn't stopped racing since she'd received the call from Hwang Halmeoni.

He was acting so weird. And I could tell Somin was afraid of something. It seemed to me like she might have even been afraid of Jihoon, Hwang Halmeoni had said. She'd always been such a perceptive woman.

Miyoung said a small prayer that Somin and Jihoon were both okay.

And that prayer was dashed as she pushed into the back room and found Somin sprawled across the floor, a smear of blood leading into the kitchen. Like she'd crawled out here to get help.

"Somin-ah!" Miyoung shouted, kneeling beside her friend. When she turned Somin onto her back, Somin groaned and Miyoung thanked all the gods in the heavens for that. At least Somin wasn't dead.

"Don't move, I'm here. I'm going to get you help." But before Miyoung could take out her phone, Somin grabbed her wrist.

"Stop her," Somin said. "She'll kill him."

Then she passed out again. Miyoung picked up Somin, carrying her outside. Junu rushed up to her. "What happened?" he gasped out.

"Watch after her," Miyoung said.

"No," Junu said. "I'm not letting you face Sinhye alone."

Miyoung started to argue when Hwang Halmeoni spoke behind her. "Leave Somin with me."

She followed Hwang Halmeoni and gently laid Somin on the wooden deck. "We'll come back for her," Miyoung promised.

"Just go help Jihoon," Hwang Halmeoni said.

"Come on," she said to Junu, and moved into the restaurant and toward the kitchen. This place was the site of one of the darkest days of her life. Second only to the day she'd lost her mother. She hated this room. But it seemed she couldn't escape its horrors as she watched Jihoon rip into his father's unconscious form.

"Jihoon-ah!"

He didn't even look up.

"Jihoon," she shouted, trying to get him to stop. "Ahn Jihoon!"

"Sinhye," Junu said.

Sinhye looked up, her face splattered with blood, and the grin she gave was one of malice and hunger.

"Stop this." Junu added command to his voice that Miyoung had never heard before.

"Do I look like I take orders from you?" Sinhye asked. And Miyoung realized that even though she spoke with Jihoon's voice, she sounded different. It was the cadence of her words and a slight accent that Miyoung couldn't place.

"I'm hoping that you'll see it as a request. A plea," Junu said. "If you're here to punish me, then punish *me*. Not anyone else."

"It seems that your immortality hasn't done much good for you." Sinhye sneered. "You're still soft and weak. Letting yourself become attached to these humans." Mr. Ahn lay at Sinhye's feet, but Miyoung could finally make out his chest rising and falling in shallow breaths. He was alive, but Miyoung wasn't sure how long that would last.

"I'm not attached to anyone," Junu said, and Miyoung recognized something in his words. He was parroting things she used to say. Things she said when she was lying to herself about being able to live with no connections. How had she not realized that before?

"I'm alone," Junu said, and now the words made Miyoung sad. "So don't punish anyone else for my mistakes."

"You really think you're capable of holding yourself separate from a world you're still so desperate to be a part of?" Sinhye asked with a laugh. "You, who always cared so much what everyone around you thought? I was wrong; you're not the same as you were before. You're worse because now you're deluding yourself. Playing at being strong, when inside you're the same scared boy I knew."

Junu's voice came out tight, choked. "You don't know me anymore."

"I don't need to know you to see right through you. Your weak heart cares about these humans."

"Leave him alone," Miyoung said. She felt a need now to shield Junu from the cruelty of this fox spirit. Because, whether she'd wanted to admit it or not, Junu had become a part of her life. A part she wanted to hold on to.

"Make me," Sinhye said with a hard grin.

Miyoung started to step forward, but Junu stopped her. "I'm asking you to leave these people alone and let Jihoon go," Junu said. "And I'll help you find another way to live."

Sinhye sneered. "You think I need your help? Don't you get it? I don't want or need anything from you except your pain."

"And how do you think this will help? I don't care about that man." Junu flung his arm toward Mr. Ahn.

"Yes, but you claim to care about this one and his friends." Sinhye gestured to Jihoon's body. "Let's see how you deal with the pain *you've* caused them."

"What?" Junu asked, but he was cut short as Sinhye's eyes rolled back and her body went slack.

42

JIHOON'S BODY FELL back, his head slamming against the hard floor. As Miyoung ran to him, Junu called for her to stop. They had no way of knowing what Sinhye would do if she got her hands on someone else. But Miyoung didn't listen.

Jihoon moaned, and Junu prepared to fight her off.

"Miyoung-ah?" Jihoon murmured, sounding distinctly Jihoon-like, but Junu was still on edge. Waiting for even the slightest hint that it was a trap. "What happened?"

"Nothing," Miyoung said, trying to block the sight of Mr. Ahn lying in the middle of the floor. But Jihoon followed the trail of gore until he spotted his father's body.

"Is that . . . ?" A gasp of horror escaped his throat. Jihoon lifted his hands as if to hide behind them; then his eyes widened as he saw the blood covering his skin. "Oh God. Did I do that? Did I kill—"

"No," Miyoung said firmly. "It wasn't you."

"Oh my God. Oh my God." Jihoon started shaking, his body jerking with agitation as he ran his red-stained hands over his face. It transferred the blood to his cheeks, stuck in his hair, made him look gruesome. His hands fisted at his temples, and he sobbed. "I remember now. I remember what happened. I'm a murderer. I killed him. I killed my own father." The last words were akin to a wail of pain so sharp that even Junu felt it.

"No," Miyoung said. "It was Sinhye, and she's gone now."

"She's not." Jihoon shook his head frantically. "She's still in here. I can hear her. She says she wants me to see what we did. She wants me to watch him die."

Jihoon's father twitched, let out a cough that spewed blood from his mouth.

"He's not dead," Miyoung said, latching on to that fact. "Look, he's not dead."

"Yet," Junu said, and she sent him an angry glare.

"You're not helping," she said through gritted teeth.

"Neither are you if you think this will help him with his guilt. There's nothing we can do for this man."

And when Mr. Ahn died, Jihoon would never forgive himself. He'd be tortured by this death for the rest of his life. And that was the punishment, Junu realized. The punishment was knowing that he was the cause of more pain. Because Mr. Ahn wouldn't be dying if not for Sinhye, and Sinhye would not have targeted him if not for Junu.

The guilt he already felt over his part in Yena's death expanded, threatened to choke him.

You can never do anything right, his father's voice echoed in his head. Angry and hard. *I'm ashamed to have a son like you.*

Junu almost lifted his hands to drown out the voice, but he knew it was coming from his own memory. And try as he might, there was no escaping it.

Let's see how you deal with the pain you've caused them, Sinhye had said. And she was right. This was a good punishment. No good came to those who associated with Junu; this was proof of that.

"There's nothing any of us can do," Junu said finally. "This man will die."

"Fine." Miyoung moved to kneel beside Mr. Ahn, whose rasping breaths were echoing through the kitchen. There was a death rattle in his chest, one that Junu was far too familiar with.

"What are you doing?" Junu asked.

"I'll kill him. This death will be on me. Do you hear me?" Miyoung said to Jihoon. "I killed him. Not you."

Then she raised her hand to give the killing blow. Junu stopped her before she could swing it down.

"No," he said. "You can't do this."

"Let go!" she shouted. Tears flowed down her cheeks as she tried to break free. "I have to do this."

"No," Junu said, kneeling down so he was eye to eye with her. "This is not your responsibility. It's mine."

He gave her a gentle push, and as anticipated, she fell back easily. Junu looked at the door leading to Somin. She would never look at him the same after he did this.

Jihoon watched him with unblinking eyes. And Junu saw it, the glint of something more beneath his irises. "Sinhye, if you're watching, then I hope you're satisfied with what you've done to us both. What you've made us both."

Then Junu wrapped his hands around Mr. Ahn's throat. His rattling breaths became haggard, choking gasps. His body shook. His hands clenched. His feet kicked. He obviously wanted to fight for a life that he wasn't yet aware had already been taken from him. And Junu squeezed his eyes shut against the burn of tears. He wouldn't let them fall. He didn't deserve them.

He held on until he felt Mr. Ahn still. He held on until the only sounds in the room were Miyoung's sobs. He held on because if he let go, he was sure he'd fall himself.

43

JUNU SAT ALONE on the cold floor.

He was in an abandoned warehouse. A place he'd sometimes come to do shady dealings with undesirables he didn't want in his home. It was also a place where the city's homeless would sometimes come to escape inclement weather.

Today, it was empty except a few stained cardboard boxes and smattering of threadbare blankets. Well, empty of anyone living. Ghosts wandered the space. They didn't seem interested in Junu as they floated through the warehouse. Spirits were often drawn to spaces that held sadness and pain. And death. Junu was sure many had died in this place. That's why it was as good a place for an unidentified body to be found. A better place than a building that Jihoon and Somin had been seen entering.

He didn't look at the body beside him, but he didn't leave either. Junu didn't feel right leaving him until . . .

The air shifted. It chilled. Like a supernatural thermostat had been turned down. Junu could see puffs of his breath as the temperature dropped. And he closed his eyes as goose bumps pimpled on his flesh.

"I knew it would be you," Junu said without looking up.

"Just like old times, huh?" Hyuk asked.

"No," Junu said, finally glancing up at the jeoseung saja. "Not like old times."

"This isn't the first time you've taken a life."

"I know."

"But this is the first time I've seen it affect you like this."

Junu closed his eyes again, afraid he felt those damn tears again. He couldn't break now. Not in front of Hyuk.

"I'm not the same person you used to know."

"I know," Hyuk said.

As he rose, pinpricks ran along Junu's legs from kneeling so long. Perhaps he'd been sitting his own form of a vigil over the life he'd taken.

"You can go," Hyuk said, laying a gentle hand on Junu's shoulder. "I'll take care of him now."

"Will he go to a good place?" Junu asked. He'd never before asked Hyuk where he took his souls. He just knew the reaper took them somewhere beyond here. "What if the tear between the worlds allows him to come back? Can you do something to make sure his soul doesn't . . . stay?"

"Afraid of being haunted?" Hyuk asked with a quirked eyebrow.

Junu shook his head and gave a forced grin. "You know me well enough to know the dead don't bother me."

Hyuk didn't return the smile. "I know you well enough to know that's what you *say*."

"What's that supposed to mean?" Junu asked. He thought he could at least depend on Hyuk to keep things light and meaningless. That was their thing now, wasn't it?

"You're the one who said you're a different person. Maybe I'm hoping you're different enough to finally accept some things you never could before." Hyuk shrugged. "It's all I ever really wanted for you. Old friend."

Then he turned to the body, reached his arms down as if scooping something out of the earth, but instead of dirt, he came away with the gauzy shape of a person. The spirit of Jihoon's father.

Junu remembered once asking Hyuk what that was like, pulling a soul free from its body. The reaper had explained that it required superhuman strength. That's why all jeoseung saja were so strong. A soul is a heavy thing.

But Hyuk had been doing this a long time and he made it seem effortless, like lifting a sleeping child. Eventually he placed the soul on its feet. Laid a hand on its shoulder as if waking someone who was sleepwalking.

"Go back to your friends, Junu. You should be with them."

"I don't have friends." And Junu felt the truth of that deep in his bones. He was alone. He was always alone.

"Go back to them," Hyuk said again before turning and fading into the shadows with the spirit, leaving Junu behind. He was always being left behind. Turning, he walked out of the warehouse, dialing 119 as he went.

"I need to report a disturbance."

44

SOMIN ACHED EVERYWHERE. *Her world was awash in white and pain.*

"Somin-ah," someone called to her.

"Hello?" she shouted, her voice echoing into a great abyss. "Who's there? Where are we?"

"Somin-ah. Be careful."

"Where are you? I can't see you. I can't see anything."

"I'm sorry I cannot protect you. That I left you."

No, it couldn't be. It was impossible. How could he be here?

A sob left Somin's chest as she whispered, "Appa?"

"My daughter. I'm sorry that you feel pain. I'm sorry that you must feel more."

Somin woke slowly. She felt the tears streaming down her cheeks as the echoes of the dream lingered.

As she regained her senses, she realized there was a throbbing ache in her back, and she turned onto her side to find a more comfortable position. But the motion made her dozen bruises throb, and she jerked upright.

Memories of the day came flooding back to her, the horror and the pain of it.

Somin blinked against the dark room. There was a single lamp on in the corner, and she realized she was lying on Junu's couch. She stood, walking to the bedrooms. All of the doors were closed, but the doorway of Miyoung's room had half a dozen bujeoks plastered to it. Odd. Why would Miyoung put those there?

She turned to look for her friends. The entire apartment was mostly dark, with only the guiding light of the kitchen to tell her where to go.

Where was everyone? What happened at the restaurant? What happened to Mr. Ahn?

She reached for a cabinet, when she heard steps behind her. She whirled around, holding out a mug as a shield or a weapon or both. But she let her hand drop when she saw Miyoung, a pharmacy bag in her hand.

"You're awake," she said, rushing forward and dropping the bag on the table. "How are you feeling?"

"Thirsty," Somin croaked out, and blinked at the strange frog-like voice that had come out.

"I'll get you water. Sit down." Miyoung took the mug. Usually Somin hated people taking care of her—that was her job—but she was already shaky on her legs, so she sat at the kitchen table.

"I have to call my mother," she said. "She'll wonder where I am."

"I already called her last night. I told her you're staying here. She said that was good. She doesn't want you spending the night worrying about her alone."

"Last night?" Somin asked.

"It's morning. You slept through the night."

Somin let out a shaky breath. "Where's Junu?"

Miyoung paused in the act of pouring water. "He hasn't come back yet."

There was something in her tone, something that spoke of burdensome things.

"What happened?" Somin asked. "How did we get back here?"

"We brought you back after . . ." Miyoung shook her head, unable to continue as she held out the mug.

Instead of taking the water, Somin latched on to Miyoung's wrist and tugged at her bloodstained sleeves. "Are you okay? Where are you hurt?" Somin pushed up the fabric to find the wound. Miyoung yelped in surprise and yanked her arm back, but Somin had already moved on, noticing blood splattered over Miyoung's shirt.

"What is this?" she asked frantically. "Please tell me what happened. Tell me who's hurt. Or . . ." Somin couldn't bring herself to say the words *or who's dead*.

"I can't."

"Is it Jihoon?" Somin finally brought herself to ask, dreading the answer.

"No. He's alive."

"Where is he? How do we get that fox spirit out of him? Can I see him?"

Miyoung seemed to fold in on herself at the barrage of questions. Her eyes couldn't meet Somin's, and her hands shook before she fisted them together.

"What is it?" Somin asked, feeling the tension coming off her friend in waves.

"I just . . . I don't know what to do for him. I don't know how to get him back, and what if this is all my fault?" Miyoung's legs shook, and she lowered herself into a crouch in front of Somin, sobbing. It tore at Somin. She'd never heard her friend sound so desperate before. So she pulled Miyoung close.

"No, you can't think like that. You're both victims here; this is nobody's fault." She stroked Miyoung's hair, holding her gently as the girl emptied herself of all her fear and frustration.

After Miyoung had cried herself out, she was limp with exhaustion, and Somin insisted that she rest.

"Did you even sleep last night?"

"I rested . . . a bit. For a few minutes," Miyoung admitted.

"You're sleeping. No arguing." Somin led Miyoung to the couch.

"But I'm supposed to be taking care of you." Miyoung's words were slurred with exhaustion.

"You are," Somin said. "I'm already feeling much better."

"Liar," Miyoung mumbled as her eyes drooped closed. Soon her breathing evened out in sleep, and Somin draped a blanket over her.

Somin surveyed the quiet apartment. Had she ever noticed before how cold it seemed? The design made it too sleek, too artificial. Like the facade that Junu put forward. Like the overly polished, pompous jerk Somin had first thought him to be. Somin's eyes traveled to the library involuntarily, the one space that held any personality. The one that felt like the Junu Somin was starting to know. Those glimpses that made Somin's heart yearn. And thinking of him, worry washed through her.

She glanced back at Miyoung's bloodstained sleeves. She should have made her friend change. But at least she'd assured herself it wasn't Miyoung's blood. And it wasn't Jihoon's.

Dokkaebi don't bleed, Somin reminded herself. *It's not Junu's blood, it can't be.*

"So you do care about him."

She spun around at the voice and stared at the beautiful boy who stood behind her. Dark, close-cropped hair. Dark, almost-black eyes in a pale face. Dressed all in black. The reaper from the street.

"How did you get in here?" Her eyes moved to the bujeoks plastered around Junu's doorway.

"Those don't work against me," he replied, his eyes following her gaze. "I'm not a ghost or a demon."

"I know what you are. What I'd like to know is why you keep hanging around here," Somin said.

"You have spirit." He nodded. "Good. He'll need that."

"What are you talking about?" Somin huffed in frustration.

"But you're not patient." He sighed. "Which could be a problem for him."

"I don't have time—"

"I could stop it for a bit. Let us have our chat without it."

Without time? Somin thought. Just exactly what could this reaper do? And how could she be sure he wasn't here to hurt her and her friends?

"I need you to be careful with him," the boy said. "He's more delicate than he seems."

"Who?" Somin asked.

"I wouldn't have imagined a human like you would be it, but I can see that you're what he needs now."

She knew now that he spoke of Junu. "I don't want to be what someone needs. I want to be what someone wants. What someone chooses. And he's made it clear he doesn't choose me."

"Even he doesn't know what his heart wants," the reaper said. "After everything that happened with his family, Junu wasn't able to handle the life fate gave him. He closed himself off. He lost himself for centuries in anything that would numb the pain. If he'd been human, it would have killed him. But instead, he was left to live his eternal life seeking out more and more ways to rip out the pain that wouldn't let go of him. That's how I found him. One who would do any job that could get him quick cash so he could buy another bottle. Every time I came to reap a soul of another he'd killed, I saw him. And came to know him. And came to care for him."

"What happened with his family?" Somin asked. "What happened to make him hurt for so long?"

"Unfortunately, even I don't know that whole story. He's never told anyone as far as I know."

Somin fisted her hands over her chest, like she sought to protect her own soul. "Why are you telling me all of this? Does Junu know you're telling me?"

"Of course he doesn't. He'd never want you to know this vulnerable side of him. But I think you need to know. He'll need you more than ever now. His soul is in danger of breaking."

"How do you know that?"

"Souls are my business."

That made goose bumps rise on Somin's skin. "What do you think I can do for him?"

"Hold on to him," the boy said.

"What?" Somin started to say, but he was gone. One second he stood before her, solid as anyone else. Next thing she knew, he'd blinked out of existence.

She turned as the front door opened and Junu entered. Blood staining his pants, his shirt, his hands.

"Are you okay?" Somin reached for him, but he pulled back.

"Don't" was all he said before he tried to brush past her, but Somin planted herself in his way.

So Junu just turned into the library, slamming the door closed behind him.

Somin debated taking the hint. He was obviously in a horrible mood, but her worry for him overpowered any restraint she had. And she slowly opened the door, peeking her head inside.

The room was empty.

Confused, Somin opened the door wider and stepped inside. She turned in a circle, just in case she'd missed something, but there was no one there.

Then Somin remembered, and she stepped to the far bookcase. It took her three tries before she found the right book again, but the hidden door swung open without a sound.

She hesitated. Was she really the right thing for Junu right now? How could she be sure? This *thing* between them seemed so volatile. Then she pushed those doubts away. Because Junu needed *someone* right now, and that someone might as well be her.

Light spilled into the library as Somin walked into the hidden studio. Junu stood among his canvases, his shirtsleeves rolled up so she could see corded muscles as he ripped a painting in half.

More paintings lay at his feet, shredded. Ruined.

With a cry of alarm, Somin tried to still his hands.

"Junu, what are you doing?"

"Get out," Junu said. Picking up a ceramic bowl covered in delicate blue leaves and lines, he let it shatter at his feet.

"I can't—"

"I said, *get out!*" Junu shouted. And if rage was the only thing she saw in his face, she would have. But there was such pain. It tore at her heart.

"What happened?" she asked.

"Nothing," Junu said, turning back to the pile of ruined art.

Somin wondered if he would burn the whole place down if he could. No, he hated fire. So maybe he'd just batter it with his hands until it was all dust.

"I shouldn't be surprised you found this place," Junu said, picking up a canvas painted to look like a sunset from a high mountain. He tore it into thin shreds so strands of orange and red rained around him. "You've always been nosy."

The words stung, but she also knew that when people hurt, they lashed out. And Junu was an expert at words. He knew how to aim them like weapons. But Somin wouldn't let him deter her.

She wrapped her hands around his wrists. He still held the fragments of canvas in his balled fists. "Junu, stop this now, okay?"

He shook his head but didn't pull away. "I don't know how to stop. I don't know how to be better." Smoke started to plume from his hands, small flames erupting from nowhere to lick at the remnants of the painting.

"Junu," Somin squeaked as his skin became searingly hot. She jerked back, letting out a hiss as it burned her hands. She glanced at her palms, red and irritated.

Junu stumbled toward a sink in the corner. He yanked desperately at the knobs until water ran over his smoking fists.

"Junu, what just happened?" Somin stuttered, staring at his hand. It looked smooth and unmarked. Like it hadn't just been holding a fistful of flames.

"You should leave me alone before you get more hurt," Junu said quietly. There was something in his words, like he wasn't talking about the fire.

"No, I don't think you should be alone. If I can help fix this—"

"This isn't something that can be fixed!" Junu yelled, swiping his arms across the counter beside the sink. Cups went crashing to the floor, smashing against the tile, spilling brushes and pens and scissors. They scattered around him as he slammed his hands onto the counter, holding on until his knuckles became white. "Don't you get it? Sometimes people can't be fixed. Not even by the great Lee Somin."

Somin wanted to tell him he was wrong. There had never been a problem she'd come up against that she couldn't defeat with sheer force of will. But she'd never known someone who had so much darkness inside of him. Centuries worth of it. This felt like a battle that had so much at stake, but it was one she wasn't sure she could fight. Only Junu could. And it looked like he was giving up.

"You don't have to tell me what happened," Somin began. "But if I can help—"

Junu let out a venomous laugh, a biting sound that made Somin's stomach tighten.

"Nothing can help me. I've been cursed for centuries. I was a fool to think it could be any different now." He stepped into the rubble that covered the studio floor, his slippers crunching on broken glass and ceramic. "What use do I have with things like this? What use are any of these to me?" he asked, picking up a half-completed bust and throwing it against the far wall. The pieces rained onto a tarp, pulling it down to reveal the faded portraits beneath.

Junu stared at the painted faces that looked back with dark eyes.

He picked up the painting of the woman looking lovingly out from her portrait. The paper was so delicate. Like it might just dissolve from being held. He stared at it intently. Like he was lost in the portrait. Like it dragged him to some long-forgotten memory.

Somin started to protest. She didn't know who this person was, but she felt important. But instead of shredding the painting, Junu slowly sank to the ground, gripping the paper so tightly it wrinkled in his hands.

Somin didn't know what to say to soothe his pain. So she didn't speak. She just knelt beside him and wrapped her arms around him, resting his head against her shoulder. She felt his hesitation like a string pulled taut. She waited to see if he'd snap or let loose. And with a sigh he relaxed. The portrait fell to his lap as his arms came around her waist and he let out a breath. One that made his whole body shudder. And then he continued to shake with silent sobs. She tightened her hold on him, trying to absorb the shock of his pain. Trying to take on some of it so it wouldn't break him.

45

SOMIN LED JUNU to his room. She'd expected him to resist, but it seemed he was too exhausted to protest. She had no idea where he'd been all night, but she was sure he hadn't slept.

She started to ask Junu if he wanted to change, when he just fell face-first onto his bed.

"At least get under the comforter," Somin said, trying to pull it free from under him. But instead he took hold of her wrist and tugged her down so she fell beside him.

"I don't need the blanket," he murmured, running his hand over her cheek. It made her skin tingle everywhere he touched.

"You don't know what you need right now."

Junu lifted a brow. "And you do?"

"I know better than you do right now."

He chuckled and pulled her close, wrapping his arms around her. She breathed him in, a musky scent she couldn't quite place. But it reminded her of his library, parchment and wood. It soothed her, and she let her shoulders relax. She hadn't even realized how tense they were. Didn't know she'd needed this, too. To be held, to feel safe.

"Jin." He said the word into her hair.

"What?" Somin asked.

Junu leaned back so he could look at her. "My family name is Jin."

"Why are you telling me this?" she asked, searching his inscrutable face.

"Because you asked," Junu said. "I didn't think I deserved the name. That's why I don't use it."

"Why would you say such a thing?" Somin asked.

"Because it's true. It was true before I ever died and became this." He nodded down toward himself. "My abeoji used to tell me that all the time."

"Then he was a cruel man," Somin said.

Junu laughed. "That's a wild understatement."

"Why are you telling me this now?"

"Because I want you to know me. All of me. You once asked why I was trying to make Changwanie like me."

"Yeah," Somin said, unsure of the track the conversation had taken.

"Because he is me. Who I used to be."

Somin was silent a moment too long.

"You don't believe me," Junu muttered.

She shook her head. "No, I do. I'm just trying to figure out how that would look."

"My human form was completely different from the one I'm in now. Short, stick thin. Couldn't build muscle for the life of me. And I had pretty bad acne. Though back then, people thought it could be a pox when it got really bad. Oh, the joys of living before modern dermatology," Junu said, sarcasm lacing his tone. "I had a weak constitution. Was constantly sick when I was young. I was never good enough for my father. Never good enough to carry the family name. And he reminded me of that every day. I guess, with Changwanie, I was trying to help him find a shield so it wouldn't get so bad for him. So it wouldn't end so horribly."

"How did it end?" Somin asked.

"They died," Junu said quietly. "Because of me."

Somin kept quiet, knowing she didn't have the words he needed. Maybe there were no words that could help him.

"After I was changed. It took me a few weeks to get the courage. But I had to see them again. I wanted to see if maybe . . . if maybe I could go back home."

There was such a longing in his voice when he said the word *home*.

"At first they didn't recognize me, so I told them things only I could know. I thought they'd be happy to see me. I thought they'd welcome me back with open arms. I was wrong. My mother broke down. Said I had turned into a demon. My nunas became cruel. Telling me I shouldn't have come back. And my hyeong . . ." Junu paused a moment, his eyes looked like they were watching something far away. As if the things he was remembering were playing out before him. "He went to get my abeoji."

"What did your abeoji do?" Somin asked gently.

"I think there was always something in him that was on the verge of snapping. I think I broke that part of him that night. He was in a rage. He said that his family had been cursed. That I was proof of that."

Somin wasn't sure anymore if she wanted to hear the rest of the story.

"He made them go into the back room, away from me. Maybe if he hadn't, they would have gotten out in time."

"What?" Somin asked, her voice shaking. "What did he do next?"

"It wasn't him," Junu said, his voice a hoarse choke. "It was me. I didn't know I could do something like that." He lifted his hands, staring at them like they were loaded weapons. "I was still so unused to this body, to controlling it. I'd forgotten the stories about what a dokkaebi could do. But even the stories didn't tell me that our abilities are tied to our emotions, especially in the beginning."

"Junu, I don't need to know," Somin said. She could tell that this was hurting him.

"There's a tale about how dokkaebi are linked to fire. Because we can create it from our very flesh. A goblin fire that burns so bright it's blue. And when the room caught on fire, I could hear them banging for my father to let them out, but he wouldn't. He said he'd rather they all burn to death than live with the curse I'd put on the family. I tried to save them. I did," Junu said desperately, as if he was trying to convince her. "But he'd bolted the door shut, and when I tried to unlock it, he knocked me out somehow. I woke up surrounded by ashes and bodies. He'd meant for us all to die together, but the dokkaebi fire didn't hurt me. I wished for so long that it had killed me too."

"You hate fire," she whispered, remembering Junu's words.

"Yeah, it took me a long time to control it, a long time to lock it away. I've never used it since that night. Until tonight."

"Your hands. The fire," Somin said.

"It's the first time in centuries that I've lost control like that," Junu said.

"That's not your fault," she said. It seemed like such an insufficient reply, but it was all she could think of. She wished she had something epic and comforting to say to him in this moment. Hyuk had told her that Junu had never told this story to anyone, but he was telling it to her. It was a responsibility she didn't take lightly.

"I killed them. They would have lived if not for me. If I hadn't been so selfish. I should never have gone back to see them."

"Wanting to see your family isn't selfish. You loved them," Somin said, and she wanted to pull him close again. But before she could, Junu shoved his face into the pillows.

"After that, I hated what I was," Junu said, his voice muffled. "I hated what I'd become. Because it had killed my family and it had forced me to survive without them." Junu turned onto his back, staring up at the ceiling now. "You know, I've never had the need for a friend until I met you all. Until I met Miyoung. There's something about that girl that makes me want to be better. She holds herself to such a high standard that it makes me worry that I'm not good enough to match her."

Somin nodded even though he wasn't looking at her. "Miyoung does have some pretty high standards for herself. But she doesn't judge her friends as harshly. Trust me, she wouldn't have fallen for Ahn Jihoon if she did."

Junu shook his head, but there was a hint of a smile, and it soothed Somin's heart to see it.

"But it's not Miyoung who made me hope," Junu said quietly. And Somin felt her heart start to race. She was anticipating his words even as she told herself not to care.

"I told myself I kept poking at you because it was fun. But in reality, I think I was hoping that maybe . . . maybe I could prove to you that I wasn't what you assumed. That I was somehow . . . more. I don't know." Junu frowned, and it still looked beautiful on his perfect lips. She wanted to trace the lines of his face with her fingertips. She wanted to memorize the shape of him.

"I know I gave you a hard time when we first met. I know that you're more than what I originally thought," Somin said slowly.

"But I'm still not as good as you want me to be," Junu said.

Somin hesitated at that because she didn't know the answer. "I know that, no matter how much I want to, I can't stop caring about you," she said.

Junu turned onto his side so they were face-to-face, mere centimeters from each other. He reached out, let his fingers trail along her cheek. Tingles raced over her skin, made goose bumps rise on her arms. She didn't dare move, didn't dare blink. His fingers trailed down her neck, tracing along some invisible pattern. She tried to remember the path, tried to hold on to each sensation.

"Is it because you're so little?" he whispered as he brought his palm back up to cup her cheek.

It would have annoyed her, but he watched her so intently.

"I think it's because you're so small that I can fit you in my heart."

"Junu-ya," Somin said, confusion overtaking her. She didn't know what she wanted to say, but Junu shook his head.

"I'm tired. Let's talk more later."

Somin let him pull her close again so her head fit under his chin. It didn't strike her as strange anymore, how perfectly they seemed to fit into each other. She just let his warmth comfort her as she hugged him close. His heart beat steady under her ear. And lying like that, she fell asleep.

46

MIYOUNG WASN'T AFRAID to dream now. She needed answers. She needed to do something. Yena had once told her to make a choice. Even if it was a bad choice, at least she wouldn't be sitting around waiting for solutions to come to her.

She needed to find a way to help Jihoon. To help Junu. To help herself.

"Mother," she called into the mist. Whenever she dreamed now, the forest was covered in fog. Like a veil pulled over her vision. Was this a bad omen?

"Mother, where are you?" Miyoung called.

"I don't know where I am. I'm lost," Yena's disembodied voice replied.

"I need to find you. I need my bead back. We need to close this tear between the worlds."

"Without the bead, I can no longer watch over you. My poor, wretched child."

"I know," Miyoung said, her voice not as strong now. "But I can't be selfish. I can't hold on to you while so many others are suffering."

"Why care about them now? I taught you better than that."

"But you also said that you have regrets. Don't you regret closing yourself off from people? I don't want to have those same regrets."

"Then why close yourself off to me?" Yena asked. "When I am the only one who loves you."

"That's not true," Miyoung said, her voice shaking.

"Perhaps it's not," Yena mused, her voice sifting through the mist that had become so cold Miyoung shivered. *"But loving you is danger-ous. Loving you kills people."*

"No," Miyoung said, shaking her head. *"That's not true. I tried to save you. I'll save him."*

"You'll try. But you're not strong enough."

"I've become stronger. I will *become stronger, if that's what it takes."*

"Then come and get me," Yena said. *"See if you can throw me away into hell!"*

Miyoung woke with a jerk, falling off the couch with a hard thud. She groaned, rubbing her tailbone as she sat up, trying to untangle herself from the twisted blanket.

The apartment was quiet, a soft light shining from under Junu's door. She glanced at the other room. Where Jihoon slept. Bujeoks were plastered around the frame. Ones meant to hold in evil things. To trap them temporarily. But she could already see the ink starting to fade, as if Sinhye's power was too great.

Her mother's words echoed in her head. She would become stronger. She would do what she had to in order to protect Jihoon.

She almost knocked on the bedroom door before she realized it probably wouldn't do much good. She felt a spark of resistance as she turned the handle. As if the bujeoks recognized that she was still connected to her bead, as if she hadn't completely shed her gumiho self. She opened the door slowly, just in case Jihoon was still sleeping. Hoping it was Jihoon—and just Jihoon—who was sleeping.

When she heard nothing, she almost backed out again, but Jihoon turned over on the bed, his eyes open. "Miyoung?"

His eyes blinked, blurry with sleep. His hair stuck up on one side, making him look mussed. It was one of her favorite looks on him.

Sitting on the edge of the bed, Miyoung ran her fingers through his hair. "Jihoon-ah?" Her voice shook, the hesitation clear.

"Yeah, it's me." He smiled gently, and she saw his dimple blink. It was like seeing an old friend again after too long apart.

"I'm so glad you're still here," she said, her shoulders sagging with relief.

"Really?" Jihoon asked, his smile spreading. "How glad?"

"What?" Miyoung asked. The light slanting into the room from the hallway made his features look harsh.

"How glad are you that I'm really me?" he asked, leaning forward. And she saw it, the sharp gleam in his eyes.

"Sinhye." Miyoung stood and backed away.

"Aw, I was hoping we could play a little more." She stuck her lip out in a pout.

Miyoung's muscles tightened. "Why are you still here? What do you want with us?"

"I want to play," Sinhye said, then flopped back on the bed, folding her arms behind her head. "Being stuck in that jar was so boring. Can you imagine it? Being locked away for centuries with no one and nothing to talk to."

She sat up again and sneered. "Of course you can't. You're so ungrateful for your power that you willingly traded it away."

Miyoung clenched her jaw, refusing to rise to the bait. She knew that Sinhye was just trying to hurt her.

"I bet Mommy loves watching her selfish, weak daughter give

up everything, even her own mother, for a chance at a boring mortal life."

"Shut up," Miyoung said, shoving Sinhye so hard that she fell against the bed.

"Well, well," Sinhye said, laughing. "I guess you're not completely boring after all."

"We'll find a way to get you out of Jihoon. And when we do, your spirit can go to hell for all I care. And with no one in this world to care about you, you'll be completely forgotten after you're gone forever." Miyoung started to turn to leave, when Sinhye's hand latched on to her arm.

"You should learn not to antagonize me," Sinhye said. "Those bujeoks can't hold me in here forever. And in the meantime, I can still hurt this body."

Slowly Miyoung turned so she was face-to-face with the fox spirit that wore Jihoon's face. "You won't." Her heart was racing with the bluff, but she had to believe that Sinhye's desire to stay in this world was stronger than her desire to hurt Miyoung and her friends. "You have unfinished business. Didn't you swear that you'd get your revenge on those who trapped you? Well, the way I see it, you're too scared to go after the sansin, and I wouldn't blame you. Mountain gods are no joke, from what I hear. And whatever shaman helped is long dead. So you're stuck poking at Junu. But he has something that you don't have."

Sinhye's jaw clenched, and the hand holding Miyoung's arm tightened. "And what's that?"

"People who care enough to help him. That's why you're here, helpless, unable to do anything. Actually, now that I think about it, you're trapped. Again."

Sinhye's hand whipped out, grabbing Miyoung's arm. "Don't push me, girl."

Miyoung swung out so fast that Sinhye didn't have time to react. Her fist connected with Sinhye's temple and sent her careening onto the bed, knocked out cold.

"No. You shouldn't push me," Miyoung said.

47

JUNU WOKE SLOWLY, reaching out for Somin. But the bed beside him was empty and cold.

He shuffled into the hallway, turning at the sound of low, murmuring voices. Miyoung and Somin sat at the kitchen table, both cradling steaming mugs of boricha. But neither drank. Junu was about to join them, when Miyoung said, "What are you going to do about Junu?"

"I don't know what to do for him. I didn't realize how much he's kept bottled inside. It scares me a little," Somin said.

Junu flattened himself against the wall, melting back into the shadows of the hallway.

"He lived for centuries before he met either of us. There's no knowing what ghosts he carries with him."

"Sometimes I can forget that he's lived through so much. Then I'm reminded of it in the way he talks or the way he thinks, and I worry that we just come from different times. Maybe too different. I know how to fight a lot of things, but I don't know how to fight that."

Miyoung gave a sad smile. "Immortality is a heavy burden to carry. For immortals and for the people who love them."

"Is that why you didn't want to be a gumiho anymore? Because you knew it would be too hard for you and Jihoon if you were?"

Miyoung let out a bitter laugh. "I don't know. I didn't give up that life just for Jihoon. I did it for me. But I like imagining what it would be like to grow old with him. To grow old at all."

"Sinhye can't hold on to him forever. We'll find a way to get her out of Jihoon."

"She has so much hate in her for Junu. It makes her powerful," Miyoung whispered. "I'm scared she'd rather destroy herself and Jihoon before she lets go of him."

"We won't let her do that," Somin said. "Jihoon's not just my friend. He's my family. I can't lose him."

"We won't," Miyoung insisted. "I won't let him go. I'll do whatever it takes."

"We all have to do whatever it takes," Somin said.

Junu slipped away, no longer comfortable listening in. There was a low pressure in his chest. Equal parts worry and guilt. He doubted anyone had ever spoken about him with the conviction they had when they spoke of Ahn Jihoon. But then again, had he ever done anything to earn such loyalty? Such love?

She has so much hate in her for Junu. It makes her powerful. Miyoung was right. Sinhye wouldn't be hurting them all if not for Junu and her hatred for him. He'd brought this on them all. He was the reason for their pain.

Frustration filled him as he shoved his hands into his pockets. His fingers brushed the edge of a business card, and he pulled it out. He was still wearing the same clothes he'd worn to the amusement park yesterday. It was the card from the little girl. The mystery number she'd been so confident he'd call. *When you find hidden the one that seeks to harm, you'll call.*

The hidden one that seeks to harm. Sinhye.

Junu cursed under his breath. And he took out his phone to call the number.

48

JUNU SAT ON the bench at the bus stop, glancing up and down the road every time a car approached. It was late enough that he'd missed rush hour, but early enough that the sun still hung low in the sky. Junu wondered, not for the first time, what he was doing here. But like every other time, he reminded himself that there was only one day left to help Miyoung. He had to do something. And he waited some more as he tapped the business card against his leg.

"You're prompt."

The woman was younger than he'd been expecting, but perhaps still old enough to be called a halmeoni. She had white streaks in her black hair. Her face was so thin that her cheekbones were prominent under her tan skin. There was something vaguely familiar about her, but Junu couldn't quite put his finger on it.

"I've never gotten such an . . . interesting message before," Junu said, still trying to place the woman in his memory and drawing a frustrating blank. "I hope you weren't breaking any juvenile labor laws."

"I heard you like to use humor as a way to shield yourself. Good to know my sources are accurate." The woman sat beside Junu on the bench.

"Why don't you give me your message instead of wasting both of our time?"

"You seek answers," she said.

When she didn't continue, Junu asked, "Do you have any?"

"You seek something you lost."

This piqued Junu's interest, and he sat up straighter. "Do you know where my bangmangi is?"

The woman chuckled. "I know how you do business, dokkaebi. And I know that you don't give anything up for free. Neither do I."

Junu chuckled. Whether or not he trusted this woman, he could at least respect her.

"What's the cost of your information?" Junu asked; money was no problem for him.

"The cost is a trade."

"What kind of trade?" Junu asked, suspicion blooming.

"The fox spirit for your bangmangi."

"And what do you want with Sinhye?"

"Not me—my family's sansin."

"Your family?"

Now the woman turned to face him, and at that angle, with that look in her eyes, he knew why she seemed familiar. "You're descended from that shaman. The one who turned me."

"She was my ancestor. And my family has faithfully served that sansin for centuries."

"Then why are you here? That sansin is not a fan of mine."

"I'm just delivering a message. You met my emo the last time you went to visit our mountain. She'll wait for you by the cave tomorrow. If you still seek your bangmangi, then she will take you to have an audience with the sansin. But in return, he wants the fox spirit."

"There's a bit of a problem," Junu said. "That fox spirit is currently possessing my friend. If I give her to you, I want her removed from his body first."

"If she is possessing a human, then she should be expelled soon enough," the shaman said.

Junu shook his head. "No, he's an ideal vessel for her."

The shaman hummed in concern. "How long has she been possessing him?"

"For almost three days."

"So you must sever her bond to the body," the shaman said. "There is a way if you're willing to pay the price."

"What price?" Junu asked.

"It requires a sacrifice."

"Like a life for a life?" Junu asked, wondering if he could do it, if he could bring himself to kill again, even if it meant saving Jihoon.

"No, not that simple. The soul you wish to sever from her vessel is immortal, so the soul you must sacrifice has to be immortal, too."

"Immortal," Junu repeated slowly.

"Yes, to cut the immortal spirit out of your friend, another immortal spirit must cut its ties to the world of the living. An even trade."

"Even trade," Junu murmured. And he knew exactly how to pay back his debt to Miyoung. How to save Jihoon. How to make sure Somin didn't lose her best friend.

He had to die.

49

JUNU WAS QUIET when he returned. Using a back door that no one knew about but him to avoid any unwanted questions as he made his way to the bedroom door surrounded by bujeoks. When he opened it, he wasn't surprised to see Sinhye sitting on the edge of the bed as if she'd been waiting for him.

"Hello, lover." Sinhye flashed a sharp smile.

"We need to talk," Junu said, closing the door behind him and flicking the lock.

"Of course." She patted the bed beside him. But instead Junu sat in the armchair across the room.

"I have a deal for you."

"Ah, I was wondering when we'd get to this part."

"Fine, if you don't want to hear the deal, I can go." Junu started to leave, but Sinhye stood up quickly.

"You might as well tell me," she said.

He heard curiosity in her voice and knew he'd piqued her interest. "I'll help you get revenge. I'll help you kill the sansin."

Now Sinhye's eyes hardened. She became completely still, like she was waiting for the trap. "And what makes you think I want that?"

"Because you want revenge against those of us who trapped you. But you never thought that you could go up against a mountain god. Not with that mortal body. I can help you."

Junu had thought this through his whole walk home. There were two things at stake here: his bangmangi and Jihoon. He had to be very careful how he orchestrated this dance. Sinhye had to come with him to the mountain if he was going to trade her for the bangmangi, but she couldn't know about the second part of the plan or else she might try to run or hurt Jihoon's body.

"What do you have that could kill a sansin?"

Junu hesitated. If he said it now, there would be no going back. But he knew he needed to do anything to convince her to come with him. If she didn't come, his whole plan would fall apart. "Dokkaebi fire."

Now Sinhye looked truly surprised for the first time. "Why would you use that, after what it did to your family?"

"How do you know about that?" Junu asked, surprise distracting him from his mission.

"Spirits talk. And I was trapped in the land of the spirits for a long time. Your mother and father were not restful souls. They lingered a long time on their hate. Perhaps they linger still."

Junu truly hoped Sinhye was just trying to mess with him. He had no idea what would happen to his soul when he died, but he knew he didn't want to meet the vengeful spirits of his parents if and when that happened.

"And why would you do such a dangerous thing? That's not like my cowardly Junu."

"You don't know what I'm like anymore. Do you want my help or not?"

"I still don't know why you want to give it."

"Because I hate that sansin as much as you do. He wasn't kind to me either back then. Plus." Junu paused. This part was delicate, and he needed to be careful. "That sansin has my bangmangi and I need it back."

"So, what? We get your dokkaebi staff and I get my revenge?" Sinhye sounded like she wasn't quite buying Junu's story. He didn't really blame her. They'd both betrayed each other. They both had proven they weren't to be trusted.

"Pretty much, and if it doesn't work, you can just go back to your original plan of making me miserable."

"You always were persuasive." Sinhye chuckled. "This sounds like fun."

o o o

Junu walked through the dark garage, bypassing the bright yellow Porsche. It was a beauty, but it wasn't what he wanted right now. This wasn't the time for being flashy. Not tonight. He pressed the key fob of a staid black Hyundai sedan. And as the headlights flashed, they lit up a dark figure.

He bit back a yelp but couldn't quite slow his speeding pulse.

"Hyuk," Junu said. "What are you doing here?"

"Whatever you're planning," Hyuk said. "You shouldn't do it."

"There really isn't any other option. I'm doing what I must to close the tear."

"You shouldn't give your life for this," Hyuk said.

"And why do you think that I'm risking my life?" Junu asked.

"I don't know your plan, but I know what the result will be." Hyuk held out a worn leather notebook.

"Is that what I think it is?" Junu eyed the journal.

"My list. The souls I must reap. And five minutes ago, your name appeared."

Junu shook his head. "Maybe it will change."

Hyuk moved closer so he could study Junu. "You don't sound surprised."

"What? Of course I'm surprised. It's not every day a jeoseung saja warns a guy he's about to die."

"Yes, that's true. Which means you should be much more upset."

"I guess I'm just a really cool guy," Junu said, trying to shrug off Hyuk's suspicions.

"What are you planning?"

"I told you, it's fine. It's going to work."

"Yes, I believe it will. I believe that whatever your plan is, you *want* to die in the end."

Junu's pulse leapt at the accusation, and he tried to step around to get to his car. But the reaper shifted, blocking his path.

"That's ridiculous," Junu said. "You know me. I'm always out for myself first. Why would I want to die?"

"You know, don't you," Hyuk said. "The price it will take to remove her soul from that human body."

Junu realized he might as well come clean. Hyuk was a reaper, which meant when he was focused on something, there was no deterring him. "You knew how to do it, and you didn't tell me. Why?"

"Because you're different now. For as long as I knew you, you always looked out for yourself first, but that's changed. I don't know if it's that human girl or that gumiho. But a part of you cares so much for them that I worried you'd do what you're about to do."

"It's my decision," Junu said, trying to move to the car again. Hyuk stopped him with a hand to the shoulder.

"Please don't do this. I do not want to reap your soul."

"When you come for my soul, can I give you something to deliver for me?"

Hyuk huffed. "That's not my job."

"I know, but I need you to deliver it for me anyway. Miyoung needs her bead back, and you need her to get it to close the tear," Junu said. "I'm trusting you, old friend." He stepped toward the car again, and this time the reaper let him.

50

SOMIN HAD ALMOST gotten used to the sleek kitchen in Junu's apartment. She at least knew how to work the complicated espresso machine now. It was still early enough that everyone was sleeping, but Somin couldn't, she was too anxious. She wanted to figure out a new plan, to find Miyoung's bead, to get Sinhye out of Jihoon. To help her friends. But no matter how she'd turned things over in her head, she couldn't find a solution. This supernatural world had too many secrets. She needed Junu's help, his knowledge, his resources. She wouldn't give up on her friends.

She carefully carried the steaming coffee to the other side of the apartment. Slowly opening the bedroom door, she knocked lightly.

"Junu?" she whispered, moving to the bed quietly. But as she approached, she realized it was empty.

"He left," a voice said behind her.

Somin let out a shout, dropping the mug. It shattered, splashing coffee all over the pristine rug. Somin glared at the reaper who now stood at the foot of the bed, pressing a hand to her skipping heart. "You have to warn someone before you do that. Unless you're trying to give me a heart attack and reap my soul."

"No, I would never influence a person's death if it wasn't integral to keep the order of things."

"What?" Somin frowned. "No, it was a joke—" She shook her head. "You know what, never mind. Where did Junu go?"

"He's in danger. And you need to hold on to him."

Her heart skipped a beat at the ominous warning, but she took a steadying breath. "What kind of danger?"

"I shouldn't be here. We do not interfere in the affairs of the living. I almost didn't come. But he'll die if you don't hold on to him."

"How?" Somin asked.

"He thinks that he can sacrifice himself to help your friend. I believe he thinks it's what he deserves."

Somin shook her head. "I don't understand."

"He and Sinhye are going to meet with the sansin that cursed them both."

"He wouldn't do that. Junu's too smart for that," Somin said.

"The sansin has his bangmangi. And I believe he has a plan to sacrifice himself."

"Now I know you're lying. Junu would never risk his life like this." But the empty bed seemed like glaring evidence.

"He's learned the way to cut Sinhye out of your friend. With the sacrifice of an immortal soul. His soul."

Somin stopped, finally looked at the jeoseung saja. There was a steadfastness about Hyuk that told her the reaper was telling the truth.

She slammed into the other room. It was empty, too. Sinhye was gone.

"Miyoung-ah!" Somin shouted, running into the living room. Miyoung was already on her feet.

"What's the matter? Why are you making so much noise?"

"They're gone. They're both gone!"

"How? Why?"

"He said Junu's going to sacrifice himself." Somin turned, but Hyuk was gone. She'd thought he was right behind her.

"You need to slow down. You need to explain it to me."

When Somin did, Miyoung cursed. "That stupid dokkaebi. Trying to martyr himself because he thinks he owes a debt."

"I don't care why he's doing it. We need to stop him," Somin insisted.

"Okay, we should leave immediately if we want to catch up."

"How? We don't know how long he's been gone. And we don't have a car." Somin felt her throat tighten with frustration.

"A car," Miyoung murmured. "I think I can help with that."

"You have a car?" Somin asked. She didn't even know that Miyoung had a driver's license.

"No, but Junu has cars, lots of them. And he loves fast ones."

"Yeah, except we don't know where Junu keeps his cars."

"Well," Miyoung said, drawing out the word, and she shrugged as if she just couldn't help herself. "When you live with someone you don't fully trust, you tend to snoop. And in snooping, I found out where his storage garage is."

Somin laughed. "Well, I guess, thank the gods for your paranoia."

"Come on," Miyoung said. "Every minute that passes, they gain more of a lead."

51

KOREA IS A country of mountains. Folktales were written about their rocky facades. The mountain that had ruled Junu's life had no such tales associated with it. It was not named in stories or poems like Guksabong or Baektu. But to Junu, this mountain was the genesis of his fate. The origin of his curse. And now it was where his long and twisting life would end.

Perhaps, knowing that, Junu should have taken his time with every step. Remembered the trees and how they climbed up the rocky mountainside. How the air became thinner as he climbed. How small rocks kicked up against his ankles, lodging themselves in his tennis shoes.

But Junu didn't concentrate on any of those things because he was too aware of the minutes ticking by. How they seemed to go faster than normal. How they might be the last ones he had on this earth.

"This place," Sinhye murmured.

Junu was surprised. They'd been silent the whole drive. And they'd been hiking for two hours without even acknowledging each other. He'd leaned into the silence. It was easier than having to talk to Sinhye, knowing that he planned to betray her. That after he got back his bangmangi and summoned Miyoung's bead, he was going to ask the sansin to take his life in exchange for pulling Sinhye from Jihoon's body.

"Are you okay?" Junu asked carefully.

"I'm fine," Sinhye mused. "It actually feels more comfortable here than being in the city. I don't know how you live like that. So much noise and bustle. It would give me a headache."

"You get used to it," Junu said. "It becomes white noise after a while."

"What's white noise?" Sinhye asked.

Junu just shook his head; he wasn't in the mood to give Sinhye a lesson on modern idioms.

"Does it bother you being back?" Sinhye asked. "I can't imagine you have fond memories of this place either."

Junu shrugged. He didn't want to have a heart-to-heart with Sinhye. He didn't want to be flooded with memories of his past. He just wanted to do what he came to do, and find some kind of peace. Whatever that looked like.

"I didn't ask them to change you," Sinhye said. And Junu thought, at first, that he'd misheard her.

"Didn't ask who?"

"That shaman. The sansin."

"Bbeongchiji ma," Junu muttered.

"I'm telling the truth," Sinhye insisted.

"Then why did they do this to me?" Junu asked. He didn't believe a word she said.

"It was to punish me."

Now Junu did stop. He stared at Sinhye, trying to discern any deceit in her face. But he couldn't find it. Was it because she wore the face of a friend?

"Why would he use me to punish you?"

"For daring to love you instead of him. He could have trapped me without you, but he wanted you to do it so I would feel what it was like to be betrayed by the one person I loved."

Junu shook his head; he didn't want to hear this. Didn't want to feel it squeezing his heart. "What we had wasn't love."

"It's all I knew of love," Sinhye said. "Before you, I'd known lies. I'd known greed. I'd known lust. But you were my first taste of love. That's why it hurt so much. Your betrayal. It's why I hate you so much now."

There. That was the first thing Junu believed. And it helped harden his resolve. He was doing the right thing. He just had to forge ahead and get it done. "Well, I guess we're both getting our revenge, then. Come on," he said, starting up the path again. "We've got a ways to go before we reach the cave."

52

SOMIN WOKE AS the car jerked to a stop. Miyoung wasn't the best driver in the world, but she'd gotten them there in one piece.

Dread filled Somin as she climbed out of the Porsche and stared up at the mountain. "We have to hike up this?"

"Yup. Come on, we have a lot of ground to make up," Miyoung said. She shaded her eyes from the sun, which was rising higher into the sky. It felt like it was moving too fast. Like time was racing against them.

Somin had tried to practice in her head what she wanted to say to Junu but hadn't come up with anything yet. She wanted to yell at him and hug him at the same time. She still wasn't sure how she felt. A part of her was so pissed that Junu would do this. That he wouldn't even talk to the rest of them before making this decision. But another part of her was so grateful he would sacrifice himself for Jihoon.

"Are you okay?" Miyoung asked, and Somin realized Miyoung had been talking.

"I'll be fine when we find them."

"Then let's get going."

53

THE TREES FELT more ominous on this climb than the last. Perhaps because Junu knew that they'd likely become the guardians of his grave. What an odd thing to walk toward. Death. He remembered a time when he'd wished for it every day. But eventually, he'd learned to drown out that depression by living however he pleased. Still it never made him truly happy.

It was only now, in the last few months, that he'd begun to feel like he was truly living. It felt like more of a life than the last few centuries. More of one than when he'd been human. This time he'd spent with this strange group of people who had somehow come to mean the world to him. Who he'd sacrifice everything for. It was perhaps the only way he knew to give a final purpose to his wayward life. He'd done no good while he was on this earth. So at least he could do one good thing as he left it.

Junu stopped and reached into his pack.

"Why are we stopping?" Sinhye asked.

"Because we have to prepare."

"What is there to prepare? We just see the sansin, get your staff, and then you burn him to ashes. It shouldn't be that hard."

"He has to trust us first. The dokkaebi fire won't hurt him unless I can get close enough," Junu said, pulling duct tape and rope out of his bag.

"I don't know what you think we're here for. But you better put that away."

"He won't believe you came willingly. He'll think something's wrong if you just walk up with me."

Sinhye scowled, but she didn't rebut his statement. She glanced up the mountain, then back toward the way they came. Like she was considering just leaving him.

Junu practically held his breath. Maybe he was pushing it. Maybe he was foolish to believe she'd go along with this. What would he do if she left? Then, with a sigh, she held out her hands.

He started to wrap duct tape around her wrists.

"Not so tight!" Sinhye complained.

"It has to look convincing," Junu said. And if he took a bit of pleasure in wrapping another tight band of tape, then he wouldn't let it show. Plus, he wasn't sure how strong she was. Taking the rope, he looped it over the tape, then around her waist, effectively securing her wrists to her own torso.

"Okay, we're good," he said, holding a bit of rope like a lead.

"Well, let's go, then," Sinhye said with an expectant look. "Since we're prepared and all now."

They walked more slowly as Sinhye struggled to balance herself with her hands tied. Twice she almost stumbled, and when Junu tried to help her, she elbowed him away. *Fine, let her do it herself,* he thought.

The trees thinned a bit. Junu began to recognize markers. And too soon, they reached the meeting place. Junu half hoped the shaman wouldn't be where she'd promised. But she stood at the entrance of the cave, dressed in a simple linen hanbok. Around her stood columns of rocks stacked on top of each other. Shrines to the mountain god.

"I thought perhaps you wouldn't come," she said, and it didn't sound like she'd have cared either way.

"I told your niece I would be here," Junu said.

"I'm not foolish enough to trust a dokkaebi's word," the shaman replied.

Instead of heading into the cave as Junu had expected, she walked past it. He followed her, Sinhye stumbling behind him. "I see you've secured the gumiho," the shaman said. "Are you sure that's enough?"

"She's in a human body. It limits her," Junu said, keeping his voice steady, his face still.

The shaman nodded as she moved through the forest. They walked almost a kilometer before the shaman stopped.

"Is the sansin coming here?" Junu asked.

"I will go alert my sansin that you have arrived. You wait here."

"Will he be here soon?" Junu asked.

"He'll take as long as he takes. It is not our job to tell him when to appear."

"The perks of being a god," Junu quipped with a wry smile.

"Be careful with your tongue, dokkaebi. My sansin does not take to humor well."

"Don't worry, I remember," Junu couldn't help saying.

With a final scowl in his direction, the shaman disappeared into the woods.

54

MIYOUNG STRAINED TO keep her pace. It was breakneck, but it was necessary. They had no way of knowing how far ahead Junu was. Or if he'd yet encountered the sansin. Miyoung wanted to be angry. But she couldn't bring herself fully to the emotion. It wasn't so long ago she'd have done something like this. Charged into something to protect Jihoon. She learned that she'd been foolish to keep everything to herself the way Junu had now done. She hoped that when they found Junu, he'd listen to reason.

And if he didn't listen, they'd find another way, because Miyoung wasn't going to lose another person she cared about.

Don't risk yourself for his mistakes. Yena's voice was a whisper in her ear, but she ignored it.

She knew what she had to do. Knowing what Junu was willing to sacrifice, it made her see things clearly. She'd been convinced that losing Yena meant that she'd lost pieces of herself, too, watched them break free and float away. But she realized now that what had been breaking free was the facade she used to hide herself away from the world.

Jihoon had broken through it. So had Somin and even Junu.

She welcomed it at first. Let herself believe that she could live a more fulfilling life as a mortal.

Then her mother died.

And she felt guilty for hoping for a different life. Her mother had worked so hard to provide Miyoung with security and safety. Miyoung tried to free herself of that life, and Yena died for it. When all her mother wanted was to protect Miyoung. So she'd allowed herself to be buried in guilt. It was easier than facing the pain of losing her mother. She decided that what she needed to do was hold on to everything of Yena. That's the only way she could survive. That's the only way she could live. But the harder she tried to hold on to her old life, the more it dragged her down.

So she would let go. She had to. Even if it tore out a piece of her, at least she'd still be alive in the end. And she'd figure out a way to survive the pain. Survival was what she was best at.

Her footing slipped on loose rubble and she almost face-planted into a sapling. She caught herself just in time. Her weakened state was going to be a problem if things got messy today. She wished, not for the first time, to have all of her old gumiho abilities again.

Taking another step forward, Miyoung suddenly froze. Something raced down her spine. A strange sensation that felt similar to when the moon hung in the sky above. A prick of power. Energy.

"What is it?" Somin asked, coming up beside her.

Miyoung held up a hand to quiet Somin. She listened intently, annoyed that her hearing was so muted now. It felt like being underwater sometimes compared to the heightened hearing she'd had before. But she finally picked it up, a strange humming sound.

"We're close to something."

"Is it them?" Somin asked.

"I'm not sure," Miyoung whispered. She turned, trying to catch her bearings, then faced east. "This way. It's coming from this direction."

55

MIYOUNG LED THEM to a cave that would have been almost impossible to find behind the thick trees that grew around it. Stone altars were piled up. And Miyoung knelt beside them, searching the ground.

"There are footsteps here," she said.

"Really?" Somin said. "How can you tell?"

"I just can. I've spent a lot of time in the forest. I can track using methods other than my senses. Thank the gods for that now."

"Was it them?"

"The shoe sizes look right. There were three people, though, not two. One set is smaller, almost shuffling. Someone older?"

"Would it have been the sansin?"

"I'm not sure, but it doesn't look like there was a fight; they left of their own free will. They followed the smaller steps. They're going that way," Miyoung said, standing again and facing a small path.

"We'll find them," Somin said, and Miyoung wasn't sure if she was reassuring Miyoung or herself.

"I can't help but wonder if I'd been kinder to Junu if he wouldn't have been driven to this extreme," Miyoung said. "Maybe if I'd just forgiven him when he asked me to, maybe he would have come to us first . . ."

Somin shook her head. "You can't blame yourself."

"I'm not blaming myself," Miyoung reassured her. "But I still wonder."

"The last thing Junu said to me was that he loved me," Somin said. Miyoung's eyes widened in surprise. "I didn't say it back," Somin admitted. "I guess I wonder if he'd have confided in me if I'd been able to say it back."

"We'll find him," Miyoung said, turning down the path. As they followed the trail, she asked, "What's the plan?"

"We find Junu, and if he's still alive, I'll throttle him," Somin said.

Miyoung laughed. "Okay, and then after that?"

"I'm working on it," Somin said. "We obviously need to get your bead back still." She paused a moment, a strange expression crossing her face. "Sinhye told me something at the restaurant. I didn't remember it at first because of everything that happened, and I'm not sure if it's true. But if it is, then I think it might be important."

Trepidation filled Miyoung. She wasn't ready for any more bad news, not right now.

"What is it?"

"Sinhye said that if a gumiho doesn't feed for a hundred days, she can sever her ties to her bead and become fully human."

"I haven't fed for even longer, and I am still connected."

"Yeah, but Junu said that you're in some kind of stasis since your bead is in the Between. Once you're reunited with your bead, you can cut your bond with it. You can become fully human."

"I never really thought that was possible," Miyoung admitted. "Do you think cutting my bond to my bead will hurt?"

"I'll be with you the whole time," Somin said, squeezing her shoulder.

Miyoung gave her a weak smile. "I don't want to think about this right now. We have more important things to take care of, like saving Jihoon. And stopping Junu from making an irreversible mistake."

Somin nodded. "The reaper said that the way to save Jihoon is to sacrifice an immortal soul. I think I might have an idea for that."

"Okay? What is it?"

"Since you can still sense energy, do you think you can still siphon it?"

Miyoung lifted her brow, surprised. "I suppose I could, since I haven't severed my ties to my bead. Why?"

"I think we're going to have to kill a god."

56

"YOU SURE YOU won't renege?" Sinhye asked. She was sitting beside Junu on the ground, shadows growing long as the day trailed on. If the shaman didn't come back soon, it would be too dark to see anything.

"I don't want to talk to you right now," he said, making nonsense designs in the dirt with a stick.

"Oh, don't worry. I'm not trying to reopen old wounds. I'm here to tell you that you need to keep up your end of the bargain. You always did let your emotions and insecurities get the best of you. If you do that now, then we're both as good as dead."

That's exactly what I'm hoping for, Junu thought.

The trees rustled as the shaman walked out of the forest again. Alone.

"What's going on?" Junu asked, searching the trees for another figure. Where was the sansin?

"Follow me," she said.

So they followed her up the path until they arrived at a small clearing where a low, flat stone stood surrounded by trees.

Junu recognized it as a natural altar, the type used for ceremonies where offerings were made to the sansin. When he was a boy, he used to participate in them himself, bringing wine and meat to offer to their local god.

The shaman pulled something from her sleeve. A yellow

paper with red writing. A bujeok. She approached Sinhye, who bared her teeth in a growl.

"Don't come closer if you want to keep your hands," she warned.

But the shaman did not hesitate; she reached out and pressed the bujeok to Sinhye's chest. The letters seemed to glow a moment as it stuck to her.

Sinhye grunted, twisting and turning like she was held in place by chains.

"You bound her? To what?"

"To me," the shaman said. "My master approaches."

She turned to face the north.

Junu did as well, and soon he made out the outline of a man in the forest beyond. He had the look of a man approaching the century mark, but Junu knew better than to underestimate him because of that. He was a god; his physical form was in no way an indicator of his power. He had a long white beard and was robed in a traditional hanbok more common two hundred years ago. Silk and satin sewn together to form a robe-like top that mostly hid white pants. But despite rubbing against low shrubs, no dirt or leaves stuck to the pristine material.

He rode on the back of a giant orange tiger. Junu wondered if it was the same tiger he'd met all those centuries ago.

"My master has decided to grant you an audience," the shaman announced.

Junu stepped forward and folded in a ninety-degree bow. "I've come to accept your deal."

"You are brave to return to this place." The sansin's voice reverberated, like it was echoing through a canyon instead of spoken out of the lips of a frail old man.

Junu reminded himself again that this god was stronger than he could even fathom. And he had a short temper. Junu had to tread lightly here.

"I am hoping that because enough time has passed, and I've reflected on my past, that you might be lenient with me," Junu said.

"I will consider it. I hear I have something you want." The sansin dismounted so gracefully, it was almost like he floated to the ground. The tiger bent, its head lowering in a bow before it loped back into the forest.

"I've brought the fox spirit, as you asked," Junu said. "In return, your shaman said I can ask for my bangmangi back."

"I see," the sansin said.

When he didn't continue, Junu cleared his throat. It seemed the sansin wasn't looking to make conversation. "But we also have an ailing friend. The one that the fox spirit possesses."

Sinhye stiffened beside Junu. This was it. If he did this, there would be no going back.

"And why should that be a concern to me?" the sansin asked.

He swallowed to wet his suddenly dry throat. He was used to bluffing and talking his way in and out of things, but this felt completely different. The last time he'd met this god, he'd been incapacitated with a single flick of the sansin's wrist. If Junu wasn't careful, would he end up with his soul trapped for a millennium like Sinhye? Maybe the punishment would be fitting after how he'd squandered his existence. But he couldn't lose courage now.

"She has bonded to this body, but it is not hers to take. I ask that you save the life of my friend. I have brought all the tools I was told you require to cut her from this vessel."

The sansin let out a low rumbling laugh that seemed to shake the trees around them. "The soul you wish to sever is immortal; to do that, you need to sacrifice another immortal soul."

"Exactly," Junu said, stepping forward on shaky legs. He really hoped this plan worked. "I have an immortal soul. Sacrifice me."

57

SOMIN WONDERED, NOT for the first time or even the tenth time, if this plan was bound to fail. Well, it seemed likely as she made her way quietly through the thick foliage. But it's all they had. So she'd have to at least try.

Somin and Miyoung had parted ways down the path, thinking they'd make less noise if they weren't together. Plus, it was smarter for them to attack separately. They didn't have the strength to go up against a sansin, so they'd use their smarts.

Miyoung had fought her on this, saying she'd be better suited to initiate a sneak attack. But it had to be Somin. It was something Sinhye had said, actually. That Somin wasn't involved in this world. That she didn't belong here. And if she didn't belong, then no one would be looking for her. She could more effectively attack from behind while Miyoung persuaded Junu to help her attack from the front in a pincer move.

Somin prayed again this would work as she heard voices. Someone spoke in a voice so low she could only make out its timbre, not the words. But the one that replied was Junu. She was close.

58

"YOU WOULD SACRIFICE yourself for this human?" the sansin asked, his eyes moving between Jihoon and Junu.

"Baesin," Sinhye said under her breath. "This was your plan all along. You never planned to kill him at all, you coward."

Junu ignored her.

"I would, but I ask first that you return my staff, for I am the only one who can wield it and we must retrieve a fox bead in order to fix a tear between the world of the living and the world Between."

"Ah, so you know the source of this tear between the worlds," the sansin said. "I have felt it."

"Then you know how dire it is and that we must fix it immediately."

"Why would I care about such things? The spirits cannot touch me here on my mountain."

Junu paused a moment, surprised by the response, but he was nothing if not quick with his mind. "But the humans who pray to you will be affected, and soon they will stop coming. Aren't there so few left already?"

Junu held his breath waiting for a reply. This was a gamble; it could just as easily offend the sansin as motivate him.

"Fine, I will return your bangmangi." The sansin held out his hand.

Junu stepped forward, not daring to look at Sinhye as he left her side.

The old man no longer looked so frail this close. Perhaps it was the aura around him that Junu could feel, like cold waves. It was power and strength so thick that it felt suffocating. This god was old, and the older a god was, the more powerful he was.

"Tell me," the sansin murmured softly so only Junu could hear. "Why should I trust one who has been willing to betray the woman he loves? Twice."

Junu wasn't expecting this line of questioning. "I'm not sure if I could call it love," he answered honestly. "Not anymore."

"So it wasn't love that stole from me what I coveted? She chose you over me because of a trivial dalliance?" The sansin's voice rose to a booming roar.

"We did love each other once. But things change with time. One as ancient as you should understand." Junu bowed his head to show deference and to hide the fear in his eyes. After centuries of negotiating, he knew that a show of fear often lost you the deal.

"Perhaps you are right about that," the sansin said, his voice calm again. "But you would do well to remember that I am the god of this mountain. My word is law here."

"Of course," Junu said.

"I give this back because its magic cannot hurt me. So do not think you can betray me and use it against me." The sansin flicked his wrist and a staff appeared. It beckoned Junu, a soft song on the wind, like a siren's voice calling to wayward sailors.

He reached out, his fingers itching to take hold. This all seemed too easy, he thought. He almost expected the god to pull back, to say that there was another price to pay. But he was allowed to take hold of the staff.

"Now, summon your bead and I will free your friend. But I warn you, if you change your mind, then I will take your life anyway and leave your friend to suffer as I take my prize," the sansin said, his greedy eyes shifting to Sinhye.

Junu gripped the staff with both hands and closed his eyes. He pictured Miyoung in his mind. Pictured her yeowu guseul. The shining bead that was like a large pearl. Small but powerful. He could feel a pull, a connection through space. He could feel the wind pulse around him, like magic sat heavy on it. His pulse lifted. The air sizzled. He could practically reach out and grab the bead. He almost held out his hand, when it faded.

"It did not work," the sansin said.

"I don't think I can find it by myself," Junu murmured, then cursed under his breath. "I'm reaching beyond this world, so I need help getting to it. If you could just give me some time . . ."

"I am tired of waiting," the sansin said. "If you cannot find the bead, then we will move on. This is the part I am looking forward to, because it is the part where you die."

"No," Miyoung said as she stepped out of the forest. "No one dies today." Then her eyes shifted to the sansin. "Except you."

59

JUNU STARED AT Miyoung in shock. "What is this?" the sansin roared.

Miyoung took off, aiming for the sansin. But the god intercepted her and flung her away.

Junu dove forward, grabbing the sansin in a headlock. But the sansin pulled free, swinging out at Junu, who dodged and grabbed ahold of the god's arm.

Before the sansin could buck again, Somin came flying out of the forest. She latched herself on to the sansin's back, beating at his head with her fists. It distracted the god enough that Junu was able to solidify his hold.

"What are you doing here?" Junu shouted.

"I'm saving your ungrateful ass," Somin said.

Junu almost lost his grip. She had really come here for him?

Miyoung had recovered by then and appeared beside Junu. "Hold him still," she said.

He wanted to give a pithy retort, but he was too out of breath from holding the sansin in place. So he just watched, sweat stinging his eyes, as Miyoung pressed her palm to the sansin's chest.

"Junu!" Sinhye shouted behind him. He turned to see the shaman holding a knife to her throat. Sinhye was still frozen in place by the bujeok, unable to fight back. In that moment of distraction, the sansin grabbed Junu's shoulder. Before he could pull free, Junu felt his flesh tighten, first along his arm, then racing down his torso and to his toes. It was like he was being stretched by an invisible force.

He screamed as agony burst along his limbs like sparklers.

The sansin lifted his fists to slam onto Junu. A final killing blow.

But before he could, the air shifted. It thickened. Waves of heat started to waft around them.

The sansin stopped mid-swing. And his hand loosened. Junu fell to the dirt, his muscles burning.

Miyoung stood above him, so focused on the sansin that her eyes looked dark as midnight. Sweat beaded on her brow from the effort.

The air sparked with energy. Then the sansin let out a roar as vapors sifted from his chest, waving around Miyoung's out-stretched arm, writhing around her like snakes made of smoke.

She was taking his gi.

"Wait," Junu shouted. "His energy is too strong. It will over-whelm you!"

"Just help Jihoon," Miyoung called, her voice strained as she focused on her hold of the sansin.

He threw himself at the shaman, twisting her arm so the knife fell from her hand. But Junu, still weakened from the san-sin's attack, overbalanced and they tumbled to the ground. Sinhye screamed as she also fell.

Junu rolled away from the shaman and crawled toward Sin-hye to pull the bujeok off. But the shaman grabbed him by the hair, yanking his head back.

Stars exploded behind his eyes as he pulled away. He felt the rip of his hair in the shaman's unyielding grip.

Behind him, the sansin let out an echoing yell that shook the trees so hard panicked birds took flight, peppering the sky.

"Junu! Get this damn thing off me," Sinhye said through gritted teeth.

Junu reached her just as a roar sounded behind him.

He spun around in time to see a flash of orange emerge from the forest. Claws and teeth leapt toward him. And he flattened himself on the ground beside Sinhye. The tiger went sailing over them, its claws barely missing Junu's nose.

Clambering to his feet, Junu turned to face the giant cat.

The shaman screamed and lunged at Junu, and he was caught off guard, with all of his focus on the tiger. He grabbed the shaman's hands, barely stopping her nails from gouging out his eyes. He heard the low growl of the tiger behind him and spun around, hauling the shaman with him. The tiger leapt in that moment. Its teeth biting into the shaman's shoulder instead of Junu's throat.

She screamed as she went down under the weight of the tiger, and Junu wheeled out of the way. He turned away from the attack, unable to stomach the sight.

"Bring her to me," Miyoung shouted, holding her hand out toward Sinhye.

Junu didn't understand at first, but when he saw the wave of energy transferring between the sansin and Miyoung, he finally realized they meant to sacrifice the sansin's soul to sever Sinhye's hold on Jihoon. They meant to save him without sacrificing Junu.

Now that Miyoung had a solid hold of the sansin, Somin leapt down from his back and raced toward Sinhye, picking up the shaman's discarded knife.

"Come on," she shouted. But Junu could just stare at her.

"Why are you doing this? Why are you risking your lives for this? It's too dangerous. You should have just let me—"

"You really think we'd let you sacrifice yourself without a fight? We aren't willing to lose anyone else we care about. So make yourself useful and help me carry her," Somin said.

"You'd betray me this way," Sinhye spit out.

"You don't belong in this world," Junu said, lifting her into his arms. But she lashed out, clawing at his face.

Junu screamed as he fell back. He rolled across the dirt and came face-to-face with the shaman. Her skin disfigured by claws and teeth. Her eyes open and unseeing. The bujeok on Sinhye had been binding her to the shaman, but now the shaman was dead. Then where was the tiger?

Junu had stood, calling out for Somin, when he caught the flash of movement.

He turned in time to see the tiger leap forward. Junu dove out of its path, barely gaining his footing again when the tiger changed course, but not toward Junu—toward Somin and Sinhye, who were struggling a meter away.

"Ya!" Junu shouted, throwing a stone that bounced from the tiger's shoulder. The beast snarled, its eyes turning to Junu. "Come and get me," he challenged as he took off into the forest. But the tiger was fast, and Junu soon reached a drop-off, the ground becoming too steep to run. If he went any farther, he'd fall. And keep falling.

Junu heard the swift steps of the tiger behind him. And he shifted to face the creature as it bore down on him. He'd only get one chance at this. It took everything in Junu not to dart away. Not to dive out of the tiger's path too soon. He knew that if he did, then the giant cat would have too much time to course correct.

So he waited as the tiger raced toward him. Fangs bared. Claws sharp. And when all he could see was fur and teeth, he jumped to the side. The tiger sailed past him. Its roar a fading echo as it fell. Junu scrambled toward the edge, glancing over. He could see the tiger tumbling along the steep decline.

"Somin! Hurry!" Miyoung's voice called. A distant plea.

Junu raced back to them, praying he'd find them in one piece. Praying the sansin hadn't gotten ahold of them.

Miyoung strained as she fought to hold on to the sansin, who writhed and twisted, trying to break free. He'd begun to chant, an old language that sounded like it came from before the time of the three kingdoms.

Somin finally reached Miyoung, dragging Jihoon's limp body behind her.

Miyoung took hold of Jihoon's hand. And the energy that had been wafting around her like smoke began to circle Jihoon, too. The energy pulled at the lines of his body, making him blur, pulling at him until another shape emerged from his back. A ghostly figure with long hair and pale skin. Sinhye.

"It's working," Somin said.

But as Sinhye's soul was pulled from Jihoon's body, smoky figures wafted through the forest. Spirits drawn to this place. Attracted to the approaching death.

Junu thought he saw a face he recognized. A white, gaping expression forming on one of the spirits moving through the forest. "Eomma?" he whispered. He almost faltered at the sight of her.

The sun was almost done setting, and the trees were illuminated in oranges and reds. The light seemed to dance. Like flames. Junu felt his skin heat. Felt his body burn.

"Eomma? Are you really here?" he whispered. But she faded away, sifting back into the shadows.

Junu started toward her, but he wasn't sure if he wanted to follow her or chase her away. He felt his entire being burning, and he stumbled, falling onto his hands and knees. The brush under his hands caught fire. Junu jumped up, letting out a yelp of surprise.

Sinhye's form was almost completely free from Jihoon's body, but Miyoung glanced over at Junu's shout and her concentration was momentarily broken. The sansin let out a guttural shout, and the mountain began to shake. The ground beneath them started to crack and break. Trees falling around them as their roots were yanked from the earth.

And Miyoung was flung back, losing her grip on both the sansin and Jihoon as she was slammed into the ground.

"Miyoung," Somin called a second before the sansin's hand swiped out at her. She danced back and lifted the knife in her other hand. Teeth bared, she crouched.

"Don't," Junu yelled, but it was too late. Somin had launched herself onto the sansin's back. She brought the knife down in an angry arc and lodged it between the sansin's shoulders. He let out a bellow.

"It's not enough. You can't kill a sansin with a human weapon," Junu yelled, but before he could reach them, the sansin dislodged Somin.

Miyoung stumbled onto her feet in time for Somin to crash into her. And both girls went tumbling across the field.

"You would dare to attack a god?" the sansin boomed. "You will be punished for your insolence."

He lifted his hands, and rocks rained down from the cliffs around the girls.

Miyoung cried out as a stone glanced across her temple. Blood seeped from a gash in her forehead.

Another volley fell, and Somin twisted in pain as one hit her in the arm. She fell beside Miyoung, bleeding.

"No!" Junu launched himself at the god, ready to use anything he could, his fists, his teeth.

But the old man turned, his eyes bright as the sun as he plucked Junu up by his neck.

Junu's feet kicked at air as he struggled.

"You have crossed me for the last time. I should have let you die a millennium ago. I turned you for my amusement, but you've become a menace."

Junu's vision blurred. Ringing filled his ears.

The shadows of the forest swam. It made the foliage turn to hazy green smoke. And he saw figures seeping out of the darkness. No, not just figures. They became opaque, faces solidifying. Faces that had haunted his dreams. Faces that looked at him with the same disgust they'd held just moments before they died. Moments before they burned.

Junu stared in horror as his mother stepped out of the shade of the trees.

No, this was impossible. He started to claw more desperately at the sansin's hold. His skin began to tingle, began to heat.

Junu watched as his sisters limped out of the forest, their forms burnt and deformed, as they stood beside their mother.

I'm sorry, he tried to choke out. Surely they were vengeful spirits come to drag him to hell with them.

Fire and death, his mother said, though her lips didn't move. Junu recognized her voice.

I didn't mean to kill you! Junu thought even as he felt that telltale burn start within him, a sweltering heat that began to fill him. *Please know that I never meant to hurt you.*

Fire and death. The end, his nunas chorused together.

I can't. His head spun. He glanced at Somin and Miyoung, lying on the ground mere meters away. *I don't want to hurt them.* His fear filled him like steam. He felt the fire within him turn blistering. Feeding on his fear. *No,* he thought. *I can't.*

It is the only way. Bring fire and death. Bring the end, his mother said, and as stars began to explode behind his eyes, Junu felt sparks race along his limbs. He closed his eyes and concentrated on holding the fire close. He couldn't stop it, but maybe he could control it. He felt it spread over him, the fire growing, brought forth by fear and agony.

And then heard the howl of the sansin as flames burst from his skin, crawling over the god, swallowing him whole.

Junu fell. The ground racing up to meet him. He smelled smoke. He felt the heat of flames, and then he blacked out.

60

JUNU WOKE SLOWLY. His throat burned. His body ached. He blinked his eyes open. They stung, like they'd been dried out by smoke.

The trees loomed above him. The sky was so clear he could see stars blinking above as twilight overtook them. Funny, he hadn't noticed before. He'd been so focused on his mission. But it was a strangely beautiful evening.

He turned his head, leaves sticking to his cheek as he did so. He saw the shaman lying where she'd fallen, and a meter away was his staff, still intact.

"Junu," Somin said.

He sat up and looked at the charred ground around him, a perfect circle, embers still burning dimly. Smoke rose like steam from the blackened ground. And beside him was a pile of burnt robes. Nothing else of the sansin remained.

Somin sat beside him, blood drying on her shirt.

"Somin-ah," he said, reaching out to her. "Are you hurt? Did the fire touch you?"

She shook her head, pushing his hands away. "I'm okay. But Jihoon." Her voice became thick, so she just glanced over.

Junu followed her gaze. Miyoung held an unconscious Jihoon in her arms, fresh blood spreading over his shirt.

61

"WE HAVE TO do something," Miyoung said, trying to stop the bleeding.

"We need to get him to the hospital," Somin said.

Junu limped over. "Let me see it." He shook his head. "The wound isn't deep enough to kill him. But his body is weak after hosting Sinhye's soul."

"What does that mean?" Somin asked.

"It means if you don't separate me from this human, he'll die," Sinhye croaked out.

"Don't try to talk," Junu said. "Save your strength."

"Trust me, that's what I'm trying to do, but you all keep jostling me around and it hurts."

Miyoung shifted to let Sinhye sit on her own. "What are we going to do?"

"We have to get Sinhye out. Having two souls is making Jihoon weak, just like when he had the bead inside of him. It's making it impossible for him to heal right now."

"How the hell are we going to get her out without the sansin?" Somin asked, wiping furiously at tears streaming down her face.

"You know what we're going to do," Junu said.

Somin turned to him, at first confused. Then her face fell. "No. That's not an option."

Warmth radiated through him at her insistence. But it also

worried him. He never thought he'd have the chance to die knowing someone would truly mourn him. But he realized he didn't want that for Somin. He didn't want her to be sad because of him.

"It's for the best," Junu said, making his voice light and conversational. "I've been messing up this whole time, and others are paying the price."

"No," Somin said again. "I can't let you go. Not this soon."

"Maybe we'll meet in the next life," Junu said softly.

"I don't want to wait that long."

"I'll make it worth the wait. I promise." Junu smiled. "In the next life, I'll work my hardest to be a person worthy of you."

Somin shook her head, but she didn't say anything; instead, she held on to him. He worried if she didn't let go, then he'd lose the courage to do what needed to be done.

"Just being yourself makes you worthy."

Now Junu felt the burn of tears behind his eyes, but he held them back. He knew that if she saw him cry, it would only make her hurt worse.

"If I'd known it would make you say such nice things, I'd have gladly sacrificed my soul earlier."

That made Somin choke out a laugh. "Of course you would say something absolutely ridiculous at a time like this."

"Be good," Junu said, leaning close, and gave her a gentle kiss. He could taste the salt of her tears on her lips.

She moved back just a centimeter, so they were only a breath apart, and said, "Don't tell me what to do, Jin Junu."

His laugh was a low rumble. Then he finally let go of Somin, and after a moment of tense hesitation, she let go, too.

"Okay, first things first. Let's call that bead."

"Junu, I can't—" Miyoung began, but he shook his head.

"It doesn't need discussion, I made up my mind."

"This doesn't feel right."

Junu laughed. "Well, you've never really approved of anything I've ever done before."

"Stop it. I'm saying that I don't think you need to do this. We'll find another way."

"Jihoon doesn't have time to wait. And I was the reason you lost your mother. I won't be the reason you lose him, too."

"You're not. I never really thought you were. I was just so angry all the time, and you were an easy target. And my mother." Miyoung paused, taking a deep breath. "My mother made her own choices. That was never on you."

Junu smiled sadly. "Thank you for that. But you're not the only person I've wronged in this life. I've spent it shamefully and now I'm paying that price. It's my price to pay."

He held out the staff. "Grab ahold."

Miyoung hesitated a moment before obeying.

"Now think about your bead. Think about the look of it and the shape of it. Make it solid in your mind."

Miyoung squeezed her eyes shut.

At first nothing happened. And Junu wondered if he'd lost the ability to use the staff. Perhaps he didn't deserve it after shunning it for most of his life. But then the staff seemed to warm. Like a low flow of energy moving through it. And the air beside Miyoung wavered.

It thickened, like a film being laid over the space. Then it congealed and shifted until it started to take shape.

"I thought it was small," Somin whispered behind them. She'd spoken Junu's own thoughts aloud. The bead should be the size of a large pearl. Whatever was forming here was the size of a human, or a beast.

It formed a head and a body that slowly filled with color. Until it became almost whole. Until it became Yena.

"Daughter." Her voice sounded like a thousand whispers emitted as one. "You did it. You've found me again."

62

MIYOUNG'S LEGS SHOOK as she rose. She wanted to do so many things in this moment. Cry in rage, in fear, in joy. She wanted to wrap her arms around the thing with her mother's face, even as she knew it wasn't really her mother, not all of her at least.

"Eomma," she said, her voice shaking. "I'm so sorry. You can't stay."

Yena's beautiful brow furrowed. "What are you saying, Daughter?"

Miyoung shook her head. "You don't belong here. Not anymore. And keeping you here is selfish."

"What if I don't want to go?"

"Be careful," Junu murmured to Miyoung as he stood beside her.

Miyoung nodded and her face became set. "You can't stay," she told her mother. "You have to move on. You have to give me my bead back and leave."

"Bead?" Yena said, and she opened her hands.

Miyoung could have sworn they'd been empty a second before, but now in her left palm lay a luminescent pearl.

"Is that it?" Somin breathed, staring at the bead. Like she'd never seen anything so powerful before. And of course, she hadn't. It was a wondrous sight. The soul of a gumiho.

"Please give it back," Miyoung said.

"No." Yena closed her hand.

"What?" Miyoung asked.

"You shouldn't have it," Yena said, her frown deepening.

That slashed at Miyoung's heart, because it was something she'd always feared, that her mother would not think her worthy of the title gumiho. "It's mine, Mother. I need it."

"No." Yena stepped back.

"If you don't give it to her, then something bad could happen to your daughter," Junu said.

Yena's eyes darted to his, sharp and angry. She growled and retreated another step.

"You are not my ally. You betrayed me."

"Yes, you're right," Junu said. "Loyalty has never been my strong suit. But I'm trying to help your daughter now. Isn't that all you've ever wanted?"

That stopped Yena. Her eyes darted back to Miyoung, and they became soft again. "Daughter. I want you to live."

"Then please, give me back my bead." Miyoung held out her hand.

Yena started to reach out.

"Please, Eomma," Miyoung whispered, catching hold of her mother's eyes. "I need it."

Yena stared at Miyoung with an unblinking gaze. Miyoung stood still, her arms outstretched as her mother moved toward her with jerking steps.

It was so close. She could almost feel the pulse of the bead. It called to her; it wanted to be reunited. Her eyes slipped toward the bead. It glowed. So bright she couldn't look anywhere else. She needed it. She didn't know how she could have been apart from it for so long.

There was a garbled cry from behind her. A sound that wrenched Miyoung from her reverie. She glanced over to see Sinhye wincing in pain, doubled over on her side.

Miyoung turned to find Yena glaring at Sinhye. "Eomma, no, just look at me," Miyoung said. "Just give me back my bead."

"No," Yena snarled. "You shouldn't have it." And she turned, fading into nothing again.

"Mother!" Miyoung yelled. She turned in a circle, searching for Yena. Then she raised desperate eyes to Junu. "She's gone."

63

"MOTHER!" MIYOUNG SHOUTED. But her mother didn't return. What were they going to do now? "Eomma!" she screamed so loud that it reverberated off the rocks.

"That's not going to work," Sinhye said.

"How do you know that?" Miyoung asked, eyes scanning the pale face that should have belonged to Jihoon.

"As someone who existed as a spirit for a long time," Sinhye panted out, "I can tell you that shouting for her won't bring her back."

"Then what will?" Somin asked.

"You have to give her a reason to come back," Sinhye said. She crooked a finger at Miyoung.

"What?" Miyoung stepped closer.

"Come here," Sinhye said.

"Why?" Miyoung asked as she kneeled beside Sinhye.

"Because I'm going to give her a reason." Then, without warning, Sinhye lunged forward and wrapped her hands around Miyoung's neck.

Despite her injury, Sinhye was strong. Miyoung fought against the choke hold, gasping for breath. But despite Miyoung's struggling, Sinhye wouldn't let go. And Miyoung started to see dots appear before her eyes.

"Let go," Miyoung heard Somin shout. Hands pulled at her, but Sinhye's hold was too strong.

"Spirits only react to strong emotions," Sinhye said as she squeezed tighter. Miyoung felt each individual finger digging into her throat. "To fear. Anger. And loss. Put the thing she loves most in danger and she'll react."

The world began to spin. Bright lights blinked into Miyoung's vision. And just as she felt like she was going to lose consciousness, a coldness washed over her skin.

There was a roar in her ears. Was that her blood trying to rush to her oxygen-deprived brain? No, it was a howl.

Stop! Yena's voice echoed around them. And Miyoung was finally freed from Sinhye's grasp. She fell back. And fell. And fell. Until darkness surrounded her.

She tried to grab ahold of something, but her arms felt so heavy she couldn't lift them. Finally, she stopped falling. Not with the hard jerk of a landing. The sensation that came with falling merely ceased.

"Hello?" Miyoung called out, her voice echoing in a void. "Hello? Can anyone hear me? Somin? Junu?"

Still nothing. Until she heard the footsteps. Turning, she saw the forest spring out of the darkness. Trees and branches twisting and reaching around her until it became the familiar terrain of her dreams.

"Eomma?" she whispered.

"Miyoung-ah." Yena stood before her. And for the first time in a long time she seemed . . . whole.

"Eomma, is this really you?" Miyoung asked.

"I don't know how to leave," Yena said. "I don't know if I can."

"You can," Miyoung said. "It's my fault you're still here. I held on to you because I was afraid of losing you. I was selfish."

"No, Daughter. I built a cage around you, one where you could only rely on me. I regret that."

Miyoung wasn't sure how true the words were, but something in her heart told her that this was truly Yena speaking, not some warped specter of her.

"You did your best," Miyoung said. "And you made me strong. Strong enough to live without you. I can accept that now. I can let you go."

Yena nodded, a small smile on her lips.

"Please, can I see my bead?"

And this time, when Yena produced it, she held it out to her daughter. "You have to make a choice now."

Taking it in her palm, Miyoung closed her eyes. She felt the pulse. She felt the pull. It would be so easy to join with it again. But she could also feel the hunger. It spread through her veins; it wanted to consume her. It wanted to connect her to the moon in a way that would give her power as well as a prison.

And she knew that this wasn't the life she wanted.

As she held the bead, she could feel her connection to it. And as she envisioned that bond, it appeared, a golden thread connecting her to the yeowu guseul. She took it between her hands. It should have been delicate, but it pulled tight and strong, like steel. She yanked at it and could feel a slice of pain. She pulled again, and the agony increased, like fire rising up to encompass her, to fill her.

With a final yank, she let out a scream. It felt like a thousand knives stabbed through her as the thread finally broke. And she felt the bead dissolve, turning to dust in her palm. And her body became numb as her energy drained. Leaching out of her until she felt hollow. Until she felt nothing.

64

JUNU STARED AT Miyoung's still body. She wasn't waking up, no matter how much Somin shook her and called her name.

Beside him, Sinhye let out a groan of pain. "Junu."

She was pale and drenched in sweat. He knelt beside her, putting a hand over her brow. "You're burning up."

"This body is too weak," she said. "I can feel it breaking down."

"What happens if he dies with you still inside him?" Junu asked.

"I don't know. But I can feel a darkness pulling me down. I can feel myself fading."

"Release him. Please, Sinhye. Or you'll both die."

She shook her head, then winced as if the slight movement brought her pain. "I can't. It's like I'm rooted in this body. I can't let go on my own."

"Somin-ah," Junu called. Urgency making his voice tight. At first, she didn't reply. She was still trying to revive Miyoung.

"Somin, please." Perhaps it was the desperation in his voice that finally got Somin to look up. She scrambled over, kneeling beside Sinhye.

"Are you okay?" But when Somin reached out, Sinhye jerked back.

"We don't have much time," Junu said, drawing Somin's

attention to him. "We need to get Sinhye's soul out of Jihoon so his body can regain its strength."

"But that would mean—" She broke off like she couldn't say the words. "There must be some other way."

"There isn't and we don't have time to sit around debating this," Junu said.

"You don't need to do this," she said. "Please, I don't want you to do this."

He held Somin close, letting her sobs shake them both.

"I can't let you lose Jihoon. He's too important to you. And he's also innocent. And he doesn't deserve any of this."

Somin's fists turned to grab hold of his shoulders. "You were innocent, too. You never chose this either."

"Even if I was innocent once, I'm not anymore."

"That doesn't mean you deserve to die," Somin sobbed.

"Perhaps not, but it's what needs to happen now."

Somin cupped his face, her eyes taking him in, boring into his like they could see everything inside of him. "You were wrong about something."

"I doubt it. I'm usually never wrong."

"You said you're broken. You said you can't be fixed. But you don't need to be fixed. You're a good person, Jin Junu."

"I'm not a person, Lee Somin."

That earned a scowl from her. "This isn't a time to make jokes."

"I think this is the *best* time to make jokes. Why be a morose bore when I'm about to die?" Junu grinned his devil-may-care smile. He didn't want to leave her with a vision of him in despair. Perhaps it was selfish, but he wanted her to remember him with joy.

He wanted nothing more than to stay here with Somin. But he couldn't. He couldn't even take a few minutes of grace to show her how much she'd come to mean to him. There wasn't enough time to show her. Even if he lived another hundred years, there wouldn't be enough time. So he pressed his lips against hers. Trying to push every part of his heart into the kiss. Trying to show her that even though his spirit would leave this earth, a part of him would stay here with her.

Before he was ready, he pulled away, turning to Sinhye.

"We're going to cut your connection to that body," Junu said. "If you try to hold on, I don't know what it will do to either of you. But it won't be punishing me anymore. I won't be here to mourn him."

Sinhye scowled, then nodded. "I'll let go. I have no need to stay here any longer. The sansin is dead. You'll be dead. I'm not afraid to move on."

Junu wasn't sure if he could truly trust Sinhye to keep her word here. But it was all he had and they didn't have time to bicker over it. So he helped her sit up.

"I see it now," Sinhye whispered into his ear.

"What do you see?" Junu asked.

She pulled back to study him with such intensity he wondered what she was searching for. "I see that what we had was not the love I thought."

"We don't have time for this."

Her eyes squeezed shut as she tried to absorb her pain. "You're willing to sacrifice everything for that girl. We pretended we'd sacrifice for each other. I would give up my immortal life and you'd give up your family. But really those were both things that didn't matter enough to us. And we were fools for that. For so many things."

Junu nodded at the truth of her words. "I'm sorry," he said. "I loved you because you helped me forget how pathetic my life had become. And I held you up in front of my family like a trophy I had won. That was selfish of me."

Sinhye's internal conflict showed in the furrow of Jihoon's brow, now so sweaty his hair stuck to his skin. "And I reveled in the fact that I was the only one who could make you happy. But I think I always knew it was because I was the only one you *let* make you happy."

"You're right."

"I'm glad," Sinhye said. "That now, in the end, we can be honest with each other."

"I hope one day our souls can forgive each other, too."

Sinhye nodded.

Junu turned to Somin and pulled out the knife she'd nestled in her waistband. "Aim for the heart like on the other dokkaebi. It's the easiest way."

"Easiest?" Somin choked out. "Nothing about this is easy. I can't do this."

When she took the knife, he placed his hands over hers like they were praying together. "I wish it didn't have to be you. But there's no one else."

Tears fell silently down her cheeks. But her face was defiant, like she would burn down the whole world to get what she wanted. It was a look that first drew him to her. It was the look that had caused him to fall in love.

"Jihoon needs you," he said. Somin took a deep breath, then nodded.

Junu held out his hands to Sinhye.

"Do it," he said to Somin.

"I can't," she whispered.

"You have to."

Sinhye's hands tightened around Junu's. Her eyes rolled back, and her body convulsed. Her whole form stiffened as she shook.

"Do it," Junu said as he caught Sinhye's thrashing body in his arms. "Somin, do it."

He heard her sob behind him. He felt the tip of the blade between his shoulder blades. He closed his eyes. He held tight to Sinhye.

The blade pierced his skin. He bit his lip to hold in a scream.

Go faster, he thought. *End it before I beg you to stop.* He wanted to be noble. To have a brave ending. He'd lived a messy, cowardly life. He'd lived a selfish life. And he knew he would never be able to erase the centuries of shame. But at least he could commit one act of bravery. One selfless thing as a final punctuation to his shameful life. And at least he could die knowing that he wasn't completely beyond the bounds of redemption. That there was still a part of him that could love and be loved.

His whole body shuddered, his teeth chattering so violently that he thought he would bite off his own tongue.

As he felt the blade dig deeper into his flesh, he tried to let go. He could almost feel his soul becoming untethered. He could practically feel himself coming apart. And he welcomed it. He held on tight to Sinhye, now unconscious. And when he thought the pain would consume him in a fire of agony, a cold hand came over his. It felt like ice. It felt like death.

He finally screamed out as the sting of the blade lanced down his back, and his eyes flew open.

Kneeling beside him was Yena. Her form so solid that he could be convinced that she'd come back to life. But her hands, holding his and Sinhye's, were too frozen to belong to someone who was living.

He realized that everything felt cold. The air around him, which hung still and heavy. The world felt like a haze around them; the colors of the mountain were leached and lifeless. He still held on to Sinhye's hands, except now she sat before him in the form he remembered. A beautiful girl, long ebony hair, light porcelain skin. She blinked in confusion as she held up her hand to glance at her slender fingers. They still sat on the mountain, except it was as if there was a spotlight on them, only three meters in circumference, and beyond the light lay a dark expanse. Where it led, Junu didn't know.

"Somin! Miyoung!" Junu called, his voice sounding garbled, like he was underwater.

"I don't think they're here," Sinhye said, her voice equally warped.

"Where is here?"

"You're in the Between." Hyuk stepped out of the darkness, shadows dancing around him. In this strange washed-out world, he looked almost vibrant in his full black ensemble. But instead of the suit he'd been wearing of late, he now had on the traditional black hanbok that had been common in Joseon times and a black gat atop his head, the kind of tall hat that Junu had once also worn over a hundred years ago. Its wide brim shaded Hyuk's eyes, but they seemed to glow as he watched Junu and Sinhye.

"So you've come to sacrifice your soul to deliver Sinhye to the underworld," Hyuk said, and he sounded morose. Like he mourned.

"I have." The voice that spoke was neither Junu's nor Sinhye's. It was Yena's. Her face serene, her eyes clear. She did not look like the rabid gwishin that had appeared on the mountain but like she once had, calm and beautiful, even in death.

"What are you doing?" Junu gasped out. It was hard to breathe in this place. But it also seemed like he didn't need to. Spirits didn't need air.

"I'm giving my daughter what she needs."

"I don't understand," Junu said.

Yena didn't reply. Instead, she held out her hand to Sinhye, who looked at Junu with confusion before accepting Yena's offered palm. The two stood together, and Hyuk approached.

"Wait, what's happening?" Junu asked. "I thought I had to die for Sinhye to leave Jihoon's body."

"In order to release Sinhye's soul from Jihoon's body, an immortal soul must be sacrificed. The energy of that sacrifice cut her soul free. As Yena's soul was still tethered to the mortal realm, her act of letting go was enough to break the bond between Sinhye's soul and Jihoon's body."

"Then what am I supposed to do now?" Junu asked. "If I'm here, then does that mean I've died as well?"

"No, you merely came to the brink of death," Hyuk said. "If there is one who wishes to hold on to you, then you can return to where you came from." The reaper motioned to the shadows that surrounded them, and Junu realized he meant for Junu to step into that unknown place.

"How will I get back?"

"If she holds on, then you'll find the way."

Junu wanted to ask more, but Hyuk took Yena's and Sinhye's joined hands in his. He led them into the shadows, and soon their forms dissolved into the darkness, leaving Junu alone.

He stood alone now, the silence almost overwhelming him.

He peered into the darkness himself before reaching out. His hand was devoured by shadows, and he jerked it back, making sure it was still whole. It was still there.

"Hello?" he called, and nothing echoed back, not even his own voice.

"Hello?" he tried calling again. And this time he thought he heard something. "Can anyone hear me? Is anyone there?"

And he saw movement in the dark. Something superimposed on the nothing that surrounded him. It shifted. It came closer. And then Junu saw a man. He had salt-and-pepper hair under a dark cap. But his face was younger than Junu expected. A young man whose face was thin, ravaged by illness. Still, there was a glint in his gaze. And Junu recognized the shape of his eyes.

"You're Somin's abeoji."

"I'm here to take you to her," he said, holding out his hand. "She is holding on to you. She is waiting for you."

Junu nodded and stepped into the dark after Somin's father.

65

SOMIN COULDN'T LET go of him even as Miyoung called her name. Even as she heard Jihoon moan and regain consciousness. Even as her friends told her that they couldn't find a pulse. That they had to leave Junu's body. She wouldn't let go.

"Somin-ah," Miyoung said. "We have to get Jihoon to a doctor. We have to make sure he's okay."

At that Somin finally studied her friend. Jihoon leaned heavily against a boulder. The bleeding from his wound had stopped, but he looked awful, with his washed-out face and bloodshot eyes. And she knew that they couldn't stay. She knew that they had to leave. But she couldn't get herself to let go of Junu. Like this, he looked like he could just be sleeping. There had been no blood when the blade had gone into him and none when she'd pulled it out. So she could almost convince herself that he was asleep.

"He hasn't turned to dust. Not like the other dokkaebi. That has to mean he's still alive," Somin argued. She'd been arguing this point for almost thirty minutes. As the moon had risen. As the night had deepened.

She wrapped her arms around Junu, trying to find a way to say goodbye. But instead she just whispered his name in small sobs as she held on. "Junu. Junu."

Somin-ah. Her name tickled her ear. A familiar voice. A flash of salt-and-pepper hair racing through her mind. A glimpse of eyes framed by smile lines.

"Appa?" she whispered.

My daughter. Be happy.

"Somin-ah." The croak of her name was spoken against her neck this time.

Shivers of hope raced through her. But she didn't let the tears fall until she pulled back and saw Junu blinking up at her.

"You held on," he said.

66

SOMIN WASN'T SURE what to do with herself. A week had passed since they'd gotten back from the mountain. A week where Jihoon had to stay overnight in the hospital for observation, despite his objections. Somin and Miyoung had told her mother a horrible excuse, that they'd gone hiking and he fell, practically skewering himself on a tree branch.

No one pointed out that Jihoon would never be caught dead hiking.

Miyoung was also recovering, gaining back her strength and looking more like the girl Somin had first met almost a year ago.

And Junu . . . she hadn't seen Junu since they'd returned to Seoul. Somin had gone to his house at least a dozen times in the last seven days. And finally, she'd stopped because it had hurt too much to feel the rejection every time his door stayed shut.

She'd tried to throw herself back into school as it started up again in mid-August. But today was Sunday and she was stuck with nothing but her brooding thoughts at home.

"You know, if you pick up your feet, you won't make that annoying shuffling noise," Jihoon said from the couch as Somin came out of the kitchen.

"You know, you're not actually a permanent resident of this house, and I'd be happy to relocate you onto the balcony," Somin bit back.

"I hate mopey-Somin. She's so mean." Jihoon pouted and went back to surfing the channels on the television. He stopped at a weekend drama, the soapy kind with melodramatic story lines and lots of slapping and water thrown in faces.

"I can't believe you watch these," Somin said, flopping onto the couch beside him. She hadn't changed out of her pajamas yet even though it was almost noon. She just didn't see the point.

"Miyoung got me hooked on them. Girl loves her dramas."

"Where is she? You two have been glued at the hip these days."

"She's going to her mother's grave. Said she needed to be alone for it."

Somin nodded. She knew what it was like to need to be alone for these things. Sometimes she went to see her father in the columbarium alone. She didn't tell her mother because she didn't know if she'd be upset to know how often Somin went.

She'd gone this week. She'd felt her father that day on the mountain. And somehow, she was sure her father had helped her hold on to Junu.

"Have you seen Junu at all?" she asked. She hated that the question made her sound so pathetic.

"No," Jihoon said. "But when he's ready, I'm sure he'll reach out."

"I'm not so sure of that," Somin said.

"He cares about you," Jihoon said. His teeth gritted, like he was reluctant to say the words. "Even I can see that. He didn't do what he did just for me. He did it because of how he feels about you. That doesn't just go away."

"He's lived a dozen lifetimes; maybe love means something different to him."

Jihoon shrugged. "Maybe," he admitted. "But I don't think you should give up on him."

"I don't know if I have your annoying tenacity," Somin said. "If someone doesn't want me around, then I can take the hint."

"That's not the Lee Somin I know," Jihoon said with a frown. "You never give up on people."

"Even I get tired sometimes. I can't fight for everyone's soul."

"I'm sorry," Jihoon said.

"Why? It's not your fault."

"I think it is. After all, I'm the one you've been fighting for the past fifteen years. And I think it's time you stopped."

"What?" Somin's heart lurched. A queasiness settled in her stomach. "I don't understand."

"Somin-ah," Jihoon said quietly. "Why did you lie to me about remembering your father?"

"Because I didn't want to hurt you," Somin said slowly. She didn't know if she wanted to dig this up, but she knew that she wanted to stop keeping secrets.

"Why would you think that would hurt me?"

"Because you had such horrible memories of your own father. It felt like I'd be flaunting my good memories if I told you I remembered. But I do remember him. And I miss him every day." Tears fell down her cheeks, hot against her skin.

"Somin-ah, I'm sorry I wasn't there for you back then."

"It's not your fault."

"Well, no matter whose fault, I'm here now. And Junu was right."

"Wow." Somin let out a choked laugh. "Hell must have frozen over for you to say that."

"Well, I've learned that the dokkaebi talks so much that statistically he has to get some things right."

Somin laughed again, and she wiped away the last of her tears. "What was he right about?"

"You have to stop holding back what you feel just to take care of the rest of us. I don't need it. Your mom doesn't need it. Miyoung doesn't need it."

"I just . . . I don't want to waste any time."

"Why would living our own lives be wasting time?" Jihoon frowned.

"When my dad was alive, I don't think I ever really appreciated him the way he deserved. And then he was just gone. I feel like I never realized how important he was to me until he wasn't there anymore. And I just don't want to lose out on the chance to make important memories with the people I love."

"Oh, Somin." Jihoon leaned forward and enfolded her in his arms. She wanted to push him away, she felt so embarrassed by the words that had come flooding out of her. Like those of a frightened child. But she couldn't hide it anymore. It was like all the fear she'd felt this summer had barreled through the walls that had always kept this hidden.

She pulled out of Jihoon's arms, averting her face. "I don't know where the worry comes from. It's just always been there."

Jihoon nodded. "Even when my parents left me, I knew they were still alive out there somewhere. I knew that they weren't completely gone from my life, no matter how much it felt like that. But now . . . after Halmeoni died, and now that my father's really gone . . ."

Somin raised horrified eyes to him. She hadn't meant to unlock this pain for him.

She started to say that they didn't have to talk about this right now.

But Jihoon saw her expression and laid a hand on her shoulder.

Comforting her even as she saw the tears pooling in his eyes. "I think I get it," he said. "I wish every day that I'd realized how much Halmeoni did for me. And I regret every day that I wasn't able to tell her that I'm so proud she's the one who raised me. I think I do fear it a bit, losing you. Because I love you so much, too."

That did it. The tears that Somin had been holding back this whole time rushed forward.

She leaned into him, and they held each other. "But," he said into her hair, "I also trust you. And I know I can trust that if you do go, you'll always come back someday."

Somin pulled back in confusion. "I never said I wanted to go anywhere."

"I'm your best friend," Jihoon said. "You don't think I can tell you want to leave this place as soon as we graduate?"

"Not forever," Somin said quickly, like she had to defend this secret dream of hers.

"I know." Jihoon nodded reassuringly. "And I think you should tell your mother."

"It's not the right time." She could feel nervous flutters in her stomach at just the thought.

"If you keep putting it off, then you'll never tell her."

"What if she gets upset?"

"You've had fights with your mother before," Jihoon said.

"I just don't know how to leave her," Somin said. "What if I leave and then something happens to her?"

"What if you stay and you start to resent her?" Jihoon asked.

Somin pouted because she couldn't argue against that logic.

"Talk to her," Jihoon said. "Don't have regrets."

"When did you become so bossy?" Somin asked. "I don't think I like it."

67

JUNU STARED AT the packing boxes. They'd been delivered ahead of the movers arriving tomorrow. Maybe he should reschedule. He wanted to make sure that the more delicate things in his apartment were prepped for transport. No, that was just a delay tactic. He'd decided to leave, and he would.

He knew leaving would hurt Somin, but it was better this way. She didn't belong in his world. He'd always known this. She could have died on that mountain because she wasn't able to let him go and he'd never have forgiven himself. Because he loved her, he had to let her go. And maybe one day she'd realize it was for the best. Or she wouldn't and she'd hate him the rest of her life. Maybe that was for the best, too.

Miyoung stepped into the foyer, then stopped short at the sight of the boxes.

"What's this?" she asked.

"I'm going to start a bowling league," Junu said. "What does it look like? I'm moving."

"Moving?" Miyoung asked, frowning. "Why?"

"I just feel like it's time. I think I've stayed way too long here. But don't worry. I own this building. You can stay as long as you want."

"Oooh," Miyoung said with a knowing nod. "I get it. You're running."

"What?" Junu said, taken aback. And surprised by the smile that spread on Miyoung's face. "I am not," he insisted. But his heart raced like he was caught doing something wrong. "This is just my thing. I go somewhere, hang around until I get bored, and leave."

"Except you're not bored this time. You're scared." Miyoung shrugged as she took a pair of shoes from the shoe cabinet.

"Don't you have school?" Junu scowled.

"It's Sunday," Miyoung said.

"Shouldn't you be killing yourself studying for the suneung exam, then? You're fully human now, why don't you act like it?"

"You just don't want me here pointing out that you're scared."

"You have no idea what you're talking about," Junu said. But he couldn't think of a way to convince Miyoung she was wrong. She just was. There was nothing else to it.

"I recognize exactly what you're doing because it's what I used to do for the first eighteen years of my life. Run away from my problems. Or let someone else clean them up for me. But you forget, I once literally left the country and my problems stayed with me. It doesn't matter where you are when your problems exist in here." Miyoung pointed to her head.

"I'm not . . . I mean, that's just not . . . What would I be running from?"

"From the looks of it, you're running from what you want because of what you think you deserve."

Junu frowned at that. "You're not making any sense."

Miyoung leaned forward so her face was lined up with Junu's, then enunciated each word. "You have feelings for people here, so you are running away because you think you deserve to be alone."

"What?" Junu practically shouted, jerking away from her. "That's ridiculous!"

"No, it's not. You care about Changwan. You can't deny that."

Junu shrugged. "Maybe. But he'll be fine without me."

"Sure," Miyoung agreed. "He'll probably be okay."

That stung, Miyoung's easy acceptance that Changwan didn't need him. Wait, that's what he wanted. He wanted to be able to leave without feeling any guilt over it.

"But it's more than just Changwan," Miyoung continued. "You said you kept trying to help me because you owed me a debt. Gaesori."

Junu raised his brows. Miyoung so rarely cursed.

"You care about me," she said. And it wasn't a question; she sounded so sure of herself. "And I have to admit, despite myself, I guess I care about you, too. I mean, I'm at least glad you're not dead, so that's progress."

Junu huffed. His throat felt tight and he coughed roughly to clear it, but it didn't seem to help.

"And you care about Lee Somin. You care about her more than you care about yourself," she said. "Don't you?"

Junu smiled wryly. "You really must be confused if you think I care about anything more than I care about me. I'm my favorite thing in this world."

Miyoung's face scrunched with skepticism. "No, I'm not buying it. You're talking to someone who spent her whole life lying to everyone, including herself. I know how to see through BS. And you're full of it."

Junu's smile faltered. There was no getting through to her.

"What do you want me to do?" Junu finally said, pacing in frustration. "I'm not used to caring about people. Or being someone others can depend on. I'm a selfish prick who thinks of his own safety and interests first. I'm not someone worth having around."

"Yeah, and I used to devour human energy every full moon. People change."

"I'm not a person," Junu said stubbornly, crossing his arms.

"Neither was I. But that can change, too." Miyoung gave him a small smile. "Come on. You'll never know unless you try. Think of it as a new adventure."

Junu groaned. "I think I liked it better when you ignored me. At least then you didn't make me face my own issues. We could just be two broken people floating around each other in blissful peace."

"Yeah, I'm not really looking to do that anymore." Miyoung rolled her eyes, then reached for the door. "Do you want to come with me?"

"Where are you going?" Junu asked.

68

SOMIN HUDDLED IN her room, letting the afternoon pass her by, before she persuaded herself to talk to her mother. Jihoon was right this morning; she had to say something or she'd always regret it. And if Somin was anything, she was a person who faced things head-on. It was her signature move.

If she could face a mountain god, she could face her own mother . . . she hoped.

Her mother was watching some soapy daytime drama that was more melodrama than substance. At least they always seemed that way to Somin.

She sat on the couch, pretending to watch the show for three minutes before she couldn't fake it anymore. "Eomma?"

"Hmm?" Her mother's eyes never left the screen.

"What would you think if I didn't go to college in Seoul?"

"College?" Her mother's eyes finally drifted away from the television. "Outside of Seoul? Like in Gyeonggi-do?"

Somin frowned. "No, like farther."

Her mother finally seemed to realize Somin wanted to have a full conversation and muted the television. "You mean outside of the country?"

Somin pursed her lips. Was that disapproval she heard? Maybe she should let this go for now. Except she wasn't sure when she'd find the courage to ask again.

Her mother stood up and walked into the kitchen, and Somin worried she'd upset her. But her mother came back with a folder. She sat, placing it between them on the couch.

Somin opened the folder and found a bunch of crinkled pamphlets for universities all over the world. She'd thrown them away at the beginning of the summer. "Why do you have these?"

"I found them a while ago when I was cleaning your room so Jihoon could stay with us. I've been meaning to talk to you, but you've seemed so distracted lately. I guess you're not as distracted anymore."

"I didn't realize you knew about these." Somin stared at the cities depicted in the pamphlets, places where things seemed so different. So new.

"Hey. I might be a bit scattered, but I'm still a mother. And mothers know what their kids are up to."

Somin dearly hoped not. If her mother knew about what she did over summer break, Somin was sure she'd have a heart attack.

"Why did you throw these away?" her mother asked.

"I just didn't know if I should be applying to places like this."

"Why? Is it the money? Because I'm doing well at the office. You don't have to worry about that."

"I guess I worried how you'd react if you knew I wanted to leave. You need me here."

Her mother let out a heavy sigh. "Somin-ah, I think I've been a bad mother."

"What?" Somin had never heard anything more ridiculous in her life. After seeing how her friends had suffered, Somin knew now more than ever how lucky she was to have a mother like hers. Not everyone grew up knowing they were loved like she did. She'd never had to doubt it.

"I should have had this talk with you a long time ago," her mother said, folding Somin's hand into hers. "You are the child in this relationship. Not the mother. And you need to stop trying to take care of me all the time."

"What?" Somin frowned. Where was this coming from?

"It's your senior year. I want you to start to think about what you want out of life."

"I want to be able to take care of you. We're a team, you and me."

Her mother nodded. "Yes, we're a team. But I think you need to realize that people on a team have different roles. My role is to be the mother. Your role is to be the child."

Somin smiled, but she was confused. "We're not a normal mother and daughter. We're different. We're special."

Her mother winced. "That's what I always told you when you were younger because I was so scared you'd see I had no idea what I was doing. And I'm sorry I leaned on you too much when you were younger. I didn't have the ability to be a strong mother for you before. But I know how to be one now."

"Don't say that," Somin said, tears filling her eyes. "You're the perfect mother. You always have been."

Her mother pushed Somin's hair behind her ear and cupped her cheek. "I'm not perfect. But I *am* your mother. And you need to listen to me. You need to do what's best for you. And I will be fine. A mother sacrifices for her child, not the other way around. Do you understand?"

Somin nodded, kissing her mother's palm. "I love you, Eomma."

"I love you, too, Daughter. That's why I want you to think about what you want from now on. Okay?"

Somin nodded.

"Will you look at the pamphlets again? Think about if you want to apply to any of these places?"

Somin smiled. She'd been right about one thing: She did have the perfect mother. "Sure, Eomma. Why don't we look at them together later?"

69

THE FOREST WAS quiet as they stood beside the maehwa tree.

Miyoung held a handful of lilies. She was unwilling, or maybe unable, to let go of them just yet.

"She saved my soul," Junu said.

"She saved mine, too," Miyoung whispered, tears thickening her voice.

"She was a good person."

Miyoung swiped away her tears. "You don't need to lie to me. I knew what my mother was. I don't need you to pretend that she lived a virtuous life."

She finally placed the lilies underneath the plaque that just had Yena's name carved in hanja.

It had been the right thing, letting go of Yena. Not only for the world but for her heart. Still, it hurt. Like a dull knife being driven further and further into her chest. And the pain had existed for long enough that it was just a constant dull throb now.

"Listen," Junu said quietly. "I'd known Yena a long time. Long enough to know dozens of names she had before she was called Yena. She was different before you were around." That got Miyoung's attention, and she finally looked up at him. His lips were pursed, his brow lowered in thought. "She was colder. There was something about her that was more frightening."

"What?" Miyoung asked.

"She didn't care. About anything," Junu explained. "But then one day, she shows up at my door and she's different. She says that she's back in town and she needs a place that's safe. Safer than anything I'd ever provided her with before."

"Are you telling me you were my mother's Realtor?" Miyoung asked.

"I find anything my clients require as long as I don't need to maim or kill to get it." Junu shrugged. "I was used to finding homes for your mother whenever she rolled back through Seoul. But this time was different. I'm really good at my job, but this time, nothing was good enough for her. And finally, I asked her why she was being so picky. I asked her if she didn't trust me. And she looked at me and said, 'I don't trust anyone when it comes to my daughter's safety.'"

"Why are you telling me this?"

"I'm telling you that Yena lived her life for you, and that was a good thing. Because before you were around, she had nothing to live for. Someone like us with nothing to live for is a dangerous thing. I should know."

"She shouldn't have dedicated her life to me like that." Now Miyoung pressed her hand against the tree, like it could bring her closer to her mother. If she pressed hard enough, she could almost feel a warmth.

"I'm telling you that you saved Yena's life. The last eighteen years of her life, she was the happiest I'd ever seen her. Well, as happy as Yena could be."

Miyoung shook her head, but some of the tension that came with guilt melted away.

"And what if I don't know if I can be happy without her," Miyoung whispered.

"You can be," Junu said. "But it won't be easy to get there."

"I had to let her go," Miyoung finally said.

"You did. It was more than just the tear between worlds. With her lingering here, you weren't able to actually mourn her. You were still holding on to the ghost of her. Just like I did." Junu let out a long breath. "I let my ghosts drag me into darkness for too long. You should learn from my mistakes. Take this time to move on."

Miyoung knew it had been right to let go of her mother. But she hated that she felt like her mother had just died all over again. It was like the pain would never abate. Like she'd live this way forever. "When will I feel better? When will I stop hurting so much every time I think of her?"

"Maybe never. You might never fully stop hurting."

"Why?" Miyoung whispered, and she didn't know if she was asking him or some heartless god.

"There's no getting over losing someone. You'll never go back to how you lived before," Junu said. "You just learn how to live a different way."

"Are you still going to leave?" Miyoung asked quietly. She hated that she was scared of losing him. Junu had become a strange part of her life. Not really a friend, though she thought she could trust him like one. And not really like family, though he annoyed her like one. Maybe something a bit in between? And after she'd lost so much, she couldn't risk letting him go without asking. At least she had to ask.

"I'm not sure," Junu said slowly.

"What will you tell Somin?" Miyoung asked.

"I don't know," he admitted. "I'm scared to say goodbye to her."

Miyoung laughed. "You should be. She'll beat the crap out of you."

"She deserves better than me."

"Isn't it up to her to decide what she deserves?" Miyoung asked.

Junu scowled at that, and Miyoung recognized the look. It was a look of someone who knew they were wrong but didn't want to admit it. "What if she doesn't want me to stay?" His voice shook, and Miyoung's heart softened a bit.

"I'm not sure what Somin wants. But for what it's worth, I want you to stay." She didn't look at him as she said the words. It was embarrassing. And she didn't want to hope that he'd say yes.

"Really?" Junu sounded surprised.

Now Miyoung did look up, her eyes meeting his. He watched her cautiously. Like he was afraid to hope, too. "Yes. I'd like you to stay."

Junu nodded. "Then maybe I should stay."

70

MIYOUNG SAT AT her desk on Monday, staring at the crisp page in her workbook. With school started again, she had something to occupy her days now. Though, she'd fallen sorely behind at the beginning of the school year from so many tardies.

Other students mingled around her since it was free period. Many of them were using the time to study since the suneung exams were closer than ever.

Miyoung still wasn't used to the idea that she was at the same school she'd attended last year.

Usually Miyoung never lasted past a few months, let alone a whole school year.

True, there was that period of time last winter that she'd been gone. Hunting for a cure to her missing yeowu guseul. She rubbed a hand against her chest. There was still a strange hollow feeling beneath her ribs, like a part of her heart had been ripped free. But she felt the beat beneath her palm, and she knew she'd be okay. She was mortal now. Truly mortal. It's what she wanted. Even if she still missed certain parts of her old life.

She jumped as hands dropped on her shoulders. Then heard Jihoon's amused chuckle.

Miyoung hadn't even heard anyone coming up behind her. That would never have happened before. But she supposed there were worse things than having your boyfriend surprise you in the middle of class. Especially a boyfriend she'd been on the brink of losing a week ago.

She turned in her seat so she could see Jihoon's dimpled grin.

"Did you get the snacks you wanted?"

"And yours," he said, holding out the honey-butter chips. Miyoung grinned and ripped into the bag. For some reason, food tasted more delicious now. Funny, she'd have thought it would be the opposite, since so many of her senses were duller after severing her connection to her bead.

"I didn't hear from you last night," Jihoon said. His voice was casual but his eyes were unblinking. Like he was watching for any signs of distress.

"I needed some time after visiting my mother," she admitted. "And I wanted to go shopping for some things for my room."

"Your room?" Jihoon frowned.

"Yeah, I figured since it's more of a permanent situation now, I want it to feel more like my space, you know?"

"So, you're staying there. With him?" Jihoon sounded surprised.

"I figure the guy deserves a break." She shrugged.

"I'm glad," Jihoon said.

"Really?" Miyoung asked. "Since when were you Team Junu?"

"I've never been anti-Junu." Jihoon shrugged. "I just didn't know if we should trust him before. But I guess, when a guy saves your life, you owe it to him to cut him some slack."

"I *am* grateful to him. I don't want to think about what I'd do if I'd lost you." She was still awkward about sharing her feelings with people, even Jihoon. "I guess I'd have hated to lose you before I could tell you . . ." She choked on the words. They felt thick and uncomfortable in her throat.

Jihoon squeezed her hands. "You don't have to say it. I know it."

"No," Miyoung said fiercely. "I want to. I want to tell you that I love you." She said it fast. Like someone admitting to a crime instead of confessing their love. But Jihoon laughed, a delighted sound.

"Of course you make love sound like you're being tortured," Jihoon said.

"Ya! I'm trying here." Miyoung scowled.

"I know," Jihoon said, pressing a light kiss to her nose.

She hunched, her eyes darting toward the other kids in the room. "Don't do that in the middle of school."

"What? I can't kiss my yeo-chin?" Jihoon asked, raising his voice.

Some of the kids looked over, rolling their eyes like they were bored with Jihoon and Miyoung's relationship antics. Then they turned back to their homework or their conversations, mostly ignoring Jihoon.

"See?" he said. "No one cares what we do. We're just normal students."

Miyoung frowned. That was also going to take some getting used to. But it seemed like being with Jihoon made her "normal" now. And she smiled at the thought. It was going to be nice being a regular teenager who didn't carry around the weight of deadly secrets.

There was a sudden bustle of activity in the hallway. Miyoung checked the time. Free study period wasn't over yet. But kids were shuffling around, hurriedly gathering into small groups to whisper. Anxiety spread through her. This was a familiar scene. Kids gossiping about someone, usually her. But they weren't looking into the classroom. They were all staring down the hall.

Then she saw him. Junu walked past the windows between the classroom and the hallway. Girls giggled as he passed them. But unlike his usually flirty self, Junu didn't seem to notice.

Every eye was on him as he moved assuredly through the hallway. His eyes glanced toward their classroom, scanning the seats. He nodded in greeting when he saw Miyoung and Jihoon. She lifted a hand in a small wave.

"You know him?" a girl asked, leaning over her desk toward Miyoung.

This girl had once been one of Miyoung's tormentors, and now she watched Miyoung with unaffected interest, waiting for a reply.

"Um, yeah, he's kind of like my cousin?" Miyoung looked at Jihoon, who gave her an encouraging nod. "We live together."

"Daebak," the girl said. "Does he have a girlfriend?"

Miyoung pursed her lips at that. "I think that's what he's here to find out."

The girl frowned in confusion, so Miyoung took pity on her. "Yeah, I'm pretty sure he has a girlfriend."

With a sigh, the girl turned back to her desk, muttering about how the cute ones were always taken.

"What do you think he's really doing here?" Jihoon asked Miyoung quietly.

"I think he's looking for Somin," Miyoung said, opening her workbook again.

"I hope she gives him hell."

Miyoung smiled to herself. Is this what it felt like to be content? To know that everyone you cared about could be happy?

To have people to care about? If it was, then Miyoung thought everything they'd gone through might have been worth it. If she was allowed to have this life now. And maybe she didn't need to just survive anymore. Maybe now she could give herself permission to really live.

"I'm sure she'll give him exactly what he deserves."

71

SOMIN STARED AT her math workbook, and nothing made sense. She was usually so good at math. In fact, she was planning to enter the upcoming math contest to increase the specs on her college applications after her talk with her mother. But try as she might, she couldn't get herself to study the material.

This study room was usually empty because it was next to the bathroom that was constantly flooding because of bad plumbing. When it was really bad, water would start to seep into this study room as well. So most students avoided it because they were squeamish. But Somin had been desperate for some quiet. Even that hadn't helped.

She closed the workbook and dropped her head on top of it with a thud.

"Ow." She let out an unhappy moan, muffled by her workbook.

"Is this normal human behavior?"

Somin jerked upright and frowned at Hyuk.

"Why are you here? To play more games with our lives?"

"A jeoseung saja doesn't play. And we're not supposed to do anything that affects outcomes in the mortal realm."

"Not supposed to," Somin said. "But you did."

"There were extenuating circumstances. We had to do what we could to close the tear between worlds."

"But you did more than help us close the tear. You wanted me to save Junu."

"I merely told you where Junu was going. I never told you how to stop him or even if you could."

"But you didn't have to tell me. Why did you?"

When Hyuk didn't answer, Somin did. "Because you care about him. He's someone special to you."

"A jeoseung saja does not have connections. In any realm." Hyuk frowned again. "But we were once human, too. Though our memories of our humanity are taken, we all know where we once came from."

"And Junu reminds you of your humanity?" Somin asked.

"He's special. I always wanted to help him defeat the ghosts that haunted him. I never could. But you did," Hyuk said. "I'm glad I was right about you."

Somin wasn't sure if he was right. After all, she hadn't been able to get in touch with Junu for a week. But she didn't want to tell the reaper that. A part of her was scared of disappointing him.

"Will we see you again?" Somin asked instead, though she didn't know what she wanted the answer to be.

"I hope not," Hyuk said. "This isn't my world." Somin saw a bit of wistfulness on his face, the first hint of emotion she'd ever seen on the reaper. "I should go."

Somin thought he'd just disappear into vapors like he had before, but instead he walked to the door. When he opened it, Junu stood on the other side, his hand reaching for the knob. Somin jumped up at the sight of him, her chair scraping across the floor. Junu froze, surprise flashing across his features as he stared at the reaper.

"What are you doing here?" he asked.

"I'm just leaving. I wish you well, old friend." Then he turned and did disappear where he stood. And Somin realized the reaper had come here to see Junu, to make sure he was okay.

Junu was staring at the spot where Hyuk had just stood. When he didn't move to step in or out of the room, Somin cleared her throat meaningfully.

He looked up and seemed to finally remember she was here. It was a blow to her ego to realize he'd forgotten about her.

"What was he talking to you about?"

"It was private," she said, primly sitting down again. Taking her time smoothing out her uniform skirt. As if it didn't matter to her at all that the last time they'd seen each other, she'd been trying to reach beyond the veil of the living and pull his soul back. That he hadn't reached out to her at all since then.

And she felt a fire lifting in her. An anger that told her that she was still Lee Somin, the ace of this school, and not someone to be played around with.

"You know, I would have appreciated if you'd have returned one of my texts or calls. The polite thing to do when you want to end things with someone is to tell them directly." The words spilled out of her like hot air, and she suddenly felt deflated. Her lips trembled, and angry tears started to fill her eyes.

She turned back to her workbook, ducking her head so he couldn't see them. She hoped with all her might that he'd just leave now. She was mortified. Crying over a boy.

"Somin-ah," Junu said. But she held up a hand to hold him at bay. If he came any closer, he'd see what a mess she was. "I wasn't trying to end things."

She let out a scoffing laugh. "You have a funny way of saying you still care, then."

Junu sighed and, despite Somin's protests, sat in the chair beside her.

"I was never planning to end things without talking to you."

"But you *were* planning to end things."

Junu's eyes squinted in thought. "I'm not used to having . . . connections. It's easier to be on my own in my line of business."

Somin snorted in derision. "Sure, because business should always come first."

"Well, maybe I also convinced myself that you were all better off without me and the baggage that comes along with me. I thought it would be better—"

"Of course you did!" Somin shouted, and Junu leaned back in surprise. "Of course you decided you knew better. Why? Because you're, like, a thousand years older than us? Well, I've got news for you. Our problems weren't all because of you. You didn't force Miyoung to lose her bead. You didn't force Yena to sacrifice herself for her daughter. You didn't create that rip between the worlds. In fact, you were the one trying to foolishly fix it all by yourself. But guess what, it got fixed because we *all* worked together. That's why you shouldn't keep things all bottled up inside like a babo, know-it-all michin-nom."

She took a deep breath that stretched her lungs, then let it out slowly. It felt good. Like she'd expelled a week's worth of anger that had been festering inside of her.

"I know," Junu said.

Somin opened her mouth to argue more before she processed what he'd said. "What?"

"I got a lecture from Miyoung yesterday. Granted, less harsh. But I understand that you're mad," Junu said. "That you have a right to be mad," he added.

"I'm not just mad," Somin said. "I'm hurt. On the mountain, you said you didn't want to leave me, but that's just what you did this last week. You left me alone to deal with everything that happened."

"I was scared," Junu whispered, his eyes lowered. "I'm still scared of how much I feel for you."

Somin found that she couldn't maintain the high level of anger she'd been walking around with all week, but she didn't want to let him off the hook that easily. "So you're here now. But how can I trust you won't get scared again and leave?"

"I'm not sure," Junu said. "But I do want to stay."

"Oh yeah? You've decided to give slumming it with the humans a try?"

"No," Junu said with a smile. "I've decided that I want to really live. That I want to let myself feel the pain that I've held back for centuries. Because if I can feel the pain, then maybe I can also feel happiness one day. And I honestly don't think anything makes me happier right now than you."

Somin forced her lips into a frown. Otherwise she'd smile like a lovesick schoolgirl and she didn't want to give Junu the satisfaction. At least not yet. She'd suffered for a week. He could suffer for another five minutes.

"So what are you proposing? We date? I'm very busy studying for the suneung exam. I wasted my whole summer break on ridiculous things like saving the world."

He laughed, but there was appreciation in his eyes. He took her hands in his. "I'm proposing that we try our hardest to make each other happy. Not really sure what that's going to look like. But I am sure that I love your hands. I love when they're holding mine." He brought her hands to his lips to kiss them. Somin's breath caught.

"I love your eyes. I love when they're spewing fire at me like you'll strike me down if I do something bullheaded or selfish." He pressed a kiss to her temple beside the corner of her eye. Somin's heart leapt, racing so fast she thought it would burst from her chest.

"I love your lips. I love when they're telling me when I'm wrong. When they're telling me that you care. When they're yelling at me." He pressed a featherlight kiss to her lips.

"Don't you dare say you want to possess everything I have," Somin said, her hands squeezing his with warning.

"Never," Junu said with a smile that lit up his handsome face so it dazzled her like the sun. "I love everything you possess. I love it because you possess it. Because I love you."

Now Somin couldn't hold back her smile anymore. "You definitely have a way with words," she said. "I don't get it. It should sound corny and horrible, but somehow you make it sound so good."

Junu leaned forward so they were eye to eye and all she could see was the warm brown of his irises. "I'll teach you how."

"You better," Somin said as their lips crushed together. She felt herself being lifted from her chair and deposited in his lap.

"You didn't say it back," Junu said against her lips.

"What?" Somin asked, but she couldn't help smiling.

His mouth trailed from hers, kissed her cheek, her jaw, the sensitive lobe of her ear. Then he whispered, "Are you really going to make me ask?"

"Yes," Somin said, though it came out as more of a breathy sigh than a command.

"Do you love me, Lee Somin?"

She turned so they were face-to-face again. Their noses touching. "I do. I love you, Jin Junu. God help us both."

EPILOGUE

SOMIN SQUINTED AGAINST the sun as she stepped outside and students spilled from the school.

Junu had declared that it was a crime for them all to stay inside on such a beautiful day. And gathered everyone to bring them out for dinner before they had to come back to school to study well into the night. Such was the life of a high school senior in South Korea.

"I don't know if I should leave," Changwan said, glancing around nervously at the other students. Most of them were first- or second-years. Almost every third-year was still cooped up inside.

"If you're hungry, then you can't concentrate. It's basic science," Junu said, throwing an arm around Changwan's shoulders.

Somin rolled her eyes. "I hate to admit he's right," she said.

Changwan and Jihoon stared at her. "Wow, I never thought I'd see the day," Jihoon said.

"What? You're surprised she agrees with me?" Junu threw his other arm around Somin, and she tried to hide her smile. "You know, I am a pretty smart guy. Somin recognizes that."

"I never said I thought you were smart," Somin said. "I said that you said *one* right thing out of a million wrong things I've heard you say. That's not really a great percentage."

"It's pretty much a failing grade," Miyoung piped up with a smile.

Junu shook his head. "I have no allies. I'm outnumbered."

"I'm your ally, Hyeong," Changwan said, forgetting his previous trepidation about leaving campus.

"You're all I have, Changwan-ah." Junu sighed.

Somin's stomach chose that moment to growl. "Come on, I'm starved. And you promised food." She grabbed Junu's hand and jogged down the school stairs. She didn't stop until they were outside the school gates.

"Trying to get some alone time with me?" Junu asked, wiggling his eyebrows suggestively. Somin just laughed.

"No. It's like I said, I'm hungry."

"Sure," Junu said, stepping toward her again. She stepped back only to collide with the security wall. "Be honest," Junu said, leaning closer. And Somin's lips parted in anticipation. Then he whispered, "Tell me what you and Hyuk talked about."

"Ya!" Somin said, smacking him on the head.

He laughed as he backed up, rubbing a hand on his head just as the others rounded the corner.

"I see you still haven't learned your lesson when it comes to teasing Somin," Miyoung said, but there was a knowing glint in her eyes.

She looped her arms through both Jihoon's and Changwan's and started leading them up the street.

"What about Junu and Somin?" Changwan asked, craning his neck around.

"They'll catch up," Miyoung said, tugging them along.

Junu turned back to Somin with a smile. "You really won't tell me?"

"It's private," Somin said. "The mortal world might depend on it."

"Oh really?" Junu asked, a playful grin spreading across his face. "I bet I can get it out of you."

"You'll have to be really convincing," she said, looping her arms around his neck.

"What do you have in mind?" Junu asked, leaning in until his lips were a centimeter from hers.

"I have a few ideas," Somin said. "But I'm really bad at explaining things. So I'll just have to show you."

Then she pressed her lips to his, humming in appreciation. And she welcomed the tingles that started in her toes and ran up her spine.

"Ya! Hurry up, you two!" Jihoon yelled from down the street.

Somin laughed at Jihoon's exasperated voice.

"So I spoke to my mother," she said as they started after their friends, hand in hand.

"Really?" he asked. "What about?"

"I told her I wanted to apply to some colleges abroad."

Junu stopped walking. "Really?"

"Yeah," Somin said. "I figured if Jihoon gets into college, he'll probably stick around this area, so it's not like he needs me around when he has Miyoung and my mother. Changwan's father has been throwing around the idea of sending him to Jeju-do to get work experience in their company factory before college, so he'll be off on that adventure. And I just started to think about what I wanted." She was rambling now, but Junu was just staring at her. She felt nervous suddenly, telling him this.

Then a smile broke free and he asked, "Well? What did she say?"

Somin grinned. "She said she thought it was a great idea." Was this real contentment? Being able to share good news with someone she loved. Procrastinating from studying to go eat with friends. Stealing kisses in the street. Such simple things that turned out to be everything.

"So where are we applying?" Junu asked.

"We?" Somin said as they approached the others, who waited in front of the restaurant.

"Well, I've been thinking," he said, hauling her close until she stood in the circle of his arms again. "I haven't traveled in a while."

"Is that so?" Somin asked. "Well, I might have a few suggestions." And she lifted onto her tiptoes to kiss him.

"Oh, come on," Jihoon said with a groan. But she didn't care. She wanted to hold on to this feeling. This love. It was so new she didn't know if it would last. She didn't know who they'd be in a month or a year. But a good friend had once told her not to worry about who they'd be a year from now.

Right now, he was what was right for her.

And right now, everyone she loved was happy.

Somin knew how rare that could be. So she'd appreciate what she had in this moment. And if she needed someone to stand with her in a storm, she knew who to call.

GLOSSARY

-ah / -ya (-아 / -야) informal name-ending implying the speaker is close to the person they are addressing

abeoji (아버지) father

ajumma (아줌마) middle-aged woman

appa (아빠) dad, daddy

babo (바보) fool

Baektu (백두산) an active stratovolcano on the Chinese–North Korean border; at 2,744 meters (9,003 feet), the highest mountain of the Changbai and Baekdudaegan ranges; Koreans assign a mythical quality to the volcano and its caldera lake, considering it to be their country's spiritual home

bangmangi (방망이) a large club carried by a dokkaebi that is used as a weapon, but also has the power to materialize anything one wishes

bbeongchiji ma (뻥치지마) slang for "don't lie to me"

bujeok (부적) talisman created by a shaman or monk, often used for luck, love, or to ease stress (see Notes)

byeontae (변태) pervert, weirdo

chonggak dokkaebi (총각도깨비) handsome "bachelor goblin" that is known to attract humans

daebak (대박) awesome, amazing

dokkaebi (도깨비) goblin; legendary creatures from Korean mythology that possess extraordinary powers and abilities used to interact with humans, at times playing tricks on them and at times helping them

emo (이모) aunt; sister of your mother

eomeoni (어머니) mother

eomma (엄마) mom, mommy

eomuk (어묵) Korean fish cakes

gaesori (개소리) bullshit

gi (기) human energy, also known as qi, chi, or ji in other East Asian cultures

gu (九, 구) nine

Guksabong (국사봉) a mountain of Gyeongsangbuk-do, eastern South Korea, with an elevation of 728 meters (2,388 feet); its name can be transcribed in Chinese characters in various ways, according to the related stories: 國思 means "national concern," 國祀 means "state ritual," and 國師 means "state preceptor," a high government post given to eminent Buddhist monks

gumiho (구미호) literally "nine-tailed fox," a mythical, immortal fox that appears in the tales and legends of Korea

gwishin (귀신) ghost

halmeoni (할머니) grandmother

hanja (한자) Korean word for Han Chinese characters that were adopted from Chinese and incorporated into the Korean language with Korean pronunciation

harabeoji (할아버지) grandfather

hyeong (형) older brother; also used for an older male the speaker is close to

jeoseung saja (저승사자) Korean reapers that are often seen dressed in a billowing black robe and a gat, a black hat worn during the Joseon Dynasty (see Notes)

jjigae (찌개) stew

kimbap or **gimbap** (김밥) Korean dish made with rice, seaweed, and fillings such as meat and vegetables; the rice and fillings are rolled into the seaweed and sliced into small discs for ease of eating

kimchi (김치) fermented vegetables, most commonly napa cabbage or radishes, served as a side dish in Korean cuisine

kkeojyeo (꺼져) fuck off

maehwa (매화나무) Asian flowering plum tree, also called a maesil (매실나무) when emphasizing the fruit

michin nom (미친놈) crazy bastard

miyeokguk (미역국) seaweed soup, often served on a person's birthday or to someone recovering from an illness

mul gwishin (물귀신) water ghost

ramyeon (라면) instant noodles

saekki (새끼) or **saekkiya** (새끼야) literally "baby animal," it's often used as slang to mean "bastard" or "asshole," though parents can use it as a term of endearment for their child as well (depending on context)

sansin (산신) mountain god

seolleongtang (설렁탕) beef bone soup

Shin ramyeon (신라면) a brand of spicy ramyeon

soju (소주) clear distilled alcohol usually made from rice, wheat, or barley

suneung (수능) nickname for the College Scholastic Ability Test, or CSAT, given to third-years (seniors) in high school in Korea every November; on the test day, the stock markets open late and bus and subway service is increased to avoid traffic jams that could prevent students from getting to testing (see Notes)

tteok-bokki (떡볶이) hot, spicy rice cake

yeowu guseul (여우구슬) fox bead

NOTES

- In South Korea, the school year is divided into two terms. The first term usually runs from March 2, unless it is a Friday or the weekend, to mid-July, with the summer vacation from mid-July to late August (elementary and secondary schools) or from mid-June to late August (higher education institutions). The second term usually runs until mid-February. Third-year high school students (equivalent to high school seniors in Western countries) all take the College Scholastic Ability Test, or CSAT (대학수학능력시험), often called the suneung exam, in November.

- When women in Korea marry, they do not take their husband's surnames, thus the different surname for Somin's mother (Moon, not Lee).

- In Korea, a person is one year old when they are born, and everyone turns a year older at the new year. Therefore, though Jihoon, Miyoung, and Somin think of themselves as nineteen years old, they are actually eighteen years old chronologically.

- Bujeoks contain letters or patterns that are believed to carry the power to chase away evil ghosts and prevent calamities. In Korean folk religion, amulet sheets are generally made by painting letters or pictures in red on a sheet of yellow paper. Nowadays, they are made with disassembled and combined letters written as abstract forms on a piece of paper. Bujeoks are often sought out before a big test or interview.

- In Korean mythology, jeoseung saja are reapers dispatched by King Yeomra, ruler of the underworld, to collect spirits of the recently deceased and lead them down Hwangcheon Road to the afterlife. In some myths, jeoseung saja were originally humans. The hero Gangrim Doryeong was ordered to capture King Yeomra, but instead became the first jeoseung saja.

ACKNOWLEDGMENTS

Thank you to everyone who helped me bring this duology to life!

First, I'd like to thank my amazing and talented editor, Stacey Barney. She helped me sift through the muck of ideas that I'd originally cobbled together to try to make this book. She helped me make sense of my ramblings and create a story that I could be proud of!

To my awesome agent, Beth Phelan. I could not have survived debuting and entering this industry without you. You're more than just my agent, you're my friend and my confidante, and I value you so much!

To Vanessa DeJesús, thank you for all the work you put into getting my books out there and making some of my bucket-list author dreams come true!

To Felicity and Shannon and all of the Penguin Teen crew! I love all the amazingly creative work you're doing and look forward to every email from Felicity that starts with "So, I'm emailing because you're willing to do weird stuff for social media . . ." (Also, sorry that I spend so long playing with the coffee machine every time I come by.)

To everyone else at Penguin Random House, Keri, Caitlin, thank you so much for your support of *Wicked Fox* and *Vicious Spirits*; it has meant the world to me!

To my friends Rebecca Kuss, Deeba Zargarpur, Emily Berge, and Alexa Wejko. You literally helped me survive some of the most harrowing professional years of my life. It's so hard to step into a new role, and you all made it so much better! I'd do it all again just so I could meet you and become friends!

To my Chicago crew: Rena Baron, Ronni Davis, Samira Ahmed, Gloria Chao, Anna Waggener, Lizzie Cooke. Thank you for your constant support and friendship!

To my friends Karuna Riazi and Nafiza Azad, you inspire me every day with your beautiful talent!

To my NYC writing friends, Swati Teerdhala and Liz Lim, I'm always so happy when we get to catch up and talk books and writing! You are such wonderful WOC talents!

To my writer cult: Janella Angeles, Erin Bay, Ashley Burdin, Alex Castellanos, Maddy Colis, Mara Fitzgerald, Amanda Foody, Christine Lynn Herman, Meg Kohlmann, Katy Rose Pool, Akshaya Raman, Tara Sim, Melody Simpson. We are legion, but it's because we all truly adore and respect each other and that is such a precious thing! I can't think of a group of writers I'd rather embark on this publishing journey with! You're all destined for amazing things and I am excited I get a front-row seat!

To my best friend and writer partner in crime, Claribel Ortega. I was so lucky to have you by my side as I debuted, and I feel honored I was able to see you debut this year as well! A good friend is someone who you can have fun with. A great friend is someone who supports you when you're down. And family is someone who pushes you to be better even when you think you've reached the end of your tether. And you are all three of those things to me!

To my cousin and fave author, Axie Oh. Thank you for always supporting me and my writing. Thank you for being a sounding board and for always wanting to make sure that we can be both great CPs and great cousins to each other! I love you!

To my family, Halmeoni, Emo Helen, Uncle Doosang, Emo Sara, Uncle Warren, Uncle John, Aunt Heejong, Emo Mary, Uncle Barry. Thank you for always supporting me and being there for me!

To my cousins, Adam, Alex, Saqi, Sara Kyoung, Wyatt, Jason, Christine, Kevin, Bryan, Josh, Scott, Camille, you're the best family I could ever ask for, and I love you all so much!

To Jim and Lucy, I love you!

To my sister and my person, Jennifer Magiera. You are my favorite person in the world (well, tied with Lucy at this point). I could not have survived the last decade without you. You are so talented and smart and good, and I am so lucky to have a role model like you in my life. You will forever be my person. And I love you very much!

To Mom and Dad. I love you. 보고싶어요.